P9-CEP-469

STRANGLED
IN
PARIS

Also by Claude Izner

Murder on the Eiffel Tower

The Disappearance at Père-Lachaise

The Montmartre Investigation

The Assassin in the Marais

In the Shadows of Paris

STRANGLED
IN
PARIS

A Victor Legris Mystery

CLAUDE IZNER

TRANSLATED BY JENNIFER HIGGINS

MINOTAUR BOOKS ❧ NEW YORK

This is a work of fiction. All of the characters, organizations, and events portrayed in this novel are either products of the author's imagination or are used fictitiously.

STRANGLED IN PARIS. Copyright © 2006 by Éditions 10/18, Département d'Univers Poche. English translation copyright © 2011 by Gallic Books. All rights reserved. Printed in the United States of America. For information, address St. Martin's Press, 175 Fifth Avenue, New York, N.Y. 10010.

www.minotaurbooks.com

The Library of Congress has cataloged the hardcover edition as follows:

Izner, Claude.
 [Talisman de la Villette. English]
 Strangled in Paris / Claude Izner; Translated by Jennifer Higgins.—1st U.S. Edition.
   p. cm.
 First published in France as Le talisman de la Villette by Éditions 10/18.
 ISBN 978-0-312-66217-2 (hardcover)
 ISBN 978-1-250-03646-9 (e-book)
I. Title.
 PQ2709.Z6413T3513 2013
 843'.92—dc23

2013020021

ISBN 978-1-250-04810-3 (trade paperback)

Minotaur books may be purchased for educational, business, or promotional use. For information on bulk purchases, please contact Macmillan Corporate and Premium Sales Department at 1-800-221-7945, extension 5442, or write specialmarkets@macmillan.com.

First published in France as *Le talisman de la Villette* by Éditions 10/18

First Minotaur Books Paperback Edition: July 2014

10 9 8 7 6 5 4 3 2 1

To our darling mother

To Monique who will always be with us

Many thanks to our friend Jacques Rougemont for his invaluable research

The past and the future slumber in the eye of the unicorn.

Adage from the Middle Ages

The pitiful, battered voices
Of the old hurdy-gurdies
First caressing, then biting
Are like the sad, reedy cries
Of a madman who sniggers and sobs
On his deathbed.

Jean Richepin
(The Song of the Beggars, 1876)

CHAPTER ONE

Sunday 7 January 1894

The storm was battering the Normandy coast. It had swept through the British Isles, attacked the Pas de Calais and had now reached the Cotentin peninsula, where it was venting its full force on the La Hague headland.

Corentin Jourdan lay fully dressed on his four-poster bed listening to the great gusts and squalls shaking the walls. The fire flickered. A piece of canvas hung from the mantelpiece to stop the smoke filling the room. The flames threw bright, fleeting tongues of light onto the copper cistern and the old grandfather clock. Two carved birds' heads seemed about to fly away from the corners of the wardrobe. A raucous miaowing briefly made itself heard above the tumult: the terrified cat was scratching at the front door. Corentin sat up. A ball of dirty fur with a pink nose and curly whiskers hurtled in through the cat flap and burrowed into the warmth of the eiderdown.

'Now, Gilliatt, is that any way for an old ship's mascot to behave? There's nothing to get excited about!'

An explosion of noise drowned out his words: the thatched roof of the shed had just been torn off. Corentin grew more and more anxious as he heard the tempest attack his stock of dry logs, and he tried to calculate the damage. He would have to get the roof seen to by old Pignol, a real crook but the best thatcher for miles around. A loud neighing suddenly erupted from the stable next door: Flip was getting nervous. Just as long as he didn't start kicking the walls down!

9

No doubt hoping to evade the worst of the weather, the old tomcat curled up under his master's arm, purring loudly. Corentin smiled.

'Chin up, Gilliatt! It's only a little shower!'

He had seen worse when he used to navigate the *Marie-Jeanneton* around the Channel Islands. If it hadn't been for that confounded spar, which had split during a squall and crushed his foot, he would never have left the navy.

He sighed deeply. Even though his house was a quarter of a mile from the shore, the sound of the breakers filled his room like the baying of a ghostly pack of hounds. The pounding of the surf reverberated inside him, soothing him. He sank into sleep.

When he woke, he felt once again the subtle stirring of fear he had battled ever since the accident. He had had to make a supreme effort to prevent the combination of inactivity and physical suffering getting the better of him. He had hated lying immobile on a hospital bed, dependent on the goodwill of others and far away from the salt air of the open sea. The enforced confinement had left him with no choice but to reflect on his past. For weeks he tried to work out whether he had made a mistake; why the stupid accident? At forty, with two-thirds of his life already gone, what did he have to look forward to? He had quickly recognised the brutal truth that no ship's captain would ever trust a cripple. At that realisation he had fallen into deep despair as he thought longingly of the familiar, reassuring atmosphere of the *Marie-Jeanneton*.

A sickly, yellowish dawn was struggling to break, and in its pale light he saw Gilliatt, perched on a cupboard with incriminating crumbs of meat and pastry stuck to his whiskers.

Corentin stretched, and remembered his dream. Once again, Clélia had appeared, transparent and inaccessible. The only woman he had ever loved, the only woman he had never possessed, still haunted him. The memory of all the others, kitchen maids or working girls, whose services were freely offered, faded as soon as his desire was satisfied: only the unattainable woman had been able to capture and hold his imagination for such a long time.

He decided to go out. There might be someone in need of his help. Despite his general misanthropy, he was careful to maintain good relations with his neighbours; after all, it had been his decision to limit his life to this little huddle of cottages.

A squall of rain whipped his face. He jammed his hat more firmly on his head, glanced at the increasingly grey sky and pushed open the stable door. Flip's tail and mane were ruffled by the wind. The mice feasting in the hay ran off, squeaking. He lit his lamp.

'Hello there, Flip!'

The horse quivered at the sight of his master. Corentin patted his flank and fed him a sugarlump from his open palm.

'A little treat from your groom, you old misery. There there, easy now, the storm's dying down.'

The horse slowly rubbed his muzzle against the wood of his stall before deigning to accept the titbit.

'Heavens above, Flip, stop looking at me like that!' cried Corentin, rummaging in the bag full of grain. Flip pawed the ground happily and plunged his nose into the handful of oats that was offered to him.

'Don't make a mess, now.'

Corentin patted his neck, put fresh hay in the rack and extinguished the lantern.

'Be good now, won't you? Don't kick anything over,' he said, fastening the door.

Outside, a cold wind raked the distant hills. Corentin walked on, past the Chaulards' farm, huddled behind its hillock like a frightened animal. The windows rattled in their frames and the whole building creaked. He couldn't see a living soul.

He staggered down the slope, tossed about in the wind like a skiff bobbing on the sea. It was at times like this, when there was a big storm, that he most regretted the loss of his own boat. On board a ship, he used to be able to grapple with bad weather in an equal fight; on dry land, he was at the mercy of the slightest squall.

Looking out to sea, Corentin could see the waves tipped with glints of silver. He crossed a stream, now a torrent, gazed briefly at the cliffs obscured by clouds of sea-spray and turned his back on them. The main street in Landemer zigzagged between fishermen's cottages and a few large villas converted for the summer into family boarding houses. The customs officer's house had lost its ostentatious ceramic decoration and the smashed remains lay forlornly in the middle of the front garden. Corentin slowed down as he reached the inn, turning up the collar of his oilskin jacket. At this time of day the fish market was usually in full swing, but today the place was eerily empty. He turned towards the beach, dodging as best he could the buffeting breath of the invisible demon.

The raging waves had thrown up a wall of pebbles at the edge of the sand, which was now gradually emerging as the tide receded. The boiling cauldron of the sea was capitulating regretfully. To the right of the fort, there was a pale patch in the water – a flock of birds? Corentin had previously spotted storm petrels here, blown off course from the Orkney Islands.

He walked on for another hundred yards, happy to find himself in the deserted spot where he had spent so many hours observing wildlife and combing the beach for driftwood and curious stones. His solitary walks here had brought him a sense of peace and security. Except for occasional conversations with Madame Guénéqué, who came to clean his little house and to cook for him, Corentin led a solitary existence.

Leaden clouds raced along the horizon, and an angry wind whipped the waves into crests before flattening them again. Corentin squinted into the distance. No, that wasn't a flock of birds, it was something much bigger. Driven against the reef, a schooner must have struck a rock, where its boom and bowsprit had shattered. The broken mast hung at a sickening angle; people on the bridge ran to and fro, dropping lines to evacuate the vessel. Small boats were bustling around the great carcass. So that was where all the inhabitants of Landemer and Urville had gone. They would have to work fast: the waves would soon pull the wreck under the sea.

He thought of all the fishermen who must have died, and of the captain of the vessel who, probably heading to France from England, had been presumptuous enough to defy the warning of such a troubled sea. Corentin, too, had often thought himself invincible.

Near Gréville, several small, wide skiffs were setting off towards the wreck, and he hurried on, impatient to join them. Suddenly, he stopped, still and attentive. A dark mass undulated in the ebbing tide. For a few seconds he stood motionless, shading his eyes, until all at once he understood, and began to run. A little girl or a woman lay in the foaming water, like a siren caught in the sticky net of seaweed.

Half carrying, half dragging the unconscious form out of the water, he staggered up onto the beach, and gazed in shock at the young woman's face. Clélia? No! Clélia had been dead for twenty years. Acting instinctively, he loosened her clenched teeth with the stem of his pipe, cleared the mucus and seaweed out of her throat with his fingers and put his ear to her chest. Her heart was beating weakly. He knelt down and, seizing her wrists, began to raise and lower her arms vigorously, pressing on her chest with each downward movement. All this came to him automatically, with an expertise gained from twenty-five years of experience. He repeated this manoeuvre fifteen times every minute, his only thought to bring the unknown woman back to life.

All at once, she was racked by a great spasm and coughed violently before falling back again, inert. He took off his jacket and wrapped it round her. As he hoisted her up, he felt something digging into him: tied around the woman's wrist was a cord with a small leather bag hanging from it.

Buffeted by the wind, he began to struggle back up the beach. Slight and fragile as his burden was, her drenched clothes made her heavy, and getting her back to his house was no easy task. The dunes seemed to have blurred into a grey mist, which danced before his eyes. He had to stop halfway to get a firmer grip on his charge, finally hauling her over his shoulder. The rain had set in again and he began to fear that the seeming calm had been misleading. When he finally reached his house, his mouth was parched and he had a burning pain in his back. Inside, it was bitterly cold.

With a sigh of relief, he laid the woman on the eiderdown and hurried to light a fire. Still limping, he rushed into the woodshed. The sodden logs would be useless. He turned back.

Ignoring Gilliatt, who was mewing for food, he grasped a hatchet and hacked two of his wooden chairs to pieces. As the flames engulfed them, he remembered that he had stored several bundles of heather at the back of the stable. He collected these, along with a crate that had once held bottles of cider: enough to keep the fire alive for at least an hour.

The woman groaned, her eyes still closed. She wore a small blue earring in her left ear but the right one was missing. He felt her pulse, which was racing. Her forehead was damp. He needed to undress her and rub her skin to get her circulation going. Quickly removing her bag and the jacket he had wrapped around her, he hesitated when confronted with her dress. So many buttons! He tore one off, undid another, and then resorted to more drastic measures. Using a knife, he cut away layer after layer of clothing. Tatters of cloth – skirt, bodice and petticoat – were strewn over the tiled floor. He felt as though he were peeling a fruit with an endless number of skins. Just as he thought he had finished, he came to a final barrier: the corset, as rigid as a breastplate. Clumsily, he undid the stays, and with a last effort separated the two halves of the armour, revealing her breasts, round, supple and generous. With trembling hands, he removed her lace drawers and torn stockings. Her legs were covered in scratches and the corset had left its impression on her skin, but nonetheless she was the most beautiful thing he had ever seen.

14

Not daring to touch any other part of her, he rubbed her frozen feet timidly.

Intrigued, Gilliatt began to sniff the woman's body, nudging his nose between her legs. With a sweep of his hand, Corentin sent the cat flying, and Gilliatt leapt up onto the canopy of the bed.

Corentin uncorked a bottle of plum brandy that he kept for special occasions and dampened his hands with the alcohol. He slowly began to massage the woman's skin, but stopped at her waist, hesitating to go any higher. The cat's mewing brought his attention back to the task in hand. Applying a few more drops of brandy to his palms, he accelerated his massage. Her breasts were soft to his touch, and he moved down to her thighs, working methodically. He was calm now, her nudity no longer troubling him. He moved over the nape of her neck, her back, curving in so delightfully at the waist, her arms, her stomach, her thighs . . .

The bottle was empty and the woman lay, still unconscious, stretched out on her side, impregnated with alcohol and pink from having been rubbed all over. When he had cleaned her wounds, he covered them with a balsam pomade scented with mint. Reaching into the wardrobe, he unfolded a sheet, placed it over the woman's body and piled several blankets on top.

The fire was dying down, so Corentin sacrificed a third chair, and hurried to the stable, where he grabbed the last bundles of heather and two more wooden crates from under Flip's nose. Throwing all these provisions into a wheelbarrow, he made his way back via the shed and managed to find two logs that were less sodden than the others. He spread all this new fuel out next to the fireplace, and leant the logs against the fire-back to dry.

He felt drained of all strength. A sharp pain throbbed in his leg, just above the knee. He leant on the edge of the table, trying to get his breath back, and began to shiver, overcome by weariness after all the tensions of the day. He changed his clothes, cut himself a large hunk of bread and reduced another crate to splinters, immediately giving it up to the hungry flames. This time, the fireplace, satisfied with the offering, gave out an intense burst of heat. Corentin poured himself a tankard of cider and sat down beside the woman.

She looked young, no more than twenty-five. She was tanned, which showed that she had lived in the sun. And were her eyes even darker than the thick curls of her hair? And how would her lips taste? It was difficult to resist the temptation to find out. He held firm, but after a few moments pulled away the sheet to reveal her body, gazing in silent admiration, then reached out to caress a shoulder, the curve of a breast, her neck. Then, springing up so brusquely that he knocked over his stool, he pulled the covers back over her.

Was he going mad? He had learnt to protect himself with a shield of indifference. He had kept to himself, avoided all intimacy and turned off his emotions. This woman was the first to threaten his serenity since Clélia. The only explanation he could find was that the exertion had affected him more than he cared to admit.

He went up the steps to his attic room, a familiar little world that he had created when his sailing days had come to an end. A homely, comforting smell of tobacco, apples and ink hung in the air, and cases filled with watercolours and sketchbooks served as reminders of his past life. Two stuffed deities reigned over the chaotic piles of souvenirs from his travels: a great black cormorant and a chough. Scattered pages related stories from his youth when, as a young sailor, he had plied the seas of North Africa and the East. The small desk was covered with clothbound notebooks along with two paperweights and a paraffin lamp. Beside the desk, a sextant and a telescope jostled for space with pots of herbs and jars of pickled samphire. The carefully reconstructed skeleton of a tawny owl kept watch over a little trestle bed covered in books. On the rough wattle walls hung several drawings by Jean-François Millet, left to him by his uncle Gaspard, who had bought them when the painter had returned to his native village near Landemer. Corentin's favourite was

16

a sketch of a shepherd herding his flock by moonlight. He was also particularly fond of the large circular map of the world that he had copied from one by Mercator. One of the cupboards was filled with dozens of nautical charts, although the chart showing the seas near his home was redundant because Corentin (like Gilliatt, the hero of Victor Hugo's *Toilers of the Sea*, for whom the cat was named) was 'born with a map of the bed of the English Channel inscribed in his head'.

Corentin lit his pipe. Without warning, Clélia appeared before him. If only he had married her, his beloved cousin! She had been seduced by a travelling puppeteer in Cherbourg, and followed him to Paris where, abandoned and miserable, she had died of puerperal fever. He had only found this out after endless searching and questioning. He had never been able to discover where she was buried.

'What does it matter, anyway?' he muttered, getting up and standing by the window. The apple trees in the paddock were bending in the strong west wind. The slate-coloured sky was indistinguishable from the sea.

He went back downstairs. Obviously in the grip of a nightmare, the woman was muttering incoherent words. Her expression alarmed him and he stroked her cheek gently. A sudden and overwhelming emotion surged through him. Had they been destined to meet? He had seen too much of life and had too many strange encounters to believe that the course of events was decided by chance alone. His gaze still fixed on the stranger, he resolved never again to expose himself to the pain and bitterness of love. And yet, and yet . . . He felt his defences crumbling, all those barriers put up during the years of solitude and despair. It felt good to have a woman under his roof.

Her eyelids fluttered.

'You're safe.'

Who could have said those words? Would this rolling and swaying never stop? Everything seemed dark, and she was floating in

17

the midst of a foaming sea, which filled her nose and mouth, choking her.

She concentrated, trying to understand this voice that seemed to be speaking, but that she could barely hear. She attempted to move, but the pain of the blood returning to her limbs made her cry out. Oh God, where was she?

'Don't be afraid.'

The voice resonated like someone calling in an empty house. She had to fight, she had to stay alive.

Could the tall figure with the head of curly hair surrounded by a halo of light be the ship's doctor? She felt hot. A sudden dizziness made the walls spin, then her confusion cleared, revealing the phosphorescent pupils of a cat and the torso of a man leaning over her.

'Are you all right?'

His voice seemed clearer now.

'Are we in Southampton?' she murmured.

'No, in France.'

She tried to sit up, but a hand pushed her back. She wanted to resist, but she was so tired. The voice again: 'You must rest.'

She pretended she was falling asleep again but managed to look about her. She could make out a fireplace, and a pewter pot filled with flowering thistles placed on a large table. To one side, rows of painted plates lined the shelves of a large dresser. The man held a globe lamp and she was able to see a large ham hanging from one of the beams. Strange forms were projected on the uneven wattle and lath walls, as lifelike as that of the large grey cat curled up in front of the fire.

Disconnected images flitted through her mind. Boarding the *Eagle* at Southampton after meeting her husband's lawyer. The captain, a squat, podgy man who stood too close to her and assured her that he knew this stretch of water like the back of his hand and that, storm or no storm, they would reach France that very day. The fear she had felt as she clung to the vessel, while it was tossed and whirled by enormous waves that all seemed intent on one thing: destroying the little boat and destroying her with it. Before that, the journey from San Francisco to New York and then the calm voyage all the way to the south of England.

At the head of the bed, Corentin was scraping his pipe out into an earthenware cup, his mind full of strange and sombre thoughts. A man like him needed something to give his life meaning. Something like a woman's love, perhaps? All that had been taken from him. He felt a thirst in his soul, as though he had lived, like a second Robinson Crusoe, on nothing but smoked herrings with never a drop of fresh water.

He was just drifting off to sleep when, heralded by a great gust of cold air, Madame Guénéqué burst in. She was a robust country woman of about fifty, the widow of a man who had devoted most of his short life to the art of brewing his own beer and cider. She had been left to bring up their numerous offspring and had earned her living as a servant in the great houses of the area. Now, she managed to get by working as a cook and cleaner.

'Hello, Captain, sorry I'm late. I didn't dare stick my nose outside earlier, on account of all that wind. It's brightening up now, though – look at the sky. Rain and sunshine all at once – it's the devil beating his missus and marrying off his daughter. It's a crying shame. A good few boats have been wrecked – it's always the same when they come. One storm, and it lasts three days! Oh, you've got a visitor?'

'I found her unconscious early this morning. I suppose she must have been a passenger on the schooner. I did my best to get her warm.'

Quick as a flash, Madame Guénéqué closed the door and scuttled over to the bed to size up the newcomer. When she caught sight of the scraps of clothing lying on the floor, her wrinkled old face lit up with a roguish smile.

'So that's why you decided to peel her like an onion?'

19

'It was either that or leave her to die. And if I'd done that I'd have been able to inspect her intimately and at my leisure.'

'Oh, don't get cross. I was only saying . . .'

'I was just answering your question,' replied Corentin in a conciliatory tone. 'Now, help yourself to some coffee.'

But it was too much to ask of Madame Guénéqué that she would leave it there.

'Ha. And what's happened to your chairs? They're in a pretty state! And is this person going to stay here for long?'

'I was waiting for you to come so that I could go out and ask the nuns at the infirmary to send someone to collect her.'

'I'd do it sharpish if I were you. When my poor old man fell head first into the cider vat, his friends did the best they could to get him to cough it all up, but in the end his heart gave out.'

'I'm going now. Keep the fire burning while I'm gone and, if she wakes up and wants to eat, there are eggs and sausages in the cupboard.'

'Don't you worry, she won't die of hunger. I'll make her some nice hot soup.' She rolled up her sleeves and set to work. 'He may be an old hermit,' she muttered, 'but he's still got a soft spot for the ladies.'

Outside, Corentin Jourdan filled his lungs with the damp air, relieved to escape the oppressive atmosphere of the house. The wind had wreaked havoc among the rose bushes and mallow plants: the trees were bent and splayed into tortured shapes, and crows fluttered to and fro among the broken branches. The bakehouse was flooded and the geese were honking in the little yard, which was white with their droppings.

He released Flip and put his harness on. The horse, an Anglo-Norman with a long nose, shook his mane in pleasure at the prospect of escaping from his confinement. With his master in the saddle, left leg hanging free of the stirrup, he walked along the shore, punctuating the monotonous calls of the seagulls with his whinnying.

They crossed the stream just as the church bell was tolling. A silent crowd gathered in front of the church doors, which were surmounted by a relief of St Martin. Urville's gravediggers would have their work cut out this evening.

He had to knock on the large double doors several times before a little hatch was pulled half open. A young nun stared at him while he explained his case. The sister retorted that the mother superior would do what she could as soon as possible but that all the beds were full because of the storm. He was insistent.

'This woman has a high fever. Who knows how long she may have been in the water? It's a miracle that she's still of this world.'

An older nun brushed the novice aside and examined Corentin, adjusting her spectacles.

'Sister Ursula is right, Captain Jourdan, we are run off our feet here. Still, I shall send Landry, the gardener's son, to collect the woman, and we'll put her up in the annexe.'

He thanked the mother superior warmly. He had earned her gratitude one winter day in 1892 when he had helped repair one of the walls of the infirmary which had fallen down, and had accepted nothing by way of a reward except for a bowl of coffee and some bread and butter.

She kept her word. Five minutes later, Landry's shock of red hair could be seen bobbing along towards Landemer behind the nuns' old nag. From a distance, Corentin Jourdan watched the cart rattling over the potholed path.

From the shelter of the stable, he observed the boy and Madame Guénéqué carrying the woman, wrapped up like a mummy, as best they could towards the cart. When Landry had disappeared round the bend, Corentin took the saddle off his horse and let it graze.

'You missed them,' remarked Madame Guénéqué when he came in. A pot hung over the fire, simmering and giving off an appetising smell of vegetables and ham. 'She didn't open her eyes or her mouth, poor thing.'

Having finished cleaning the ground floor, Madame Guénéqué was putting on her shawl. The loft was forbidden territory, except when her employer was away.

'I'm going to see old Pignol.'

'Don't forget to tell him about the roof. The weather's settling down now, but still . . .'

'Don't worry, I will. See you on Wednesday, Captain. And remember to dig out that washtub for me – there's a ton of washing to be done.'

She shot a poisonous glance at Gilliatt, spread-eagled in the middle of the bed.

When she had gone, Corentin Jourdan let out a sigh. A few short hours had been enough for a stranger to turn his routine upside down. He lay down next to the cat, overcome with fatigue.

In the middle of the night he got up, poked the remains of the fire and added the remnants of one of the crates. He served himself a bowl of warm soup and sat down in the chimney corner. At his feet, Gilliatt lapped at a saucer of milk. The regular sound of the cat's little pink tongue flicking back and forth sent Corentin off into a daydream. He recalled a vision he had once had: a naked water sprite was holding him in her arms, and a blue aura hung around her jet-black hair.

What was happening to him? It was the first time in twenty years that he had become so obsessed by something. Ashamed of behaving like a dreamy adolescent, Corentin got up and was about to make for the attic when he saw something under the bed. He bent down and picked up the woman's bag. Madame Guénéqué's broom wasn't always very thorough.

He lit a candle and went up to the attic. Uncertain what to do, he looked thoughtfully at his find. Should he open it? If he did, he risked becoming attached to the woman, rather than freeing himself from her. He had resolved never to leave his home here where his frugal way of life, combined with the money left by his uncle, meant that he was independent, almost rich. He was entirely at peace with the world, because his heart was not pierced by any thorns of emotion, and because he hardly ever saw other people and only had a horse and a cat to look after.

'Is she married?'

Unable to resist, he picked up the bag. The leather had protected an address book, a bulging purse and a wad of papers tied up in a triple layer of oilcloth. Where to start? He began with a crinkled beige envelope, pulling out a blue notebook whose pages were covered in small writing. He settled himself on the trestle bed, began reading and didn't stop until he had read the whole thing.

When morning came, he put the notebook back where he had found it and went to stand by the window. In the courtyard below, a timid ray of sunlight projected the black shadow of the chimney onto the wall. Between two buildings, there was a glimpse of the sea, calm as a millpond. He looked at it for a moment, his pipe in his mouth, lost in thought. The clear horizon seemed to bode well for the day and he set off to take the woman's bag to the nuns.

He was told that, after a difficult night, the woman seemed, according to the doctor, to be out of danger. Her name was Sophie Clairsange. A sailor from the *Eagle* had brought her suitcase, full of beautiful clothes. The poor woman was still fragile, but had managed to swallow a few mouthfuls of food. Would the captain like to see her?

Corentin instructed the novice not to reveal his identity if Sophie Clairsange should happen to ask about him. Surprised, the novice promised to do as he asked.

He left. At Urville, he bought *La Lanterne Manchoise* hot off the press. A front-page article on the wreck of the schooner recorded that there had been no casualties. Elsewhere, the newspaper bemoaned the uprooting of trees in Cherbourg, which was causing chaos on the main road into the town.

He set off back to the sanctuary of his own home.

'What about that washtub?' grumbled Madame Guénéqué, when she saw that Corentin hadn't obeyed her instruction.

Without replying, he went up to the attic. Where had he left it? Ah yes, under the bed. He pulled out a wooden box and took off the lid. Inside he found 420 francs, which he hoped would be enough for his needs. After all, the journey there and back in third class cost less than forty francs. The trip to Cherbourg wouldn't cost much and Landry would be delighted with even such a small sum, which he would go and spend straight away in one of the bistros at the port. Then it would just be a case of renting a cheap room – would twenty francs a month be enough? – and cutting back on his meals. Luckily, he had never had a big appetite.

Paris! A noisy island, a crowded continent as mysterious as the ocean, where he could get lost for ever.

He put the money in his pocket, filled a haversack with clothes and then went back downstairs, dragging the washtub with him.

'Madame Guénéqué, I'm going away for a few weeks – urgent business in Paris. As soon as I know my address there, I'll send it to you in case you need to contact me.'

'You'd be wasting your time – I can't read or write.'

'Then you can ask the nuns to help you.'

'I'm surprised at you, Monsieur Corentin. For years and years you've never been further away from here than a rabbit from its warren. People will be talking about this all the way from here to Val de Saire!'

'I'm counting on you to keep all those busy tongues from wagging, and to make sure the farrier mends that shoe of Flip's that's wearing down. The main thing is, don't forget to give him some water before you feed him his oats, and brush him every day.'

Madame Guénéqué eyed him mischievously.

'You don't need to give me all these instructions, Captain, you've told me a hundred times before. Ah, Paris, Paris, everyone's got Paris fever! That lovely lady you scrubbed up so carefully, she's going to Paris too. The doctor told her over and over that she shouldn't go, not in the state she's in, but she's as stubborn as a mule! They wouldn't be linked, would they, your two journeys?'

'Wherever do you get your ideas from? I don't know anything about her – who she is, where she lives. It's business, as I said, to do with my uncle's investments.'

'Whatever you say. I'll look after the animals, but it'll mean me trailing over here every morning . . .'

'I'll give you forty francs. If I'm not back by the end of January, I'll send a postal order.'

'Oh, no need for that, Captain, no need for that. Forty francs is a tidy sum!' she blustered, her eyes round at the thought. She spirited the notes away as soon as he put them in her hand.

With a stroke for Gilliatt and a friendly pat for Flip, he was off. He was clutching the blue earring he had found under the table. Despite the black clouds and the occasional gust of wind, the storm had left the Cotentin peninsula and gone to wreak its havoc further south.

Why had he ever opened that confounded bag? Now, he knew things he wished he didn't and, if he refused to act on what he had read, it would poison his very existence. He would not rest until he had found the woman whose secrets he had stolen. Come what may, he would seek her in that immense city, full of dangers far more deadly than the storm.

CHAPTER TWO

Friday 9 February 1894

It was nearly five o'clock and Paris was succumbing to dusk. Sprawling Paris of the grand houses, the brightly lit avenues, the shady districts, the bustling streets, the sinister streets, the empty streets. Corentin Jourdan knew exactly what he had to do. Either the two women would emerge from the house together, or one would come out alone. Depending on whether it was the brunette or the blonde, he would put the first or the second of his plans into action.

From his garret room, he could see all of the houses along Rue Albouy,[1] but the one he was interested in was the building on the corner of Rue des Vinaigriers. If the brunette Sophie Clairsange emerged, he would easily have enough time to get to the stall where his horse was waiting. The carriage station was on Boulevard Magenta and it would take the young woman five minutes to get there. He was familiar with the streets now and would be able to catch up with her.

Chance, destiny and luck had all worked in his favour so far, and fortune seemed to be smiling on his endeavour. Living alone and seldom speaking to anyone had been the best way of gathering information discreetly.

He'd realised he would have to tail carriages or omnibuses at short notice, and so would need his own mode of transport. His budget would not stretch to hiring a carriage and horses; the twenty-five or perhaps forty francs a day necessary would have swallowed up his savings in no time. But fortunately he had discovered a removal man who operated nearby. In exchange for a small sum, the man had allowed Jourdan to hire an old mare who still had some life left in her, and a cart which would be at his disposal any time of the day or night.

Immediately on arrival at Gare Saint-Lazare, he had made for the address he'd found in the notebook belonging to the young woman whose life he'd saved. When he got to Rue des Vinaigriers, the little shop painted in garish blue seemed to beckon to him. There was a sign outside:

THE BLUE CHINAMAN
Madame Guérin
Fine Confectionery since 1873

His heart pounding, he had put down his haversack. Now all he needed was to find a hotel or a furnished room, anything as long as it was nearby, and wait. He had looked at the rows of glass jars lined up on the shelves: caramels, sugar-coated almonds, pralines, Turkish delight, aniseed balls, barley sugar, humbugs, gumdrops, marshmallow and liquorice. The symphony of colours had washed over him like a memory of childhood, of freedom and innocence. His vision blurred and he saw again the slender young girl running towards him across a beach, as clearly as if she had actually been there.

The rays of the setting sun glinting on the shop window had brought him back to his senses. *Clélia is dead. You're looking for Sophie Clairsange.*

She was there, behind the sweet-shop counter, with a middle-aged woman standing next to her. Should he go in? Push open the door of the gingerbread house? No. He had come so far, and was so close to his goal – so close to her! He must be patient, and not fall into the trap of accosting her too soon.

He had sat at the bar in the Ancre de Fortune café, beside a bakery on Rue des Vinaigriers. It was a tiny place with a provincial air and

27

he felt as though he were back in Cherbourg. Outside, a long, drab strip of fencing partially concealed a warehouse built from tarred wood. The light of a gas lamp cast its spindly shadow across the road and into the gutter. Two stray dogs were playing in the street, and a tow-haired boy was carrying a large jug filled with cheap beer. There was no noise except the puffing of trains coming from the Gare de l'Est.

'Do you know if there are any rooms to rent near here?' he had asked the barman.

'How long do you need it for?'

'A month or two. I can pay in advance.'

'Maman!' the barman had called. 'You've got a customer.'

An old woman had stuck her nose out of the kitchen.

'If you're not too fussy, I've got an attic. The water's from a pump and you'd have to go down three floors to get it, and there's no heating.'

'That's fine. How much?'

That evening he had stood daydreaming, gazing at the sky above the huge, dark warehouse, with no thought of what was to come. On the horizon, windows began to light up, casting a wavering glow over the tiled roofs. She was so close by, just behind one of those curtains that fluttered in the night air, his lovely siren.

Over the next few weeks, Sophie Clairsange had not left the house. Corentin Jourdan had questioned some of the neighbours and learnt that the man with a large bag who visited the house each morning was a doctor, and that the woman lodging there was ill. One evening he had caught sight of her briefly, standing at the window. She was well again! He felt relieved.

He was always on the alert, ready to intervene when the time came. He didn't know exactly what had happened, but his imagination filled in the gaps and led him to gloss over some of the details. Who was the blonde woman? A nurse, most likely, or a friend, nothing more.

All the while that Corentin Jourdan kept watch over the lit window on the second floor, he thought about Sophie Clairsange, her body which he had glimpsed so briefly and the secrets hidden in the blue notebook.

An old drunk slumped on a stool in the Au Petit Jour bar on Rue d'Allemagne² let out a loud hiccup, like a bottle being uncorked.

'They serve short measures here . . . it's a well-known fact!'

Martin Lorson fixed his gaze on the Views of Paris calendar that was pinned to the peeling wall, picked at a stringy ragout and did his best to block out his surroundings. But it was to no avail: to his right, an ex-clergyman with a beard sprinkled with lumps of fried egg declaimed a line from Ecclesiastes, 'The thing that hath been, it is that which shall be', and to his right, a scrawny girl, a mother at just sixteen, was prattling to her baby: 'Whose are these little hands then?'

A man with a wooden leg leered toothlessly at the ruddy baby and hailed his fellow drinkers. 'The Middle Ages, now that was a good time to be alive! On Friday, I was sitting right up against the big heater in Église Saint-Eustache, and the sexton shows up. "What's going on here?" he says. "I'm just getting warm," I say. "This isn't a warming house, you know, this is God's house, and you'd better leave."'

'The Middle Ages? You must be joking!' mumbled the ex-clergyman.

'Churches were places of sanctuary, Mr Preacher! You think you're so clever. I might be on my uppers now, but I'm an educated man!'

In desperation, Martin Lorson craned his neck to look at a niche in the wall where, with one hand on her hip and a suggestive look on her face, an Egyptian dancing girl made of wax, rotated slowly to the strains of 'Plaisir d'amour'. For a moment he dreamt of putting his arms round the dancer and escaping with her from all the ugliness around him. The hoarse voice of the ex-clergyman interrupted his reverie.

'"There is nothing new under the sun!" I don't hold it against society, but really, for someone of my background to be reduced to a career on the stage, playing bit parts at the Châtelet. Five changes of costume every performance, and I only get forty sous for it! Ecclesiastes was right, "What profit hath a man of all his labour?"'

The landlord, bilious and sharp-tongued, with a dirty cap askew above his hatchet face, a menacing mouth and hard eyes, gathered up a stack of plates. On his way past, he flicked Martin Lorson with his dishcloth and addressed the listening audience.

'Now, take this bloke, he's fallen off a pedestal too. Haven't you, Swot? That's what they used to call him when he was still a pen-pusher at the Ministry of Finance. Look where it got him!'

Everybody turned to stare at the object of his disdain, a bloated, balding man in his forties, whose fraying suit was shiny with grease and dirt.

'And d'you know why?' continued the landlord. 'Debts! Oh, the little Swot wasn't lazy, and if he'd hung on for another eighteen years he could have worked his way up to being the office boss, which is more or less a rest cure! Oh yes, only going to work three days a week, to read the paper and stamp a few documents. But he hadn't counted on his dear lady wife!'

A crumpled-up dishcloth landed on the bar. Martin Lorson hurriedly paid the bill, jammed an old top hat onto his balding head and grabbed a coat that had seen better days. He tried to hurry, but his ample stomach and equally impressive posterior impeded his progress. He thus had the pleasure of hearing all the landlord's venomous comments, like an animal caught in a trap.

'Her ladyship wanted a posh house and all the trimmings. She wanted to be kept in the style to which she was accustomed, didn't she? A new dress here, a pair of shoes there, not to mention the servants and the private box at the theatre. Was he rich, though, the Swot? No! So he had to borrow, left, right and centre. And then boom! Creditors rolling up at the Ministry on pay day – it looks bad, doesn't it? Once, twice, ten times, the cashier agrees to give him an advance, but the eleventh time, he gets fired!'

Martin Lorson had finally reached the door when he realised that he had forgotten his scarf. With burning cheeks, he laboriously made his way back across the room. Suddenly cheering up, the ex-clergyman didn't feel as bad about himself as usual and the young girl caressed her baby, sure that he would never end up in such a terrible state.

'"Vanity of vanities, all is vanity,"' brayed the ex-clergyman.

'Someone get me a drink!' roared the old drunk.

'As soon as Madame Lorson got wind of her penpusher of a husband's disgrace, she chucked him out. It's just a blessing they never had any children!' the landlord concluded, eyeing the girl and her offspring.

'And now?' asked the ex-clergyman.

'Now? He's a pauper dressed as a gent!'

'"All is vanity and vexation of spirit!" says Ecclesiastes. "That which is crooked cannot be made straight."'

Suddenly aware of noise outside, Corentin Jourdan got up quietly from his chair. Down below, a streak of orange light fell across the pavement, spilling from the open door of the basement of the bakery. Within, a group of young men, bare to the waist, stood with their arms thrust into the dough, seizing it and kneading it as they chanted rhythmically, like natives around a campfire. Corentin looked at his watch: eight o'clock. The baker's boys had already begun their night's labour. Sitting down close to the window, he picked up his book, *Treasure Island*.

This here is a sweet spot, this island – a sweet spot for a lad to get ashore on. You'll bathe, and you'll climb trees, and you'll hunt goats, you will; and you'll get aloft on them hills like a goat yourself . . .

31

He had read and reread Stevenson's novel, and each time this paragraph brought tears to his eyes. 'Bathe . . . climb trees . . . hunt . . .'; for him, all these things were impossible now. But then it occurred to him that the situation in which he now found himself was rather like having a map of a desert island in the South Seas, but not knowing where the buried treasure was hidden. He was Jim Hawkins, sailing alongside Long John Silver aboard the *Hispaniola*.

A creaking interrupted his reverie. He pulled back the curtain and saw that the metal gate of the house on the corner had just opened. A woman in a gold-sequined cloak, her hair coiled into a chignon and covered with a velvet cap, was hurrying towards Rue Lancry. He jumped up, pulled on his coat and hat and, despite the pain in his injured leg, ran down the three flights of stairs and raced to the courtyard where his horse, already saddled, greeted him with a stamp of its foot.

He caught up with the woman on Boulevard Magenta just as she disappeared into a carriage, which turned round and drove up Quai de Valmy. Corentin followed on his horse, keeping his distance. At the far end of the canal, in the dim light of the lanterns illuminating the locks, a large cylindrical building loomed, like an ancient monument.

Night was closing in on the La Villette meat market, headquarters of butchery and metropolis of steak, mutton and offal, through which Martin Lorson wandered, his spirit wounded by the landlord's biting remarks. He would have to get a grip of himself.

'The fish rots from the head first, after all. I should despise these fools. I'm head and shoulders above all of them.'

For a moment, he thought he could hear the piteous cacophony of terrified beasts, brought by blue-overalled drovers to the entrance of the biggest abattoir in Paris, but it was only the roaring of blood in his head. In this strange landscape, where the capital's lunches and dinners were prepared, the atmosphere was permeated with the fear of the animals about to be sacrificed. Fear was a constant companion to him now. Had it not been at his side ever since his dismissal from the Ministry? Fear and resentment, fear and loneliness, which lasted far longer than the sudden fright caused by the clatter of a passing cart laden with coke or animal fodder. The weight of his fear would sometimes lift for a while, only to return with renewed force. He hoped that he would eventually escape from it by dint of sheer stubbornness.

A lamplighter was making his way down the street, repeating the same series of movements again and again: lifting the lever on the gas tap and squeezing the rubber air pump at the bottom of his pole. The glass mantles lit up one by one, and the neighbourhood echoed with the sound of the rubbish carts doing their rounds. Martin Lorson knotted his scarf more tightly round his neck; the air was unpleasantly damp despite the mildness of the winter.

As he walked on, he planned his movements for the next twenty-four hours. Stand in for Gamache. Then to bed, with a lie-in the next morning. Sprint over to the piano maker's and stand in for Jaquemin. Lunch at the cheap canteen in Rue de Nantes. Stand in for Berthier, Norpois and Collin at the abattoir. Dinner at Au Petit Jour. Go back and meet Gamache again.

The career he had invented for himself as a stand-in provided regular work and he was rather proud of it. The people whose jobs he took over could go and have a drink or a bite to eat, and in return they gave him a few centimes, enough for him never to be short of food or tobacco. And, thanks to Gamache, he even had somewhere to sleep. Had he not, all things considered, found a jolly good solution to his problems? No senior clerk breathing down his neck, no promotion, no wife, no rent and no furniture or possessions except the few odd things he kept stored in the shack where he slept. This was true independence. So what did he care about the base insults of a common waiter? Now that he had had a taste of this life, no amount of money would have persuaded him to change it. His colleagues at the Ministry were welcome to their struggles to make ends meet before payday, moonlighters taking their jobs, and the treacherous attentions of women!

No sooner had these thoughts run through his mind than a wave of vague anxiety broke over him and his breath seemed to catch in his throat. Stopping in front of the public wash-house (only twenty centimes for a bath), he lit a cigarette. Smoking calmed his nerves. He set off again, his protuberant stomach leading the way.

In the centre of the La Villette roundabout, the impressive rotunda that marked the toll barrier at the old city gates loomed up like a huge fortified tomb, with its circular gallery and arcade supported by forty columns. The mausoleum of a building had been built by Claude Nicolas Ledoux,[3] and now contained offices and stocks of goods held as surety. A general air of dirt and decrepitude added to its funereal aspect. Below a triangular pediment were some rusty railings with a sign attached:

NO ENTRY

By the light of a streetlamp, Martin Lorson could just make out a figure in a kepi armed with a bayonet, on guard near one of the large colonnaded porches of the rotunda. He was twirling the ends of his enormous moustache and pacing up and down. As soon as he caught sight of his stand-in, he pulled on his cape and handed over his bayonet and kepi, which was embroidered with the emblem of a red hunting horn on a dark background.

'I was starting to wonder where you'd got to – I haven't got time to stand around kicking my heels, you know!'

'I came as fast as I could!'

'Well, 'scuse me! I might stay away for longer than usual tonight. I've got an assignation with a nice little bit-part actress from La Villette Theatre. I've promised her a slap-up meal and I'm hoping for a bit of slap and tickle in return. Ah, that Pauline, she's perfect!'

He joined his thumb, forefinger and middle finger and kissed them, but his friend merely grunted disapprovingly. Martin Lorson had no interest in Alfred Gamache's little intrigues, and besides he was anxious to get rid of the man and settle down to drink the rum he had bought earlier in the day at La Comète des Abattoirs.

He set the bayonet down as far away as possible, and began swigging the rum, which quickly lulled him into a state of exquisite bliss. From Boulevard de la Chapelle, the faint strains of a barrel organ could be heard, droning out *La Fille de Madame Angot*.[4] Curled up against the railings, he soon dozed off. There was silence all around him, broken only occasionally by the click-clack of heels tapping along the tarmac. Even the canal seemed to slumber, tired after the incessant to-and-fro of barges loaded with goods destined for the factories in the port or for delivery to one of the nearby warehouses.

In his drunken haze, Martin Lorson didn't notice a carriage draw up on the pathway separating the rotunda from the canal. A woman in a ball gown and wrapped in a gold-sequined cloak got out and the carriage drove away. She considered her surroundings, her face hidden behind a black velvet mask. A second carriage clattered down Rue de Flandre and stopped just out of sight, and this time the commotion woke Martin Lorson from his trance. The passenger, a man wearing a soft felt hat, hesitated for a moment under the pale glow of a gaslight, a cigarette in his mouth. He watched the woman skipping down the pathway and avoiding the cracks between the paving stones. Eventually, he accosted her.

'If this is where the toffs meet up for their smutty shenanigans, I'm in for a long night,' Martin Lorson muttered.

But he soon realised that these two weren't a pair of lovebirds. Otherwise, why would they be so offhand with one another? There was no embrace, no tender caress; they only talked, in voices too low to be overheard. Now the woman was waving an envelope she had produced from her bag. The man tried to take it from her, but she whisked it away, laughing, and made off towards Rue de Flandre. It was four or five seconds before the man reacted, and then everything happened so quickly that Martin Lorson didn't even have time to brandish his bayonet. The man leapt towards the woman, grabbed her by the neck and squeezed and squeezed. His victim's body jerked like a puppet and then sank down lifeless into his arms. He let her slide to the ground, looked at her stiffened body for a moment and then bent down, rifled through her bag and ran off. Then a horse could be heard trotting away.

On Boulevard de la Chapelle, the barrel organ was still playing, but *La Fille de Madame Angot* had given way to *La Fille du Tambour-Major*.[5]

Suddenly a man appeared from behind the rotunda.

I must've had one too many, Martin Lorson thought to himself, his heart beating wildly. I'm seeing visions . . . It's all over, isn't it?

It wasn't all over. The killer had returned. Bending over the woman, he lifted her mask. Kneeling over her, transfixed, the man studied her face minutely before replacing the mask and melting into the shadows.

Martin Lorson was too terrified to utter a sound. He dared not move or even swallow, sure that the man must be watching him as a cat watches a sparrow, delighting in its fear. Would he jump out from one side, or from directly opposite him? Panic kept Martin Lorson curled up in a ball, shrinking against the railings. Was that creak the muffled sound of a knife being drawn? Was that shadow the fist of an assassin about to attack?

Panting, he screwed his eyes shut and clenched his jaw. After what seemed like an hour but was only a few minutes, he managed to convince himself that there was nobody around. He tiptoed over to the woman, freezing at the slightest sound. He nudged her body with his foot. A corpse. As he greedily gulped down air, a medallion stuck between two paving stones caught his eye. Crouching down, he slipped it into his pocket, and noticed the remains of the cigarette that had fallen from the man's mouth as he'd committed his crime. Lorson lit it and filled his lungs with smoke. The rotunda gazed at him hollow-eyed, daring him to carry on keeping watch. Why should he hang around here while Gamache was off carousing? A draught of rum revived him, and he decided to hide the kepi and bayonet behind a column as a sign that his departure had been carefully considered. Alfred was wily enough and would realise that his friend had judged it best, for whatever reason, to slip off quietly. He would see the dead woman, alert the police and, with any luck, omit to mention the name of the only witness to the crime.

Martin Lorson made his stumbling way back to the wooden shed on the quayside that was currently his home. Here, he jostled for a little space to sleep among piles of goods confiscated at the toll barrier. In the midst of the jumble of boxes and crates, a simple mattress, a horsehair pillow and two eiderdowns, along with a sawdust stove, a pitcher and a basin, constituted the sum of his worldly possessions. He sank down on the mattress, still fully dressed and, huddled under his double layer of feathers, soon began to snore sonorously.

Beyond the streetlamp, Rue des Vinaigriers was lost in shadow. The clock in the bar hummed and then chimed ten. The landlord lit a second lamp. As he sat at the bar and looked out at the house on the corner of Rue Albouy, Corentin Jourdan felt as though the groups of men playing cards were speaking a foreign language. The two glasses of cognac he had drained one after the other had not been enough to stop him shaking. He went and sat down closer to the door.

Dazed with shock, he had brought the mare back to her stall, fed her and brushed her down before collapsing here, a few yards away from the house, whose shutters were all closed.

He was obsessed with one thought: he had got the wrong one!

37

How could he have known that the blonde had died her hair black?

He paid the bill and crossed the street, still lit by the red glow from the bakery, went up the three floors to his room and lay down. He was tired, but sleep eluded him. What had happened at the La Villette tollgate seemed not to belong to any chronological sequence of time. He remembered having followed Sophie Clairsange for several days. How long, exactly? He could not remember. First, she had gone to a street near the church of Saint-Philippe-du-Roule. She had stopped the carriage in front of an elegant house, but had simply looked at the building without getting out. Then she had done the same thing opposite a large town house in Rue de Varenne, and then again in Rue des Martyrs, outside a residential building.

Corentin Jourdan had carefully taken note of all three addresses, hoping to identify the residents and match their names to the information he had found in the blue notebook.

A train whistling broke the silence, and all of a sudden he felt unbearably lonely. He missed his home, Gilliatt, Flip, even old Madame Guénéqué. He had neither friends nor confidants in his quest, only the certainty that he must do everything in his power to achieve his end. Eventually, he fell asleep. His dreams were filled with the image of Clélia.

At daybreak a series of violent blows threatened to break down the door of the wooden shed. Martin Lorson, yawning and scratching his aching head, opened the door to Alfred Gamache, who was fuming with rage.

'Is that the way you thank me, eh? And to think that, if I hadn't helped you, you'd be sleeping under a bridge by now! D'you think I'm stupid? The police found a stiff by the canal, so they came looking for me and what did they find? My hat and bayonet abandoned in the dust! Good thing I turned up sharpish just after. I told them I'd responded to an urgent call of nature, leaving the symbols of my authority to keep guard in my place. I said that whoever had throttled the poor woman must have perpetrated the dreadful crime while I was otherwise distracted.'

'Did they believe you?'

'I should hope so, because thanks to you I'm in a fix! Apparently, they're going to summon me to the police station for questioning some time soon!'

'You . . . you'll keep me out of it, won't you?'

The knot in Martin Lorson's stomach seemed to rise up to his throat, and he began to stammer, terrified to admit that what he had persuaded himself was a hallucination brought on by the rum had actually happened, and that he had witnessed a murder.

'Yes, you imbecile, but it's not as a favour to you. If they find out about my escapade, I'll lose my job. Now, spit it out.'

'What?'

'Tell me what happened, by God! They didn't just invent it, did they?'

'The truth is . . . I'd dropped off for a moment. I'd had a bit to drink, and then I just fell asleep. When I woke up, I saw a man standing next to a woman, all stiff and stretched out, and I was so afraid that I—'

'Blind drunk, I'll bet!'

'No, I swear, I was just tired. I promise it won't happen again, Alfred!'

'Well, there's no point fretting about it now. One of the *flics* is an old army pal. And, in any case, stiffs turn up all the time around here, so one more now and again doesn't cause a stir . . . Go on, you old scoundrel, go back to sleep, and, word of honour, it'll be our secret. We've been mates for so long, we won't fall out over a crime of passion.'

When Gamache was gone, Martin Lorson stayed wide awake. A crime of passion? He kept seeing the villain in the felt hat rifling through the bag, indifferent to the fate of the woman spread-eagled on the pavement.

Something didn't fit.

Martin Lorson struggled to order his thoughts. It was a laborious process, but eventually he managed to piece the jigsaw together.

A masked woman plays hopscotch in front of the rotunda.

An unseen carriage stops behind the toll barrier. Someone jumps out and, after a brief exchange of words, strangles the woman and disappears. The carriage drives off, *clip-clop clip-clop clip-clop*.

'That much I'm sure of. So why did the bloke come back again straight away?'

Martin Lorson finished off the last dregs of the rum and all of a sudden it hit him like a slap in the face: the killer couldn't be in two places at once, so there must have been a second criminal lying in wait. Yes, that was it! And it was this second man who had come back to peer at the dead woman's face.

'Unless . . . unless the strangler never got back into that blasted carriage. What if he saw me? If he did see me . . .'

Martin Lorson thrust his trembling hands into his pockets. His fingers closed round the medallion. He stifled a curse.

CHAPTER THREE

Wednesday 14 February

A man was loitering outside 18, Rue des Saints-Pères. Dressed in a tightly fitting overcoat and a black velvet beret, rather like a latter-day Van Dyck, he was feigning an interest in the window of the Elzévir bookshop. On the left-hand side, several books about famous criminal cases and how they were solved were on display, with the complete works of Émile Gaboriau taking pride of place. The right-hand side was filled with old books illustrated with engravings, and other more recent ones, many of them English, including *The Picture of Dorian Gray*, *Tess of the D'Urbervilles* and *The Adventures of Sherlock Holmes*.[6]

It was a dank, gloomy morning, and a persistent drizzle was making the paving stones damp and treacherous. The streets were deserted. The same could not be said of the bookshop, though, which had been invaded by a quartet of society ladies all decked out in their winter finery. There was an old man with them who had the look of a poet about him: his forehead was marked by fine lines and the corners of his mouth were curled into a sardonic expression, only partly masked by his luxuriant beard.

Maurice Laumier peered in through the window. Kenji Mori, one of the owners, was making a discreet exit up the stairs leading to the flat above the shop, whilst Joseph Pignot, his assistant, was leaning against a fireplace adorned with a bust of Molière, reading a newspaper. There was no sign of the other owner, Victor Legris.

Making his way over to the porch of the adjoining building, Maurice Laumier deliberated for a moment before resigning himself and knocking on the door of the concierge's room.

41

'Be brave,' he adjured himself. 'Mustn't fall at the first hurdle!'

Micheline Ballu abandoned her pile of carrots and turnips. The scandalous corruption of these final years of the century had spawned more than its fair share of eccentrics, and since she and her late husband had begun working as concierges in this neighbourhood full of bookish types and students, nothing surprised her any more. She hardly batted an eyelid at the sight of the damp and dishevelled dandy. By the look of him, he was probably trying to sell her something.

'O keeper of the gate, goddess of this vestibule, please be so good as to tell me where the venerable Monsieur Legris is currently residing.'

The concierge had been about to rebuff her unwelcome visitor, but to be addressed as a goddess, when secretly she had always thought of herself as having a lot in common with the Queen of Sheba, was music to her ears. How could she resist? She quickly took off her apron and smoothed her hair, before pointing upstairs and murmuring, with a little curtsy that made her arthritic knee twinge, 'First on the left.'

But when the young whippersnapper bounded off up the stairs without so much as a 'thank you', she bellowed after him, 'They probably won't let you in, you know! They're all as lazy as each other, and the apartment's knee-deep in filth!'

With a face like thunder, she retreated back into her lair.

'Sheba Ballu! Really, you should be ashamed of yourself – at your age! You're nothing but a cracked old jug, you silly fool,' she muttered into her vegetables.

Standing in front of the apartment above the bookshop, Maurice Laumier hesitated for a second time. He was not on the most cordial terms with Victor Legris, and he baulked at the idea of begging for his help. Finally, he rang the doorbell.

An imposing, thickset woman, her hair drawn into a tight bun bristling with pins, appeared at the door armed with a ladle. He recoiled, awestruck, crying, 'Incomparable Aphrodite, guardian fairy of this castle, might I humbly request an interview with Monsieur Legris on a private matter?'

Euphrosine Pignot frowned, trying to remember where she had seen this young firebrand before. She was sure he was some sort of artist, but his name escaped her.

'He moved out ages ago. And, anyway, he'll be in the shop at this time of day.'

Before the visitor had time to protest, she closed the door in his face and went back to the stove.

'Who is he, anyway, the big beanpole? Not a respectable person, that's for sure! And what was all that about dying for a cup of tea? I've already got enough to do and now they want me to start serving tea? If Monsieur Mori thinks I can turn myself into one of those creatures with ten arms like that horrible Hindu statue on his dressing table, he's got another think coming! Me, the mother of his son-in-law!'

She locked herself in the kitchen. When she had all her pots bubbling away on the stove and stood over them singing hymns, nobody could cross the threshold of her culinary fortress, even if they were part of the household. The principal victim of this eviction, Kenji Mori, had resorted to making his tea on a small stove in his sitting room. In her new role as head chef for the family, Euphrosine was becoming skilled at slipping meat or fish into the mashed or puréed vegetables that she prepared. Now that she was about to become a grandmother at long last, she watched over her daughter-in-law as keenly as any midwife. She was tormented by the idea that her future descendants would have weak constitutions because Iris Pignot, née Mori, was a vegetarian. Every evening, holed up in her little flat on Rue Visconti where she now lived alone, she racked her brains to come up with nutritious recipes to nourish the baby who was to continue her family line. The child's Japanese ancestry mattered little to her, and she did not even consider the fact that it might turn out to be a girl.

43

She now had time to sit and think about all these things, because since her son's marriage she was no longer burdened with looking after the flat above the bookshop or the one at Rue Fontaine, where Victor and Tasha Legris lived. Monsieur Mori had taken on Zulma Tailleroux, a dreamy young woman employed to do the housework, which she did with all the finesse of a bull in a china shop. It had long since become impossible to keep count of the number of vases, glasses and plates that she had smashed. For Kenji Mori, the fact that he had got rid of a tyrannical housekeeper only to replace her with a clumsy girl was endlessly irksome, but he was determined not to let his annoyance show: Euphrosine would be only too delighted to point out that he had nobody but himself to blame. She had seen straight away that this Zulma girl didn't amount to much, but Monsieur Mori, so high and mighty, and hoodwinked by this little temptress – like all men, only one thing on their minds – had taken her on.

'A good thing too! If she smashes all his precious things, that'll teach him a lesson! Just as long as she doesn't lay a finger on the baby!' she muttered between hymn verses, hacking away at a slice of calf's liver.

The terrible vision of a baby suffering at the hands of the new employee appeared before her. Always quick to imagine corruption and deficiency in others, she kept a journal in which she noted down people's failings. She promised herself that she would add some juicy details to the section on Zulma Tailleroux, as well as describing the ridiculous flatterer in a beret whom she had just seen off.

Despite the shrill tinkle of the bell, no heads turned when Maurice Laumier entered the bookshop. He hid his face inside a copy of Octave Mirbeau's *Tales from the Village*, which he had picked up from a pile of new arrivals, so didn't see the expression of annoyance on Joseph Pignot's face.

'Do carry on, Monsieur Pignot!' cried a woman with a face like a goat.

Joseph continued to read aloud from the newspaper:

'After an inspection by the magistrate and the head of the municipal laboratories, the Terminus café is once again open for business. For part of the day and the evening, Rue Saint-Lazare was obstructed by a crowd hoping to join the customers already there and hear the witnesses' testimonies. For our part, it must be admitted that we entered through one door and left immediately by another, more amused by watching the crowd than by being crushed in it. Police Sergeant Poisson, who was shot twice in the chest as he tried to bar the terrorist's way, received a visit from Lépine, the Chief of Police, who awarded him the Cross of the Légion d'honneur.'

'That man is a hero – they should put up a statue of him!' intoned a woman who was wearing a dress of aubergine silk and carrying a fur muffler from which emerged the leads of two miniature dogs, a Schipperke and a Maltese.

'Did you hear that, Raphaëlle? An attack in the station where I had been just a few hours earlier, with Mademoiselle Helga Becker and my cousin Salomé!' complained a plump woman.

'These anarchists don't even know themselves what they'll dream up next! It was lucky that this maniac's device, apparently a pot filled with gunpowder and bullets, collided with a lampshade, which threw it off course so that it landed on some tables. Otherwise, there wouldn't have just been twenty injured, there would have been deaths!' cried Blanche de Cambrésis whom, privately, Joseph Pignot referred to as 'the nanny-goat'.

'Finish the article, Monsieur Pignot,' ordered a majestic woman, whose face on one side was twisted into a painful grimace.

Renouncing his anonymity, Maurice Laumier tried to attract Joseph Pignot's attention, but Joseph cleared his throat and continued.

'Police Sergeants Bigot and Barbès also deserve to receive a Cross. The libertarian attacked them on Rue de Rome, and they fought with him hand to hand until they eventually succeeded in immobilising him, with the aid of several doughty passers-by. And, dear readers, did I neglect to mention that our rough and ready pyrotechnician appears to be a music lover, who decided to act while the orchestra was playing *Martha* by Flotow, or some similar minuet? When summoned to state his identity at the police station, this eighteen-year-old upstart, with only the slightest hint of a moustache, declared, "I am X from Peking.[7] That is all you need to know."'

'What a nerve! I'd have him beheaded without a trial, this little Pekinese! Or else I'd send him to the front line wrapped in dynamite, and he could be a flare for our brave soldiers fighting in the colonies! Sooner or later Madagascar will be ours,' piped up the old man.

'Madagascar?' said the plump woman. 'You share the beliefs of Colonel Réauville then?'

'I am rarely wrong in my predictions, my dear Madame de Flavignol. I have contacts in government. Madagascar will adopt French culture very easily as soon as we have conquered it.'

'Indochina will also become French before long, no matter how rebellious, Chinese and anti-Western it is at the moment, provided we can root out their yellow culture by substituting French for their Annamite dialects, which are an inferior sort of chatter. Those are the terms used by Monsieur Gabriel Bonvalot, the famous explorer,' declaimed the woman with the twisted face.

'I see, Madame Brix, that you too are keen to see the expansion of our culture,' replied the old man approvingly.

'Certainly. Following my stroke and my marriage to Colonel Réauville, I decided to start an artistic salon in my home in Rue Barbet-de-Jouy. I organise dinners there, which the members of the Dupleix Committee[8] often attend. They are experts in these matters. As my fourth husband never ceases to remind us, "The Celestial Empire and its satellite states have no real language – so let us give them one!"'

'Bravo! Where there is effort, success will follow.'

Exhausted by the conversation of the battle-axes – the name he gave to the windbags who surrounded him – and by the persistence of Maurice Laumier who, the previous year, had tried to seduce Iris, Joseph sought to conceal himself behind his newspaper. He noticed an advertisement at the bottom of the page.

Modern! Unprecedented!

Ever in search of the most exciting serials for our readers, *Le Passe-partout* is proud to be the first to publish the second work by Monsieur Joseph Pignot, *Thule's Golden Chalice*. The first instalment appears next month and those who enjoyed *The Strange Affair at Colombines* (published as a novel by Charpentier & Fasquelle) will love the gothic adventures of the intrepid Frida von Glockenspiel and her dog Éleuthère, on the trail of the evil amber. It is a story that will enchant our male readers just as it will delight the ladies and our younger readers.

Taken aback, Joseph folded the newspaper, set it down next to the bust of Molière, and scratched his head, muttering, 'Those swine! I've been waiting for a reply since October. They could have warned me! We haven't even discussed the contract. All they gave me was two hundred francs – that's nothing! Next time, I'll demand a thousand francs! Although Clusel won't like it, that's for sure. I'd go down to eight hundred francs, but that would be my last offer, otherwise…'

He rubbed his hands.

'Soon, fame, acclaim and the whole caboodle! What a bunch of rotters … They've delayed publishing my masterpiece to keep that scribbler Pelletier-Vidal happy! His style's terrible and his plots are totally insipid. They only like him because he knows Paul Bourget!'

Maurice Laumier was approaching the fireplace when a new arrival, with a hat bristling with feathers and a mouth like a parrot's beak, pushed him out of the way and bore down on Joseph.

'Olympe, what a surprise!' twittered the battle-axes.

'Monsieur Pignot, be so kind as to fetch me *Sophie's Misfortunes* by Madame la Comtesse de Ségur née Rostopchine. I want to read it to my niece Valentine's twin sons, Hector and Achille.'

'I think that must be down in the basement.'

'Then don't dilly-dally, young man! Run and fetch it!'

'But who'll look after the shop?'

'Do you doubt our integrity?' exclaimed Olympe de Salignac.

Casting a conspiratorial glance in Joseph's direction, Raphaëlle de Gouveline, the woman with the dogs, thought it judicious to intervene.

'Such a charming story, and such wholesome reading! Who could not delight in the chapter where Sophie, anxious to cure her doll of a terrible migraine, decides that she must bathe her feet in hot water? But the doll is made of wax and Sophie's doll becomes a cripple! It was so moving – didn't it make you cry?'

'My dear, are you sure that such a thing happens?'

'Positively, Olympe. And then there is the famous part about the goldfish, where the unfortunate creatures are beheaded alive by the little innocent Sophie! I still tremble at the memory.'

'Hmm. I think I shall buy them some tin soldiers instead. Yes, that's an excellent way to teach them a sense of duty and patriotism. Will you come with me, ladies?' she proposed, without taking leave of Joseph.

With a rustle of skirts and a draught of cold air, they all left, including the old man, who followed Madame de Réauville-Brix like a little dog.

Maurice Laumier and Joseph were left facing one another like two duellists about to set upon each other, but they had to content themselves with verbal jousting.

'Good Lord, it's the Rubens of the boozer himself.'

'I'll eat my hat if that isn't the Dumas of the down-and-outs! How fares your lady love, by the way?'

'Sorry to shatter your dreams, but Iris has become Madame Pignot.'

'Paris is heaving with unattached muses. Pass on my condolences to your wife.'

'Why should I do that?'

'She has traded in her precious liberty in return for the austerity of matrimonial life. So sorry to have disturbed you.'

'You certainly have disturbed me! So clear off!'

'With pleasure – as soon as I've seen Monsieur Legris. On an urgent matter.'

'Then I can finally get rid of you – my brother-in-law is at his apartment on Rue Fontaine.'

'You're his brother-in-law and yet you're still a shop assistant? They're taking you for a ride!'

'I absolutely forbid you to—'

'Farewell, happy husband!' trilled Maurice Laumier, lifting his beret. 'And tell your better half that I'm ready to sketch her in profile or full face, dressed or in the altogether, whenever she chooses!'

Joseph looked around for something to throw at the bounder's head, but he suddenly found himself alone.

His anger evaporated and he felt crushed by a mass of black thoughts. He was no good, either as a bookseller or a writer. Iris's love for him was just a delusion, and their newborn would be a hunchback. What was the point?

'My pet, I've made your favourite food for this evening. You need to feed yourself up,' called his mother. 'I've hidden it away at the back of the cupboard – all you have to do is heat it up.'

The prospect of a carnivorous feast restored his faith in the future.

'Hooray! A rare steak with fried potatoes!'

*

Tasha nibbled at her thumbnail, unable to choose between two paintings: one a nude of a seated man viewed from behind, and the other a Parisian cityscape at dusk. She was tempted to seek advice from Victor, who was over in their apartment at the far side of the courtyard, developing his photographs. She resisted.

'The cityscape's definitely better.'

Shortly after their wedding, which had taken place in a registry office in the autumn of 1893, with no witnesses except their close family, they had worked out a strategy that allowed both of them to pursue their own activities independently. They devoted the mornings to their respective passions: books and photography; painting and illustration. Whenever their busy schedules allowed, they had lunch together in their apartment in Rue Fontaine, where they had employed a former butler, André Bognol, to cook and clean for them. This efficient man had liberated them from the indiscreet Euphrosine Pignot.

When they hadn't had time to see each other at all during the day, they dined together in the evening. Tasha often returned home late, however; either because she was held up in town by meetings with other artists, or because she had stayed longer than planned at her mother's house, where she still gave lessons in watercolour painting. Tasha sometimes had a prick of conscience about this, because although Victor denied it she feared that he felt neglected by her. She therefore made sure that her Sundays were devoted to him, frolicking in bed, strolling along the banks of the Seine or travelling to the outskirts of the city for a breath of fresh air.

Having previously dreaded the thought of being married, she now had to admit that she had not sacrificed any of her independence. Victor was more attentive than ever, and their desire for one another was far from diminishing.

'Managing married life is like tending to a stove: too much air and the flames get out of control, not enough and it fills up with smoke,' Kenji always said. Nevertheless, she feared that their perfectly regulated life might give rise to the pernicious boredom of a straight and narrow path.

For goodness' sake, have a bit of faith in your beloved, she urged herself. He hates obeying the rules and doesn't give a damn about wagging tongues. Carpe diem!

She dismissed these worries from her mind. Now was not the time for procrastination. Thadée Natanson, the driving force behind *La Revue Blanche*,[9] to which she had recently begun contributing, had agreed, following a recommendation by Edouard Jean Vuillard,[10] to display twenty of her paintings in Rue Laffitte at the end of the month.

'Twenty, you understand? Show us your very best paintings!'

She had to get her selection right, and to choose from among her successive periods Parisian skylines, masculine and feminine nudes, funfairs and recreations of antique scenes.

She placed two pictures, one of a family of acrobats and another of a lion-tamer, side by side. Did the lion look a little bit like a large stuffed cat? There was a loud mewing as if to confirm her suspicions. Kochka, the tabby cat rescued by Joseph from the street the year before, waved her tail in the air, eager to go out.

'You're right, kitty, the acrobats win hands down.'

She opened the door of the studio to let her out and, when the cat had crossed the courtyard, she picked up a lace glove and ran her fingers over its delicate material, fighting back the temptation to go and embrace Victor.

Kochka lumbered through the cat flap with some difficulty. As soon as she got into the apartment, she made a beeline for the kitchen. Cloistered in his dark room, Victor heard a vigorous scratching sound and guessed that, having relieved herself, the cat was now noisily expressing her satisfaction. Leaning over a zinc tank, his face illuminated by a paraffin lamp with a red cover, he rinsed the prints, put them to one side to dry and emerged from his ivory tower.

Apart from his laboratory, the apartment consisted of a kitchen, a bathroom and a huge bedroom where he had managed to find space for his roll-top desk and a large chest of drawers, after moving out of the apartment in Rue des Saints-Pères. Several Constable watercolours hung on the walls, as well as two portraits by Gainsborough and some pen sketches by Fourier, the social visionary. A red chalk drawing of his mother, set in an oval frame, hung next to a small nude of Tasha and a portrait of Kenji. Although Victor had been left with no choice but to get rid of his large dining table and six chairs, he had kept his glass-fronted bookshelves. He pulled out a slim volume, settled himself comfortably on the bed and began to leaf through Verlaine's *Fêtes Galantes*, in search of his favourite poem:

> *Les hauts talons luttaient avec les longues jupes,*
> *En sorte que, selon le terrain et le vent,*
> *Parfois luisaient des bas de jambes, trop souvent*
> *Interceptés! – et que nous aimions ce jeu de dupes.*[11]

A gently sensual feeling of wellbeing crept over him, and he was sinking into a pleasant daze when he was brought back to reality by Kochka. She had jumped into his lap and begun to massage his legs with her paws and outstretched claws. Victor cried out in pain.

'Stop that, you horrible creature!' he grumbled, but he had a soft spot for the cat, and didn't try to move her.

He inspected her stomach cautiously, wondering when she would have her kittens. Tasha thought it wouldn't be long now. What were they going to do with a litter of kittens? Would they have to fall on the mercy of Raoul Pérot at the La Chapelle police station, guardian angel of abandoned dogs and tortoises?

An image formed in Victor's mind: Tasha pregnant. Iris's stomach was looking so round now that he suspected his sister and Joseph of having disobeyed Kenji's orders and consummated their union early, with a blithe disregard for the blessing of the curate of Saint-Germain-des-Prés. Although Victor and Tasha had long since stopped taking any precautions of their own, Tasha remained as slim as ever. He was relieved: the idea of becoming a father didn't fill him with enthusiasm.

'Can we really change the way we feel?' he asked Kochka, who was curled up and purring contentedly.

At thirty-four, he was getting on a bit. Although he was managing to curb his possessive feelings towards Tasha, surely the arrival of a child would bring them all back? Naturally, he never said a word when she talked to him about this exhibition coming up with *La Revue Blanche*. On the contrary, he encouraged her, which made her happy but did not stop him worrying about it – what a hypocrite he must be! All those men flocking around her and undressing her with their eyes. The knowledge that three of his photographs would be displayed alongside her paintings did nothing to ease his qualms.

The fact that he constantly had to lie to Kenji was another weight on Victor's mind. He was behaving like a schoolboy inventing any old story to explain why he was missing school.

'Dourak![12] Face up to him! Admit that you're fed up with the deadly dull routine in the bookshop and that you want to spend all your time on your photography!'

Somebody was at the door. Three loud knocks sent Kochka scuttling under the bed.

'It's open!' shouted Victor.

A tall bearded man in a velvet beret leant nonchalantly against the doorframe. It was a full minute before Victor could collect himself enough to say, 'Tasha's not here.'

'That suits me – this is a confidential matter, Legris. Sorry to interrupt your siesta. I've been running around all morning. May I?'

Without waiting for permission, he flopped down on the bed next to Victor. The two men considered one another coldly, and as Victor made as if to get up Maurice Laumier gave him a coarse smile.

'You're right, Legris, better get up. Tasha could come in at any minute and find us here together. What would she think, the poor innocent girl?'

Nerves jangling, Victor leapt up, straightened his clothes and lit a cigarette, despite his promise only to smoke outside.

'Calm down,' said Laumier, pointing to an armchair.

As Victor insisted on remaining standing, Laumier rose too, and began to inspect a series of photographs propped up on the dressing table.

'Well, well, are you getting a social conscience? You surprise me! I had no idea that you were so fascinated by the seamy side of our modern Babylon. I thought you preferred more edifying subject matter.'

'And you, Laumier, still churning out your pictures of dingy darkness?'

'My poor Victor, when it comes to painting, you're behind the times! Don't you know what Renoir says to all those clever-clogs who are throwing their tubes of black paint into the Seine? "Black is one of the most important colours. Perhaps the most important." Mind you, it's in his name . . .'

'I couldn't agree with him more, hence my penchant for the darker side of Parisian life.'

'Well, now I come to think of it, grey is in your name, so no surprises there! Oh, come on, you have to admire my little word play,' said Laumier teasingly.

'Spit it out, for goodness' sake! What do you want?' Victor barked.

'So calm! So in control of the situation! I'm overcome with admiration—'

'Out with it!'

'Oh, now you're really scaring me. It's a somewhat delicate matter that I rather regret having to bring to you. If Mireille Lestocart hadn't forced me to take these measures, I'd never—'

'Mireille Lestocart?'

'You must remember, Legris – two years ago, Rue Girardon, you got an eyeful. The well-endowed brunette. Mimi, in fact! My model, my muse, my little sweetheart. Ah, woman, the artist's saviour!'

Maurice Laumier assumed an expression of beatific ecstasy.

'And what does this Mimi want from me?'

'She wants your brains, my good man. She loves to read about your daring and perilous investigations. You have become her alpha and her omega. Luckily, I'm not a jealous man. By the way, have you got anything to drink?'

'Just water. Are you going to tell me why you're here or not?' fumed Victor.

Laumier settled himself comfortably in the armchair.

'I shall be brief. Her cousin Louise Fontane, more commonly known as Loulou, hasn't been seen now for about three weeks. She's left her job, her home likewise, and not a day goes by when Mimi doesn't nag me: "Go and see Monsieur Legris! Beg him to do something! He'll find her, I know he will!" In a word, she's driving me mad, and I've surrendered. You can name your price, within reason . . . Don't look at me like that! Our materialist society works on the basis that each man has his price. I am simply asking what yours is. I wouldn't dream of taking up your precious time without offering you a modest sum in return.'

'What on earth are you talking about?'

'You do work as a private detective, don't you?'

There was a clatter of footsteps and Tasha burst in.

'Darling, I know I promised not to disturb you, but I couldn't resist—'

She stopped short at the sight of Laumier.

'Good morrow, my charming fellow artist. Have you any idea of the rumours that are flying around Montmartre? It's a scandal! People are actually suggesting that the superb and talented Tasha

Kherson has got hitched to a bookish type who prides himself on solving crimes. She has confused love with the illusion of security and now she's trapped; she's done for! I denied it all, naturally.'

'How did you hear we were married?'

'Bibulus on Rue Tholozé is a veritable den of gossip. The owner, Firmin, is in cahoots with the deputy mayor of the ninth, and he spends all his time playing billiards at the Chien Qui Tête. Anyhow, my dear, anybody could have read the banns outside the mayor's office. You could at least have invited me to raise a glass of champagne with you. I would have brought some confetti.'

Looking very pleased with himself, Laumier examined his fingernails.

'I bet you've been going around telling everyone!'

'I, speak ill of friends? Never! You wound me.'

'Did you come all the way here just to tell me that? What do you want?'

'You, darling girl.'

Tasha could smell smoke in the air, even though Victor had stealthily stubbed out his cigarette and hidden it behind a pile of books. She eyed them suspiciously. What were they plotting, these two, who were usually at daggers drawn?

'Darling, when you have a minute, could you possibly come and give me some advice?' she asked Victor.

She left, followed by Kochka, who had just emerged from under the bed.

'You're a lucky fellow, Legris. She's got some character to her, your little woman. Ah, true love! A cure for solitude or a ball and chain?'

'No, no and no!'

'That doesn't answer my question, Legris.'

'No to Mademoiselle Lestocart's request.'

'Mimi, just Mimi. She'll be awfully disappointed and will make my life a perfect misery.'

56

'Why do you stay with her, if you despise the married state so much?'

'Out of habit. For me it's a cure for solitude and a ball and chain, but as soon as it doesn't suit me any more, it'll be goodbye Mimi, *adios*, *ene maitia*,[13] I'm off to Spain and I'll send you a pair of castanets. Won't you think again, Legris? If I dig deep into my pockets, I can dredge up twenty francs to offer you – I've just sold a painting.'

'Money isn't the problem.'

'You're lucky. I never have enough of it. Well, I'm going to take my leave. Until we next run into each other, Legris. And for goodness' sake, try to smile – life's a tremendous joke, you know.'

He caught sight of the painting of Tasha on the wall, which was his own work.

'At least admit I have some talent! And the model really is very alluring!'

As soon as he was alone, Victor opened the window and, with trembling hands, lit a second cigarette.

Maurice Laumier crossed the little garden with its withering roses at top speed, and the stray cats which made their home there bolted as he passed. He reached his ground-floor apartment and turned the key in the lock. Mimi had vanished, and he decided to make the most of the time to add a few final touches to the portrait of the writer Georges Ohmet, which he had promised to deliver at the end of the month, and which was vital to the health of his finances. He hummed to himself as he concentrated on the tricky details of a curled moustache. The stove was burning, proof that the curvaceous brunette, already the subject of about fifteen of his paintings, would shortly return. And before long she did return, carrying a pot of soup and a four-day-old newspaper swiped from the fruit seller on Rue Norvins.

'Did you speak to him?' she asked, with a tremor in her voice.

Maurice Laumier wiped his hands on his sweater and poured the soup into a pan which he placed on the stove.

'He says no.'

'Even if we pay him?'

'Especially if we pay him. It would be an insult to his honour. In any case, it's better that way. Until they finally show me the colour of their money for this painting, we're going to be living on the proverbial shoestring.'

Not listening to him, Mimi was crumpling the pages of the newspaper into little balls, to keep the fire in the stove going. Suddenly, she froze and pointed to a paragraph on one of the pages.

'It's her, I'm sure of it! Oh, how awful!'

'What's the matter, my poppet?' asked Laumier, as he filled two bowls with soup.

'They've found a girl strangled near the La Villette abattoirs. Her body's in the morgue. We've got to go there!' she squealed, shaking her lover by the shoulder and making him choke on his soup.

'But it's miles away! Mimi, think about it, little bits of skirt like Loulou are ten a penny in this city – why should this particular one be her, exactly?'

'I can just feel it. And it's the first time she's disappeared like that for so long. Ever since I came up to Paris, we've seen each other at least once a fortnight. We grew up together; we were like sisters!'

'It's true that "sister souls will find each other out if only they wait for one another". Beautiful, isn't it, my poppet? But I didn't write it – Théophile Gautier did. Calm down and turn that tawdry rag into fuel.'

Mimi stamped her foot, seized one of his brushes, rubbed it on the paint palette, circled the article in red, folded the page into a small square and wrapped a shawl round her neck, over her warm woollen cape.

'That's so typical of you, that is!' she burst out. '"Little bits of skirt like Loulou are ten a penny in this city." Own up! As soon as my back's turned, you're carrying out a close inspection of some of those little bits of skirt, and still I stick with you! Nine times out of ten, the girls who prance around in this studio haven't got a stitch on them by the time you actually start painting them!'

'Come, come, these are big words for a little woman! How do you expect us to live if I don't earn us a few pennies? Would you rather be on the . . . well, anyway, you know what I mean.'

'Oh, I see! And I'm supposed to get down on my knees and thank you because you let me share your bed? The arrangement seems to suit you, as far as I can tell!' she cried, gesturing at the portraits of her that filled the studio.

'Yes, my poppet, you took your clothes off too, like any self-respecting artist's model.'

'You don't love me. You're a brute!' she wailed, her voice choked with a sob.

Then she rushed out of the apartment.

'Damn it! What about the soup? What's wrong with people? The trials of love . . . Where are you going, you little idiot?'

'Idiot yourself! To the morgue.'

He jammed his beret onto his head, pulled on his coat and rushed after Mimi, who had made off towards Rue Girardon.

'Off to the morgue, off to the morgue, what a lovely little stroll!' he grumbled, hurrying to catch up with her.

The weather was getting steadily worse and snowflakes now fluttered in the cold wind, covering the streetlamps. Victor had stayed later than usual at the Elzévir bookshop, and was now trudging home, cursing himself for being so stupid. Why hadn't he thought up some lie that would have saved him from tearing himself away from the cosy warmth of his apartment? He carried out his duties as a partner in the business more and more unwillingly, even though he tended to offload many of them onto Joseph, who was more than happy to oblige.

He almost collided with a couple who had emerged from a porchway. One of them grasped his arm.

'Monsieur Legris, I'm begging you, please help!' cried the woman.

'Loulou is dead – murdered. We've just been at the morgue. It was a horrible sight,' the man gabbled. 'Mimi is terribly upset, and I'm not much better . . . Do us a favour, Legris, buy us a drink. My shoes are letting the rain in – I'll catch my death of cold.'

In the yellow gaslight, Maurice Laumier's face wore an unusually serious expression. Victor could tell that he was really shaken and, under a fresh flurry of snow, he led them to a bar on Rue de Douai.

They settled themselves at a table near the fire, and waited until the waiter had finished pouring three glasses of red wine before they began to talk. Victor recognised the famous Mimi by her statuesque figure, principal source of so much of Laumier's artistic inspiration. She sat twisting a handkerchief between her fingers and every so often used it to wipe her eyes. She managed to pull herself together and, between two sobs, said, 'I've got a silver brooch that my old grandma left me. I'll pawn it, and give you as much money as you want.'

'Mimi, you're embarrassing Monsieur Legris,' whispered Laumier.

'I don't care if it'll make him say yes! You will say yes, won't you, Monsieur Legris?'

Victor stared down at his glass uncomfortably.

'It's completely incomprehensible,' said Laumier. 'She was more or less broke, was our Loulou, and yet they told us that she was wearing a dress that would have cost a fortune. And there's another thing – her hair's dyed black.'

Victor looked up, admitting defeat. It was impossible to resist Mimi's red eyes, her trembling lips, her stricken face. If Tasha had been there, she might have felt a stab of jealousy.

'What colour was it before?' he asked.

'Pure Venetian blonde, a real Botticelli! They found a velvet mask near her body. The whole thing has an air of mystery about it that you should find impossible to resist, Legris.'

'Do you take me for some kind of sadist? There's nothing irresistible about a woman's murder,' Victor retorted sharply.

'You're right there, Monsieur Legris, it's atrocious. This brute is completely oblivious to other people's feelings!'

'That's a bit much, my poppet. I felt very nauseous just now.'

'You certainly did, but not because of all the dead bodies. It was the smell of the formaldehyde that gave you a nasty turn, but as for me, as soon as I saw poor Loulou stretched out on the cold stone, with her neck all purple . . . My God!'

She burst into tears again and buried her contorted face in her shawl. Victor stretched out a sympathetic hand to her and she grasped it feverishly.

'Thank you, thank you! At least you have a heart, Monsieur Legris!'

'I've got one too!' muttered Laumier.

He kissed Mimi's forehead and she snuggled up to him.

'Have you told the police about this?'

'The police! Are you mad, Legris?' cried Laumier. 'We took great care not to let on at the morgue that we recognised her. The police! That would get us into all sorts of trouble. I'm as clean as you like, nothing to hide, but Mimi . . . Before we got together, she used to trade on her charms, and the police have a file on her. Well then, is it yes or no?'

'Very well, Mademoiselle, I'll look into it,' replied Victor, disengaging his hand. 'I'll need your friend's address, wherever she used to . . . ply her trade.'

He coughed discreetly and rummaged in his pocket for a pencil.

'Oh, she earned an honest living working for a clothing manufacturer at 68, Rue d'Aboukir. She rented a room in Rue des Chaufourniers, number 8, two minutes away from the coach station.'

'Where was her body found?'

'In front of the La Villette rotunda. It says so here.'

She handed him the page torn from the newspaper, an issue of *L'Intransigeant* dated 10 February. Victor quickly read the paragraph outlined in red.

'I'll hold on to this.'

'Will you help us then?'

'I'll do what I can.'

'How much will it cost?'

'Keep your grandmother's brooch, Mademoiselle Mireille. Laumier is an old acquaintance. We met in '89, at the exhibition at Café Volpini, and after all, if you can't help out a friend, what can you do, eh, Maurice?' replied Victor, as he paid the bill.

'You're a true gentleman, you really are!' gushed Mimi, her eyes shining.

Laumier pushed back his chair and offered her his arm.

'It's jolly good of you, Legris. If I can do anything in return . . .'

'You can, actually. Tasha must hear nothing about this business, so keep your trap shut.'

'I shall be as silent as the grave, dear Victor.'

They were now back on Rue de Douai, where a ragged-looking man was struggling to shovel away the snow that had piled up on the pavement.

'I'll let you know what happens,' said Victor, touching his hat. 'It has been a pleasure, Mademoiselle Mireille.'

CHAPTER FOUR

Thursday 15 February

Never in all his life had Alfred Gamache been as worried as he was now. Even thinking about the sight of Pauline's generous breasts as she unlaced her bodice was not enough to calm him down. If he had known that their amorous rendezvous would lead to so much bother and trouble with the police, he would have left well alone. And all this because of some silly fool who was completely unable to take any responsibility for things himself!

Through half-closed eyes, he observed the column of two-legged ants hunched over unloading a cargo of bricks from a barge whose full belly was blocking the whole of the La Villette dock. His attention was caught by someone approaching him. It was a young man with regular features and a neat black moustache, dressed in a tweed suit and a felt hat set at an angle on his head.

'This looks like more trouble,' he said to himself as the stranger accosted him.

'Excuse me, could you direct me to the person who found the body of the strangled woman?'

'I knew it! First the inspector in the hussar's jacket, like something out of an operetta, then the tall, mysterious chap with a limp, and now you. Everybody's looking for him – shame he's gone!'

Victor raised an eyebrow. The mention of the hussar's jacket had made him think of his corpulent rival, Inspector Lecacheur.

'He's already cleared off, the rascal!'

'I'm sorry? I don't think I follow you. Is Monsieur Gamache no longer here?' Victor asked the uniformed man.

'I'm Gamache.'

'Ah, you're the watchman at the tollgate and, unless I'm very much mistaken, you take your duties seriously!'

A flicker of doubt crossed Alfred Gamache's mind. Despite his relaxed air, this fellow could be some kind of plain-clothes official, one of those mysterious superior beings who moved in such distant spheres that trying to picture them in his mind was rather like trying to picture the gods of Olympus. In which case, it would be no use covering for an imbecile and jeopardising his own job.

'I only reported the death. As for the other bloke, the actual witness of the crime, I didn't tell anybody about him because he's a little bit simple, and I'd have felt like a swine if I'd brought him into it. He's scared out of his wits, poor old Lorson.'

'Lorson?'

'Martin Lorson. He used to live around here, but he's upped sticks and gone to live in the abattoirs, or at least he sleeps there, anyway. During the day, he doesn't stay in one place – a real nomad! He must have set up camp with one of his friends.'

'Who are they?'

'Berthier, Norpois, maybe Collin. Unless he's gone as far as Jaquemin's place, on Rue de Flandre, at the Érard piano factory. Why are you writing that down? Who are you?'

'Victor Legris, your humble servant. My wife does illustrations for a newspaper, *Le Passe-partout*. She draws the latest news items for the front page, sometimes for pieces on politics, sometimes on crime. She's also a painter, and is preparing for an exhibition soon, so she asked me to come and find out the facts of this case.'

'Oh, she's a painter!' exclaimed Alfred Gamache, as a huge weight suddenly lifted; he was so relieved that he put aside his bayonet, leaning it against one of the columns of the rotunda. 'I've got a friend who's a painter – a colleague of mine. He's been a customs officer for more than thirty years at the Vanves tollgate. In his free time, he does a bit of painting. I'm not very taken with his pictures – they look like a cross between a child's drawing and those advertisement posters; you know the sort. The ones that say "Nasty cough? Géraudel loz-enges", or "Julius Maggi consommé", except that his pictures have titles like *The Artillerymen*, *The Revolutionaries*, and the like...'

'Really?' mumbled Victor, in a hurry to get away.

'Yes, yes. Every time he has an exhibition, I go along with my old lady – it's a nice outing for us. Last year, we went to the Inde-pendent Salon, and there were some real jokers exhibiting there! Perhaps you've heard of him – Henri Rousseau, otherwise known as Le Douanier Rousseau?[14] His colours and shapes aren't half pe-culiar!'

'My wife must know him, I'm sure. Thank you.'

'Hey! Monsieur, seeing as you hang around with journalists, try not to mention Lorson's name. It may be no big deal to you, but he'd go barmy with fear if you did!'

'Don't worry. If he tells me his story, I'll say it came from an anonymous source. My wife can do a very impressionist rendering of the whole scenario.'

Alfred Gamache went back to his guard duty, happy to have es-caped the vigilance of the police bigwigs and to have contributed to the production of a work of art.

Large wet snowflakes were falling from a heavy sky and turning to slush as soon as they touched the pavement of Rue de Flandre. Victor took care not to slip, feeling glad that he had taken public transport rather than his bicycle. The low grey cloak which seemed to envelop the city gave the morning a twilight feel. He kept on having to step aside to avoid passers-by wrapped up in mufflers. Commercial vehicles rumbled along the dirty roadway in a steady stream, and were occasionally sprayed with mud by a passing om-nibus or carriage that seemed out of place in this industrial zone. Everything contributed to the melancholy atmosphere, and yet a feeling of excitement was gradually creeping over Victor. If he had stopped to analyse it, he would have recognised the thrill of a new investigation beginning.

Near the abattoirs, the ground floors of the buildings contained an astonishing number of little cafés: À l'Amiral, Au Veau d'Or, Au Mouton Blanc, Au Bélier d'Argent. The strains of a merry-go-round barrel organ blended with the clanking of the railway that ran nearby, and a series of hideous papier-mâché cows revolved in time to the music, pursued by equally hideous cockerels in an endless round.

Victor came to the vast expanse of the abattoirs. There was an imposing pillar with a clock and behind it five wide avenues opened out before him. He felt uneasy. Which way should he go? Should he take the avenue named 'Pigpens', or one of the ones simply called 'North', 'Centre' or 'South', or the one named 'Coaches'? Either way, he would have to penetrate deeper into this hell of wails, groans and cracking whips. What insatiable demons reigned over this place of torment? Men, nothing more: butcher's boys in clogs and stained aprons, armed with mallets and cleavers.

Directly ahead was a succession of numbered sheds. A group of slaughterers was hoisting a skinned cow onto a large iron hook. Carcass-cutters, gutspinners, blood collectors, scourers and knackers moved busily around the dead animal in a gruesome ballet that could have been set in an ogre's kitchen.

Victor set off, his eyes fixed on the ground, plunging into the maze of streets, scattered with piles of debris. With clenched teeth, jostled and scolded as he went, he made his way past sheds strewn with the unspeakable by-products of butchery. He stopped to catch his breath on the threshold of a large low-ceilinged room. Five strapping young men, with their sleeves rolled up above their elbows, were working around a long table and, a terrible sight to behold, their arms were red with blood. Victor's stomach churned and he had to look away, but what he saw next was even worse: on a wooden tray, a pile of sheep's heads gazed at him. In their eyes he saw a terror which was to haunt his dreams for many nights to come. He drew back, unable to wrench his gaze away from the animals' empty stares. He swayed and nearly fell against two men who were extracting tongues and brains just as though they were removing the stones from fruit. Victor felt as though he had been transported back to the time of the Inquisition, into a torture chamber where innocent victims were being interrogated. He was still trying in vain to gather his thoughts when he heard the sound of his own voice.

'Norpois, Collin, Berthier?'

'In the tripe-house!'

He beat a hasty retreat. As he went mechanically from one room to the next, his only thought was that he should try to forget all this, and pretend he had never been here.

The first room was full of workers sorting piles of horns and hooves, destined to become combs or buttons. The tufts of hair from the ends of the cows' tails would be turned into cushions or plumes for military helmets. The hairs pulled from inside their ears would go to make fine paintbrushes.

Victor reflected that humanity relied for its comfort on the daily annihilation of millions of living creatures. No historian had every documented this particular martyrdom. Civilisation rested on an immense mountain of suffering and fear. He would have given anything to be elsewhere, but he continued on his way.

In the third room he came to, his luck finally changed. About twenty men were dealing with piles of stomachs: future slippers and bandages. Others were handling ewe foetuses, soon to be made into household soap.

'Monsieur Norpois! Monsieur Berthier! Monsieur Collin!' he cried.

One of the workers pointed to a red-haired giant washing down a heap of entrails with a hose.

'That's Berthier.'

'Are you Monsieur Berthier? I'm looking for Martin Lorson – it's important.'

The giant nodded and showed him to a courtyard surrounded by small huts.

'The third from the left.'

Victor had to knock at the worm-eaten door for a long time before it was inched open.

'Monsieur Lorson? Martin Lorson?'

The man, as fat at the front as he was behind, peered at him with bulging eyes from beneath a moth-eaten old top hat.

'I'm a friend of Monsieur Gamache's. I've come to ask you about the terrible scene you witnessed. As a detective, I shall be able to ensure your safety.'

Feeling suspicious, Martin Lorson blocked the door with his foot.

'Why should I believe you? Show me your badge.'

'I'm a private investigator, and I work freelance, Monsieur Lorson. I'm not employed by the police, but you are free to enquire into my good character – here's my card.'

'You work in a bookshop?'

'Yes, I do. It's up to you, Monsieur Lorson. You've got my address,' said Victor, doffing his hat.

Martin Lorson considered the card for a moment, and then his visitor, who was walking away now.

'Monsieur, wait! Come back!'

The hut stank of manure. Victor forced himself not to cover his nose with his handkerchief. They remained standing in the dim light.

'Will Gamache really answer for you?'

'Yes, I told you, he's a friend of mine.'

'What's his first name?'

'Alfred.'

Victor's instantaneous reply dispelled Martin Lorson's suspicion. He heaved a sigh and whispered, 'You won't go telling the police?'

'You have my word.'

'You haven't got a cigarette, by any chance?'

'Of course.'

'I'd give anything for a few puffs.' With his hand outstretched, Martin Lorson suddenly became still. 'Excuse my bad manners, but I've been living off what I can steal for nearly four days now, I haven't got a penny left and I've lost my job. Would you mind . . . ?'

'Keep the packet.'

'I'm sorry to be indiscreet, Monsieur . . . Legris, but I'd like to know why you're concerned for my safety.'

'The reason may surprise you. I'm not only a bookseller, I also write stories for serials in the newspapers, and I'm interested in unsolved cases. I use them to test investigation methods that I want to write about. I don't ask for any money, naturally.'

'I'm extremely grateful to you,' said Martin Lorson.

'And, now that you've questioned me, I hope you won't mind if I ask you something in return?'

'Not at all.'

'What exactly did you see?'

Martin Lorson lit a second cigarette.

'I need to talk about this, get it off my chest. I'll tell you the story as I remember it. But just because I say it happened a certain way, that doesn't mean that it was actually like that – I was awfully drunk and it was dark . . .'

He described the masked woman playing hopscotch, the sudden appearance of the man in the felt hat, the murder, the flight of the assassin, followed by his immediate and incomprehensible return. He mumbled, swallowing half his words. When he had finished, he rummaged in the pockets of his threadbare suit and pulled out a chain with a medallion hanging from it, on which there was an engraving of a unicorn shown in profile, seated on its haunches and surrounded by a black border.

'I picked this horrible beast up next to the corpse. Please take it – it gives me the creeps. It's a talisman and it has some kind of malign influence,' he said in a low voice.

'What makes you say that?'

'Ever since I picked it up it's been bringing me bad luck.'

Slowly, concealing his excitement at being the first to see this concrete clue, Victor put the trinket in his pocket.

'Are you going to stay living here for long?'

'Why?' asked Martin Lorson, becoming suspicious again.

'I might need to contact you. This investigation still has a long way to go.'

'I'll get in touch with you.'

'I'll only contact you if it's absolutely necessary,' Victor insisted. 'Would it be of any use to you if I . . .'

He held out a five-franc piece. Martin Lorson hesitated, took the coin and then, looking shamefaced, made as if to give it back, but Victor said, 'No, keep it.'

'Thank you. What a life. I haven't always lived like this, Monsieur, if only you knew—'

'I had guessed as much. Goodbye.'

'Freeloaders, and women's meddling, that's what brings down a ministry!' Lorson muttered to Victor's receding back.

Victor had nearly reached the exit to the abattoirs when he came across a mob of people. He stopped, unable to believe his eyes. A group of men and women were waiting their turn to sip from a bowl of red liquid that a butcher was holding out to them.

Beads of sweat stood out on his forehead. He had never seen anything as bad as this.

'Get in line!' a policeman warned him.

Victor made a faint gesture of refusal. He felt as though he were losing his grip on reality. He leant against the railings and closed his eyes. He had heard of this practice: a dose of warm, fresh blood was reputed to cure nervous disorders and tuberculosis.

Trembling, and revolted by the sickly smell, he walked along past a cold store and found himself back at the Ourcq canal. A stray dog eyed him for a moment before going back to foraging among the contents of a bin. The snow had stopped falling.

*

Kenji had been careful not to let his irritation show when, for the hundredth time, his business partner had not arrived at work until almost midday. Kenji had sat down at his desk and carried on working imperturbably on his spring catalogue. Although on the outside he was a picture of serenity, on the inside he was outraged.

'No respect! Part of the furniture! I'm just part of the furniture! Everyone has abandoned me!'

Iris, his precious daughter and the centre of his universe, had become a stranger to him, enamoured of his shop assistant, who was infatuated with himself: Joseph had become even more insolent since his marriage. A little brat would soon arrive and turn the household upside down with its screaming and its tantrums. Euphrosine Pignot had extended her despotic rule over the whole family. And, to cap it all, Victor clearly begrudged the time he spent working in the bookshop. It seemed to Kenji that growing old was indeed like swallowing a bitter draught of tea. Was this a transition period? Had he been alone for too long? He felt himself becoming intellectually weaker, as the passing years relentlessly sapped his enthusiasm, and yet he still wanted to see more of life.

The voice of youth seemed to whisper: 'Throw off your ties! Live your life!' Torn between his love for his family and his desire for independence, he could not quite resolve to leave Rue des Saints-Pères and the Elzévir bookshop, the fruit of so many years' work.

There's nothing to stop me renting a room in town, he thought.

This vision of escape had begun to occupy his mind at the beginning of the year. He had received a letter from the disconcerting Eudoxie Allard, alias Fifi Bas-Rhin, alias the Archduchess Maximova, who assured him that she had not forgotten him in icy St Petersburg, and that soon she would be coming to Paris to embrace him. Kenji's thoughts, however, had turned away from

Eudoxie Allard. Instead, he was building castles in the air for Tasha's mother, Djina Kherson, whom he imagined crossing the threshold of the room he could not quite resolve to rent.

That's all very well, but how will I persuade her to come and see me, he wondered. How should I play it with a woman as intelligent, cultivated and slightly puritanical as she is? A woman who has passed the first flush of youth but still seems so youthful. A woman who would accept me as I am?

First of all, he would ask her advice about trifling details to do with the decoration or the colour of the curtains in his bachelor flat. Then he would try to get closer to her, tell her more about himself, make her laugh . . . In his mind, he began to construct an intimate relationship, rich in shared pleasures, emotions and promises.

When the time came for the family to gather for the midday meal, a minor incident confirmed his decision. Victor had stayed to eat and Euphrosine, annoyed by this unforeseen eventuality, had grumbled that she had made enough for four, not five, and that the portions would all be too small. She had prepared a celery salad followed by broad beans in a béchamel sauce, a feast of vegetables that suited Iris but left the three men feeling rather disappointed. Nevertheless, they ate heartily, careful not to offend their chef, who served them with such authority and refused to sit down herself until they had finished everything on their plates. The moment had finally come when they were about to tuck in to an eagerly anticipated orange blancmange, when Iris suddenly stopped chewing and, after a discreet exploration with her index finger, pulled a morsel of food out of her mouth and examined it suspiciously.

'This looks . . . This looks like a piece of ham!'

Euphrosine responded with a bellow like an enraged bull.

'Anybody would think I was trying to poison you! Oh, nobody knows the efforts I go to!'

Iris looked to Kenji and Joseph for support, but they maintained a diplomatic silence, although they had rather enjoyed the rich fla-

72

vour of the ham in amongst all the vegetables.

'And they call themselves men!' cried the young woman indignantly. 'I can't count on anyone!'

She jumped up and ran off to shut herself in her bedroom. Joseph plucked up the courage to brave his mother's wrath.

'You know perfectly well she can't stand meat!'

'It's not for the meat, it's for the fat! She's as skinny as a rake, that girl! I'm just trying to help the poor little baby!'

Victor chose this moment to interject.

'If everybody who ate meat took the trouble to have a look at what goes on in abattoirs, they'd be permanently cured of their taste for a juicy steak. Luckily for them, they never do!'

'Jesus, Mary and all the saints!' cried Euphrosine. 'Is that the way it is now? In that case, you can all make your own food!'

A second door slammed. Looking pale, Kenji quietly folded his napkin. 'Well done, Victor, nicely timed. I'm going out and I'll be back late,' he muttered.

'I'll look after the shop,' said Victor.

Joseph listened for a moment to Iris's loud sobs and to his mother's curses, and then he opened the door of the cupboard where the remains of a plate of roast beef and some cold potatoes still sat, looking a little forlorn by this time. As he chewed his way through it, he began to think about the second instalment of his serial, *The Devil's Bouquet*, in which the unfortunate Carmella was destined to be murdered by the dastardly Zandini. Such literary concerns allowed him to rise above life's little trials.

The afternoon passed without mishap. Euphrosine had taken refuge at her home in Rue Visconti with the dignity of a queen who has been severely wronged, and Iris hadn't reappeared.

Victor was going over various theories about the murder of Louise Fontane and turning the unicorn talisman over and over in his hand, when the door opened and Horace Tenson, otherwise known as Pocket Size, also known as Abridged Edition, burst in.

'I bring fresh news, Legris. I've got a petition here against the proliferation of velocipedes. The bicycle is killing the book trade! Devotees of this form of transport no longer have time to discover the wonders of literature! You agree, I assume?'

'Of course, of course. I support your demands and will put my stamp on your petition.'

Satisfied with this response, Horace Tenson straddled a chair and began to recount the strange tale of the manuscript of *Le Neveu de Rameau*, which had been bought three years earlier by Georges Monval from a colleague of his.[15] Meanwhile, Joseph was distracted by having to answer the telephone twice and promise the caller, who happened to be the Comtesse de Salignac, that he would order the book by Dr Lesshaft that she wanted to give to her niece, Valentine.

'Yes, Madame la Comtesse, *On the Education of the Child in the Family, and its Significance*. No, I haven't forgotten. Yes, I've noted it down. Goodbye, Madame la Comtesse.'

He put the phone down, muttering that the battle-axe was going soft in the head. Victor hardly raised an eyebrow, cornered as he was by Horace Tenson's endless tirade.

Joseph heard the sound of footsteps upstairs and, suddenly feeling a surge of desire for his beloved other half, decided to close the shop. He was pulling the first shutter to when Kenji appeared.

'Already? It's not time yet!'

'It's only five minutes to closing . . .'

'All right, carry on,' said Kenji, and made his way towards the back of the shop, whistling.

There was a sudden cacophony of crashing and clanking.

'Victor! How many times have I told you to keep your bicycle somewhere else?'

Victor coughed sheepishly as Tenson froze and eyed Victor with all the haughtiness he could summon.

'Traitor!' he bellowed.

He swept out of the bookshop under Kenji's amused gaze.

'I fear I may have committed a faux-pas,' he remarked sardonically.

'You did it on purpose.'

'Of course I did it on purpose! It was the only way I could rid you of that agitator. His petition is doing the rounds of the bookshops, and I've had the privilege of signing it too. I bet he subjected you to the saga of *Le Neveu de Rameau*.'

'You seem to be in a good mood,' said Victor, who suddenly noticed that his adoptive father's hair was turning grey.

'Yes, I am feeling rather sprightly. This morning, I was down in the dumps and this evening everything looks rosy. I have no idea what the reason for this change might be.'

He was lying shamelessly but didn't feel any remorse. The reason was a certain widow, Madame Duverger, owner of a small apartment to rent at 6, Rue de l'Échelle. Negotiations were already well under way and a decision would probably be made the next day.

He's getting old, thought Victor. He's pretending to be happy, but he can't pull the wool over my eyes. I've known him for too long. He still has a childlike side. He needs us to look after him.

Choked by a flood of emotion, he cleared his throat and, for the first time, dared to stretch out his hand and put it on Kenji's shoulder. The gesture made Kenji jump, with its unexpected tenderness. He looked at the son of his now-dead beloved, Daphné Legris, with a strange pleasure. He had nursed him through all his childhood illnesses, and had taught him to love literature, to face up to his fears and his inhibitions. He had also given Victor his love of mystery.

'You who are the embodiment of learning,' said Victor, removing his hand, 'do unicorns have some kind of special symbolic significance?'

Joseph, still wrestling with the final shutter, stopped short and listened. Kenji looked up, the hint of a smile playing on his lips. His gaze passed from Victor to his son-in-law and then back to Victor.

again.

'You flatter me,' he said 'I'm not as knowledgeable as all that. Unicorns ... unicorns ... Some say that it's nothing more than an idealised or sublimated version of a rhinoceros or a narwhal. I've seen some ... Let me think ... It was in an illuminated bible ... Ah yes! The Petrus Comestor Bible.[16] A very rare book, a real gem, printed in 1499.'

'And?'

'He depicts the unicorn between Adam and Eve, under the tree of knowledge. It's the same theme as the tapestries in the Musée de Cluny.'[17]

'Is that all?'

'If I remember rightly, alchemists associate this mythical animal with sulphur and mercury. Does that satisfy your curiosity? On that note, good night. I've been working on a new combat technique with a friend just back from Japan and I'm worn out.'

'Aren't you a bit old for that sort of thing?'

'You must be joking! There's nothing old about me!' retorted Kenji, bounding towards the staircase.

Joseph waited until his brother-in-law had left the room before locking up the shop. As Victor, pushing his bicycle, was about to leave, Joseph barred his way.

'Boss – I mean, Monsieur Legris – I overheard your conversation. There are two places in Paris where you could find more detailed information about unicorns: the Supernatural Bookshop, run by Monsieur Chamuel, on Rue de Trévise, and the Independent Art Bookshop on Rue de la Chaussée d'Antin.'

'Thank you, Joseph. Just a moment.'

Victor handed his steed to Joseph, emptied his pockets onto the counter and took down the addresses in his notebook.

'Why are you interested in this horned creature?'

'No real reason, just a funny dream I had. Good night, Joseph. See you tomorrow.'

'Look how fast he skedaddles on that thing! He'll be lucky if he doesn't come a cropper one of these days. I'm sure he's hiding something from me. I could swear it,' muttered Joseph, walking back towards the counter.

Victor had left his pen and a folded piece of paper near the telephone. Intrigued, Joseph saw that it was a page torn from *L'Intransigeant*.

'Hmm, he reads that now, does he? What's this all about?'

He noticed that one article in the 'news in brief' section had been circled in red.

'Gosh!'

This morning at dawn, two police officers on their beat around the La Villette area discovered the lifeless body of a young woman of about twenty-five, elegantly dressed and wearing a black eye mask. She was lying, strangled, near the rotunda, not far from the canal. She has not yet been identified. Alfred Gamache, the watchman at the tollgate, was questioned by the police but said that he had not seen anything. The body was taken to the morgue.

A few names had been scribbled in the margin; Joseph recognised Victor's handwriting.

Maurice Laumier. Mireille Lestocart. Louise Fontane, her cousin, blonde hair dyed black. Alfred Gamache. Martin Lorson at the abattoirs or at the Érard piano factory.

I bet the sly old dog's started on a new investigation! This time, he's going to collaborate with me whether he likes it or not, right from the beginning! I'm sick of always being ten steps behind him.

He checked the date on the newspaper: Saturday 10 February 1894. The scent was still fresh! Feeling buoyed up, he went upstairs and into the kitchen. Sitting opposite each other at the table, Iris and Kenji were nibbling at a dandelion salad. He kissed his wife chastely on the forehead.

'You should go to bed, my sweet. I'll do the washing up and then I'll come and join you.'

When they were alone, Kenji and Joseph pushed the salad away and polished off the blancmange that had not been eaten at lunch time.

CHAPTER 5

Friday 16 February

Victor's bicycle drew up outside the bookshop just as Joseph was opening up.

'Did Tasha chase you out early this morning? There's no point hurrying anyway – I've still got to sweep the floor and dust everything. Maman usually does it, but she's shut herself away in her apartment after that row yesterday. She's lucky she can cut herself off like that.'

'Nothing's stopping you getting your own place!' retorted Victor, who had put his bike away and was now rummaging around under piles of papers.

'Thanks for the advice. I'd never have thought of that without you. What are you looking for?'

'A piece of paper. I must have dropped it when I wrote down the addresses of those bookshops you told me about.'

'Is it a page of *L'Intransigeant* that you're after? It's under Volume Four of Anquetil's *History of France*.'[18]

'How the devil . . . So it was you . . . ?'

'Yes. And you may as well know that I read it. So, dear brother-in-law, are we wallowing in sordid crimes again? Unless . . .'

Joseph trailed off and contemplated his feather duster in silence.

'Unless what?' snapped Victor, pocketing the scrap of newspaper.

'Unless you're already well into the investigation, and are just trying to convince me there's nothing going on?'

'What makes you think that?'

'I wasn't born yesterday. Those names you've scribbled in the margin—'

'Friends I'm planning to visit.'

'Maurice Laumier, a friend of yours? Now that I can't believe! You're telling me—'

Joseph didn't finish his sentence. The telephone rang and Kenji shouted, 'It's for me!'

He bounded down the stairs in his dressing gown, grabbed the receiver and smiled when he heard the voice at the other end.

'Perfect, my dear lady. I look forward to seeing you this evening,' he said.

He hung up and, without noticing the knowing looks exchanged by the two younger men, went back upstairs, whistling. Halfway up, he remarked, 'I've rented an office in town so that I can work in peace when I need to. Oh, it's nothing really, just a bolthole, only big enough for a chair, a table and a little bed. When I go there, one of you two will have to cover for me, naturally.'

With a spring in his step, he disappeared into the bathroom, murmuring an old Japanese proverb to himself: 'The bitterest tea is sweet when it is made with fresh leaves.'

Flabbergasted, Joseph and Victor stood stock-still for a moment, then Victor burst out laughing.

'Good old Kenji! "Perfect, my dear lady. I look forward to seeing you this evening"! His cancan dancer must have surfaced again.'

'An office, honestly! An office, my foot! A bachelor flat, more like, with a double bed and the whole caboodle!'

'Our friend has had the same idea as you, Jojo, except he got there first.'

'You shouldn't use that nickname any more. It's disrespectful,' interrupted a surly voice.

They stepped aside to let Euphrosine past. Her rabbitskin coat and feathered hat gave her more than a passing resemblance to a Mohican on the warpath. She was struggling with two huge bags full to the brim with cabbages, pumpkins, squashes and Jerusalem artichokes.

'On the contrary, Madame Pignot,' Victor replied; 'he's part of the family now. And so are you, of course,' he added hurriedly. 'And may I say that you're looking extremely elegant today.'

'Hmm. Don't try to sweeten me up. I'm going to cart so many vegetables into this house that you'll be able to convert your bookshop into a grocer's! Get out of my way!'

Kenji reappeared, impeccably dressed and trailing a cloud of lavender perfume.

'Even monks need their little bit of privacy,' he said, seating himself at his desk.

'Who knows what schemes this monk's got hidden under his cowl,' muttered Joseph. Then, in a louder voice, 'Monsieur Mori, Monsieur Legris wants me to go with him to value a collection of books in Vaugirard. It's terribly inconvenient because I've got so much work to do, but we'll be gone until about three or four o'clock. Could you let Iris know?'

Kenji nodded.

'Yes, go on then. It's a good thing we've hardly got any customers at the moment. Don't be late back – I've got to go out myself.'

Joseph put on a hat and a checked jacket.

'Come on, Victor, it's on the other side of Paris!'

Victor did as he was told, sighing irritably.

'You're completely out of your mind!'

'Far from it! You're on an interesting case, I can tell, and I insist on being part of it. Listen, just to show you that I'm a good egg really, I'll buy you a coffee at the Temps Perdu, and you can put me in the picture. Don't forget that you're the future uncle of my child. That means we have to get on.'

Victor looked at him out of the corner of his eye. Joseph was becoming an adult, an equal, and henceforth a force to be reckoned with. He tried one last counterattack.

'Iris Pignot won't be very pleased . . .'

'My sister-in-law, Tasha Legris, won't either. But we don't have

81

to spill the beans to them. We should just swear not to tell, like the knights of old, cross our hearts and hope to die.'

After Victor had told Joseph everything he knew, they decided to go first to Rue d'Aboukir, because it was closer to Rue des Saints-Pères than Rue des Chaufourniers.

The cab dropped them at Place des Victoires, near the imposing statue of Louis XIV on his horse. Dozens of signs with large gold lettering disturbed the harmony of the façades, whose ornate arcades were surmounted by Ionic columns. At the corner of Rue Étienne-Marcel, Victor grimaced at the sight of two buildings that had recently been built right next to a very old one. Modern nineteenth-century Paris was worming its way in amongst the historic city, and there was no doubt that each year it encroached a little more on the old buildings so beloved of the illustrator Albert Robida. Eventually, these soulless new constructions would stifle the entire city.

They turned onto Rue d'Aboukir, which was almost entirely given over to shops selling cloth, silk, lace and tulle, but also contained several workshops producing the very cheapest kind of clothes. Sandwiched between an artificial-flower factory and a milliner's premises was a five-storey building that housed a dimly lit shop on its ground floor, which they now entered.

Rows of tables buckling under the weight of piles of clothes stretched into the dark recesses of the shop. From floor to ceiling, the walls seemed to be clothed in stacks of greyish material, which gave off a sickly smell. Here and there, buyers were deep in discussion with shop assistants while their impatient fingers, like burrowing insects, tested remnants and offcuts.

Victor introduced himself to the manager, a man wider than he was tall, whose cheeks were sprinkled with moles.

'My friend and I are writing an article about the fashion industry. We've been astonished by some of the clothes prices in the shops: two francs fifty for a pair of trousers, a suit for nine francs. How do you manage to sell your wares so cheaply when they're often made of good, durable material?'

The manager was flattered and offered to show them around.

'All five floors are full, so full that we constantly have to shift the bundles around in case one of them falls on our heads. That's the major drawback of our Parisian premises. We often have to store things vertically when actually we'd rather have them out on display.'

They walked through a series of corridors and up staircases worn away by the steps of countless shop assistants weighed down with stacks of pattern pieces. In the midst of this hive of activity, they reached the sewing and finishing workshops, where thirty or so women worked in cramped conditions, some on sewing machines, some making buttonholes, some working on oversewing. Others did nothing but stitch hems.

'These women seem to be treated as no more than needle-pushers or factory workers,' remarked Victor. 'What do they earn for doing these repetitive jobs?'

'Oh, they get by. It's three francs a day. They just need to know how to be thrifty.'

'And how to tighten their belts, and go without new clothes or any little luxuries,' murmured Joseph, who was standing a little way off.

'How many hours a day do they work?' asked Victor.

'Fourteen. The people to blame for this state of affairs aren't the producers or the wholesalers; it's the customers in the department stores. We constantly have to cut our prices, so salaries suffer. And now it's the summer off-season.'

A bell rang: it was time for the lunch break.

The women scattered. Victor and Joseph took their leave of the manager and followed a group of young women to another building on the same road, where they flocked into a cheap canteen run by Protestant women. For ninety centimes they could buy a meat dish with vegetables and a dessert, served with a glass of wine, beer or milk. The majority of the girls, seamstresses, cutters, trimmers, finishers or embroiderers, made do with a bowl of soup for fifteen centimes or with a stew for thirty.

Joseph noticed a bench where a freckled redhead was chattering cheerfully to a stuck-up-looking girl with blonde hair, who kept adjusting her ringlets in the mirror that ran along the wall. He dragged Victor over and they sat down opposite the pair.

'May we join you, ladies?'

The redhead giggled.

'You're not shy, are you?' the blonde exclaimed.

'We'd love to buy lunch for you, if you don't have any objections,' suggested Victor.

They consulted one another, with a good deal of whispering.

'There's no harm in a bit of lunch, is there, Pétronille?' the redhead concluded raucously.

'Pétronille – what a lovely name! Mine is Joseph and this is Victor.'

'And mine's Florine. Waiter, four menus, please, and some bread and wine! What's for afters?'

'*Îles flottantes!*' barked the waiter on his way past.

'We'll have coffee too. If that's all right with you two, that is?'

'Of course,' replied Joseph. 'We're friends of Louise Fontane. Do you know her?'

'Loulou? She's gone – threw in the towel three weeks ago. She just dropped everything. Really excited, she was. Told us she'd had enough of this slave labour and that she was sick of ruining her eyes sewing seams. I don't blame her.'

'She must have found herself a rich bloke!' said Florine, getting ready to devour her tomato and parsley salad.

'It's better than that. An old childhood friend of hers just back from America has given her a job. Apparently it's easy and she gets paid a fortune. A load of money without all the trouble of having to have an affair with someone. Oh, this salad's lovely. I could eat it all day!'

Pétronille devoured her tomatoes, and Victor and Joseph followed suit. Between two mouthfuls, Victor asked, 'What's this rich friend's name?'

'No idea. But Loulou sent Lionel packing. He's our foreman and he's a dirty old so-and-so with wandering hands. She grabbed her chance, our Loulou! If an opportunity like that ever came my way, I'd make the most of it too.'

'Where does she live?'

'The friend from America? I don't know – do you, Florine?'

Florine shook her head.

'She never told me anything.'

'And Loulou? Do you know her address?'

Victor tried to nudge Joseph's foot under the table to remind him that Laumier had already given them Loulou's address, but his foot slipped and collided with Florine's shoe instead. She burst out laughing.

'Wait a minute, I thought you were friends of hers. You're not pimps, are you? What are you up to?'

The arrival of a lentil hotpot mollified her, and while she gobbled it down, Joseph tried to reassure them.

'I'm practically her brother – we were brought up together by the same nurse, in Charente.'

'That's funny, she told me she grew up around Flanders,' remarked Pétronille, who, having cleaned her plate, was eyeing Victor's with envy.

'That was later, when her mother moved to Paris,' said Joseph.

'Are you going to eat all of that, Monsieur Victor?'

'I'm not really very hungry. If you'd like it . . .'

Pétronille didn't wait to be asked twice. Her excessive appetite betrayed a life of daily deprivation and chronic hunger.

Joseph's winning smile combined with Victor's generosity overcame the redhead's reticence.

'She lives at number 8, Rue des Chaufourniers, in a furnished room. I went there once and I can tell you I'd never set foot there again! What a neighbourhood! An awful place.'

Guessing that he would probably get no more out of these two, Victor pushed back his chair.

'It's time to go, Joseph.'

'What, already?' cried Florine. 'What about our afters? And our coffee?'

'I'll pay the bill and ask them to give you our desserts as well as yours.'

'Oh, go on, stay a bit longer; we're having a good time. You're not like the usual idiots and gropers, you two.'

Florine twisted her napkin in her hands, still thinking about Victor's accidental foot signals. Joseph got up to follow Victor to the tills.

'Come back tomorrow!' called Pétronille.

Out on the street again, where errand girls, seamstresses and telephone operators hurried back to their servitude, Victor decided on the next plan of action.

'Joseph, you go back to the bookshop, and I'll go and find Loulou's old room. I'll join you later.'

'Why not the other way round?'

'Tasha's at *La Revue Blanche* all day today, but Iris is at home waiting for you,' replied Victor, hailing a cab.

Rue des Chaufourniers branched off Rue Bolivar and ran all the way up to the scrubby, terraced hillocks of Buttes-Chaumont park, where it ended in a semicircular cul-de-sac. At the top of the road an open sewer spewed out its foul water. The place reeked: sour, sickly and vinous odours blended in the heavy atmosphere. An air of desolation had settled over the whole area. Children riding in broken prams tore down the street at high speed between peeling façades, screeching to a halt in front of Monsieur Smith's bar and then climbing back up the hill, dragging their vehicles along behind them.

In this neighbourhood, the arrival of a cab caused quite a stir. A mob of curious onlookers wandered out of the bar, the head-quarters of a pawnbroker where the poor could get a couple of sous in return for their cast-offs. The baker, the laundry woman, the rag and bone man, their clientele and their assorted offspring crowded around Victor.

At number 8, a furnished lodging house claiming to offer 'all mod cons', an imposing woman with the suspicion of a beard re-plied to Victor's enquiry.

'Loulou? She paid her last rent on the dot three weeks ago. She wasn't the sort to flit without paying. I usually won't rent rooms to single people, but she was different, a lovely girl and, anyway, Father Boniface said he'd answer for her honesty, so we weren't worried!'

'Where does she live now?'

'She kept herself to herself in that way, and I didn't ask her to tell me.'

'This Father Boniface, might he know?'

'He might do – Loulou was a favourite of his. Before she moved in here, she lived in a hostel for seamstresses that was run by nuns, on Rue de Maubeuge. She was sick of sleeping in a dormitory and just wanted to find a little place of her own, not too expensive, ten francs a month maximum. She talked to Father Boniface about it. He's a real guardian angel for the poor folks around here – always does what he can for people.'

'Where can I find him?'

'It's easy. From here you can see the coach-hire company. On the other side of that, you go down Rue Asselin,[19] and don't dawdle because it's full of shady characters, then go down Rue Burnouf. The clinic is near Boulevard de la Villette.'

Victor set off down a slimy passageway no more than a few feet wide. On the right-hand side was a palisade of rotting boards, and on the left, a row of sordid hovels with holes where the doors and windows should have been, surrounded by mounds of detritus.

At the intersection of Rue Asselin and Rue Monjol the Hôtel du Bel Air, painted a garish red, seemed to invite those unlucky in love to set off on a new amorous journey, judging by the scantily clad women who were hanging around on the pavement outside.

Two identical buildings, the Hôtel Bucarest and, at the top of the steps at the end of Rue Asselin, one called 56 Marches, formed the outer edge of a large area in which some crazed architect had piled up flimsy shacks, mouldy sheds and a heap of worm-eaten buildings whose windows were gaping holes open to the elements and whose roofs were worn away by wind and rain. The unpaved streets were gradually disintegrating, leaving large craters filled with mud and rubbish. This cramped and dirty cesspit was home to gaggles of pale children, mangy dogs, prostitutes, pimps, the unemployed, old men and tramps.

Victor walked past a group of prostitutes whose old, shapeless dressing gowns barely concealed their bodies, some plump and some dangerously thin.

'Hello, handsome, you after some fun? I'll give you such a seeing to you won't know what day of the week it is! Not interested? It'll only cost you twenty centimes and a beer!'

Victor turned back, pursued by their jibes. He thought he was safely beyond reach when a figure with an orange scarf and a pointed cap suddenly barred his way.

'I need a partner to play cards with. Make up your mind, sunshine: either you play, or you do the decent thing with one of these ladies. I can recommend Supple Sarah or Charity Box Margot – both well worth a visit!'

'Thank you, but the answer's no,' answered Victor calmly.

A blade flashed in the man's hand. He braced himself and was making as if to lunge forward when a fist hit him squarely in the chest.

'Put your knife away, Little Louis, and watch your mouth. Irregulars like you need to stay out of the limelight. Make yourself scarce – go on, go and have a snooze! And I'll keep the knife.'

The person who had just spoken so roughly was a large, open-faced man with weather-beaten skin and a tonsured head. He wore a grubby white cassock over a patched shirt, and his stomach hung over his belt a little. His shoes were made of old, battered leather. He took Victor's elbow and led him away.

'A piece of advice, Monsieur: keep away from these parts. You're too well-dressed, and that gives people ideas. They're not all ruffians, but sometimes they get rowdy and that's when bad things can happen.'

'Father Boniface?'

'Yes, my friend, that's me.'

'Thank you for stepping in there. I . . . What's an irregular?'

'It's someone who's broken their parole. Little Louis is no angel, but he has got a heart. Last year, when a horse without a harness fell into the Saint-Martin canal, he saved it from drowning by jumping in and hoisting the animal out using a rope. Then he sticks a knife in a rival and he becomes an outlaw.'

'Are you sheltering him?'

'Yes, it's part of my faith. But they do respect me – I know how to handle the awkward ones.' He held out his fists. 'Don't worry, I hardly ever use them. I prefer treating my fellow creatures' illnesses, and I studied medicine as a young man. As for moralising, I leave that to the rich. Their mouths are full of it, whereas here everyone is more intent on filling their stomachs. Here we are at the clinic, my domain.'

They went into a clean, whitewashed room where three female patients were waiting. One had a black eye, another was suckling a sickly-looking baby and the third, a girl with piercing blue eyes, was rocking a one-legged doll in her arms. Father Boniface sighed.

'Two years from now, this flower which has bloomed in the mud will become one of the thousands of prostitutes who satisfy the bestial desires of men from all walks of life.'

He motioned to the women to sit down, and led Victor to a tiny consulting room.

'This is where I work, and where I try to alleviate the sufferings of my patients. I've hardly got anything to offer them, though – everything is so expensive! My pharmacopoeia is rather limited.'

Victor examined the contents of a glass-fronted cupboard. Borage, mustard powder, tincture of iodine, hydrogen peroxide, strips of gauze, boric acid, arnica, a few cupping glasses and some thread constituted all of Father Boniface's weapons against tuberculosis, malnutrition, ulcers and the whole litany of the afflictions of the poor.

'How can I possibly treat syphilis and miscarriages with that! But just listening to their troubles is in itself a small comfort to some of these poor women.'

'They could choose a more honourable profession.'

'Have you been living on a different planet, my friend? The laws are made for rich people. Think about it: the civil code doesn't allow a girl to marry before she is fifteen, but the penal code authorises her to sell her body from the age of thirteen! Working-class women, who aren't allowed to get divorced, become destitute when their men abandon them. Their daughters are easy prey – they're taken in by the romantic nonsense of the first man they meet. After the first child, this man beats them, and after the second, he leaves them.'

'And the women replace these husbands with pimps. What exactly do they gain by that exchange?'

'They have to live somehow. Here's an example, Monsieur. One of my patients managed to obtain a court order which obliged the father of her daughter to provide her with a little money every so often. Except that Céline hasn't got a father. Result: her mother gets nothing.'

'I don't follow.'

'Although the man responsible for the pregnancy is in actual fact the father, he isn't the father by law: the civil code forbids attempts to trace the fathers of abandoned children.'

He shrugged his shoulders, took up a flask of arnica and went into the waiting room.

'So, Fernande, banged your head against the cupboard door again, did you? You've got a good old shiner there.'

His manner was gentle and comforting. Fernande blinked quickly.

'There you go, young lady. Put some of that on three times a day. Careful, close your eye – it stings. I'll be back in a moment.'

He smiled, and his forehead furrowed a little, but by the time he had turned round and gone back into his office, his expression was entirely neutral again. Victor knew the saying that generals in wartime must only show their emotions in the privacy of their tents, and never let their men see them.

'Do you belong to a missionary order?' he asked.

'I did serve as a missionary in Africa many years ago. I was in charge of a hospital. But now I'm here, and I've made it my mission to lessen the sufferings of these outcasts from society and . . . Well, I'm not going to tell you my life story! How can I help you, Monsieur . . . ?'

'Victor Legris.'

'Are you intending to make a contribution to support my work?'

'I was just going to suggest it,' replied Victor hurriedly, pulling out his wallet.

'That is most generous of you. I suppose that it wasn't pure altruism that brought you here, though.'

'No, indeed, I was given your name. I'm interested in the cousin of a friend of mine, Louise Fontane.'

'Loulou? She's a real gem. Responsible, hardworking – I've been keeping an eye on her ever since she was twelve years old.'

'Three weeks ago, she was—'

The door creaked open. The woman with the baby was standing shyly in the doorway.

'Just a minute, Marion.'

Father Boniface hung a stethoscope round his neck.

'Go on, Monsieur.'

'Loulou has moved away.'

'I know. She came to tell me. I hope to see her again soon – she often brings medicine for the clinic.'

'I'm afraid she won't be doing that any more. She's been strangled, near the La Villette tollgate.'

Father Boniface was still bent over the chrome counter where he dispensed his remedies. He straightened up and turned a devastated face towards Victor.

'Are you sure?'

'Yes. Her cousin identified the body at the morgue. Louise Fontane had dyed her hair black.'

'I've seen plenty of sick people die when I could have done something to help them. They just fade away quietly and give up hope. But Loulou . . . Loulou . . .'

His voice faltered, and there were tears in his eyes. Victor was surprised by the sensitivity hidden behind the tough exterior of this man, who looked more like a market porter than a priest.

'May she rest in peace, O Lord, and may your eternal light shine upon her, amen,' murmured Father Boniface, as he crossed himself.

'Monsieur Legris, I feel as though you haven't said everything you wanted to say. What do you want from me?' Father Boniface fixed his piercing gaze on Victor.

'Do you know the address of the last place she was living?'

'No. What a terrible waste! Such a wonderful girl!'

There was a painful silence in the room. For a full minute, Father Boniface did not say a word or move a muscle, and his eyes remained fixed on Victor.

'No, Monsieur, she didn't tell me anything about her plans and I didn't ask her. I should have. She seemed happy.'

'I'm sorry to have brought you such terrible news,' said Victor, in a low voice. 'I'll leave you to your work now.'

As he was leaving, he bumped into Marion. She seized his arm.

'I heard what you were saying. There is someone who might know something about Loulou. She lives on Rue Monjol. Her name is Éliane Borel but they call her La Môminette. She works near the Enseigne de l'Élysée café. You can say that I told you where to find her.'

Victor had to screw up his courage to go back the way he had come, and he went into the Fort Monjol neighbourhood[20] as though he were entering a jungle bristling with hostile beasts. Ragged clouds were racing across the sky now, and the paraffin lamps were glowing faintly behind their cracked glass mantles. A melody floated through the air.

> *When hope returns*
> *And winter seems far away . . .*[21]

Victor caught sight of a little café on the corner of two alleys. When he went inside, all eyes turned to him. He feared the worst, but the customers eventually carried on with their conversations.

'I couldn't care less – he wouldn't even pay for the whole night!'

'. . . she had a senator die on her right in the middle of it. Had an aneurysm, he did. So now they call her the Gravedigger.'

A stocky man wearing a rough woollen sweater was drowning his sorrows with the help of a glass of cheap plonk.

'Excuse me – where can I find La Môminette?'

'You've got good taste, Monsieur! In the house opposite, fifth floor, on the left.'

> *I'll see my Normandy again!*
> *The place where I was born.*

The entrance to the building looked like the mouth of some underground tunnel. Victor was reminded of the Court of Miracles in Victor Hugo's Notre-Dame de Paris. Half suffocated by the foul smell emanating from the latrines on the landing, he rushed up the stairs two at a time. As he reached the upper floors, an even more nauseating smell filled his nostrils, coming from the pipes which ran through the stairwell. On the fifth floor, a tall, bony woman, semi-naked and covered in tattoos, slammed a door behind her and elbowed her way past Victor. He found La Môminette's door and knocked.

'Come in, there's no one here.'

At first he thought he would hit his head on the ceiling it was so low. The half-light of the winter afternoon gave the room a melancholy feel, and the atmosphere was heavy and stifling. Victor could just make out a forlorn-looking iron bed with a worn-out mattress, its sheets reeking of lily of the valley. A few ragged clothes hung from the rafters and a basin placed in the middle of the floor dominated the small room. A half-naked woman was pouring water into the basin from a jug with a cracked spout.

'Make yourself at home. I'll just have a wash and then I'm all yours.'

Victor stood stock-still. The nearness of this woman made him feel like a flustered adolescent. His heart began to beat faster.

'I haven't come for that. There's something I want to talk to you about.'

She was very young, and rather beautiful under her heavy make-up.

'Oh, is there now! Well, you've come to the wrong place. I don't run a confessional!'

'I'll pay you.'

She gave him an appraising look, pouting flirtatiously.

'Five francs.'

He put the money on the bed.

'Marion told me to come here. Do you know where Louise Fontane is living now?'

'Loulou? Now she's a real friend! When they fired me from the workshop, she lent me a few bob, or rather gave me, because I never paid her back. Well, she got her reward a hundred times

94

over – she's living like a proper lady now, in Rue des Vinaigriers, with someone called Madame Guérin. She told me that before she scarpered.' She bit her lip. 'I said I'd keep it a secret . . . You won't do anything bad to her, will you?'

She came up close to him, and he jumped, feeling a shiver run down his spine. She seemed so vulnerable. He breathed in her smell, and she pressed her chest against him. He gazed down at the vision of her velvety shoulders.

'I'm a friend of hers.'

She gave him a scrutinising look.

'Yes, I believe you. You're like someone out of a book, you are. Are you sure you don't want to? It'd be a little bonus . . .'

She was pushing him towards the bed. She was so slim, so alluring . . . A voice deep inside him protested, 'Are you just a body? Does nothing mean anything to you except possessing this body that you desire?'

'Don't you like me?' she whispered.

'Yes, I do like you.' He made a supreme effort, and gently pushed her away. 'I'm married, and I love my wife.'

'Well, you're a funny one. And your wife's a lucky lady! Go on, get out of here.'

'Thank you so much, Mademoiselle, and good luck.'

Through the door, he heard the sound of splashing water. He caught a whiff of the smell of lily of the valley coming from his clothes.

'I'll have to have a bath.'

He thought of Tasha and felt ashamed.

CHAPTER 6

Saturday 17 February

That morning, the Parisian sky seemed to be every possible shade of off-white, from a turtledove's wing to a mouse's coat. Tasha had got up very early to take some things to be ironed at the laundry on Rue Lepic. She dropped off a bundle of bedclothes and a pink velvet dress with grey inserts, a wedding present from Victor.

As she was walking back up Boulevard de Clichy, a surge of happiness ran through her, an inexplicable bubble of emotion, one of the mysteries of human life. When she got to Rue Fontaine, the bubble burst, leaving a feeling of uncertainty in its place. She remembered Laumier's visit, and Victor's embarrassed expression. What were they plotting? She imagined Victor hurt, or dead. A sudden anxious tenderness made her rush into her husband's arms, and he only just had time to put down his razor.

'Help! An Amazon!' he said, laughing.

He wiped away the foam on his cheeks with a crumpled handkerchief before embracing her.

'What's the matter, my darling?'

'I missed you,' she murmured, leading him towards the bed.

She would have liked to say, 'I think Maurice has got you caught up in some shady scheme. You wouldn't admit it for the world, but I can tell.' Yet all she could do was cling to him, and then take off her camisole and press herself against him. Experiencing his own surge of emotion, Victor kissed her again and again, covering her breasts with his hands. As his caresses explored the rest of her body, she threw her head back with a little cry. Without removing his lips from hers, he laid her on the bed and took off the rest of her clothes and then his own. The shifting shadows cast on the wall by the washing drying in the courtyard merged with the shadows of their bodies. Everything receded except the present moment.

When they caught their breath again, they stayed fused together. Kochka watched them curiously. With half-closed eyes, Victor saw the cat drag her heavy body up onto the eiderdown and begin to wash herself. He pushed her away with his foot.

'Scram, you brazen hussy!'

'She's hungry,' said Tasha. 'Me too – aren't you?'

'I'm going to be late, my pretty.'

'You already are!'

She ruffled his hair, jumped out of bed and ran to the kitchen. There was a banging of cupboard doors and she shouted at the cat, 'You little thief! If the cobbler's moggy hadn't got you in the family way, I'd put you on bread and water for ever and ever! Victor, she's eaten all the cheese!'

'At least you'll stay nice and slim!'

There was something affectionate in his voice, as though he found her charming and childish. She was happy that she could make him feel that way about her.

When she came back with bread and coffee, Victor was sitting up in bed smoking a cigarette.

'You promised not to smoke inside any more.'

'A man who makes promises, breaks promises. Come here. What have you got planned for today?'

'I'm having lunch with Thadée Natanson. He's nice but so intimidating, with his big black beard and his fiery eyes. Thanks to you, I'll be on top form, though,' she whispered.

'You're so selfish! I'm just going to be called a shirker by you-know-who!'

'Your father is too indulgent with you. And such a handsome man …'

She pointed to the picture she had painted of him four years earlier. Lounging nonchalantly in an armchair, a slight smile playing on his lips, Kenji stared out at them.

'Do you find him attractive?' Victor asked.

She gave him a playful look.

'Who knows? If he'd shown an interest in me before you did, perhaps I would have succumbed. I'd like him to pose nude for me.'

Victor could not disguise a pang of uneasiness. He had been feeling nervous since the previous day, sure that he was going to let slip a word or a phrase to Tasha that would reveal the temptation he had felt when he had almost given in to La Môminette's advances.

She put his discomfiture down to the fact that he was nervous about the forthcoming exhibition, and said to him gently, 'People are going to love your photographs at the exhibition, my love.'

'What are you going to wear?'

'That beautiful dress you bought for me.'

'I should have bought something more frumpy!'

'Don't worry. Thadée is married to a beautiful young woman and he's completely mad about her.'[22]

Victor thought about La Môminette and reflected that the most ardent passion didn't put a stop to feelings of desire for other people.

'Listen to me, Victor Legris, are you going to tell me the truth about Laumier? What are you cooking up together?'

'That coxcomb? I absolutely refuse to listen to his whining any more. He can keep his distance. Come on, duty calls!' he cried, scratching Kochka under the chin and completely avoiding answering the question.

The cat craned her neck and purred voluptuously.

Iris opened one eye and could just see Joseph getting dressed near the window, which was still closed but let in a few rays of grey morning light. She looked at the uneven line of his shoulders. Far from being repulsed by this imperfection, she found it touching.

How fragile he was, this man whose child she was carrying! Although she was younger than him, she felt stronger and more mature than this husband of hers with his slightly hunched back and naïve eyes. Because he had read a lot and written a little, he thought himself more mature than her. Iris, however, was convinced that she was the more sensible one of the couple.

She made herself more comfortable on the mattress, her palms resting on her stomach as she thought about the new life inside her, which was both real and unreal. Soon, it would take up a central role in this apartment and in the daily lives of those around it. Was it a boy or a girl? What would it look like? What would be its strengths? Its weaknesses?

Still half asleep, embroidering all sorts of imaginary details into her musings, she was barely aware of Joseph leaning over her. An excess of love almost made him wake her to give her a kiss. That she should have agreed to share her life with him, misshapen as he was, and nothing but an obscure shop assistant – although he did have the makings of a literary master – filled him with gratitude.

Bearing a loaded tray, Euphrosine strode into the room, cutting short any further loving reveries.

'Maman? Already?'

She set her burden down on a pedestal table.

'I've been thinking it over: this young lady needs a bit of pampering. Lord knows, expecting a baby is no joke! I remember my own pregnancy. You weighed a ton, my pet! And I had all sorts of cravings. Just think, I once absolutely had to have black pudding with apple sauce in the middle of the night!'

'Don't ever make that for Iris!'

The subject of this conversation had heard every word of it, even though it had been enacted in stage whispers, and she tried hard not to laugh. Despite Euphrosine's exasperating ways and her insistence on taking charge of the whole household, Iris had come to feel the sort of respect for her that she might have felt for a grandmother. Having lost her own mother at the age of three, she enjoyed having an older woman look after her, even if all of this solicitude was sometimes rather suffocating.

Iris waited until Joseph had left the room and then sat up.

'Euphrosine, I want to apologise about the meat yesterday. I understand your concern and I've come up with a compromise. I'll agree to eat ham once a week, some fish on a Friday, and a chicken breast once every so often. Dr Reynaud did say that it would be a good idea.'

'At last! I'm so pleased. I hope you haven't got anything against eggs either, because I've made you two soft-boiled ones. You must be peckish. There's some toast too, and homemade plum jam, a present from Micheline Ballu, some croissants, a brioche, a hot chocolate and some orange juice.'

Feeling suddenly nauseous, Iris allowed her mother-in-law to plump up the pillows and place the tray on the bed.

'Eat up while it's hot! I'm going to let a bit of air into this room – it feels like a greenhouse in here.'

While Euphrosine opened the curtains, Iris quickly stuffed the croissants, the brioche and the bread into an empty biscuit tin hidden in her bedside table.

'Please, don't make my father, my husband, my brother-in-law and you yourself go without meat because of me. And do sit down and eat with us – that way we'll be a proper family.'

'Y–you're a good girl,' stammered Euphrosine, her eyes moist. 'So kind to relieve me of the cross I bear. Oh, you've run out of bread! I'll go and get you some more, to make soldiers with.'

As she went into the kitchen, Euphrosine saw Kenji rushing to his apartment, kettle in hand. She only had time to catch a flash of blue dressing gown with red spots before he had closed the door behind him.

'Like father, not like daughter,' she grumbled to herself. 'He survives on nothing but tea!'

Downstairs in the shop, Joseph was giving an impromptu rendition of the Savoy regional anthem.[23]

> *'I salute you, hospitable land,*
> *Whose charity all ills allays,*
> *Where freedom's flag rests in the people's hand;*
> *Your constitution I come to praise.'*

As he finished opening the shutters, he bellowed the chorus at the top of his voice:

> *'Valiant Savoyards, I salute you!'*

The sound of the telephone ringing cut short his moving performance. He resisted the temptation to bellow 'I salute you!' into the receiver, realising that the Comtesse de Salignac was on the other end, asking about the delivery of the book about the education of children that she wanted to buy for her niece.

'By Dr Lesshaft,' she enunciated, in her best German accent. 'Don't let me down!'

'*Jawohl*, Madame la Comtesse!' said Joseph.

He replaced the received, muttering to himself, 'There's no need to keep on at me! She'll get her manual eventually.'

He wrote the order down for a second time in Kenji's ledger and the lanky figure of Boni de Pont-Joubert, the husband of his former sweetheart, Valentine, who also happened to be the Comtesse's daughter, came into his mind. 'That pretentious, overdressed prince of fashion! When I bring up my son, I'll do it without an instruction book, or an English nurse either! Seriously! In any case, English or not, if I employ a nurse, Maman will kill me!'

A little man with a sallow complexion came into the shop, a newspaper under his arm. While he rummaged among the shelves, Joseph quietly removed the newspaper, which the man had left on top of a pile of dictionaries.

'Well, I'll be damned!' he exclaimed. Hurriedly, he cut out an article and slipped it into the notebook where he kept short news items, without noticing that the little sallow-faced man was cramming a hardback into his pocket.

The bookshop was full of customers all of a sudden. It was one of those days – was it because of an unexpected ray of sunshine? – or had each passer-by, struck by a thirst for knowledge or simply by curiosity, decided to come in and look at a book, perhaps even buy one?

At that moment, Victor and his bicycle came to the rescue. The little man had just rolled up his newspaper and was about to leave when, leaning his steed against the counter, Victor called to him.

'Monsieur, that book that seems to have got caught in your coat … my assist— my brother-in-law will be most happy to help you if you wish to buy it,' he said, pointing at Joseph.

The thief paid up without a murmur for the volume of Ronsard's poetry that had taken his fancy and, having checked that Joseph had given him the right change, he sauntered out casually.

'What a nerve!' muttered Joseph.

'I saw you through the window – your scissors were working away at that newspaper. What news?' asked Victor.

He greeted a few acquaintances as he went to put his bicycle away. When he got back to the counter, he winked reassuringly at Joseph.

'Don't worry about it. These things always happen when you least expect them,' he whispered.

'In any case, it was worth it. Have a squint at this!' retorted Jojo.

He handed over the article.

MAN SERIOUSLY INJURED
AVENUE DU BOIS-DE-BOULOGNE

The Marquis Saturnin de La Picaudière was driving his phaeton in the park, according to his daily routine, when he noticed a body lying on the verge beside one of the avenues. It was Baron

Edmond de La Gournay, who, despite being a skilled horseman, must have fallen off his horse, a fine Württemberger called Priam, who was later found wandering along the Champs-Élysées.

The Baron's face was covered in blood, and he was found to have a wound at the back of his head. He was taken home as quickly as possible, and the victim is now in a critical condition, although the doctors say that the danger of a stroke is, in all probability, very slight.

We would like to remind our faithful readers that the Baron is a friend of Jean Lorrain, whose play *Yanthis* opens tonight at the Odéon Theatre, and that a few years ago the Baron founded one of the most famous occult societies in Paris, the Black Unicorn, whose professed aim is to 'probe the realms of the invisible and illuminate the obscure labyrinth leading to the philosopher's stone'. If only the society could have sharpened the poor Baron's vision a little, then he might not have had this terrible accident.

'What's so interesting about this?' asked Victor.

'What's so interesting? Well, the medallion with the black unicorn that the fat chap at the abattoir gave to you – he found it near Loulou's body, didn't he? Maybe she knew the Baron—'

Victor signalled to Joseph to be quiet as he heard Kenji's footsteps on the spiral staircase.

'Monsieur Mori, what a pleasure to see you again!' trilled a generously proportioned woman whose hair was arranged in tight ringlets. 'Have you finally got the *Songs of a Country Man* by Déroulède that you've been promising me ever since it came out a month ago?'

Joseph hid behind a row of shelves and was eventually saved by the ringing of the telephone, which drowned out Kenji's reply.

'Hello, Legris? It's me,' said a voice which Joseph immediately recognised as belonging to the loathsome painter.

'The shop's full of people,' he said, in a low voice.

'Have you given it any more thought? Can I really count on you? Mimi won't stop pestering me.'

'"By time and toil we sever, What strength and rage could never."'

'Save your preaching, Legris, and tell me what you mean!'

'It's from a fable by Jean de La Fontaine, and I think its meaning is clear!' Joseph slammed down the receiver. 'To think that we're going to all this trouble for that cretin . . .'

'Joseph, what's this you've put in the ledger? It's illegible,' said Kenji.

'Oh, it's just an education manual for Madame de Salignac. It's the second time the old battle-axe has asked us for it.'

'I thought I'd strictly forbidden the use of that word.'

Victor quickly put his arm round his brother-in-law's shoulders, saying, 'Do you remember those two bookshops you told me about? Well, I think it's about time you went along there, to see about that big order from the Baron de La Gournay.'

'What order?' chorused Joseph and Kenji.

'The one the Marquis de La Picaudière told us about,' replied Victor, brandishing Joseph's newspaper cutting in his free hand.

'Oh that, of course! I'll go straight away!'

'Where's he going? The Marquis de La Picaudière? A customer? You and Joseph have endless confabs and I'm never in on the secret,' grumbled Kenji. 'And now he's off again. What about you? Will you deign to stay or are you going to make up some excuse about having photographs to develop?'

Victor looked around the shop. The more irritating customers had all left, leaving only a few well-behaved bibliophiles browsing.

'Listen, Kenji, don't you think it's time we reassessed Joseph's status in the bookshop? After all, he's your son-in-law now.'

'I'm all too well aware of that. There's no need to twist the knife in the wound.'

'So he can't be just a shop assistant any more.'

'But he insists on behaving like one! I wanted to employ a new assistant and he was categorically opposed to the idea! So here we are in a pretty pickle, with an ex-assistant who refuses to be replaced, and his mother who insists on playing housekeeper!'

'I could take over the purchasing side of things, and he could look after sales and delivery, in exchange for a share of the profits.'

'If apple trees bore fruits of gold, man's burning greed would soon turn cold. In other words, money doesn't grow on trees!' Kenji said, before being accosted by a customer.

'But a new assistant would be expensive too,' Victor objected.

He gave up. 'There are none so deaf as those who will not hear,' he reflected, determined to take up the point again at the earliest opportunity.

Joseph jumped off the omnibus at Rue Bergère and, walking past the National Savings Bank, headed towards number 29, Rue de Trévise. Victor had had the bright idea of continuing their investigation at the Supernatural Bookshop, owned by Lucien Chamuel, a native of the Vendée, who was also a publisher and had a little back office behind the shop, which served as a meeting room. For fifty centimes a day, readers could consult key texts on hermeticism.

An imposing figure, adorned with exotic fur-trimmed draperies, shook his dark hair and beard as he declaimed a text of his own devising.

> *All praise to you! Intangible Eros,*
> *Uranian Eros! All praise to you!*
> *O deliverer from banal tenderness,*
> *Great alchemist of impure desire,*
> *Athanor of the great work in the world of souls*
> *All praise to you, Androgyne!*[24]

Joseph saw that the rest of the audience were applauding devoutly and resisted the urge to burst out laughing.

A stocky, jovial man with a curly beard came into the bookshop. The speaker bowed stiffly to him and made his exit, followed by his admirers.

The man narrowed his malicious eyes and knocked at the editor's door. A voice called him in.

Feeling rather lost, Joseph went and stood next to a young, delicate-looking man with a halo of blond curls who was engrossed in a slim volume of verse. Joseph coughed quietly to attract his attention.

'I'm sorry to bother you, but who was that old chap?'

'What? Didn't you recognise Sâr Péladan?'

'Sire Péladan?'

'No, he takes the title Sâr from the kings of Assyria. He's a highly respected writer – his fictional character Merodack is fascinating. I recommend that you read his book *The Supreme Vice*. It was published ten years ago, but is still fresh and instructive today.'

Joseph remembered having placed a few books by this man on the shelves of the Elzévir bookshop, but he had been put off by their convoluted style and had never actually read any.

'And the other man, who the, er, Sâr seemed to want to avoid?'

'Oh, that was Dr Encausse, commonly known as Papus,[25] the name of a spirit in the Nuctemeron by Appollonius of Tyana. He and Péladan haven't been on good terms since the War of the Two Roses broke out.'

'The one fought in England?' Joseph hazarded innocently. He had once flicked through an abridged history of the House of Lancaster.

The young man put his volume of poetry back on the shelf and looked at him pityingly.

'That's got nothing to do with it. I assume that the name Stanislas de Guaïta[26] also means nothing to you?'

Joseph gave a subdued nod of the head.

'Six years ago Stanislas de Guaïta, a great admirer of Péladan, suggested that they should found the Cabalistic Order of the Rosicrucian together. Papus became a member. However, on 14 May 1890, the Sâr decided to create his own brotherhood, and gave himself the title of "Imperator and Supreme Hierarch of the Catholic Order of the Rose and the Cross". From then on, Papus replaced Péladan in Stanislas's eyes, thus all the resentment. Last year, the supreme council, to which de Guaïta and Papus both belong, condemned Péladan as a usurper, a schismatist and an apostate. It's a great shame, because in my opinion they're all talented investigators. Ah! If only he could succeed in discovering the secret of the philosopher's stone, as he so passionately desires!'

This last comment caught Joseph's attention. Suddenly alert, he cried, 'He'd definitely be able to tell me something about the Black Unicorn, this Papus!'

The young man curled his upper lip, giving him a curious air.

'The Black Unicorn! A band of imbeciles, the dregs of society!'

'But they're seeking the philosopher's stone!'

'They couldn't even begin to guess at its whereabouts. You, on the other hand, dear boy, seem extremely talented. What would you say to taking a little glass of the Green Fairy with me? Unless you'd prefer to inhale some ether in my humble abode?'

The young man was pressing himself so close that Joseph, terrified, abandoned his plan to talk to Dr Encausse, alias Papus, and escaped as quickly as he could.

He went down Rue La Fayette, and continued, his forehead still damp from this unsettling experience, until he reached Rue de la Chaussé d'Antin, where he managed to find the Independent Art Bookshop. He tore a page out of his notebook, scribbled the title *The Supreme Vice* on it, and waved it under the nose of one of the shop assistants, a stooped old man who made up for his baldness with a flowing white beard and moustache. The assistant said that it was a shame that Joseph had arrived when he had, because he had just missed Stéphane Mallarmé and Claude Debussy, who were both interested in esotericism and friends of Sâr Péladan. Feeling reassured by the fact that he was the only customer in the shop, and relieved to be safe from the young man's clutches, Joseph enquired about the Black Unicorn. It transpired that the old man was rather hard of hearing.

'Speak up!' he shouted.

'The Un-i-corn,' Joseph enunciated.

'Ah, yes, the beautiful animal. Three thousand years ago, the Chinese believed it to be sacred and called it the *kilin*. In Sanskrit, it was known as *ekasringa*; in Tibetan, *tso-po*; and in Vietnamese, *lân*. The Arabs knew it by the name of *kurkadann*. Its traces can be followed to India, where the *sarabna* haunts the snowy mountain summits, and to Palestine, where the name *re'em* recalls the Assyrian name, *rimu*,' the old man quavered.

'I want to know about the Black Unicorn!' bellowed Joseph.

'Bah! A sect of charlatans who can only follow in the wake of the great work. They claim to have unearthed part of the horn of a *tusson* or a *texon*.'

'What's a *tusson*?'

'Why, a unicorn! They ground it up into powder and use a pinch of it, mixed with sulphur and mercury, at séances reserved for their inner circle. In fact, they exploit credulous nincompoops, whose money they take to fill their coffers.'

'Who exactly are "they"?' Joseph roared.

'I have absolutely no idea. Ask Monsieur Satie, who's just come in. He must know – he is the Chapel Master for the Order of the Rose and Cross, and he composed a set of chimes for them, to be played on the piano.'

Joseph walked over to the man who had just entered. He was around thirty, wore a shapeless velvet hat and had long brown hair and a neat brown beard. He had a well-groomed moustache, which was curled up at the ends, and was smiling facetiously. His dark eyes scrutinised Joseph through a pince-nez as he leant on his umbrella.

'Monsieur, I am a friend of Sâr Péladan,' said Joseph.

'Do you like my compositions?'

Embarrassed, Jojo twisted the sheet torn from his notebook in his hands.

'Yes, that is … I … yes, your chimes!'

'My chimes, just so. But what about my three *Fils des Étoiles* preludes, and my *Danses Gothiques*? And what did you think of my *Gymnopédies* and my *Gnossiennes*? There's no need to lie. I'm well aware that neither Péladan, whose ideas I nonetheless admire, nor his entourage are capable of truly appreciating my music. My lot is a melancholy one – born so young in such an old world.'

'To tell the truth, Monsieur, I, er … I'm trying to find out the address of an alchemist, Baron Edmond de La Gournay, so that I can deliver a message to him.'

'De La Gournay,' mused Erik Satie, stroking his beard. 'One of those men who make me think that the more I know men, the more I admire dogs. Alchemist is rather an ambitious title for him! Fine words, abracadabra and open secrets, more like … I once went to a concert at his house with Debussy and Huysmans. What an appalling evening! He lives at number 34a, Rue de Varenne, in a rather rundown house. The building is on its last legs and sooner or later it's bound to fall down. They keep servants to a minimum, and the footmen have all left, in any case, because they never got paid. As for Madame de La Gournay, she does provide an injection of something, but it's something other than high spirits, if you see what I mean. It's not really surprising, given that she's the wife of a hopeless addict. Their cosy abode reeks of ether and morphine.'

'Why? Are they using them to disinfect his wounds after his fall?'

Erik Satie's smile became more pronounced.

'Either you are a simpleton, or you have a singularly eccentric sense of humour. I prefer the second theory. Goodbye, Monsieur,' said Satie, and he disappeared into the recesses of the bookshop.

'What did I say that was so funny?' wondered Joseph, as another cab took him over to the Left Bank.

The vehicle had to stop before the appointed place because the roadway, which was paved with wood, was strewn with bales of hay.

109

'One of the rich toffs who live around here must be ill – they don't want anyone disturbing their sleep,' grumbled the coachman.

On Rue de Varenne, nothing except a few cracks in the façade and the peeling shutters revealed the state of decrepitude into which the De La Gournays' home had fallen.

The bell rang several times before a thin, aristocratic-looking woman with pale cheeks appeared at the door. She was draped in a plush mantle embroidered in fuchsia pink, and wore a yellow bird of paradise as a hat. She seemed overcome with irritable fatigue, and considered her visitor without displaying the slightest interest in him.

'Good morning, Madame. Monsieur Chamuel, the bookseller, sent me with an enquiry about some books that the Baron de La Gournay has ordered.'

'My husband? He is at death's door,' the woman replied tonelessly.

Nevertheless, she did reach for a bell, which she rang imperiously. A coarse-featured servant with a wart-studded chin responded to the summons.

'Octavie, take this visitor to my husband. I am going out. My friend Blanche is receiving today. Then I have a dress fitting at Doucet's.'

'Will Madame take the tilbury?'

'No, Priam is too unsettled. I shall hire a carriage.'

She bowed almost imperceptibly to Joseph, and he climbed the front steps under the hostile gaze of the servant, in her black dress, dirty apron and old pattens.

'She's off her rocker, Madame Clotilde is! Does she think that Monsieur Edmond's receiving today too? He's already had that madman with him for more than an hour, the one who doesn't know when he's not wanted! If it was up to me, I'd send all these characters packing – to think they all come and torment him, in the state he's in!'

This speech was pronounced as though Joseph didn't exist. Still grumbling, Octavie led the way through a vast room with cracked walls and faded furniture, which looked onto a courtyard filled with mossy statues. They arrived at the bottom of a huge marble staircase, every step of which was cracked and crumbling. The muffled notes of a distant piano followed them up the stairs.

They walked through a series of cramped rooms, full of old fireplaces, plaster busts, armchairs and tapestries where the dust of many generations had accumulated in a thick layer. Numerous family portraits hung over Louis XVI writing desks or bronze pendulum clocks, which they seemed to guard jealously.

Finally, they stopped in a hall that was even more dilapidated than the rest of the house, and Octavie issued some haughty instructions.

'That crank is with him now. He'll clear off eventually, and you can go in, but don't be too long – the doctors say he mustn't get tired!'

The pattens retreated into the distance, clattering on the parquet floor. Left to himself, Joseph breathed a sigh of relief before inspecting the surroundings, a clutter of rickety chairs and threadbare Persian carpets. As well as the door he had come through and one leading to the Baron's bedroom, there was a third door that aroused his curiosity. He slipped through it into a corridor with a spiral staircase at the end. The place reminded him of the overly ornate home of Fortunate de Vigneules.[27] Joseph was about to explore the corridor when he heard the sound of raised voices behind a door, which he inched open as quietly as he could.

'... need it, it brings me such relief!' a high-piched voice implored.

'... madness ... get your nightmares again ... destroys your innards and your soul ... better to follow Lorrain's advice ... a bit of bromide ... feel better,' replied a low voice.

'A gulp of ether, I beg you! I'm in such pain!' wailed the first voice.

111

The bass resounded again.

'... extremely serious ... blood ... my dolls, they're ruined! ... Crucial to know whether your ... blood everywhere ...'

Opening the door a little further, Joseph saw a man in evening dress bending over a bed in which someone with a bandaged head could just be made out: the Baron.

'One mouthful, just one ... the bottle is in my desk,' the Baron pleaded.

The crank straightened up and Joseph softly pulled the door to. When he dared to open it again a few minutes later, the air was heavy with the odour of phenol.

'Where have you hidden the key with the unicorn's head?' scolded the crank. He bent down still further. 'The key to your private chamber ... must have it ... Edmond ... the key ... just tell me ...'

'Please ...'

'Answer me. I must know whether your collection has also been stained with blood! Will you answer me, in the name of—'

'You'll be the death of him!' rasped a harsh voice just behind Joseph's head, giving him such a shock that he jumped back into the corridor.

Slowly, he turned round to face the largest nurse he had ever encountered. He barely came up to her shoulder.

'She was right to warn me, that maid. Get a move on in there, and clear off!' she thundered, bearing down on the bed. 'What with that blow to the back of the neck, he needs absolute rest! We've already had that policeman in here questioning him without permission ... Out you go!'

Joseph took cover behind the third door and caught sight of the crank, an angry-looking man with a square, clean-shaven face and a slit of a mouth. The hairy fingers of his right hand twisted a suede glove convulsively. He had an impassioned argument with the invalid before he left, and the nurse ejected Joseph from his hiding place and shoved him authoritatively towards the exit.

'You too, lad, get lost.'

Joseph contemplated her imposing bulk and obeyed without a murmur.

At the bottom of the huge staircase, Octavie stood, hands on hips, savouring her victory.

Victor had taken a cab instead of his bicycle because of the ice, and he was struggling to stay awake as it gently jogged along. He hadn't had a chance to say a word to Joseph, who had been impatient to relate the morning's events, but unfortunately the constant presence of Kenji had obliged them to keep their mouths shut. As Tasha was away for the day, Victor had been invited to lunch with the family, and had sat down with them to sample Euphrosine's *gratin dauphinois*. There had simply been no opportunity to interrogate Jojo. As soon as dessert was finished Victor had, as planned, made his excuses, to Kenji's intense displeasure.

Stuck in a traffic jam, the cab driver dropped Victor at the corner of Boulevard de Magenta and Rue de Lancry. He made his way to Rue des Vinaigriers via Quai de Valmy, and spotted a little café called L'Ancre de Fortune. At the back of the tiny room, a solitary customer was sitting opposite a large speckled mirror.

Victor ordered a vermouth cassis at the bar, and struck up a conversation with the owner. He mentioned Madame Guérin's name.

The solitary drinker glanced quickly at the newcomer's reflection in the mirror.

'Old Madame Guérin?' exclaimed the owner. 'Of course I know her! Certainly – she's an old friend, and she's always lived around here. She runs the sweet shop a bit further down the road – it's called the Blue Chinaman, in memory of her father, who was killed at Palikao.'

'Palikao? Where's that?' Victor asked politely, his eyes already on the exit.

'In China. He served under General Cousin-Montauban. It was years ago.'

Corentin Jourdan felt a shiver run down his spine. He looked at the mirror suddenly certain of an imminent threat, just as a hare in a field pricks up its ears at the first sound of a poacher. The new-comer had disappeared. Corentin paid his bill and took up his position underneath the awning of the bakery.

When Victor walked into the Blue Chinaman, a woman and her daughter were using a little silver shovel to fill bags of sweets.

'It's more than just a baptism, Madame Hermance, it's a family party, and my nephews just love your mint pastilles and your barley sugar. Bastienne is the same – she adores your almond brittle.'

'Maman, I love fondants,' the little girl lisped.

The woman behind the counter weighed the bags. Her black lace cap covered a bun that could not completely tame her curly, copper-coloured hair, streaked with grey. Although her porcelain-blue eyes were as clear as a doll's, the wrinkles on her cheeks betrayed Madame Guérin's age.

Nonetheless, the voice with which she addressed Victor when the customers had left was unexpectedly childlike.

'And you, Monsieur, how may I help you?'

'I'm not here to buy sweets. I need some information about Louise Fontane. My name is Maurice Laumier and I am a painter. My fiancée, Mireille Lestocart, has asked me to track down her cousin, Loulou, and her colleagues at the workshop on Rue d'Aboukir told me that she had moved to live with you three weeks ago. However, I have recently discovered that this young woman has been strangled.'

Since embarking on the sad business of investigating tragic deaths, Victor had come up against so many suspects that his instincts were now finely tuned when it came to judging their reactions. Although Madame Guérin had remained impassive while he made his little speech, she had not been able to stop herself blinking and tensing her jaw, which were just as revealing as a confession. It was obvious that she knew Louise, even though she replied in an acid tone, 'I've never heard that name before.'

Victor held the cutting from *L'Intransigeant* out to her. As she read the article circled in red, her hands began to tremble slightly, confirming his suspicions. This woman was lying.

'I've just been at the morgue and I'm sorry to say that there's no doubt about it: the victim is Louise Fontane.'

'Monsieur, I can only say again I don't know anyone of that name. You must have been misled, or perhaps you have made a mistake. There are plenty of Guérins in Paris. Also, my business means that I deal with dozens of people for communions, weddings, all sorts of ceremonies, really. I cater for so many well-to-do customers, and Christmas and New Year are my busiest times of the year. Somebody must have mixed my name up with that of one of my customers. No, I have never met this ... what was her name again?'

'Louise Fontane.'

'I'm sorry, Monsieur,' she replied, handing back the newspaper cutting.

She had regained her composure.

Twilight was enveloping the city. Victor stood smoking a cigarette in a porch, his eyes fixed on the sweet shop.

The unusual behaviour of this stranger had not escaped Corentin Jourdan's vigilance and he, too, kept watch outside the bakery. He could only partially make out the man's face – he seemed to be about thirty. He had seen him go into the Blue Chinaman, show the shopkeeper a piece of paper and then come out again after about ten minutes without having bought anything. Instead of going away, he had hidden in the corridor of a building and had not taken his eyes off the shop since. When old Madame Guérin had put the catch on the door and hung up the closed sign, he had shrunk back against the handrail of the staircase. Apparently, he wanted to see without being seen.

115

With a cape wrapped round her shoulders, Madame Guérin had paused for a moment in her doorway, as people do when they are about to leave a warm interior for the cold and damp outside. She had looked around her and then, reassured, she had hurried to the corner of Rue des Vinaigriers and Rue Albouy, pushed open the gate of a little garden, and disappeared into a narrow building with closed blinds.

Victor threw away his cigarette butt and, with his hat pulled down low on his forehead, approached the house. As he passed by, Corentin was able to see his face: regular features and a dark moustache which gave him a confident, youthful air. This man was obviously keeping watch on the house, but why? Leaning against a lamp-post, he had unfolded a newspaper and was pretending to read it. Who was he? A rejected suitor? A policeman? A lunatic? God knows there were plenty of those about in this city!

In order to allay any possible suspicion, Corentin bought a croissant and chatted to the baker for a moment, without taking his eyes off the stranger. He saw him fold up the newspaper and look at his watch.

Corentin didn't stop to think; what he did next was a purely spontaneous reflex over which he had no more control than he did over the irregular pounding of his heart. He rushed to where his horse was stabled and harnessed it to the cart; painted on the side in neat letters were the words:

LAMBERT REMOVALS

Then he put on a blue sailor's jacket and a cap, and pulled up a few yards away from the house. In the growing darkness, the memory of Clélia, faded with time, suddenly appeared before him, like a guard dog intent on tearing him apart. Why was he running all these risks? Corentin was frustrated by the enforced inactivity, and did his best to resist the temptation to force his way into the retreat where his beautiful Landemer siren was lying low. Clélia's death

116

had been almost impossible to bear and he had suffered so much that he had tried to stifle his grief completely, telling himself that time would heal his wound. Alas, time seemed to mock him, and his pain, although less intense now, was more persistent and more frightening. He was losing his appetite and, he sometimes felt, his mind. Afraid of no longer being in control of his life, Corentin knew that he needed to finish this business once and for all if he was ever to free himself.

Victor made a mental note of the layout of the house, unsure what to do next. Should he wait? To do so was to run the risk of not getting back to Rue des Saints-Pères until the shop was shut, which would make it impossible to snatch a conversation with Joseph. A shower of melting snow had now started. What was the point of defying the elements if he had no idea how long he would have to lie in wait there? 'Let's just hope it'll be dryer tomorrow.'

He made an about-turn towards Boulevard de Magenta, looking for a cab.

A short distance away, a removal cart moved off.

In the bookshop, the lamps were all lit and Kenji was talking philosophy with a professor from the Sorbonne. Victor signalled to Joseph to follow him down to the stockroom. As soon as the red bulb above the bust of Molière lit up, Jojo picked up a pile of books and joined his brother-in-law. They whispered their news to one another like conspirators.

'I bet you don't know what the War of the Two Roses is.'

'That's where you're wrong, Joseph. I was brought up in England. Unless I'm very much mistaken, it took place around 1450, when the Houses of Lancaster, whose armour bore a red rose, and York, with the white rose, fought over the crown. Henry VII, a Lancastrian, won the day, and married Elizabeth of York.'

'You're not even close, Boss – I mean, Victor!'

Bursting with pride at his news, Joseph related the story of the quarrels between the followers of Stanislas de Guaïta and Sâr Péladan, and then all that he had seen and heard during his visit to the Baron de La Gournay.

'He was pushed off his horse – the nurse claimed that he'd had a blow to the head. And then the other chap, the one who was in the bedroom for ages – you must admit that he's rather interesting: dolls, blood, a key decorated with a unicorn's head – perhaps he's a sorcerer!'

Victor suppressed a snort of impatience, angry at the prospect of being caught up with occultists yet again. He had already met one of those cranks, a certain Numa Winner.[28] The supposed message from his dead mother, which this clairvoyant had transmitted to him, still rang in his memory: *His death freed us, you and me. Love. I have found it. You will understand. You must ... follow your instinct. You can be reborn if you break the chain. Harmony. Soon ... soon ...*

'In any case,' continued Jojo, 'his lady wife doesn't care one bit about his misfortunes.'

'We're not going to stop there. A second visit is called for.'

'Well, it'll have to be you this time – I've blown my cover with the maid and the nurse. She's a real sergeant major. What about the woman in the sweet shop?'

'She needs watching too.'

'The trouble is, I'm stuck tomorrow: Iris is insisting that I stay at home when Dr Reynaud comes to examine her.'

'Never mind, I'll manage.'

'You will tell me all about it afterwards, won't you?'

'Never fear, I'll give you a full report, as always,' Victor replied, laughing.

His definition of 'full' isn't always quite the same as mine, thought Joseph. *If he thinks I'm going to play second fiddle again, he couldn't be more wrong!*

CHAPTER 7

Sunday 18 February

At the corner of Boulevard de Magenta and Rue des Vinaigriers, there was a lamp-post where all the local dogs came to mark their territory. Nearby, the orange glow of a stove lit up the gloom of the leaden morning. An old woman, wrapped in shawls and with her face nearly hidden by a large scarf, was selling cups of wine to passers-by. Victor's fingers were frozen in spite of his gloves, and he warmed them against the hot porcelain as he sipped the bitter brew. Reinvigorated, he walked down the road as far as the Blue Chinaman, where he glanced inside to make sure that the shop-keeper with the lace bonnet was behind the counter. She was there, sitting next to a stove and knitting a brown muffler.

He went straight to the house he had seen her go into the night before, and rang the doorbell. Several minutes later, it creaked open.

'What do you want?'

He looked down and saw a slip of a girl, only about thirteen or fourteen, her face smeared with dirt, gazing at him inanely and fiddling with a strand of hair that had escaped from her crumpled bonnet.

'Hello, Mademoiselle. I'd like to speak to the lady staying here.'

'M'dame Guérin? She's in the shop now, like always.'

'No, not Madame Guérin – a young American lady.'

The girl looked flustered. Concerned that he was frightening her, Victor took off his hat and, smiling, bowed respectfully.

'Are you the housekeeper?'

She squared her shoulders, drawing herself up proudly.

'What's it to you?'

'I'm sorry?'

'I'm Aline, the maid!'

'May I come in?'

'It's against the rules. M'dame Guérin is always telling me the story about the nanny-goat and her seven baby goats who got gobbled up by the wolf 'cos he disguised himself as the nanny-goat.'

'My name is Maurice Laumier and I am a respectable artist,' Victor assured her, stooping as he tried to see behind her into a dark entrance hall that led to a kitchen.

'The wolf in the story covered himself in flour so he looked like the nanny-goat.'

Victor sighed. He wished he could give the girl a good shake. But then Madame Guérin might appear at any moment.

'I am the American lady's fiancé.'

'You must've got the wrong house – there's no Americans here. There's just Mam'selle Sophie, except she's gone.'

'Sophie who?'

The girl twisted the strand of hair more violently, and tried to push the end into her ear.

'Don't know.'

'Can you try to remember where Mademoiselle Sophie went?'

'Even if I could, it's against the rules to tell you.'

The girl's mulish expression enraged Victor. He made a supreme effort to remain calm. Feigning surprise, he rummaged in his pocket and pulled out a coin.

'You're obviously an excellent maid, Aline, and you deserve a reward.'

Her face lit up.

'Is that for me?'

'Yes, it's for you.'

Clutching the coin in her hand, she jigged from one foot to the other, making her skirts balloon out underneath her smock, which was far too big for her. She decided that the wolf wasn't so bad after all.

'She was poorly for two weeks, Mam'selle Sophie was. The doctor came and looked after her, and he put poultices on her that burnt her. I helped her to get better.'

'That was very kind of you.'

'Yes, because really my job's just doing the housework, the ironing, the shopping and the cooking. But she gave me a pretty chain with a medallion on it.'

She pressed her closed fist to her chest and, in his excitement, Victor had to resist the urge to pull it away.

'My fiancée is very generous,' he simpered. 'When she likes somebody, she's not happy until she has given them something. Would you show me the medallion?'

The girl hesitated, still mistrustful. Her skirts swished from side to side and she studied their movement with serious concentration, as though she were a yogi about to demonstrate the art of levitation. This show of reluctance was more than Victor could stand.

'This is really very important, Mademoiselle. My fiancée gave me a medallion too and, if yours is the same as mine, it means she wants to marry me.'

The girl let go of the chain and stood up on tiptoe. The medallion was a one-dollar coin fixed on a chain. Although he had hoped for a unicorn, Victor still rejoiced: the reasons that linked Louise Fontane to a mysterious American acquaintance and to Madame Guérin would surely become clear soon.

'Where is Mademoiselle Sophie now?' he asked in a calmer voice.

'Monsieur Bricart turned up early this morning, with his horse and cart. He loaded up all her things, except one suitcase, which is still down in the cellar.'

'Do you know where he took them?'

'A hotel near the station.'

'A hotel near the Gare de l'Est?'

121

'Yes. I heard M'dame Guérin say the name of a town or a country when she was telling Sylvain where to go.'

'Sylvain? Who's Sylvain?'

'The Millionaire, silly!'

'Who's the Millionaire?'

'I've already told you, it's M'sieu Bricart. He's scary. He always shouts, "Clear off, stop hanging around," but when there's no one else in the room, he pushes me up against one of the cupboards and pinches me all over. One day, he invited me to a dance at the Tivoli-Wauxhall,[29] but I said no. There are loose women there. Since then, he's stopped giving me little cakes from the bakery.'

'Do you know the name of the hotel?'

'All I can remember is that Mam'selle Sophie went off in a carriage as soon as M'sieu Bricart turned up. M'dame Guérin gave him a kiss and he put his hand on her bottom and said she was getting plumper by the day. Then they lugged all the cases into the cart, and that was when she gabbled out the name…Well, I've got to go upstairs and polish the brass, otherwise M'dame Guérin will go mad.'

The door slammed shut.

Deep in thought, Victor walked back to Rue Lancry. He stopped in front of the Barbedienne foundry and, oblivious to the comings and goings of workers weighed down with bronze decorative pieces, he copied down everything the girl had told him into his notebook.

He returned to Boulevard de Magenta, then turned off into Boulevard de Strasbourg, with its brightly coloured shops and crowded brasseries. He stopped opposite Rue de Strasbourg,[30] waiting for an opportune moment to dart across the road, which was teeming with omnibuses, carriages and cyclists. The cacophony of cursing cabmen, clattering wheels, hooting horns and policemen's whistles paralysed him for a moment. Straight ahead, the Gare de l'Est, with its triangular pediment dominating a semicircular courtyard surrounded by railings, looked like a prison or a courthouse. This impression was reinforced by the large clock face on the front of the building, surrounded by allegorical figures of the Seine and the Rhine.

Ever since childhood, stations had attracted and repelled Victor in equal measure; they were the frontier between actual journeys and those that existed only in the imagination for as long as one remained on the threshold. But once inside, on the huge station concourse, the porters, the cab-runners and the chaotic flurry of departures and arrivals threatened the stability of everyday existence. Always uncomfortable with goodbyes, Victor had, nonetheless, often stood and waved his handkerchief at a departing train. Although he felt very attached to his adoptive city, he sometimes found himself dreaming of escaping to some far-off country. This Sunday, it was impossible not to fall under the spell of the trains. He bought a copy of *La Revue Blanche* at a kiosk, and began to lie shamelessly.

'What a mess! I'm well and truly lost. I've arranged to meet my niece, but the name of her hotel has completely slipped my mind. All I can remember is that it had the name of a town or a country in it.'

The newspaper seller rubbed her surprisingly hairy chin with her index finger, before replying, 'There are plenty of those around! At this end of Rue de Strasbourg, there's the Hôtel de France et de Suisse, then a few steps further down the road you've got the Hôtel de l'Arrivée and the Hôtel Français. On Rue Saint-Quentin, there's the Hôtel Belge, and the Hôtel de Belfort is on Boulevard de Magenta.'

Victor thanked her and began his search. He struck gold at the Hôtel de Belfort.

The decor in the foyer was a mixture of ancient and modern. An enormous painting of the château of the Comtes de Bar-le-Duc hung in state over a medieval-style fireplace with sculptures

123

on either side: on the right, a copy of Mercié's patriotic *Quand même*, and, on the left, Bartholdi's famous *Lion*.

At the reception, Victor recited his story again.

'My niece checked in here this morning. Did she leave a message for Maurice Laumier? That's me.'

The man behind the desk was annoyed at being disturbed just as he was about to persuade a rich guest to stay for another week. He looked at the register.

'Laumier? I'm sorry, Monsieur, we haven't got any guests by that name.'

'Well, really, that's a bit much! She definitely said Hôtel de Belfort, like the château. Are you sure?'

The receptionist nodded.

'Sophie is such a scatterbrain! I was sure of it, and now my suspicions have been confirmed: my brother and his wife have brought her up terribly.'

'Sophie, did you say? Mademoiselle Sophie Clairsange? That young lady did let me know that her luggage was arriving. Are you—?'

'No, absolutely not, it's Laumier, Madame Sophie Laumier! L.A.U.M.I.E.R.' He spelt out the name, blustering now. 'She's married to Field Marshal Laumier! Check again.'

'She isn't here, Monsieur. We only have one woman on her own staying with us, Mademoiselle Sophie Clairsange. The other rooms and suites are occupied by men or by couples. She must be somewhere else.'

Although he didn't add, 'And to the devil with you,' his eyes said it clearly.

'Thank you for your help. May I use the telephone?'

'At the back of the foyer,' muttered the man, already returning to his conversation with the rich guest.

Corentin Jourdan felt feverish and nauseous. His heart was beating too fast and he was gripped by fear. What was that man doing at the hotel? He must think, control himself. Surely it was impossible that the man had noticed him. No, he couldn't possibly even be aware of his existence! When he had followed the stranger over to the Left Bank the night before, he hadn't even got down from the cart. He had seen the man get out of his cab in front of a shop and disappear inside. He had just been able to make out the writing on the window:

ELZÉVIR BOOKSHOP
V. Legris & K. Mori
Since 1835

Then the man had vanished into thin air.

Hunched up on the seat in his cart, Corentin had waited in vain for him to reappear. After half an hour, he had decided to risk moving a little closer, and he saw the man talking to another man who had his back to him, before going up a spiral staircase which presumably led to the first floor. Was he one of the owners? If so, was he Legris or Mori? Neither of those names appeared in the blue notebook, but, in any case, this man was certainly pursuing the beautiful Landemer siren. But why?

Hidden behind a voluminous newspaper, sitting nonchalantly in an armchair near Bartholdi's *Lion*, Corentin Jourdan saw the man head for the telephone booths.

'"Shrouded in many-coloured veils, Carmella pirouetted across the stage like a distracted dragonfly ..."'

Click clack click clack ding! tapped the typewriter's keys.

'"She was about to begin a sensual fandango ..."'

'You dictate too fast,' Iris complained.

She stopped typing, while Joseph continued to pace up and down the room.

'Is something wrong, my dear?' Joseph asked.

'"Shrouded" doesn't sound very nice … "Adorned" would be much better,' Iris replied.

'Is that all?'

'No. "A distracted dragonfly" sounds rather strange. Why not an "impetuous dragonfly"?'

Joseph stopped in front of Tasha's full-length portrait of his wife.

'You're logical, as ever.'

'And also, what's a fandango doing in a show that's supposed to be set in Italy during the Renaissance?'

'Oh, does it really matter? I like the word, and there was a vogue for all things Spanish, whence my heroine's name.'

'It would make more sense to have your Carmella dance a branle, or a galliard, or else to change the century.'

'All right, make it a galliard. "She was about to begin a sensual galliard …" Damn! The telephone.'

Joseph hurried downstairs.

Corentin Jourdan watched the man in the foyer wrestling with the telephone. He had pressed the wrong button three times and ended up having to speak to the operator, and now he was waiting to be put through, tapping his fingers on the glass of the booth. If only he could read the man's lips and get a better idea of this character and the dangers posed by his presence!

The man replaced the receiver, went over to the reception desk and paid for the call. Should he follow him? Corentin had vowed not to abandon his watch at the hotel. He stayed glued to his seat.

Iris had tiptoed towards the staircase, but hadn't been able to catch anything more than a few muffled words of Joseph's conversation. When he reappeared, she was back in the low chair near the table where the Remington stood in all its glory. Relieved that Dr Reynaud had already examined his wife, Joseph began to explain why it was absolutely necessary for him to go out yet again.

126

'Victor insists: there's a collector who's got a whole set of books by Grolier and Thouvenin, and, of course, it's miles away in the suburbs, out at Bourg-la-Reine . . .'

'So it'll take the whole day. Strange – Tasha and my brother are usually so protective of their Sundays together.'

'You're right, my darling! It's very unusual for a customer to flush him out of Rue Fontaine on a Sunday!' agreed Joseph, sounding so innocent that he was even beginning to convince himself that he was telling the truth.

'Well, in that case, don't hang around – off you go.'

'What rotten luck. It's Zulma's day off too, and your father's made himself scarce . . . Should I go and fetch Maman?'

'No, certainly not! Don't worry. I'll have another look over *The Devil's Bouquet*, eat a bit of that chicory gratin and the walnut cake that Euphrosine made this morning, and then have a lie-down . . .'

'You're right, my dear, you must rest and get plenty of sleep.'

He kissed her for rather longer than he had intended, his hands beginning to stray underneath her black silk kimono.

'You're going to be late,' she murmured.

'Yes, but . . .'

She pushed him away gently. He blew her a kiss and hurried out of the room.

Alone at last! She got up and stretched, delighted to have the apartment all to herself. What detective mischief had Victor got himself embroiled in this time? Should she warn Tasha? Was Joseph putting himself in danger? And Kenji, gallivanting around at his age! But why shouldn't he, after all? Love was such a sweet invention! And so is freedom, she thought. Leave them to their investigating, and leave him to his seducing. This day of solitude is a gift from heaven.

She got out her work basket and unfolded the table runner that she was making for her mother-in-law, who was soon to celebrate her forty-second birthday. She snorted with laughter at the thought that Euphrosine had been born in the year of the dragon. It suited

127

her domineering character well, as did her Western star sign, Aries the Ram. In giving birth at a young age, Iris was following in the older woman's footsteps. Euphrosine had become a mother at the age of seventeen, and Iris was not yet twenty. She decided to embroider a multicoloured dragon amongst the chrysanthemums that covered the material. A sudden feeling of heaviness forced her to stop. The child was growing inside her.

She glanced lazily over the sheet of paper still wound into the typewriter. Writing seemed to be rather like a game. One simply had to choose the right words and then set the imagination free, weaving the words together into a bright tapestry. Then, Iris, who never read anything unless she had to, took up a pencil and began to scribble in the margin of a crumpled sheet of paper.

Once upon a time, there was a dragonfly who had fallen in love with a butterfly …

*

His appetite sharpened by the cold, Victor had eaten his fill of fried eggs and potatoes in the Duval café where he had summoned his brother-in-law to a meeting. At a nearby table, a red-faced man with large sideburns was eyeing the anisette cocktail, which the waitress, dressed in a dark merino-wool dress, had just set down in front of him. Joseph burst in, quivering with excitement, and bounced into a cane chair, where he unfolded the illustrated supplement of *Le Petit Journal*.

'From Scylla to Charybdis!' he announced, at the top of his voice. 'Look! Read that!'

Annoyed at finding himself the centre of attention, Victor took the newspaper impatiently.

MYSTERIOUS DEATH

We have just learnt that Monsieur le Baron de La Gournay, member of the Pegasus Society for the protection of horses, owner

128

of several thoroughbreds and co-founder of the esoteric society of the Black Unicorn, died yesterday as a result of injuries sustained when he fell off his horse. According to the doctors who confirmed the death, the blow to the head he received could have been caused by a fast-moving projectile. Was this a deliberate attack? His widow, Madame Clotilde de La Gournay, has refused permission for an autopsy to be carried out. Will the police launch an investigation which might turn out to be extremely complicated?

The man with the sideburns lit a cigar. As soon as the bitter smell reached Joseph's nostrils, he covered his nose with a handkerchief. Victor folded up the newspaper.

'If he was killed, then we need to consider the possibility that there is a link between this death and Loulou's murder, I suppose. Still, it's rather a tenuous connection. All we have to support our theory is one word: unicorn. Are you feeling ill?'

'Just a b-bit nauseous,' stuttered Joseph, now enveloped in a cloud of cigar smoke.

'You haven't had much to eat all day – have a bite now.'

While Joseph consulted the menu, Victor studied his notebook. Each was confronted with a tricky problem: one torn between sweet and savoury while the other weighed up various hypotheses.

Joseph called the waitress.

'A quince jelly and a cup of mocha coffee, please.'

'So frugal! Congratulations. I think we're going to be forced to pay a second visit to the La Gournay residence. We can put it off until tomorrow, though – there are more urgent things to do now.'

Victor described the morning's events to Joseph.

'The American friend who was staying in Rue des Vinaigriers is using a French identity as a disguise and calling herself Sophie Clairsange.'

Through a mouthful of food, Joseph voiced his objections to this.

'That dollar on a chain doesn't prove anything. I bet we could easily buy one at any old second-hand dealer in Paris. And another thing – if I remember rightly, Pétronille's comment about the friend just back from America doesn't necessarily mean that the woman must be an American citizen.'

'Pétronille?'

'Yes, don't you remember? Rue d'Aboukir, the cheap canteen!'

'Oh yes . . . but you're splitting hairs, Joseph. Whichever way we look at it, Madame Guérin is acting suspiciously, you must admit. Here's what I suggest: you take over the watch outside the Hôtel de Belfort, and follow any lone woman who so much as sets foot outside it, in the hope that it turns out to be this Sophie Clairsange. You'll need to be very discreet – that goes without saying.'

'As always, Boss, I mean Victor! I'm a master of concealment!'

'And of bragging. I've just realised that Martin Lorson's account of Loulou's murder is rather ambiguous. He seemed amazed that the murderer should return so quickly to the scene of his crime. But what if there were two men? What if the Baron de La Gournay – and this is far-fetched, but not impossible – strangled Loulou, and then an accomplice came along and finished off the job?'

'We're clutching at straws now!'

'But, to quote Kenji, "The surest way to reach the light is to journey through darkest night."'

'Yes, well, I'm like dear Professor Lidenbrock:[31] I prefer to light my way with a Ruhmkorff lamp. The more clues I have, the more clearly I can see. What's the name of the man with the cart, who took Sophie's things?'

'Second name Bricart, first name Sylvain, otherwise known as the Millionaire.'

'Why the Millionaire?'

'I have no idea. My interview with the maid drove me mad. It seems that he and Madame Guérin are more than just friends.'

'Do you know where Lorson is holed up?'

Victor nodded as he paid the bill.

'It's best if I telephone you at the bookshop this evening. I hope Iris doesn't suspect anything. She's incapable of holding her tongue.'

'Poor thing, all she thinks about at the moment is the baby,' Joseph replied, relieved to be outside and to fill his lungs with the smell of horse manure and the dusty streets.

Djina Kherson arranged the flowers that a courier had delivered to her in a vase. The flowers seemed to have been chosen according to a code that she wasn't completely au fait with. The white roses meant 'I am worthy of you', she had recently read in an English book on the subject. A sprig of fern, didn't that mean 'fascination'? Red carnations . . . 'love'! And, as for the meaning of the lilies, she would have to check.

The blend of colours was irresistible. She opened the card that had come with the flowers.

Chateaubriand said that 'the flower in its divine language is the daughter of the morning, the charm of spring nestled against winter's breast, the source of all nectars'. I shall never have a poet's gift for expression, but I hope I can still make pleasant conversation. Would you come to tea with me at five o'clock this afternoon, at Gloppe's, on the Champs-Élysées? I shall be waiting there for you.

Yours devotedly, Kenji Mori

This missive piqued her curiosity: to refuse would be ridiculous, and she would always regret it if she did. Although her divorce from Pinkus had not been finalised, the fact that he had gone to live in New York and intended to stay there had long since put an end to any vestige of their life together. A simple meeting like this was perfectly innocent and in no way implied infidelity to her distant husband, the father of her children and a friend for whom she still had a great deal of affection. How sad it was that a marriage could fade away like that! She and Pinkus had rarely quarrelled, but their views on many important matters were radically different. As the years went by, politics had gradually alienated them from one another. Although they were both horrified by the criminal violence of the anti-Semitic activities of the tsarist government, Pinkus worshipped revolutionary ideals, while she simply wanted to find a place of exile where she could live safely and with dignity. Following Tasha's lead, she believed that she had found that place in France, and she only regretted that Ruhléa, her younger daughter, who was married to a doctor called Milos Tábor, had decided to go and live in Krakow.

Despite their differences, perhaps she and Pinkus would have managed to stay together if they had not had a more private problem to contend with. Devastating as it was to accept the reality of her feelings, she nonetheless had to face the fact that as an intimate relationship, their life as a couple was a failure. Once she had come to this realisation, she had told Pinkus, without beating around the bush, that they must separate.

She stood musing in the workshop, which had been left in a state of joyous disorder by the students she took for watercolour classes. Pinkus had left his little Hester Street hovel and rented an apartment in Manhattan. His business was doing so well that he would occasionally send her postal orders to ease her financial situation. She was grateful to him. She still couldn't understand how it was possible to get rich by selling kinetoscopes. Her son-in-law, Victor, had explained to her that the famous Thomas Edison had invented a machine which showed moving images. In Djina's eyes, these big rectangular boxes were an obscene form of amusement fit only for fairs and arcades. You put a coin into a slot and looked into two little holes fitted with an eyepiece. When you turned a handle, you could see miniature versions of cock fights, boxing cats, wrestling dogs and dances from the Samoan Islands . . . but usually you just saw hussies taking off their clothes in front of some shameless man. Luckily, the film reel ended before the final revelation. Why had Pinkus given in to the attraction of such pornography?

She went back to her room and put the latest letter covered in American stamps away in a box. There was an ocean between her and her phantom husband. She was free to meet Monsieur Mori.

'I'd better make myself pretty.'

She looked at herself in the mirror, and ran her fingers through her auburn hair, which was now streaked with grey.

'Anyone would think you were about to fly off on a broomstick! All these wrinkles, this sagging neck . . . Somebody must have given that charming man a love potion, and he's forgotten what you really look like. You're mad! At your age . . .'

Djina washed her face, put on some make-up and chose a simple watered taffeta dress with peacock-blue and rose-pink stripes, which would go with her only coat. The wrists of the dress were so worn that she had hidden them under some lace frills. She put on a tulle hat decorated with primroses, and suddenly she remembered: lilies represented purity. Such irony! And she was a respectable woman with a family! Was he making fun of her? She looked again at her reflection, all decked out from head to toe, ready to run after a man with whom she had only ever exchanged a few banal words and some highly charged glances! She was filled with shame, but still unable to entirely overcome her excitement, feeling like a girl about to accept the advances of her first suitor. So many years of battling on alone, of dreaming, of stifling her dreams . . . Resolutely, she turned her back on the mirror.

The cab journey had seemed to last for ever and, judging by the size of the buildings occupying numbers 110 and 112, Rue de Flandre, finding Martin Lorson was going to be a little like searching for a needle in a haystack. This time, Victor had not had to lie to Tasha about where he was going because she had been invited to lunch by the Natansons, so it was with a clear conscience that he could devote himself to his favourite hobby. Today he could work without remorse, taking his time. A huge sign above him read:

ÉRARD
Makers of the Finest
PIANOS AND HARPS
Founded in Paris in 1780 by the Érard Brothers[32]

This was where matters became more complicated. Where should he start? In the grand piano workshops and the buildings where the piano actions were constructed, or in the upright piano factory, or in one of the warehouses?

As he stood indecisively on the threshold of a huge courtyard surrounded by several four- and five-storey buildings, he examined the drying sheds, which were full of planks, strips of wood and veneer facings made of exotic and European woods. He waylaid an adolescent boy struggling under the weight of a huge block of sycamore.

'Where is Monsieur Jaquemin, please?'

'Down the boozer, I should think!' cried the apprentice, making off in the opposite direction.

An older worker came up to Victor.

'He's a stupid boy, and insolent too, but you must excuse him – there are more than five hundred of us working here. Still, I can give you the information you need: Jaquemin works on the grand pianos. Are you a concert pianist?'

'Yes, I am. I'm looking for an instrument that's as finely tuned as … as a racing bike.'

'An apt comparison, Monsieur. Our pianos are marvels of precision. You won't regret the expense.'

Victor resigned himself to searching the whole factory. At least here the air wasn't heavy with the odour of carcasses or cigar smoke. He wandered from room to room, past work benches and wooden frames, enjoying the smell of sawdust all around him. Amongst all this febrile activity, nobody objected to his presence. He left the rooms where the outer casings of the pianos were built and climbed the stairs to where the soundboards and brackets at the very heart of the pianos, were made. When he asked after Jaquemin, no one seemed to be able to help. He went back down to the ground floor, where craftsmen were covering bare wooden frames with veneers of maple, mahogany, thuja and rosewood. Jaquemin was nowhere to be seen.

Sweating now, and out of breath, Victor walked past still more rooms where piano actions, sound boards and strings were put together with painstaking care. He would never have dreamt that so many different operations went into the creation of one of these huge instruments, from which some virtuoso would one day coax magical sounds. Out of interest, he stopped to watch seven or eight men at work varnishing about fifteen instruments. He admired a particularly rare creation, a baby grand sculpted by Charpentier and painted by Besnard. A workman remarked matter-of-factly that the instrument had taken two years to complete and that a rich foreigner had purchased it for the modest sum of thirty thousand francs. Victor whistled and once again asked after Jaquemin.

'He's at the showroom, right at the other end of the factory. Just follow the noise!'

When Victor pushed open the showroom door, he was greeted by a cacophony of scales. He remembered how, as a child, he would perch on the revolving stool in front of the hated keyboard where his father, who had never been to a concert in his life, tried in vain to teach him the basics of musical theory. Every time he pressed a key, he would imagine that he was decapitating an invisible enemy. Now, he pitied the young girls who were testing the accuracy of freshly tuned pianos. This din was a far cry from Schumann's *Arabesque*!

A tall man in overalls, with a shock of messy hair and an unruly beard, was listening attentively to all of these soloists.

'Monsieur Jaquemin?' bellowed Victor.

The man pointed to himself and then to a nearby office.

'I'm sure to end up as deaf as a post with all this racket. What can I do for you?'

'A friend has asked me to contact Martin Lorson.'

Jaquemin's face darkened.

'You'll find him near the entrance. He's made a lair for himself inside one of the warehouses where we stock wood. Don't let on, though. If anyone knew I was looking after him, I'd be in trouble. I felt sorry for him, so I was really far too charitable. We carved our names on the same desks at school. Poor bloke's in a sticky situation now.'

Finding himself back where he had started, Victor threaded his way from one warehouse to another, and eventually heard the sound of a tipsy voice singing out of tune.

> *'Dear friends, embrace the bottle, forswear the carafe …'*

A shadow wider than it was tall was jigging about behind a thin, windowless partition, by the light of a paraffin lamp. Victor walked around a wall built of sacks and planks of wood. Martin Lorson was keeping a careful eye on a sausage sizzling over a brazier and nursing a litre of rum, from which he occasionally took a swig. A particularly large gulp preceded the conclusion of his song:

> *'And you shall become more learned in geography with each quaff!'* [33]

Victor's appearance cut short this alcoholic ode.

'Who's there? Jaquemin?' Martin Lorson barked.

'Legris, the bookseller. We talked at the abattoirs.'

'The detective bookseller? . . . Are you soft in the head, rolling

136

up in broad daylight? When are you bloody well going to leave me in peace?'

'I've brought you some cigarettes.'

Mollified, Martin Lorson took the pan off the brazier and balanced it on a board, before pocketing the cigarettes.

'I won't keep you long. There's just one detail of your story that I can't stop thinking about. You said that the murderer ran away, and then came back straight away – and you found that incomprehensible.'

Martin Lorson burped sonorously.

'Are you too drunk to think about this?'

'No, 'sall right. If I was tiddly, I wouldn't be able to string a sentence together.'

'Think: could there have been a second man?'

Martin Lorson warmed his hands over the coals.

'It's funny you should stumble on that idea just today. I've been going over and over it in my mind, until my head spins. Now, I'm convinced: the one rascal was actually two rascals.'

'Are you sure it's not just the alcohol that makes you so certain?'

'No, no. Their hats! They were different. The one who strangled the girl was wearing a felt hat. The other one was wearing a cap.'

'The assassin would have had time to change his hat.'

'Why, though? He had no idea I was there and, even if he did know, do you think he'd be stupid enough to come back for more?'

'People crack under pressure …, they do stupid things.'

'Well, you know best, it would seem …' Martin Lorson sniggered. 'Seeing as you thought it was so important to come and sniff me out here, you must think my opinion's worth something, even if I am just a poor old drunk. Trust my instinct then! Let's shake hands and say goodbye! If you keep coming here, you'll jinx me.'

Victor withdrew, satisfied that Lorson had confirmed his intuition. He looked back and had a momentary vision of the drunken form metamorphosing into a string of Russian dolls inside the giant silhouette.

Djina alighted from the omnibus. Somebody bumped into her and she apologised. The city seemed to accost her from all sides. A sea of carriages flowed down the Champs-Élysées from the Arc de Triomphe, a tumultuous spectacle reminiscent of an army returning from war.

The street around her began to spin, and she leant against a tree for support. She absolutely must escape from this crowd and get back to the safety of her apartment. She caught sight of her reflection in a jeweller's shop window and thought herself ugly. A stream of elegant people walked past her: carefully made-up women, and men, both young and old, with confident, indifferent expressions. 'Nobody knows who you are,' they all seemed to be saying to her. 'Nobody knows anything of your desires, or of what you have endured. You don't belong here.' She was ashamed of her clothes, ashamed of having lived so many years without becoming more worldly and experienced.

The Gloppe patisserie looked like a fairytale castle. She began to panic. She would never even dare to go through the door of a place like that!

She breathed deeply.

I don't want to be frightened. I must do what I have to do, she told herself.

She hung back for a moment, torn between conflicting emotions. She was embarrassed by her own girlish feelings, but nonetheless it was nice to know that men like Kenji Mori existed, and it was nice to have pretended that he could find her attractive.

'Are you lost? I'm so sorry – there are far too many people here. It's race day at Longchamp, and the winners and losers are all out in force.'

He was there, smiling, at ease. She looked at him. He wasn't playing games. He emanated a calm wisdom, which betrayed none of his inner conflicts.

'I'm so glad you came,' he said. 'Take my arm, dear lady.'

138

Joseph stood fretting in front of the Hôtel de Belfort. He paced up and down the pavement and kept looking at his watch, as though he suspected that he was being stood up by his sweetheart. He wished that he had eaten more at the Duval café, and he urgently needed to urinate. He would have given anything for a public toilet just there in front of the hotel. At this rate, he was going to die of hunger and cold and, what was worse, wet his trousers. He persevered. Twice, he saw a man with a slight limp go up to the reception and talk to the man behind the desk. Who was he, this limper? The second time, the limper wrote a note, and he seemed to have asked the receptionist to give it to one of the guests, because he rang a little bell and a page-boy came running.

The limper quickly left the hotel, and Joseph stared into a furniture shop window, whistling. He looked at the stranger out of the corner of his eye, and saw him stop a few yards away and feign a passionate interest in a stationer's window display. Joseph made a mental note: pleasant face, thick head of hair, sideburns, about forty, a handsome man.

Joseph walked nonchalantly back the way he had come and stopped for a moment to glance inside the hotel. He caught sight of a strikingly beautiful young brunette with tanned skin and full lips, standing, hesitating, in the middle of the foyer. She unfolded a piece of paper that she had been clutching in her left hand, read it and quickly looked up. Her expression was fixed, as though she had seen something that frightened her.

Intrigued, Joseph continued his pacing. Was this Sophie Clairsange?

Sophie Clairsange called to a page-boy standing near the lift.

'Who left this message?' she asked him.

'A man.'

'What did he look like?'

'I don't really know, Madame, it was Monsieur Delort who took it, and Monsieur Delort has gone home.'

'Where can I contact him?'

'Monsieur Delort? Oh, he lives out at Argenteuil, Madame.'

Sophie felt her legs giving way beneath her. How did they find me? she thought to herself. She read the note again:

> *You are in danger. Be careful — you are being watched. If I were you I would move somewhere a good distance away from this hotel. Don't delay, I beg you. And, above all, do not speak to anybody you don't know for a little while.*
>
> *A friend*

Who could have written it? Hermance? No, she would have signed her name . . . 'A friend'? Which friend? That big fat man sipping a tonic wine in the corner? That skeletal dandy talking poppycock to a little goose who couldn't stop clucking?

She shut herself in the lift and hurried back to her room on the third floor. Since Loulou's death, her life had become a nightmare. Who could have left this note? She had been just about to go out, feeling reassured by being in a new place, and now a lead weight had fallen on her and crushed her new-found confidence.

Somebody had wanted to kill her and had got the wrong woman. Who, though?

Joseph realised that the limper had gone back inside the hotel. He was standing next to the lift, just as the lift door opened and the beautiful young woman emerged, covered up from head to toe and followed by a page-boy weighed down with suitcases. While she was paying her bill, a carriage drew up outside. The page-boy loaded up the suitcases and shouted to the cabby, 'Hôtel de l'Arrivée!'

The young woman climbed into the carriage.

The limper was leaning over the reception desk. He pushed a few coins under the receptionist's nose and seemed to be listening carefully to what he was saying. Satisfied with the information, he straightened up, looked around him and then walked calmly towards the revolving doors.

Joseph waited five minutes and then rushed into the foyer waving his watch.

'This really is beyond the pale! Women are all the same – incapable of telling the time! Please be so good as to tell Mademoiselle Clairsange that Maître Pignot's secretary requires her presence urgently.'

'Impossible, I'm afraid,' said the receptionist, shrugging his shoulders.

'And why, may I ask?'

'Because she left a few minutes ago. Her husband has been asking for her too. What a waste of a perfectly good room, to leave as soon as you've arrived!'

'Her husband? Where did she go?'

'To another hotel – one of our competitors.'

Fortunately there was a urinal on Rue de Strasbourg: Joseph's torment was over. Feeling much better, he began to keep watch near one of the hotel doorways. He wasn't surprised to see the limper take up a post in a recess of the foyer. Was he the husband? No, that was ridiculous – why would he be hiding like this? And, in any case, his note had made Sophie Clairsange decide to leave, but she didn't seem to know who had sent it. Had the limper told her that a young blond man was following her? If that was the case, then the truth was about to be revealed, because the man was heading straight towards him. Joseph was preparing to defend himself when the other man walked right past him and made his way towards Boulevard de Strasbourg.

The walk warmed Joseph up but didn't alleviate his hunger, which was made worse by the sight of rows of inviting restaurants. He grumbled as he followed in the wake of the man, who found his way unhesitatingly. Who was he? A betrayed lover? A policeman?

A hired killer? Loulou's murderer?

They turned into Rue des Vinaigriers, where it was much darker, away from the lights of Boulevard de Magenta. Joseph's heart skipped a beat as he saw a sweet shop.

THE BLUE CHINAMAN
Madame Guérin

He slowed his pace. The limper had gone inside a dilapidated building opposite a bistro. Hanging around was becoming a sport in itself. At least the man had the decency to reappear almost immediately. He had swapped his frock coat for a heavy coat with a long collar. He set off towards Boulevard de Magenta. Surely he wasn't going all the way back . . .

'Yes, he did, Victor, I'm telling you! The limper rushed off to the Hôtel de l'Arrivée as though his life depended on it, and he sat himself down in a chair, once he'd greased the receptionist's palm. I bet he's going to sleep there! I gave up in the end,' Joseph said, in a low voice.

'That's very inconvenient. We might lose him now. You'll have to go back there first thing tomorrow morning. I'll think of something to say to Kenji if he asks where you are. Is he there?'

'He isn't back yet. And what am I supposed to tell your sister?'

'Invent something.'

'You know as well as I do that she won't believe me.'

'Well, at least she has the tact to pretend that she does. So is it yes or no?'

'It's yes.'

Just as Joseph was putting the receiver down as quietly as he could, Iris's voice made him jump.

'Were those antiquarian books worth the trek out to Bourg-la-Reine?'

Victor stared pensively at the telephone and stroked Kochka, who had jumped onto his lap. The word 'limper' troubled him. He pushed the cat off his knee. She licked herself angrily while he rummaged in his jacket pocket for his notebook. Ah, there it was. He had been right to note it down: Alfred Gamache had mentioned a 'tall, mysterious chap with a limp'. Was this the man Joseph had been observing?

'We're getting warmer,' he announced to Kochka, who, thinking that he was about to give her some tasty leftovers, ran ahead of him to the kitchen at top speed.

CHAPTER 8

Monday 19 February

Joseph ruminated as he nibbled on a croissant, trying to make it last as long as possible. Why did people say 'He who sleeps forgets his hunger'? He had slept extremely well, but the breakfast he had eaten with Iris hadn't filled him up. Was it because of the cold? And, also, what had Victor been thinking of, sending him to brave this Siberian gale on Rue de Strasbourg? Would Kenji be satisfied by the excuse they had invented, an exhibition of art books in Drouot? It was difficult to read his emotions, if indeed he had any. As for Iris, she had complained of a migraine and gone back to bed.

Growing tired of watching the entrance to the Hôtel de l'Arrivée, where, for the moment, there was nobody to be seen except delivery boys, Joseph indulged in an extended reflection on the subject of popular sayings. Most were idiotic – for example, 'He who loves well, punishes well.' Neither his father-in-law nor his brother-in-law would be very impressed with a dressing-down from him, no matter how lovingly it was administered.

He shivered, and wished for a moment that he could swap places with his beloved wife, snuggled under the eiderdown. But she was pregnant, and he certainly didn't want to suffer that terrible fate. Briefly, he imagined carrying a child inside him, and the ridiculousness of the idea amused him. He moved straight from this vision to one of all the guests of the hotel who were, at this moment, stuffing themselves with food and warming their toes on cast-iron stoves. Was the limper among them? His prolonged presence in the foyer the previous evening seemed to indicate that he didn't intend to budge until the morning.

While Joseph was preoccupied with these thoughts, a strange character appeared pulling a cart flying the French flag, and came to a halt on the pavement. The man was well past the first bloom of youth, and dressed in an extravagant get-up: dented top hat, threadbare black frock coat, wide blue belt and red shoes. His small eyes and jutting chin made him look a little like a bull terrier. His shoulders were sore from the shafts so he massaged them for a moment before disappearing into the hotel. Joseph followed him and, through the half-open door, clearly heard an angry voice.

'By heaven! Tell her it's Bricart, Sylvain Bricart, Uncle Bricart! I lugged her trunk all the way to the Hôtel de Belfort for nothing, and now here I am at the Arrivée, and it's a good thing she chose a hotel called the Arrival, because this is my terminus! Well, what's the matter? I'm not dragging Gouffé's suitcase around with me![34] It's just full of her things! And now, by God, you can keep the damn thing!'

He came hurtling out of the door again, and began to tug fiercely at the straps securing a tin trunk with copper bands round it. Joseph noticed that on the side of the cart, large orange letters advertised:

STALE BREAD – FRESH TODAY!

'Do you need a hand?' he asked.

'I need at least four hands,' barked the man. 'That snotty hotel boy's a halfwit. I keep telling him that Sophie Clairsange is expecting me, and he says she's not receiving visitors. Another bumpkin from out in the sticks somewhere!'

They struggled to drag the trunk into the foyer, under the haughty and disapproving gaze of a page-boy in a resplendent uniform.

'Here it is. Do what you like with it. I wash my hands of the damn thing,' Sylvain Bricart concluded.

'I wanted to meet Sophie Clairsange too. She ordered a book from me. The woman is nowhere to be found,' Joseph improvised, planting himself in front of the cart.

'Ever since she married a rich American and left California, she hasn't been the same, it's true.'

'She's married? What's her married name?'

'Mat something or other. You don't pronounce it as it's spelt – it's a funny kind of a word. In any case, I deserve a bit more gratitude from her.'

'Are you close to her?'

Sylvain Bricart spat copiously.

'Close? Sophie used to sit on my knee when she was still young enough to be sucking her thumb. I was more or less a father to her for years, because her real one had made himself scarce and I wanted to make my sweetheart at the time happy. Then we drifted apart, the little girl and I, but as soon as she got into difficulties I was there quick as a flash to help her. Sorry, but I've got to go – a load of bread crusts to collect behind Saint-Jean-Baptiste church. I don't quite trust the verger. I wouldn't put it past him to give them all away to the parish poor – what a waste! I'm going to stir my stumps and store them all at Sentier de l'Encheval.'

'Excuse my prying, but by what miracle is your stale bread fresh today?'

'It's just a manner of speaking. Bakers give me their stale bread – brioches, sweet pastries, barley cob loaves, all as hard as rock. Real offensive weapons, if I was so inclined! There's no way they can sell them. I've invented a way, though. I put them back in the oven for a bit, stick them into crates, load them into my cart under a blanket to keep them warm and then I sell them on to the punters as snacks! *Adios, amigo!*'

With a supreme effort, he lifted up the shafts of the cart.

'Just one more thing, please! You mentioned difficulties ... Did Sophie, er ... Clairsange have a brush with the police?'

'That's all ancient history now. It was a trial, and a lot of dirty linen got washed in public, some of it more dirty than the rest. Sponges, candles, ergot, a whole lot of things. Now I've really got to make tracks. I need to catch the children coming out of school and I haven't got long ...'

As he moved off, he bellowed, 'That's my best earner in winter!'

'Married! Mat something or other, ergot, whatever on earth that might be,' Joseph murmured. 'Might as well add yeast and wheat flour, while we're at it. All his tall tales have ended up driving him dotty. If he's the Millionaire, I'm the King of Prussia!'

A flurry of fine hail was bombarding the La Villette roundabout. His fingers numb with cold, Alfred Gamache was trying, with fumbling determination, to peel the hot chestnuts he had just bought from an Arab whose nearby stall wafted enticing smells. His bayonet was leaning against the wall, its point securing a leaflet vaunting the attractions of the new revue at the Folies-Belleville, called *V'la l'funi qui grimpe*.[35] He had promised Pauline that he would go and applaud her as she pranced about in her scanty costume and flesh-coloured tights.

He popped a golden chestnut into his mouth and chewed ecstatically, the flavour bringing back a flood of memories from his childhood, when his mother, a manicurist, would buy him a bag of roasted nuts on cold winter Sundays. He would try to make her eat some, but she always said that she wasn't hungry, even though she was as skinny as a rake.

A quiet cough interrupted his reverie.

'Hello – do you remember me? My wife is an artist, she works for the—'

'*Le Passe-partout*, I remember. I got hold of a copy: nothing, nix! Something tells me you were lying,' the customs man said, through a mouthful of chestnuts.

'I assure you I wasn't. I've been wondering about the man with a limp that you mentioned the other day.'

'I mentioned a man with a limp, did I? Well, I never. I read somewhere that when the weather gets really cold like this, it can cause all sorts of hallucinations, just like in the tropics. You should see a doctor.'

While Gamache stuffed himself, Victor carefully folded up a banknote and slipped it into a crack in the wall of the rotunda. Alfred Gamache feigned indifference.

'Who are you?'

'I work for the tall policeman in the hussar's jacket who's always sucking on lozenges to hide the smell of tobacco.'

'Good grief, you're a policeman!'

'Did you mention the man with the limp to Inspector Lecacheur?'

'Even presuming that this limping bloke does exist, I'd have had trouble telling your boss about him.'

Victor lit a cigarette and exhaled a cloud of bluish smoke into the customs man's face.

'Why?'

'Because there's a chronological order to things; first the cause, then the effect. Example: suppose a man is visited by an apparition in human form. There's no way that man would be able to tell a *flic* about it if the *flic* questions the man before the apparition's even appeared. Who knows, I may well have had a daydream about a man with a bit of a limp, and he may well have asked me if I saw anything on the night of the murder. It's also possible that I said to him, "Listen here, mate, I wasn't playing gooseberry" . . . I may just have dreamt all that after my encounter with your inspector.'

'And what did this apparition look like?'

'Brown hair, side-whiskers, no moustache or beard.'

'And what was he wearing?'

'You've got me there. Something about the apparition told me I should be careful. What if it's a *flic* or a journalist trying to catch you out? I thought to myself. So I was on my guard, and didn't size him up too carefully. It's funny, the things you find growing on the walls around here,' he remarked, pocketing Victor's banknote.

'I didn't notice a thing. Must have been a trick of the light.'

'That must have been it. Do you want a chestnut?'

148

*

A stack of papers fluttered on the desk. Kenji just managed to catch them before they blew away, and he sneezed as the icy blast from the street whipped past him.

'Close the door!' he shouted.

Fräulein Becker and her bicycle had just burst into the shop, and were now blocking the exit of two other customers. The impasse would have gone on for ever if Euphrosine had not intervened. With one decisive hand, she pushed the betrousered woman and her steed firmly out of the way, and with the other, she shooed the two bibliophiles out of the door.

'You missed your vocation, Madame Pignot. It's a shame that the police don't admit women into their ranks,' Kenji remarked.

'Women make excellent chefs, though, so woe betide anyone who objects to the whiting and lentil stew I'm making for lunch!'

Kenji made no reply except to sneeze again. As he blew his nose, a few cake crumbs fell out of his lawn pocket handkerchief. He picked one up and tasted it.

'Raspberry tartlet,' he murmured.

How lovely their meeting at the Gloppe tea room had been! He found Djina's agitation enchanting, and delighted in observing the trembling of her fingers, which turned the simple gesture of raising a teacup to her lips into a perilous undertaking. He studied her sweet face, and did his best to contain his joy as he perceived that its timid expression was mingled with an attraction that she could not hide. When he had passed her cup to her, their fingers had touched and she had blushed and lowered her eyes. Bowled over, he felt his own shyness increase in response to hers. The rather superior, off-hand manner he had assumed with all women since Daphné's death melted away. By the time he kissed her hand at the end of Rue des Dunes, after he had insisted on walking her to her door, he was completely under her spell. He did his best to conceal this from her,

149

even though the sensation filled him with a new energy.

'I am like Esau, Madame Pignot. I would gladly give up my birthright for a mess of pottage, or even a bowl of whiting and lentils!' cried Helga Becker.

'I thought you were an only child.'

'It was just an image, Madame. I'm feeling carefree this morning, as light as air! Just think, my compatriot, Dr Otto Lilienthal,[36] has pulled off yet another victory. Last October, he had already become airborne and floated down the slope of a hill near Rhinow, in Germany. And now, in Steglitz, near Berlin, he has just launched himself off a platform in his flying machine and managed to land three hundred yards away!'

'Does he think he's a bird?'

'He most certainly does! He believes that it will one day be possible for man to create artificial wings like those of birds, which he has been studying for more than ten years, especially swans' wings. Despite the swan's weight, it is able to glide while barely moving its wings. That's because their wings are concave and, when fully extended, they are carried on updraughts in the air around them. They use their tails as rudders to steer with, and off they go!'

Her arms outstretched, Helga Becker was about to knock over a pile of books when Euphrosine blocked her way.

'So it follows that if you attach two geese to an elephant, take them to the Alps and launch them off the Aiguille du Midi, they'll fly right over the mountains? What a load of rubbish!'

'How dare you mock such impressive technological advances? *Unverständig!*'[37]

Kenji couldn't resist getting involved.

'Although I am a great believer in progress, I must agree with Madame Pignot. When it comes to aeronautics, we are already well supplied: hot air balloons, gas balloons, airships …'

Helga Becker drew herself up and, nostrils quivering, fixed her eyes on a point high above their heads.

'I guarantee it: today, the engine; tomorrow, independent flight!

And no amount of cynical mockery will rob me of that conviction!'

'What, has there been another robbery?' cried Joseph, rushing into the shop with his cheeks reddened by the cold and by unaccustomed physical exertion.

'What are you talking about? Has something been stolen?' asked Kenji, raising his eyebrows.

'Er, no ... I meant ...'

Euphrosine came to her offspring's aid.

'Guess what Madame Becker has been predicting, pet: we're all going to have a pair of wings strapped on us, and be forced to beat them until we go fluttering off, away from God's earth!'

'Well, if that's the way it is, I'm leaving,' Helga Becker retorted, but as she made to leave she met Victor and his bicycle coming in the opposite direction.

There was a clash of metal, an exchange of tight smiles and obsequious apologies, and then, finally, everything was quiet again.

'The Teuton has admitted defeat – now the kitchen calls,' said Euphrosine.

Joseph went to the back of the shop, where Victor was polishing the handlebars of his bike with a shammy leather.

'I should have taken a cab – the roads are like one big ice rink. But it was worth it: the customs man confirmed that a man with a limp was asking about the murder. What about you? I wasn't expecting you back so early. What happened?'

'Mission accomplished, Boss. I came back because Sophie Clairsange had her things delivered to her, so now we know that she's going to stay at the Hôtel de l'Arrivée for a while. As for the limper, no trace of him at all. But we're all right, because I've got his address. Oh, and I also met—'

'Not so loud! I'm proud of you, Joseph. Good work – you're a first-class sleuth.'

Joseph did his best to look modest. He studied the glass case full of quivers and blowpipes attentively, but his face shone with happy pride.

'We must go back to Rue de Varenne and offer our condolences to Madame de La Gournay. I want to find out who this man with the square face is,' Victor whispered, out of the corner of his mouth.

'Don't forget that he was particularly interested in a key decorated with the image of a unicorn, so that he could get to the Baron's collection and see whether it had been covered with blood, just like his own dolls – dolls, at his age! Shall I copy all that down for you?'

'No need, Joseph, it's all up here,' said Victor, tapping his forehead.

'When shall we go?'

'I'll have lunch quickly with Tasha, and then I'll go straight away.'

'Where shall I meet you?'

'I'll go by myself. I'll telephone you later.'

Joseph seemed to be struggling to understand what Victor had just said. He stood absolutely still, holding his breath, his eyes wide. He knitted his eyebrows and said quietly, 'What have I done to deserve this punishment?'

Victor replied in a honeyed tone, 'Oh, nothing whatsoever. You deserted your post when it was crucial not to let Sophie Clairsange slip through our fingers, and you made me look like a fool in front of Monsieur Mori, to whom I had carefully explained that you were spending the day at the Drouot exhibition. Do you know what, Joseph? You're nothing short of useless. So if I go without you this afternoon, it'll be good riddance.'

He pushed the door open angrily, slipped on the parquet, nearly fell and staggered back into the shop.

Joseph clenched his fists, suddenly roused to anger.

He really has got a nerve! he fumed. Well, never mind! He shall know nothing of what Bricart told me. Nothing at all. I'll keep that firmly under my hat! Ergot, the candle, the trial, the whole lot! Really, what's the world coming to? Bother and blast, he can just go without, Monsieur too-big-for-his-boots Legris!

'Lunch time!' roared Euphrosine.

*

His eyes fixed firmly on his shoes, Victor twisted his hat in his hands, almost as disconcerted as he had been when he had met La Môminette. The maid with the warts had shown him into a room filled with dark upholstery and draperies, which seemed to blot out the light. Three candelabra cast a dim glow over some sofas arranged in a semicircle, on which several lethargic-looking women were lounging. The women's faded complexions, their bluish eyelids and their dazed expressions gave their faces a mask-like appearance of intense fatigue. The light of the candles revealed several small dressing tables on which lay, among bottles of perfume and powder compacts, an array of hypodermic syringes made of silver and gold, in leather cases encrusted with precious stones.

One of the women, propped up on her elbow, let out a sigh, which quickly turned into a wild laugh.

'Clotilde! A handsome stranger has come to fall at your feet! I didn't know that you had reconciled yourself to the opposite sex!'

She sat up and, without the slightest embarrassment, hitched up her skirt and petticoats, rolled down her stocking and plunged a needle into her thigh. Madame de La Gournay rose calmly, adjusted the widow's cap which covered her hair, smoothed her plain grenadine silk dress and straightened the short cape she wore over her shoulders. She was as tall as Victor. As she drew closer to him, he could see her chalky complexion and the dilated pupils that betrayed her addiction.

'Madame, I was terribly sorry to hear of your husband's unjust and untimely death, and may I—'

'That is a pleonasm, Monsieur: death is always unjust,' she observed in a neutral tone which showed that she was not entirely under the influence of the morphine. 'I am astonished to see that, despite his numerous misdemeanours, Edmond managed to retain some friends. For you are a friend, unless I am mistaken?'

153

'Certainly. I used to provide him with books about alchemy. We met—'

She silenced him with an upraised hand.

'The details do not concern me. Nothing about my late husband is of the slightest interest to me. If you wish to pay your respects, the body is laid out upstairs. Octavie will show you the way.'

She rang a bell and the maid reappeared. The clatter of her pattens was not enough to drown out the sniggers of the women as Victor left the room.

After following a series of winding corridors, they came to the antechamber that Joseph had described. Octavie stopped and stared at Victor. The crepe bow attached to her collar added to her forbidding appearance.

'Madame is ruining herself with that drug. She may well say that it's a remedy to calm her nerves, but she'll soon be a wreck if she carries on with it. Sometimes she sleeps for hours, sometimes she paces up and down all night. It spoils her appetite and her brain's got more holes in it than a sieve!'

'She seems not to care about her husband's death.'

'She doesn't give a damn. I'm the only who ever cared for him here. And even I lost my nerve when it came to calling a priest to give him the last rites and absolve him of his sins. Our priest, a good man, took the initiative himself and sent his cousin just as Monsieur was about to pass. Thanks to that, he may still go to heaven despite his faults. Madame and her great oaf of a son certainly couldn't be counted on . . . they're a pair of heathens! They abandoned him. And he dares to play the piano on a day of mourning! That boy is heartless.'

The sound of a clumsy pianist murdering a Chopin polonaise drifted from some far-off room.

'Did the Baron leave a large legacy?'

'Not on your life! The fortune has all gone – there's just a pile of debts where it used to be. And the house is mortgaged to the hilt.

154

Madame and her son are lucky that Monsieur's family, in Orléans, are going to take them in. As for me, at my age, references don't mean much any more, and it'll be difficult for me to find another position . . .'

She looked sheepish, and Victor felt obliged to reply, 'I'm only a bookseller, but I'll keep my eyes open.'

'Oh, thank you, Monsieur, thank you!' cried Octavie, and she showed him into the bedroom, stepping aside as soon as she had opened the double door.

The stuffy atmosphere of the room, with its closed shutters and macabre setting, made Victor feel slightly uneasy. The body looked huge, stretched out on the bed and dressed in riding gear. The Baron's hands were joined over a large ivory crucifix. A row of candles cast wild flickering shadows over the walls.

'Is it true that somebody smashed his skull?' Victor asked Octavie, who was in a hurry to escape from the room.

'The doctors finally admitted the truth of what the nurse had said all along: somebody knocked him off his horse, the poor man. A real-life game of Aunt Sally, except they were aiming for the back of his neck instead of his head. And they didn't even take his money!'

As she made off down the corridor, she delivered a heartfelt monologue on the treachery and cowardice of the perpetrators, which gradually faded into the distance.

Left alone with Edmond de La Gournay, Victor swiftly sought out a paraffin lamp and lit it. The corpse regained its normal proportions, and its outfit became almost grotesque: silk hat, morning coat and jodphurs. The boots and whip were waiting close by, laid out on a rug. Was the horse pawing impatiently in a nearby corridor?

Victor glanced around the room with some trepidation: it was filled with innumerable Louis XVI cupboards and sideboards, each one of which could have concealed a multitude of keys. Where to start? He pulled open a drawer and a pile of letters and bills spilt out. Next, he knelt down in front of the bookcase, and was worried when he felt a sudden cramp flash through his right calf – was he already getting old? Standing up again, he pushed his hat back and scratched his forehead, perplexed. It would take at least three days to sort through all this.

He tried to gather together everything he could remember.

'Look deep into your memory,' Kenji used to tell him. Now then, where did his father used to hide the key to the larder, to stop his son stealing sugar and apples? Victor frowned, and the image of a richly decorated vase standing on the mantelpiece in the dining room came to him. The father had underestimated the son's perspicacity: Victor had quickly discovered the hiding place, but hadn't taken advantage of it, so fearful was he of the punishment that would inevitably ensue.

Of the three vases that stood in a row, looking down on all this bric-a-brac, the second proved to contain the prize. Victor fished a key out of it, and saw that it had a tiny golden unicorn inlaid in its ornate head. He was full of childish triumph, until another thought stopped him short: which lock would it open?

Once again, the furniture seemed to crowd round him hostilely. Was the answer even in this room? Would he have to comb every inch of the whole house? Discouraged, he began to ferret around in the death chamber, the presence of the corpse no longer perturbing him at all. Wherever the man who had been called Monsieur de La Gournay was now, the torments he had endured, his taste for ether, the occult and money, the very reasons for the criminal act which had caused his death – all these had disappeared when he had breathed his last breath. And what did it matter if a curious ghost was observing Victor as he turned around and about like a hamster in a wheel?

The toile de Jouy wallpaper depicted shepherdesses watching over herds of pale-blue sheep. Amorous musketeers popped out from behind an infinite number of small hillocks. The galloping of their steeds began to make Victor feel dizzy, and he stopped his feverish searching. There was something odd about the wallpaper. He examined the wall opposite the window and gradually realised what it was that seemed strange. Each little pastoral scene was exactly the same, except for one, which contained a sheep that seemed to reflect the light. Was it a nail? Without taking his eyes off it, he moved closer. A lock! He raised the lamp and noticed that the edges of the strips of wallpaper were uneven. He traced the join with his fingertips, and found that it formed a rectangle, about five feet tall and two feet wide. He put down the lamp and knocked: it sounded hollow. There must be an empty space on the other side.

He turned the key in the lock and a corridor opened up in front of him. He took a candle and, stooping beneath the low ceiling, began to make his way along the dark passage. The door closed behind him. He had only taken a few steps when he came up against another wall. The candle guttered and went out. He wanted to turn round and go back, but there was no longer any escape that way. Victor slid to the floor to rest his back, and suddenly retched: he felt seven years old again, and his father was all-powerful, imposing, threatening, without pity. The implacable sentence had been passed. What crime had he committed to deserve being locked in the cellar? The cellar: darkness and solitude. He couldn't stand it. He would surely die.

Crouching with his knees up against his chin, Victor searched desperately through his pockets and finally found his lighter. The candle wick lit straight away, but then smoked and flickered. He felt a slight draught on his forehead.

'Oh God, please let there be . . .'

A breath of air was coming through a tiny crevice in the woodwork. He put his hand against it and heard a click. A panel slid to one side.

Bent double, he clambered through and found himself in a narrow room full of even more jumble than the death chamber, lit only by a faint ray of light filtering through a tiny bull's-eye window. At first, all Victor could see was piles of books, but as his eyes grew accustomed to the dim light he was able to make out serried ranks of unicorn sculptures, in bronze, marble, amethyst, agate and china, prancing on shelves and display cases. Several of the statuettes were broken. The air was stale, but he also detected another, sour smell which turned his stomach. Had he been transported straight into a unicorn's belly? Then he saw the brownish stains, like mould, infecting the whole room and giving it the appearance of pock-marked skin. He looked more closely: it was dried blood. Overcome with nausea, he saw great splashes covering the floorboards, the rug and the walls. He held the candle nearer to some of the books, and deciphered their titles: *The Origins of Alchemy* by Berthelot, and tracts by Nicolas Flamel, Albertus Magnus, Eliphas Lévi, Roger Bacon, Basil Valentine, Paracelsus and Helvétius, all stained with scaly mould.

'A shame – they're all originals, and they're ruined,' Victor murmured.

A sudden flash of light hurt his eyes. On an oval mirror in a frame decorated with acanthus flowers, some words had been scrawled in white, in capital letters:

IN MEMORY OF BRUMAIRE
AND THE NIGHT OF THE DEAD
LOUISE

Victor leapt back and knocked over a table, sending several unicorns flying. To stop himself falling, he caught hold of a handful of medallions that were fixed to the wall: they were exact replicas of Martin Lorson's unlucky talisman. The fatal mystery which had been troubling him and Joseph was beginning to make sense: the La Villette medallion had belonged to Edmond de La Gournay who, like Louise, had been brutally murdered ... She couldn't possibly have written this abstruse message. So who had? The mysterious Sophie Clairsange, in a fit of vengeance? Hermance Guérin? The limper? The Millionaire? The man with the square face? He looked at the key to the room, half expecting it, too, to be covered in blood like the key to the forbidden room in Bluebeard's castle. He put it in his pocket and tried to open the tiny window to let in some fresh air. He pulled, but the latch had seized up. He staggered backwards and bumped into the door he had come through, which slid shut before he could stop it. Victor screwed up his courage and searched the narrow surface for some kind of hidden mechanism. He caught his foot on a poker lying on the floor and, bending down, discovered a few chips of wood that seemed to have been knocked off one of the bookshelves. A second door, disguised by a covering of fake books, was right in front of him. It gave easily when he pushed it – somebody had forced it open.

He came out into a corridor that led to a spiral staircase, where there was a pervasive smell of cauliflower. He felt sick at the thought of food, and went down the stairs in a comatose state, emerging next to the kitchen, where the maid was trudging around in her pattens. When she realised that he was standing behind her, she gasped and brought her hand to her heart.

'You gave me such a fright . . .'

'Please tell your mistress that I'm going to leave now.'

Madame de La Gournay seemed reluctant to speak to Victor for a second time in the presence of her companions, so came out onto the front steps. She had a little more colour in her cheeks and her behaviour was almost normal. Only her voice retained its apathetic tone.

'Has your husband had many visitors this morning?'

'Three or four,' she said evasively.

'I read in the newspapers that you refused to give permission for an autopsy to be carried out. I think you were wise.'

'I also refused to let the police come and search the house.'

'I found this near the bed. It might be best to shut up the room in

159

question,' Victor advised her, handing her the key.

'The secret room . . . Thank you,' she whispered.

'I would like to come to Edmond's funeral.'

'It's tomorrow at ten o'clock, in Montparnasse cemetery, where we have a vault. All of his dear companions will be there, with tears in their eyes and pompous words in their mouths, even though none of them ever really liked him. They're all mad, especially that Gaétan.'

'I shall bring Sophie with me, Sophie Clairsange.'

'Sophie? Is she one of your conquests? Or one of Edmond's?'

Her surprise was genuine. He did not insist further and only said goodbye, adding, 'She's just a young relative of mine who's interested in the Black Unicorn.'

'I shall be glad to see you, Monsieur. You seem not to be like . . . the others,' she replied.

Victor set off to find a cab, reflecting how tragic it was that morphine had a similar effect on Westerners, especially women, as opium did on the Chinese. His musings were interrupted when he caught sight of a familiar podgy figure. He could only see the man side-on, but there was no mistaking him; that rolling gait, that ancient brown suit, that worn bowler hat, could only belong to Isidore Gouvier, the phlegmatic and perspicacious reporter from *Le Passe-partout*.

'Monsieur Gouvier!' he cried.

'M'sieur Legris! Fancy seeing you – it must be two years since we last met! Ah, M'sieu Legris, it's a pleasure to see you! Are you still working away at those detective stories?'

'Not me, that's Joseph Pignot, my assistant.'

'I heard that he's married, and that the lucky lady is your half-sister.'

'How did you know?'

'I always scan the announcements of marriages and deaths in *Le Passe-partout*. And you? What news?'

'I'm very well. Can I buy you a drink?'

'Thank you, but I've got an appointment with a lady. No, no, it's not what you think, it's all in the cause of work,' he said, pointing to the Baron de La Gournay's decrepit house.

Victor thought for a moment and decided to tell a half-truth.

'What a coincidence, I've just come from there. The deceased was a customer of ours. I've just learnt of his death. It seems that he fell off his horse and came down hard on his head.'

'Well, yes, that is what they're saying, but the doctors are telling a different story. You should go and ask them about it – the answer will make your own head ache. I find it all very perplexing that such an accomplished horseman as the Baron should . . . Anyway, I've come to nose around. You know my boss: when Antonin Clusel smells a scandal, he goes straight for the jugular. What he really likes are the juicy details. Anything on that secret society, the Black Unicorn, will sell a lot of newspapers.'

'I've heard people talking about that society. What is it exactly?'

'A bunch of lunatics, devotees of Nicolas Flamel. They're searching for the philosopher's stone! Philosopher my foot!'

'Madame de La Gournay is a puzzling woman. Are the police going to get involved?'

'Who knows? According to my sources, the police are scratching their heads over this one and can't decide how to proceed. This occult society includes a good few bigwigs, so the police want to avoid causing too much of a stir. The Baron was one of the three founders of the society.'

'Ah, I wasn't aware of that.'

'Now there are only two of them left to keep the whole thing going: about twenty toffs and members of the gentry, a few famous actors, political schemers, magistrates and even some prominent egghead or other!'

'What do you mean?'

'A member of the Académie Française . . .'

'And who are the Baron's co-founding cronies?'

'The president is Richard Gaétan.'

'The couturier from Rue de la Paix?'

'The very same. A rival to the great Worth, father of fashion.

161

It's all frills and flounces, feathers and sequins! The third crony tops the bill at Franconi's Winter Circus.[38] His acrobatics and his daring leaps are renowned for their virtuosity. He likes all things exotic and goes into the ring decked out in all sorts of costumes – Russian, Chinese, Japanese, Moroccan, Hindu, you name it. His name is Absalon Thomassin. You should see the act where he hangs from a wire and spins round a hundred times.'

'The Great Absalon,' Victor murmured. 'Will you mention them in your article?'

'Why shouldn't I? That's what I'm paid to do. If they try to sue me, Clusel can pick up the bill.'

'That's a shame.'

'Why?'

'It's bad publicity for the Elzévir bookshop. They're regulars there.'

'That's where you're wrong. It'll attract more customers! Are you still in the detective line, by the way?'

'Since I married Tasha Kherson, I've been behaving myself a bit more.'

'Maroussia? Bravo, well chosen. That reassures me, because if you'd carried on in that line you'd have ended up in some kind of trouble. It's nearly been the death of you once already. I've got to go, M'sieu Legris. Come and see us one day at the offices. My regards to your lady.'

Lying next to Iris, Joseph couldn't get to sleep. The sibylline words of the stale-bread seller were going round and round in his head like a swarm of fireflies.

A trial which involved some respectable people, some less respectable, and Sophie Clairsange-Mat! Which trial? When and where did it take place? If only I had a date, just a date, I could look it up in my collection of newspapers.

He suddenly remembered that his mother had converted his

162

study at Rue Visconti into a playroom for her future grandson. All his piles of magazines and newspapers were now stored in the basement of the bookshop, and he had had to negotiate long and hard with Monsieur Mori even to be allowed to keep them there.

'I could ask my friend Bichonnier . . . No, it would take weeks of searching. What can I do?'

Iris turned over, dragging the sheet and blankets with her. He got up, lit a candle and crept into the kitchen on tiptoe. Perhaps a bit of bread and cheese and an apple would stimulate his mind.

When he got back into bed and snuggled up to his sleeping wife, it was one o'clock in the morning and he had resolved nothing. There was also a sartorial question to be answered: what on earth was he going to wear to the Baron de La Gournay's funeral? He silently struggled to win back a bit of the blanket for himself, and finally dropped off to sleep. He dreamt of a sea sponge appearing before a jury of bulrushes and candles all wearing top hats.

CHAPTER 9

Tuesday 20 February

Joseph and Victor made their way stiffly up the central avenue of the cemetery. Their formal suits were too tight round the armholes, and trying to look nonchalant in their heavy, ill-fitting top hats was nothing short of torture. As they splashed through large puddles in their polished shoes, it was hard not to imagine that the drizzle falling on the long symmetrical rows of plots had been ordered especially for the occasion. Joseph was putting on a brave face after Victor's comments the day before, but he was determined not to reveal anything about his meeting with Sylvain Bricart. There would be no collaboration between him and his brother-in-law without a heartfelt apology. Four words went round and round in his head: ergot, candles, sponges, trial. Yet another puzzle. Was it the chatter of a madman or a cryptic clue? He would have liked to go and look at Guy de Maupassant's tomb, the great writer having taken his place there only the previous year, but he did not dare ask Victor to make a detour. They passed by the monument to the historian Henri Martin, with its pyramid decorated with palm leaves, and rejoined the Northern Avenue where several men dressed in black were standing near the tomb of the celebrated lexicographer Pierre Larousse.

'The one in the middle in the chic get-up, with the bulging eyes and fingers covered in rings, that's the writer Jean Lorrain,' Joseph whispered. 'And in fact I recognise almost all the others too: Papus, the Sâr, that mad composer . . .'

'Is the man with the square face one of them?'

'Yes, the one on the right.'

The group had broken up now, and the men formed a line. As they approached the grave, each one took a red rose from a basket and threw it onto the coffin, before crossing themselves. Then they kissed the widow's hand. She had assumed a pose of dignified mourning and hid her impassive face under an opaque veil. The men also shook hands quickly with a youth whose spotty face was set in a self-conscious grin, before making their escape, their shoulders hunched against the rain. Victor skipped the formalities and bore down on his prey, touching the square-faced man's sleeve just as he, too, was about to make off.

'Allow me to offer my condolences, Monsieur . . .'

'Gaétan, Richard Gaétan,' the man replied gruffly, shaking off Victor's hand with an impatient gesture.

'My name is Maurice Laumier. I hope it isn't too late to . . .'

'Too late? What for?'

'To join the ranks of the Black Unicorn, now that its founder is no longer with us.'

Richard Gaétan seemed to relax, and his lipless mouth attempted a smile.

'I shall be taking over, and enrolling new members. I wish that we didn't have to charge a fee, but, as you can imagine, the running costs are considerable: we hire a meeting room, provide our members with our special insignia and manuals, and we also subsidise society dinners . . .'

Swindler, thought Victor, but he only said, innocently, 'Is it expensive?'

Richard Gaétan grasped his chin in his hand, and there was a short pause while he evaluated the possible income of this new recruit.

'A thousand francs a year.'

'A tidy sum! But we have to spend our money one way or another, don't we? I have heard great things about your work.'

165

'Here's my card, Monsieur Laumier. Come to my office and settle the fee as soon as possible – you're far from being the only aspiring new member, and the number of places is limited.'

'I would have thought it was in your interests to enrol as many people as you can. At that price . . .'

'Mass recruitment? Certainly not. We despise the common herd. Our aim is to form an elite dedicated to complex spiritual endeavours. We cannot simply admit people willy-nilly.'

Gaétan, his nose in the air, walked away before Victor had time to say anything else.

'Mission accomplished?' asked Joseph. 'Did you get his address?'

Victor showed him the card:

Richard Gaétan
LE COUTURIER DES ÉLÉGANTES
10, Rue de la Paix, Paris 2nd
Office: 43a, Rue de Courcelles, Paris 7th

'This fellow seems to me to be a scoundrel of the first order,' he said.

'Jean Lorrain spoke to me!' Joseph burst out. 'I told him that I write and that I've had work published, and he told me to go and see him and show him my new story.'

'Just in case you weren't aware, he is known for his predilection for the male sex.'

'You think you're so clever! Of course I knew that – the whole of Paris knows. Still, it's flattering; the author of "Fleur de Berge"[39] wants to see me!'

He began to sing, imitating Yvette Guilbert's wry tone:

'In the evening, with my lover at the Golden Lion, in the
*   firelight's glow,*
When it's dark and snowing,
I try every trick and spell I know
To try to get him going . . .'

'Well, that's nice, very clean, coming from the father of my future nephew!'

'Oh, come on, don't play the prude, dear brother-in-law! I know all about your special interest in curiosa[40] – had you forgotten?'

'I have a professional interest in curiosa,' Victor replied curtly.

'Yes, well … Apart from inviting me to a funeral, you haven't told me anything about what happened when you visited Madame de La Gournay.'

'I was waiting for the right moment. Can I tempt you to a slap-up meal? I know a little restaurant where they serve particularly good tournedos in Béarnaise sauce. That way, we can escape the vegetable feast at the bokshop, and exchange all our news. I've picked up some new clues. And lunch is on me, naturally.'

All of Joseph's strict resolutions evaporated.

'Me too! I've had some rich pickings. Sophie's married, and Sylvain Bricart told me that . . .'

Corentin Jourdan was sitting near the window of his hotel room on Rue de Strasbourg, looking out at the bustle down below, where teams of horses stamped and snorted. He had paid for his hotel room in advance. One night would be enough. He read the newspaper article yet again.

This morning, Monsieur le Baron Edmond Hippolyte de La Gournay's funeral was held in Montparnasse cemetery. Among the mourners were Dr Gérard Encausse (known as Papus), Messieurs Huysmans and Mallarmé (writers), Messieurs Claude Debussy and Erik Satie (composers), and Monsieur Richard Gaétan, the famous couturier of Rue de la Paix. Madame Clotilde de La Gournay requested that there be no eulogy . . .

One down, he thought. Two to go. I need to tread carefully now. First: get my siren away from her entourage. Second . . .

He alternated between excitement and cold reasoning. Rather

167

than this headlong rush towards almost certain failure, perhaps he should jump on a train and go home.

The silly idiot! Why didn't she go to a hotel in a completely different part of town, he wondered. That would have made things much simpler. Time is running out, and so is my money.

He looked at his watch.

There's nothing for it – I'll risk it.It's now or never.

He got up, and tore his shirt down the front. Then he took off his cap, pulled on his sailor's jacket and opened his door a crack to make sure the coast was clear. He locked the door behind him and walked cautiously up to room 14, her room.

He took a deep breath and threw himself against the door, hitting it hard with his shoulder and making no attempt to protect himself. He fell to his knees and huddled on the floor.

The door opened. He could see a woman wearing a soft dress that showed the curves of her body. She hesitated for a moment and then seemed to slide forward between him and a lamp. He stood up, hitting his head against the wall. She was there at last, so close. She didn't speak, but stood with her head lowered, and he could hear her breathing fast. He blinked in the light. In a very low voice, she said, 'What are you doing here?' Her voice trembled.

'I've been attacked,' he groaned, as a ridiculous thought crossed his mind: I'd have made a good actor!

'Don't move, Monsieur. You need a doctor.'

'No, no doctors!'

'But you're injured!'

Corentin felt the blood throbbing at his temples. He grasped the woman's hand, and she tried to release it.

'Help me to stand up. You've already been of great assistance to me. It's nothing serious, just a few bruises.'

He caught hold of her elbow.

'Listen carefully. It is vital that you trust me. You are in danger. Get away from here, and take as little as possible with you. Don't hire a carriage.'

'Who are you?'

'A friend.'

'Did you leave the note at the Hôtel de Belfort?'

'Yes. I can't tell you any more. Go back to the house in Rue Albouy – you'll be safe there. Lock the doors and don't receive any visitors. Ask them to leave your meals outside your bedroom door. I'll contact you.'

'But . . . you must be mad!'

'No, I'm telling the truth!' He was almost shouting. 'Please, do as I say,' he said, more calmly.

'Tell me your name.'

'I saved you at Landemer, in January.' He let go of her arm. A feeling of intense unease and worry crept over him. He had no idea what she would do next, or how far she was prepared to go in her reckless state. 'You must believe me!'

Sophie Clairsange watched him stagger away down the corridor and disappear round the corner. Going back into her room, she knocked over a chair in her haste and, with a feeling of rising panic, shot the bolt. Was this stranger who had begged her to leave really a friend? Who had attacked him? And why? Had he really saved her at Landemer? What if he had wanted to kill her?

I'm going mad, she thought – he could have killed me easily just now if he'd wanted to. Could he have read the blue notebook? Should I trust him? Dangerous . . .

Even so, the familiarity of Rue Albouy was preferable to being shut up in this hostile hotel.

The sun was setting. She ran the whole way. When she reached the garden, she feared that a fist would strike her from behind. She turned the key in the lock.

Five minutes later, a light flickered briefly behind one of the blinds on the first floor.

Corentin Jourdan stood stock-still near the glowing windows of the bakery. Thank God she had obeyed him.

The weather had grown milder. Workers and shop girls flocked onto Rue de la Paix. A shadow fell on number 10 just as a swarm of apprentice milliners poured out, hurrying to catch their omnibuses. Going against the flow, the shadow flitted into the building. Nobody paid the slightest attention to this figure, half hidden as it was by a roll of material that it abandoned surreptitiously against a doorframe. The shadow quickly slipped towards the back stairs and shut itself away inside a broom cupboard. The long wait had begun.

The concierge was busy extinguishing all the stoves, moving from one workshop to the next. Heavy shoes clattered on floorboards and young female voices cried out, 'So, Père Michon, what are you looking in the stove for? Have you lost your wife?'

'Watch out, Père Michon, you know the Bible says it's better to marry than to burn in the furnace!'

The girls were all in cahoots when it came to jeering at the concierge, a ribald old widower with wandering hands. Permanently tipsy on cheap spirits, Michon grumbled that they all treated him like a doormat, and it wasn't just these dirty hoydens, but the big boss too. He maintained that in thirty years of honest work, he had never suffered the insults of such a cruel mob.

The shadow held its breath in the cramped space, listening to the confused sounds from all around. That door banging meant that the concierge had gone back to his lodge, and the quiet humming came from the cleaning lady at work in the crystalware shop next door. The sewing workshops would not be cleaned until early the next morning.

It was becoming difficult to breathe, and it was vital not to get cramp now. Only a few steps separated the cupboard from the mezzanine landing. From there, it was possible to see down to the ground floor and the bottom of the stairs. Too much haste now would be dangerous: observations made on previous days had revealed that the big boss liked to linger after his troops had retreated, and that he often had a prisoner with him. A creaking sound soon confirmed this to be the case. Somebody was coming down the stairs. They paused for a moment and then continued, making gurgling noises that sometimes sounded more like laughter, sometimes more like sobs.

Quickly, the shadow crouched behind a ficus plant in a terracotta pot.

In the half-light, a young girl appeared. As she clung to the banisters, she was shaken by a great heaving sob. She pulled herself together, breathed out slowly with a quiet moan, and hobbled down to the tiled hall. Lamplight filtered in through the fanlight above the front door and was reflected in a tall mirror hanging on the wall. The figure of a seamstress, who was no more than fifteen, appeared in the mirror, her hair messy, her cheeks scratched and her stockings falling around her ankles. When she saw her pitiful reflection, she burst into tears of despair. She let a bundle of crumpled clothes fall to the floor, and then gradually her sobs subsided. Eventually, she smoothed down her skirt and bound the cotton strips which were all she had in the way of underwear more tightly round her bony chest. She buttoned up her blouse and pulled on her cape. She wiped away her tears with her arm, put on her hat and turned towards the door. The concierge had not padlocked it, so she only had to lift the latch. A good escape route.

The shadow checked that the leather pouch and its contents were in place, even though their weight was proof enough, and then set off, step by step, slowly. Only a few more feet. Stop. Carefully forward. Don't think about the little seamstress.

The shadow reached the first-floor landing, silent and agile as a cat, as though an invisible wire were there to guide it in the right direction. Now, turn right, past the rooms where clients came to inspect their new dresses, and then the bathroom. Perfect, perfect. It had been easy to bribe the young pattern cutter, who had been fired a month before. She had provided an accurate sketch of the layout of the whole place. There was, just as she had said, an office at the end of the corridor, where the head seamstress brought certain lucky clients who had been invited to take a glass of curaçao with the big boss. There was no need to look around: the pattern cutter had described the room in minute detail, also relating how, one evening, summoned to share a glass of wine with the boss, she had fought tooth and nail when he threw her down on the satin divan. There was a jug for hot chocolate on a side table, and an ornate bowl full of sweets. Two squat armchairs in front of the stove, a vase full of artificial flowers, a Chinese screen and a terracotta nymph dancing on her pedestal completed the decor. The whole room was suffused with the orange light of a Rochester lamp. And there he was, sprawled on the divan, a spider in the middle of his web, replete with the evening's savagery, and exhausted because he wasn't young any more, and raping a little girl required an awful lot of energy.

This time, it would be possible to take aim and strike in one fell swoop. The big boss would not suffer, would not even know what had happened, and when he found himself in the next world he would surely think that his end had been quite merciful, given the terrible acts he had committed. And how pleasant it was, this final caress of the heavy object that was about to dispatch the enemy on his final journey!

Richard Gaétan stretched and yawned, overcome with fatigue. This sort of sport was too much at his age, and his heart wasn't what it used to be. And, damn it, the divan was covered in stains. He would get them to send the loose cover to the laundry before the workshop opened. Never mind; that yellow bedspread, pressed into service on several previous, similarly messy occasions, would do the job for a few days. Solange, the head seamstress, would give him a roguish look, but a few banknotes would ensure that she forgot the whole episode. He would summon the little seamstress discreetly, give her notice and buy her silence with a well-filled envelope. What a tedious performance, all in the name of a few paltry seconds of pleasure!

He tucked his shirt-tails in, buckled his belt and combed his hair in front of a swing mirror surrounded with stucco cherubs. Then he froze in the act of smoothing his hair. He thought he had seen a face over there in the shadows. Ridiculous – that little minx would never have dared come back. He turned round and took a sweet from the bowl. All he wanted now was to bathe, go home and change his clothes, have something to eat on the Boulevard and sleep, sleep . . . He started combing his hair again.

The shadow took aim. There was a brief gasp. Struck on the back of the neck, Richard Gaétan fell heavily, his mouth still full.

The shadow bent over the inert body, looking for signs of life. Nothing. This could justifiably be called a great leap forward in the mastery of the weapon. Practice, it would seem, did indeed make perfect. Where had it rolled away to? Here, next to the comb.

The iron ball was carefully picked up, and the lamp extinguished. There was nothing left to do, except to take one's leave and to concentrate on the next step of the plan.

CHAPTER 10

Wednesday 21 February

Solange Valier, the head seamstress at Le Couturier des Élégantes, was feeling greatly relieved. The visiting dress for Madame de Cambrésis was ready on time and, thanks to a few final touches, looked even more beautiful than she could have hoped. She carefully arranged the black skirt, with its moss-green inserts on either side, on the wicker dummy. The bodice was gathered round a delicate ruff, and its voluminous sleeves tapering down to narrow wristbands were really something special. All that remained was to attach the beaded satin rosette, and the ensemble would be perfect.

The junior seamstresses were taking their places in the workshop, chattering and giggling. Solange Valier sent one of them to tidy the boudoir: it was strictly out of bounds to the cleaning ladies, but had to look immaculate because the boss would sometimes entertain a client there after she had given a new outfit her seal of approval.

'And don't forget the toffees and the sugared almonds, Marguerite – you know how much he likes those. The boxes are in the little side table.'

The girl in question, a young apprentice with a mop of curly hair, pushed back her chair eagerly, only too happy to have the chance to set foot inside this sanctuary usually reserved for the elite of Parisian high society.

'I'll need a lamp, or I won't be able to see a thing!'

'There's always something, isn't there? Hurry up!'

Marguerite slowed her pace as soon as she was out of sight. She wanted to make the most of this unforeseen treat, which would transform her humdrum day into something magical. She was no longer a slave to the needle, but a tragic heroine just like her namesake, Margot, the lovelorn queen in the stories her mother used to read to her from the big illustrated edition of the works of Alexandre Dumas. She crossed the storeroom where rolls of velvet, silk, shining taffeta, and tussore and surah from India waited, ready for the big boss to transform them into reception dresses or dinner gowns. She went down some steps and came out of a hidden door which led to the main staircase. The boudoir was adjacent to the fitting rooms and the bathroom. The light of the lamp revealed all sorts of luxury items lined up on the shelves of the bathroom, and she found the sight of them utterly bewitching. She reached up and touched the coveted bottles and boxes, savouring the privilege of possessing such objects, even if only for a moment, running her fingers over a scented soap or a silk handkerchief. She felt like a queen.

Much as she would have liked to linger there, the thought of being reprimanded made her move on. She pushed open the door of the boudoir, and once again felt as though she were entering a dream world. Now she was a princess dressed in sumptuous robes, about to awaken her prince, who lay slumbering on the divan. She was so absorbed in her role that she curtsied respectfully to the terracotta nymph, but as she did so, she froze.

Somebody's watching me, she thought.

She glanced down to the floor. Lying on his side, head thrown back and lips stained with a dark-brown liquid, Richard Gaétan seemed to stare at her with eyes that glinted with a strange amber light. She drew back, unable to tear her gaze away from his. Somewhere inside her, a hysterical voice told her to act as if nothing had happened. She lost her nerve, whirled round, staggered and caught hold of the terracotta nymph, which fell and shattered into a thousand pieces.

*

These battle-axes! Did they turn into vampire bats, hanging upside down from gutters, ready to swoop on the bookshop the minute it opened? Joseph was pondering this question just as Mathilde de Flavignol and Raphaëlle de Gouveline entered the shop, brushing their wet coats against the bookshelves. Thank goodness! The wet weather meant that the Schipperke and the Maltese had been left at home.

Which is ironic, given that it's raining cats and dogs, thought Joseph.

Mathilde de Flavignol was criticising the ceremonies marking the bicentenary of Voltaire's birth and Raphaëlle de Gouveline was describing the details of a charity tombola in the town hall of the ninth arrondissement when the telephone rang and put a stop to their chatter. It was Isidore Gouvier, wanting to speak to Monsieur Legris.

'He's not in the shop at the moment, but, whatever it is, you can tell me,' Joseph said. 'Yes, I'm married, and going to be a father soon … What? … Murdered? … When? … Good heavens! … Yes, I'll tell him … Yes, he was a regular customer of ours. Thank you, Monsieur Gouvier, goodbye.'

No sooner had he put down the receiver than the cry went up.

'A murder?' gasped Raphaëlle de Gouveline.

'Which regular customer?' squealed Mathilde de Flavignol.

'Please, Mesdames, a little calm. It's a nasty business involving a rather prominent person. A crime of passion. The details will all be in the newspapers.'

He bounded up the stairs.

'Mesdames, hold the fort, if you would be so kind.'

They acquiesced, open-mouthed. He hammered on one of the first-floor doors, which opened slightly to reveal Kenji in his blue dressing gown with red spots.

'Victor needs me urgently – a fabulous set of first editions! Can you tell Iris I'll be back as soon as I can? The battle-axes – that is, Mesdames de Gouveline and de Flavignol are eager to talk to you!'

Kenji's eyes were narrow with anger and he was about to protest vehemently, but Joseph had already careered back down the stairs. Under the astonished gaze of the two women, he grabbed his coat and bowler hat from a peg and dashed out of the shop.

The day that Tasha had been dreaming of for so many weeks had finally arrived. In a few hours, Thadée Natanson would open the *Revue Blanche* exhibition – her exhibition. Five years' work would be exposed to public scrutiny. Would it attract compliments, criticism or indifference? Would she succeed in dazzling one or two buyers? Even that might be too much to hope for, given that Vincent Van Gogh had only managed to sell one painting during his lifetime. Now that she was called Legris, she was protected from malicious gossip, but this dependence, which Victor seemed to find completely natural, wounded her pride. He was possessive and jealous of other men, and no doubt always would be, but he was also so thoughtful and so unselfish in his behaviour towards her that she longed to be a success and make him proud of her.

She examined her reflection in the mirror. It was impossible to tame her red hair: no matter how many pins she used, a stray curl would always escape. She buttoned up the embroidered bodice of her pink velvet dress. She would have to hold her stomach in to make up for the absence of a corset, an instrument of torture which she could not bear to wear. Finally, she pulled on her lace gloves, powdered her face and put on a little scent, conscious of André Bognol's admiring gaze.

This former butler, with his curious combination of efficiency and stiff dignity, was busy tidying the large room that Tasha used as her studio.

'We are almost ready. There is a ragoût with fresh herbs ready in the kitchen, and now all we have to do is dust the studio.'

At first, his use of the royal 'we' had astonished Tasha, but she had soon got used to it.

'There's no hurry, André, we – I mean, I am going out now, first to the framer's and then to the *Revue Blanche* offices. I promised to be there before midday.'

Most of the paintings selected for the exhibition were already in place, but she needed to make a second trip to arrange the transport of four particularly large canvases.

She stroked Kochka, who was curled up next to the stove. Victor was developing some photographs, and would go on to the bookshop before joining her at Rue Laffitte towards the end of the afternoon. She thought that a goodbye kiss would bring her luck, and hurried towards the apartment, but before she got there she had the misfortune to bump into Joseph.

'What on earth are you doing here?'

'Victor sent for me – a collector has some first editions . . .'

'Where is he?'

'In his laboratory.'

'I meant the collector,' she said.

'43a, Rue de Courcelles,' said Joseph, immediately regretting having blurted out the first address that came into his head.

He gave her a winning smile, hoping to soften her up, thinking back with nostalgia to the time when she used to call him 'my little *moujik*'.

She hesitated. She assumed that Joseph was lying, but knew that it was useless to contradict him. He and Victor had demonstrated often enough that, despite their frequent disagreements, they were as thick as thieves when they were investigating a crime. Was that what they were doing? She didn't want to confront Victor just now, and, in any case, she might be mistaken.

'See you this evening, darling!' she called to Victor.

'Good luck, my love!' he called back cheerfully.

She left the apartment, casting a rather hostile glance in Joseph's direction.

'Dear brother-in-law, I think that your wife smells a rat,' Joseph said.

178

Victor came out of his lair.

'Well, as long as she keeps quiet about it … Tell me again, word for word, what Gouvier told you,' he said, selecting a waistcoat.

Richard Gaétan's home stood out from its neighbours with its neo-Gothic architecture groaning with ogives and gargoyles. A skinny butler wearing a tail coat, pinstripe trousers and a stiff white cravat fixed the two visitors with a baleful gaze, the corners of his mouth contorted by a nervous tic. When Victor informed him of his master's demise, the tic stopped for a moment, but this was the only sign of emotion he betrayed.

'Will you be needing to question me, officers?'

Preferring not to correct this misapprehension, Victor and Joseph followed him into a large, comfortable library. With his hands solemnly behind his back, Joseph eyed the titles of the books that filled the room, with their green and red spines embossed with gold. Although most of the great names of literature were represented, he realised that the books were all fakes, and retreated, disappointed.

The butler began to dust a vase mechanically.

'It wasn't unusual for Monsieur not to come home of a night, but last night I felt as though there was a great weight upon me and I couldn't sleep a wink.'

'How many staff are employed here?' Victor asked.

'There's the cleaning lady, Sidonie Mandron. She only comes in the mornings and cleans a different room each day. There's Madame Couperie, the cook, but she never goes up into the rooms. Then there is me. I've been in service here for twelve years now, but recently he got himself so worked up – I'd never seen him like that before.'

'What do you mean?'

'It was on the ninth of this month, a Friday – I distinctly remember because that day Madame Couperie's son Arnaud had got married. He's a butcher and he married a fishmonger's daughter, a stuck-up thing who hasn't the first idea about how to run a household. I foresee a disaster. Madame Couperie had prepared a cold collation and I had laid a place for Monsieur Gaétan here at this very card table near the fireplace. He had come back late and seemed tired. I served him, took my leave and went back to the office where we do the accounts. Suddenly, I heard: "Didier! Didier! Come quickly!" Didier Godé is my name. I ran back here and found Monsieur as white as a sheet. I thought he was going to have a nasty turn.'

The butler's face twitched convulsively, but he took a deep breath and mastered his emotion.

'Monsieur pointed to a panel in the wall that had been pulled back, just between Balzac and Beaumarchais. He was stammering, but he managed to say, "Did you open it?" I was indignant! "Good God, no, Monsieur," I cried. "I had no idea that this chamber existed." We went inside it. What chaos! As though a tornado had passed through. There were dozens of dolls of all shapes and sizes, dressed like the pictures in fashion magazines, all torn apart and broken. The worst thing was . . .'

He seemed to be feeling giddy.

'I'm sorry . . . The worst thing was the blood. For a moment, I thought that Arnaud Couperie, the butcher, had overturned a bucket in there. The dolls were all crimson!'

'Was it blood or red paint?'

'It was blood, Messieurs, blood! You can't mistake it: so thick, with that sickly smell that I can't stand. That's why I thought of the Couperie lad – he always has that terrible smell about him. I always have to air the room after he has come to deliver the meat.'

Godé wiped his face with a handkerchief and cleared his throat several times.

'Go on,' said Victor.

'There was something written in green chalk on one of the walls. I didn't have time to read it because Monsieur Gaétan rubbed it out as though it were some kind of terrible spell. I do remember one word vividly: Angelica. We spent half the night picking up the debris and scrubbing the place clean. Then Monsieur Gaétan closed up the passage to the secret chamber, and demanded that I swear on all that is most dear to me to say nothing about it. I swore on the life of my Aunt Aspasie. She was like a mother to me after my parents died of suffocation because of a faulty heating system. She brought me up and—'

'Please carry on with your story.'

'In my line of work, one has to be devoted and discreet, but now that Monsieur is no longer with us . . . Such a talented man! He invited me to sit down and take a cognac with him. I declined – it wouldn't have been seemly. But I listened to what he had to say. He told me that those dolls were precious to him. Milliners and couturiers often send such dolls abroad to advertise their creations. It's an old custom. Queen Isabeau of Bavaria used to send alabaster dolls dressed in the latest French fashions to the Queen of England. The dolls were so popular in European courts that during the wars of the seventeenth century a treaty was signed which allowed them to be transported freely across national borders. Monsieur Gaétan had spent years building up his magnificent collection, and he loved it more than anything. As he was telling me all this, I felt responsible – I should have been more vigilant, what with Monsieur receiving so many visitors, men as well as women. They used to slip in through the tradesmen's entrance – Monsieur would let them in if they rang the bell in a special way: two long rings and one short one. So I never knew who they were. Sometimes – although not often – customers would come to the front door, respectable people. Should I have been more wary of them? I offered to resign, because of my negligence, but he refused. "I have enemies, Didier. There are jealous people everywhere and they can't forgive my success." There you are. It's a sad case. I'll have to take another position, but I'll always remember Monsieur Gaétan.'

'Did you ever let anyone in while he was out?'

'A lady. That was the same day as he made that macabre discovery. It was already dark when she came, and she waited in the sitting room. I thought that Monsieur would be back at any moment, as he usually ate at about eight o'clock. The lady told me she had an appointment with him. I went down to the kitchen for a few minutes to check the menu, and she left without telling me.'

'What did she look like?'

'Like any well-to-do lady – a hat with a little veil, lots of frills and flounces.'

The shrill tinkle of the doorbell interrupted their conversation. Immediately on the alert, Victor signalled to Joseph that they should make themselves scarce. They hurried up some stairs to the mezzanine, and as they went, they heard the butler exclaim, 'Police? But the police are already here!'

The unmistakable voice of Inspector Lecacheur began ranting about simpletons who couldn't see through the most blatant lies.

They raced back downstairs and found themselves in the laundry where a surly-looking girl was dragging a basket full of dirty laundry over to a large tub.

'Sidonie Mandron? I'm Inspector Lecacheur. We're checking all the exits – open that window please!'

There was a shed with a flat roof a few feet below the window. Victor climbed over the windowsill and jumped down, sure that he was about to sprain an ankle or at least crack some tiles. He landed on his knees, safe and sound. Joseph dropped down next to him. They ran to the edge of the roof, slid down a drainpipe and ended up on a small lawn where a gardener was standing, clipping the hedge.

'Police! We're chasing a thief!' shouted Victor, dashing towards the gate.

Their chase ended near Saint-Philippe-du-Roule church. Behind them, several passers-by were eyeing them curiously. Joseph hailed a cab.

He and Victor were silent for a while, watching the driver's greatcoat jogging up and down in front of them. By the time they had reached the top of the Champs-Élysées, they had both got their breath back.

'As you can see, Joseph, I'm still agile,' Victor remarked, rubbing his calves.

Their cab got stuck between two omnibuses. Joseph let out an exhausted sigh.

'Well, at least when I want to write about tricksters and cat burglars, I'll have some real-life experience to draw on!'

'As Kenji always says, "Experience is the nectar of creation"!'

'But there are some days when one would prefer to die ignorant!'

They exchanged a conspiratorial glance and burst into gales of laughter. Still letting out the occasional giggle, Joseph managed to stammer, 'That makes two now! No, three!'

'Three what?'

'Three stiffs!'

'You should show a little more respect, Joseph. They were people, you know. This is real life, not a story.'

'I'm sorry, Boss, it's just that we've seen so many! And laughing about it helps me not to think about it. But you mustn't imagine that it doesn't mean anything to me. You know, I sometimes think I can't stand all this any more. I'm soft-hearted.'

'I know, Joseph. Do you want us to stop?'

'I didn't say that. It's just that I'll be a father soon . . .'

'We'll have this all sewn up in no time, or at least we'll try.'

'All right, come on then. What are your thoughts, Boss?'

'Gaétan's murder is identical to the Baron's. They both received a fatal blow to the head, and the two crimes were staged almost identically: the splatterings of blood, the destruction of the two men's most precious possessions and the messages signed Louise and Angelica.'

'Well, I'm blowed if I can piece any of it together! Gaétan's butler couldn't read the whole message, but perhaps Louise might have appeared there too?'

183

'Unless we start believing in ghosts, that line of thinking doesn't lead anywhere: Louise Fontane is dead. These two murders, as well as the vandalism, were carried out by somebody who knew how to gain access to the secret chambers … Somebody who knew the victims.'

'That takes us back to Sophie Clairsange.'

'But we have to be careful here – the women's names could have been put there precisely to throw any detectives off the scent. Don't forget what Martin Lorson told me: there were two men near the La Villette rotunda on the night of Loulou's murder. One of those men had a limp. Either he is the criminal, or Sophie Clairsange and the man with the limp are in cahoots.'

'We need to go right back to the beginning: let's winkle some more information out of the stale-bread seller and Madame Guérin, and get our hands on the limper.'

The cab stopped in front of a large coach builder's showroom, next to a horse dealer's premises. The sound of whinnying broke Victor's train of thought, and if, at that moment, he could have transported himself to a desert island, he would have done so in a flash.

'They should put up a monument to silence,' he grumbled.

Joseph scowled, feeling annoyed.

'Come on, let's concentrate,' Victor said. 'La Gournay and Gaétan ran an occult society. Gaétan's dolls were vandalised before he was murdered, but he didn't tell the police. That must have been because he suspected he knew who had done it. And, in fact, there's a third person in charge of that society – Gouvier told me his name. It's Absalon Thomassin, the star acrobat at the Franconi circus. Is he in danger? Is he guilty?'

Joseph would have continued to sulk if Victor hadn't given him a friendly slap on the back.

'We're going to grill every single person we can think of. Just you wait – we'll get to the bottom of this!'

'But we need to be quick, or we'll have another corpse on our hands!'

'You must be joking! There are only so many hours in a day! Tasha's counting on me being there this afternoon, and Iris is counting on you too. We'll have to suspend operations until tomorrow. Although I must admit that I sometimes wish I could speed up time!'

'Well, I don't, otherwise I'd be a grandfather before I'd even got to know my children! . . . Well, I'll be . . . That woman who visited Gaétan, she turned up on the evening of the ninth, the night of Louise Fontane's murder!'

Sophie Clairsange had spent the morning tidying her bedroom. Menial tasks were a useful distraction from her anxiety, and for a short time she was able to rediscover the person she used to be, the person who had to look after herself, not a rich landowner's wife trying to control a crowd of mercenaries on a Californian orange plantation. Her bedroom, a rather joyless place decorated in shades of yellow, brought back melancholy memories. She disliked the Henri II-style furniture but, nonetheless, the cramped room with its four-poster bed covered in old tapestries, and the sideboard converted into a dressing table, was an oasis of peace, where she was protected from harm. There was a bad gouache painting on one of the walls, in which an old woman sat huddled close to a fireplace, poking the glowing embers. The picture evoked the serenity of a home in which people lived their daily lives without incident. The stocky figure of Samuel Mathewson seemed to her to form a ghostly presence in the background. She had never felt the slightest hint of desire for her late husband, so complacent and well-meaning, but he had nevertheless provided her with the means of living a comfortable, even happy existence, now that he was dead. She felt a sincere gratitude towards her guardian angel of a husband.

She ventured out onto the landing, where a tray had been left for her with a cold meal and that day's newspaper, which carried the headline:

Avidly she read the article and then, breaking her promise to stay in her room, ran down the stairs.

Hermance Guérin had eaten her lunch in the sitting room, where two windows with coloured glass seemed to keep light out, rather than letting it in. She was now asleep in a cretonne wing chair, her cap askew on her head, her slippered feet resting on a footstool. Opposite her was an upright piano with a marble clock and a pair of Renaissance candlesticks on top of it. Her knitting had slipped off her lap onto a felt rug on the floor. As Sophie bent down to pick it up, Madame Guérin awoke.

'You promised to stay upstairs.'

'I read the newspaper.'

'So did I. He only got what he deserved.'

'Oh, I can't stand this! How much longer will I have to stay hidden away?'

'Patience, my dear. What is begun must be finished. You should have something to eat – you look pale.'

Sophie contemplated the pattern of black and white tiles on the floor. She was tormented by doubts.

'What if somebody did go through my bag?' she murmured.

'You shouldn't worry about that.'

And, as if to convince her, Madame Guérin started knitting again.

'While I was ill—'

'I was in the room every time the doctor came to examine you.'

'And Sylvain?'

'He doesn't take the slightest interest in anything except his business and his lady friends. And Aline's a simpleton – she can barely read a shopping list.'

'I'm worried about that man who says he saved me on the beach. He keeps on turning up.'

'Don't worry; nothing terrible is going to happen. I'm looking after you,' Hermance said with a smile.

The ball of wool went bouncing away again and rolled underneath a *tête-à-tête* sofa. Sophie ran after it, like a cat chasing its prey. Hermance's smile became a grimace, her lips set in a tight line, and her whole expression hardened.

Djina had excused her students from their usual lessons. The pretext for this treat was a visit to the Louvre, where they could search the galleries for a painting, which they would then reproduce in watercolour.

Despite her usual aversion to siestas, today she couldn't resist lying down for a moment. A courier had brought her a message from Kenji, and she put it on the bedside table. Lying with her eyes shut, she thought she could hear him speaking the words he had written:

> *Would it be possible for you to accompany me to a shop between two and four o'clock? I would like your advice on the purchase of some curtains. Afterwards, we could go and admire your daughter's paintings together . . .*

Before she knew it, Djina was asleep. She was walking through a forest whose trees were laden with all sorts of delicate blossoms. When she reached out to pluck a red flower, a warm wave of arousal broke over her. She was walking in the midst of a tangle of veils, through which she could see a shape that she knew she must reach. But, however much she hurried, she remained alone and full of yearning. At the same time, though, she was aware of an intense sensuality that seemed to be connected to a drawbridge covered in snow, which she dared not approach because she was naked. She sheltered in a doorway and saw that there was a pile of clothes on the floor next to her. As soon as she put them on, they disappeared, and she only managed to keep hold of a camisole which barely covered her breasts.

She woke herself up and was ashamed to discover that her right hand had found its way underneath her skirts and slipped between her thighs. She fought against her desire, and a glance at the clock told her that it was nearly two o'clock.

When Kenji rang the doorbell, smartly dressed in a charcoal-grey suit with a mauve cravat, his walking stick with its jade knob slung jauntily over his shoulder, Djina hurried out of the apartment and walked down the stairs in front of him, ignoring the arm that he held out to her. She continued to give him the cold shoulder in the cab all the way to Boulevard de Sébastopol, replying in monosyllables to his best attempts to make conversation. Kenji was unruffled: she had agreed to accompany him, and that was all that really mattered.

Was his choice of shop, À Pygmalion, an attempt to tell her that, like many men, he wanted to mould her to his design, as the sculptor Pygmalion had done with his statue of Galatea? No, Kenji wasn't so sly. He explained to her that this enormous department store between Rue de Rivoli, Rue des Lombards and Rue Saint-Denis had fascinated him when he and Victor had first come to France, and that he had bought everything he needed there when they moved to Rue des Saints-Pères. He also loved the Friday concerts dedicated to French chansons, which were held at the Éden-Concert, next to the shop. He had heard Yvette Guilbert sing there before she had moved on to a more risqué repertoire.

The front of À Pygmalion was decorated with a large figure of Punch, which had been left there after the New Year celebrations, much to the delight of all the children coming into the shop. The sight of it made Djina relax somewhat, and it was with something approaching gaiety that she finally accepted Kenji's arm as they passed underneath the bronze chandelier hanging in the huge doorway.

Crisscrossing rows of waxed parquet tiles marked out walkways in front of long counters overflowing with goods, and women stood assessing the merchandise under the beady gaze of the shop assistants.

'Let us not follow the example of those La Bruyère criticises in his chapter "Des Esprits Forts": "They are undecided as to which cloth they want to buy: the large range of possible choices makes them feel indifferent and, instead of coming to a decision, they leave without even taking a sample,"' Kenji whispered.

'Bravo, your memory is impressive.'

'It's all part of my job,' he replied modestly. 'In fact, I told you a little white lie, because I do already have an idea of which fabric I like best, but I wanted to know whether you approved. I shall be entirely guided by you in my choice of decor. You see, I intend to use the little apartment that I've rented to work on my catalogues, but, if you would consent to come, I would be most honoured to invite you there. So it's natural that you should have some say in the decoration.'

He made his request so lightheartedly that it seemed impossible that he should have any ulterior motive, and Djina followed him without a murmur to the counter where the bolts of damask were kept. A liveried shop assistant, his hair parted in the middle and carefully plastered down on both sides, was standing at the foot of an ornate ironwork staircase, eyeing them over his half-moon glasses. Were these two browsers, kleptomaniacs or serious customers?

'Here we are. I can't decide between this damask brocaded with flowers, or this green satiny one.'

'What colour is the wallpaper?' asked Djina, running her fingers over a bolt of ornately patterned chintz.

'Ivory,' Kenji whispered, and his fingers touched the same roll of cloth, advanced crab-like towards Djina's, hesitated, and then grasped hers.

'In that case, you should choose this warm shade, with the flowers,' she advised him, her heart pounding, astonished at her own temerity.

He nodded his head gravely, as though she had just imparted a

189

pearl of wisdom, and beckoned to the shop assistant.

'Would Monsieur like to order some curtain fabric? What are the measurements? Two windows? I'll call a sales assistant.'

A young woman armed with a tape measure and a pair of scissors cut out four sections of cloth and folded them meticulously.

'Is there anything else Monsieur desires?'

They avoided looking at each other, as the possible meaning of the words struck them.

'We'll take a set of ties for the curtains, in the same material but without the pattern, and a set of copper rings and rods,' Djina decreed.

They formed a small procession as they followed the sales assistant to the tills, the male assistant bringing up the rear, making swift calculations in his counterfoil book. Kenji paid the bill, and a second copy of it was stuck on a large metal spike on the counter. The man wrapped up the parcel and asked for the address to which it should be delivered.

'Monsieur Kenji Mori, 6, Rue de l'Échelle, first floor on the left,' Kenji recited clearly, casting a meaningful glance at Djina as he did so.

CHAPTER 11

The same day, in the evening

Euphrosine Pignot was keeping Iris company at 18, Rue des Saints-Pères. Since their reconciliation, they had begun to spend many hours together preparing for the arrival of the new baby. Despite indulging in considerable speculation regarding its sex, they chose a white layette, suitable for either. Euphrosine, queen of protocol, had planned everything down to the very last detail. The newborn's maternal grandfather would be its godfather, and it would have its paternal grandmother as a godmother. As for names, she had accepted a compromise: Daphné Euphrosine Jeanne, if it turned out to be a girl, or Gabin Victor Kenji, if it was a boy.

The bookshop was deserted, and Joseph hadn't sold a thing all day. There was still an hour to kill before setting off for Tasha's exhibition with his mother. Iris had decided to stay at home, unwilling to expose her small round belly to public scrutiny.

Joseph sat ruminating behind the counter, slumped on a stool, certain that he was not equal to the task he had taken on. He would have done better to devote his free time to his wife instead of tormenting himself with yet another complex riddle, even though it did give him new material for his writing. Suddenly, the tension he had been holding in check for so long seemed overwhelming.

'The sixth of March! Only two more weeks to champ at the bit! It'll be on the second page of *Le Passe-partout*: *Thule's Golden Chalice*, by Joseph Pignot! They'll all be laughing on the other side of their faces then! Iris will be bowled over, Maman will buy every single copy from the newsstand, and Madame Ballu will tell the whole neighbourhood all about it. As for Victor and Monsieur

Mori, I know perfectly well what they'll think: "His style isn't worth much, and his imagination is worse. He's bombastic half the time, and just plain silly the rest of the time." They think even less of my work than they do of the stuff churned out by those scribblers the battle-axes are so enamoured of. I don't give a damn – Ollendorff has taken a chance on me.'

He hadn't dared ask for a larger fee, for fear of being sent packing, and had even agreed to make some changes to his manuscript to keep Antonin Clusel, publisher of *Le Passe-partout*, happy. 'My dear Pignot, your novel is set in Transylvania, but no one's ever heard of it. Simplify: stick to sentiment and intrigue, and let's have a bit less of the descriptions and the psychology.'

'My time will come. Then they'll see that a true artist never lets criticism shake his resolve.'

He leafed through his notebook.

Bricart, Sylvain, stale-bread seller, ergot, candle, trial …

That blasted trial! If only he could get at his precious stock of newspapers, stashed away in the basement.

'You can't turn back the clock,' he sighed lugubriously.

A tiny light flickered at the back of his mind.

'Your brain's scrambled, my friend! You haven't got the newspapers from 1891. You stopped collecting them the year you got the job at the bookshop, in 1885, you idiot!'

The light grew stronger. He was suddenly filled with optimism. He would make it a point of honour to extract the answer from his brain, using forceps, if he had to. Now then, concentrate …

He frowned and bent over his notes, looking through them methodically.

19 February. Victor went to Rue de Varenne without me. I'll get even with him for that. He met Isidore Gouvier as he left the La Gournays' house. Gouvier is going to write an article on …

'Good heavens!' he cried.

He leapt up and grabbed the telephone, tapping feverishly to alert the operator.

'Hello, Mademoiselle, put me through to Monsieur Isidore Gouvier, reporter at *Le Passe-partout*, 40, Rue de la Grange-Batelière, please.'

He talked for about ten minutes, and then pulled down the shutters and closed the shop.

Although they were on the small side, the two exhibition rooms next to the *Revue Blanche* offices showed off Tasha's paintings to great advantage. The first room held her Parisian cityscapes, together with the still lifes and the male nudes – with the exception of the one of Victor. The second was devoted to modern scenes showing the influence of Nicolas Poussin, and to depictions of fairgrounds, alongside the photographs that had inspired them.

With her new departure into the realm of acrobats and the circus, Tasha was working towards a more personal style executed with fluid brushwork and luminous colours, which blended dream and reality.

There were many artists among those present, some unknown, some famous, some disdainful, some delighted. Édouard Vuillard and Maurice Denis were full of praise for the paintings' rich palette and the sense of rhythm in their composition. Toulouse-Lautrec had just returned from travelling through Belgium and Holland where, with his colleague Anquetin, he had sampled the museums and the beer. He was more reserved in his judgement of Tasha's work.

'All rather vapid,' he murmured to the satirist Maurice Donnay, who reproached him for being so harsh.

'Well, it's only to be expected. I've just been having lessons from Rembrandt and Hals,' Lautrec replied, in his nasal tone.

He was nonetheless charming to Tasha, hoping that if he couldn't actually seduce her he could at least persuade her to pose for him.

Pierre Bonnard arrived bearing bad news: Gustave Caillebotte, who had caught a cold in his garden a few days earlier, had suffered a stroke and was dying. It was thought that he could breathe his last at any moment.

'Such a delightful man, so selfless . . . And he's only forty-six! Fate really does seem to have it in for artists at the moment. We've already lost old Tanguy,' said Lautrec.

'If Caillebotte goes too, what will become of their collections?' asked Maurice Laumier, who had appeared behind Bonnard.

'Tanguy's will certainly be sold.[41] As for Caillebotte, rumour has it that he has appointed Renoir as executor of the will . . .'

Tasha glanced around the room, looking for Victor, disappointed that his photographs weren't attracting anything more than a few polite comments. He was talking to Joseph, who disappeared off into the crowd. Next, Victor was accosted by Euphrosine Pignot and Micheline Ballu, whose extravagant dresses, embellished with flounces and feathers, attracted some amused attention. There was more laughter when Fräulein Becker made her entrance in a kilt and tartan cape, topped off by a hat covered with grapes and vine leaves. Mathilde de Flavignol and Raphaëlle de Gouveline were more elegant, in their fashionable dresses decorated with sequins. They stood slightly apart from the others in order to be able to gossip in peace.

'My dear, have you heard, Colonel de Réauville went to see the tidal bore at Quillebeuf-sur-Seine with Adalberte yesterday, and he fell into the water!' whispered Mathilde de Flavignol.

'Did he drown?' asked Raphaëlle de Gouveline.

'No, he just swallowed a mouthful of water, and they say he'll get away with nothing worse than a bad cold.'

Helga Becker was following Lautrec's movements, and looking very perturbed.

'The other day, I carefully peeled one of his posters for the Moulin-Rouge off an advertising column. Do you think he would agree to sign it for me? I collect all the posters I can – I've got about sixty already,' she whispered to Mathilde de Flavignol. Mathilde, however, only had eyes for Victor, whose charming smile made her feel rather flustered.

Victor was amusing himself by standing behind people and listening to their comments. He had stopped near a painting of a group of women sitting at an open-air café.

'Goodness me, how vulgar! And the colours are simply atrocious!'

He realised that it was the Comtesse de Salignac and her nephew, Boni de Pont-Joubert. He knew that, as far as they were concerned, it was scandalous to use such trivial subject matter for a painting. They could no more recognise its hidden power than they could understand that its power lay precisely in its vulgarity.

'Oh! That fellow again! What a cheek! Walking around shamelessly like that, a divorced man!'

'Who are you talking about?' Helga Becker whispered.

'Anatole France, the novelist. Last year, he and his wife separated, no doubt because she had grown tired of his affair with Léontine de Caillavet. In court, the blame was all laid at his door, not hers! Since then, he's been living at the Villa Saïd, on Rue Pergolèse, but only in the mornings. After lunch, he goes to see his mistress, and spends the afternoon writing in a room in her house that she has set aside for him. Then they have dinner together.'

'What about her husband?'

'Monsieur Albert Arman de Caillavet? Why, he sits down to dinner with them! He's the philosophical sort – he gets on so well with his rival that people call him "France's domestic affairs minister"!'

Victor was revolted by what he had just overheard, and as a great admirer of France, author of *At the Sign of the Reine Pédauque*, he couldn't help commenting.

'The Caillavets would have divorced long ago, but they're afraid of damaging their son Gaston's career prospects.'

As soon as Victor moved off to welcome Kenji and Djina, Olympe de Salignac expressed her righteous anger.

'I'm not surprised he's playing devil's advocate, given the sort of life he leads! And do you know, his Japanese friend has had a bathtub installed in his apartment – it's disgusting!'

'They are used for washing, you know,' Raphaëlle de Gouveline reasoned.

'But first you have to be completely naked!' retorted the Comtesse.

Anatole France was standing in front of a painting of a tightrope walker balancing on his wire high above a busy street. France's asymmetrical face, with its mischievous eyes, wore an admiring expression. He twirled his grey moustache.

'It's very finely observed. Did you draw it from life?'

'Only the background. I took the figure of the acrobat from this photograph,' Tasha said.

'Superb. I shall buy them both,' the writer announced, and went off to greet Thadée Natanson.

Tasha blushed with pride, and hurried over to tell Victor the good news. Victor was also feeling pleased, having heard Lautrec announce to Vuillard that he had moved from Rue Fontaine to Rue Caulaincourt.

Now there's some good news! You won't keep turning up at Tasha's studio all the time! he thought.

'Where has my son got to?' said Euphrosine.

'He's gone to see a customer. He told me to tell you to go home with Madame Ballu.'

'He could at least have said goodbye to me!' grumbled his mother.

'Or hello to me,' Tasha said.

Victor gazed contemplatively at a sunrise over the Île Saint-Louis, thinking that Joseph had done well to take the initiative, and that he would have liked to go with him. His reverie was broken by Maurice Laumier, who tapped him on the shoulder.

'A brilliant idea of yours, Legris, to put all those photographs next to the paintings. That way, we can all see how the artist appropriates the real.'

'I'm only too glad to do anything to help Tasha,' Victor replied tersely.

'Don't worry, Legris, I'm not criticising your work. Especially now that you're making real progress.'

'I'm so honoured that you like it.'

'And your investi—'

He broke off as Tasha appeared. He praised her work enthusiastically, but only got an ironic smile in return.

'Dear sister artist, I was just telling your husband that Lautrec and Bonnard are showering praise on your genius.'

'Oh, do be quiet, or I'll collapse under the weight of your compliments.'

The Comtesse de Salignac had been lurking nearby, and seemed to be on the point of suffocating. Mathilde de Flavignol, too, was quite overcome.

'Her husband? Her husband?' she kept repeating. 'So they're married then?'

'Surely not in church, a pair of heathens like that!' gasped the Comtesse, fanning herself energetically.

'You must admit, Olympe, they do make a handsome couple.'

'If it weren't for my love of reading and for Monsieur Mori's exceedingly polite manner, I would boycott that bookshop! Come, Boni, we're leaving.'

She pushed past Tasha, who was making her way over to her mother.

'Do you really like it, Maman?'

'I think it's wonderful, my darling. What progress you've made over the last six years! Such finesse!'

'I should have hung some more neutral material on the walls before we put up the pictures. This horrible lilac wallpaper ruins

197

the contrasts. And what about that big grey curtain with the mauve sash right in the middle of the room there – do you think we should have it removed?'

This last remark was aimed laughingly at Kenji, who was standing in front of a rather severe male nude, envying the young man's well-developed muscles. He and Djina exchanged glances, and began to smile despite themselves. Their faces took on contorted expressions as they did their best not to burst out laughing.

I seem to be suffering from an advanced case of curtainmania. Thank goodness decorum prevented him from showing me his collection of Japanese prints! Djina thought to herself, feigning a coughing fit.

'What's so funny?'

Tasha was moving off, feeling somewhat disconcerted, when she heard a woman's voice behind her.

'I just hope your friend Legris has got what it takes. I'm counting on him, so he'd better come up with the goods. Those police couldn't care less about Loulou now that she's out of sight, chucked into some communal grave.'

'Try one of these canapés, my sweet,' said the man she was with.

Tasha turned round, just in time to see Maurice Laumier shoving a biscuit into Mimi's mouth, almost choking her. He tried to drag her off in the opposite direction, but Mimi resisted and cornered Victor instead.

'When are you going to solve this mystery for us, Monsieur Legris?' she managed to say, still trying to swallow the biscuit.

'It's still too soon. Be patient. I promised you—'

Mimi squeezed his arm.

'You're such a hero. I do trust you – and if there's anything you want from me, you only need to ask!'

This time, Laumier pulled her away so forcefully that she nearly fell over.

'Have you lost your marbles?' she squealed.

Lautrec cast an appreciative glance in Mimi's direction.

'A fine specimen!' he remarked.

'Who is Loulou? What are you and Laumier up to? And what have you promised to do for that little tart?' shouted Tasha, enraged.

Several heads turned. Embarrassed, Victor led her towards the door.

'You're mistaken, my darling. This woman's cousin died recently at the hospital – of tuberculosis. And I've known Laumier for a long time—'

'I know that! I introduced you to him, and you've always hated him!'

'I've changed my mind – he's not so bad. I promised to try to recover this Loulou's belongings, because they seem to have been stolen by another patient or a nurse.'

'Do you really think I'm going to fall for that? I'm sure you and Joseph have been bitten by the detective bug again. Where have you sent him off to, anyway?'

She was red in the face now, determined to expose his lies. He adopted an affectionate expression and nodded towards the room full of her work.

'Nowhere. I love you, that's all that matters now. This evening is your triumph and I'm delighted to have played a small part in it. Don't spoil it all.'

He was a master of the art of evasion. She could have insisted and forced him into a confession, but instead she banished her suspicions about Laumier and Mimi from her mind. It was better to remain in a state of blissful ignorance.

As they were making their way back into the room, they met Euphrosine Pignot and Micheline Ballu on their way out, eager to get the long trip home in the omnibus over and done with.

The journey had proved to be an arduous one. The only available seats on the omnibus had been on the upper deck, where an icy wind had frozen their cheeks and found its way under their coats.

Madame Ballu's feet, squeezed into a pair of narrow boots, were begging for mercy by the end of the journey. When she finally came within sight of her street, she felt like a thirsty explorer who spies an oasis on the horizon. Her satisfaction would have been complete had it not been for the removal cart, parked on the pavement opposite the bookshop.

'There's something fishy going on,' she said to Euphrosine. 'This is the third time in a week that Lambert Removals have graced us with their presence, but every time, once it's parked, the cart stays in exactly the same place, and the driver just sits there, with his cap pulled down over his ears. I've had a look and the cart's empty, and it's always still empty when he finally pushes off. And another thing – he limps. I noticed that when I saw him pacing up and down one evening, smoking his pipe.'

Euphrosine rolled her eyes.

'Is it a crime to have a limp now? You've been spending too much time with Monsieur Victor. Mind you, so has my Joseph – that's why we had to get an omnibus instead of coming home with him in a cab. He's rushed off to goodness knows where, when he should be at home looking after his pregnant wife. A customer indeed! At this time of day, honestly! A little outbreak of detective fever, more like.'

'I wasn't born yesterday, you know. I know something suspicious when I see it,' said Madame Ballu, piqued. 'The removal man even followed me into the courtyard once.'

'What?'

'Yes, he … he …'

Micheline faltered as Euphrosine fixed her with an incredulous stare. She wished that she had kept that detail to herself.

'He did what? My poor Micheline, if you hadn't already had the change, I'd say you were having some kind of hallucination, or that you'd started confusing your desires with reality. Why on earth would any man follow you? It's absurd. You're getting yourself all worked up over nothing!'

200

'I saw what I saw.'

'Oh, and what has that clumsy great oaf gone and done now?' Euphrosine cried, as Zulma Tailleroux crept out of the building carrying a canvas bag which clinked with the sound of broken pottery.

'It wasn't my fault, Madame! I was cleaning Monsieur Mori's room when a book fell off the shelf. I bent down to pick it up and I kicked the chamber pot. Luckily it was empty—'

'You're a walking disaster! It'll be taken off your wages!'

Zulma burst into tears and ran off towards the Seine.

'What an old curmudgeon you are! And all for a chamber pot, which your boss doesn't use anyway, not since he had his own "water closet" put in!'

'My boss? My daughter-in-law's father, more like. We're equals now, I'll have you know. If he wants to have a chamber pot there in case of emergencies, that's his business, and nothing to do with a silly gossiping woman who dreams that all the men in Paris are running after her!'

Micheline Ballu felt as though some kind of earthquake had knocked the Queen of Sheba off her pedestal and was scattering the broken fragments in the gutter. Dethroned, the noble Sheba was nothing but a lowly concierge. Her face contorted with anger, she retorted, quick as a flash, 'Sling your hook, you old trout!'

'Isn't it past your bedtime, Madame Methuselah?' Euphrosine roared.

Micheline opened her front door and slammed it behind her.

'And to think I was kind enough to see her home! Talk about pearls before swine,' Euphrosine thought to herself, as she made her way back to Rue Visconti. She conveniently forgot that she had only walked along with her friend because she had also wanted to interrogate Iris about Joseph's desertion. Following the spat with Micheline, it had completely slipped her mind.

'An old trout? I'm only forty-two, and I'm not over the hill yet!' she said to herself, once she was back in her own apartment.

201

She threw her hat and cape onto a chair, unbuttoned her flounced dress and ran her hands over her hips.

'I may have a little bit of extra padding, but no more than what you see on those big amazons in the museums! They were on every wall when Tasha dragged me to the Louvre. Strong thighs, generous bosoms, and a good womanly behind! I'm a bit like them. But Micheline Ballu, well, she's just flabby. Take off her corset and she looks like a blancmange!'

She glanced at the portrait of Gabin Pignot that hung over the sideboard, and let out a sigh. He would always be like that: leaning against his bookstall by the Seine, thirty years old and full of bonhomie.

'Why do men have it so much better? Monsieur Mori must be well past fifty but he's still a ladies' man, and women love him. And why is it that women get uglier as they get older, but men get more handsome?'

She felt the urge to note down some of her observations. On the page devoted to Zulma, she wrote:

Zulma broke a chamber pot. She'll have to pay for it. That girl will find any excuse not to do a stroke of work. And her royal highness Micheline Ballu defends her. Micheline's not so keen on working either – she never even so much as sweeps the corridors! She'll pay for that too!

Suddenly, her pencil stopped moving, and she nibbled on the end, overcome with anxiety. Where could Jojo have got to? Was he chasing some woman? Oh, nobody knew the cross she had to bear! She lifted her head and gazed once more at her Gabin Pignot, the love of her life and Joseph's father, called to God before they had even got married.

The tram from Nation to the town hall at Montreuil went down a series of bleak roads lined with factories, building sites and warehouses. The two horses, whose driver kept nodding off, struggled to pull the vehicle with its half a dozen or so passengers. It passed the premises of Bébé Jumeau, an enormous china-doll factory.

What was it that Gouvier said? wondered Joseph, get off at Rue du Pré, in the middle of the allotments.

The light was gradually failing. Here and there, gas lamps cast shadows that looked like ragged cloths clinging to the façades of the houses.

With his hat pulled down low and his hands thrust deep into his pockets, Joseph plunged into a maze of small streets.

'The fourth house on the right. This must be it, this bungalow. It's a bit of a dump.'

Isidore Gouvier had inherited the house from his parents, lowly shopkeepers who had spent their lives saving up enough money to buy this little plot of land where he had been born, grown up and grown old. Joseph crossed a tiny, overgrown garden with a wooden table and two benches on one side. Perhaps someone had once thought that this would be a good place to relax, sip an aperitif and enjoy the scenery.

Gouvier opened the door, after fiddling for a while with the rather capricious lock. The coat pegs in the hallway were groaning under the weight of the clothes piled on top of them. The kitchen was relatively clean: Gouvier enjoyed his food. He showed Joseph into his office, where all his books were piled higgledy-piggledy on the shelves.

'Only people who never read keep all their books shut up behind pretty panes of glass,' he said, chewing on a cigar.

The room was full of trinkets and pictures, and there were hundreds of files covering the floor. An antique clock that looked as though it must have stopped years ago blocked one of the windows.

'It kept time in my parents' day, and since then it's been resting. Have a seat, Monsieur Pignot. I've made a cassoulet. Can you smell it? It's already a veritable feast for the nose!'

Gouvier went into the kitchen. He owed his limping gait to a few nasty kicks from a burglar, who had broken one of his shins while he was still working as an ordinary bobby on the beat. Joseph thought of the limper at the Hôtel de l'Arrivée. He looked around the room. A blackened paraffin lamp stood on the corner of a dresser, among a jumble of skeleton keys, handcuffs and crowbars, which had belonged to noteworthy criminals. Joseph could never have dreamt up such a treasure trove; this eighth wonder of the world was a true goldmine for a writer.

After a boozy meal, he began to feel euphoric. He was eager to find out whether Isidore Gouvier, with all his years of experience, might be able to help him.

'So you want to know what the words ergot, candle, sponge and trial might possibly mean, is that it, M'sieu Pignot?'

'Yes.'

'Ergot ... ergot. Really, M'sieu Pignot! It's a fungus that's often used to bring on contractions and get rid of unwanted offspring. Sponges and candles can have the same effect.'

'How awful!' Joseph cried.

'Well, yes, one of those everyday horrors. As for the trial, I seem to remember ... One moment.'

Gouvier bent down to read the dates on some of the files.

'I know it's recent. Two or three years ago. We can check.'

He pulled a few files bursting with loose papers out of the pile.

'I keep everything. I've never been able to throw things away ... Ah, it's coming back to me now. It was the year of the Fourmies massacre! My brain is just like a piece of M'sieu Edison's wax – even tiny details are inscribed on it! Here's the year: 1891. It was Clusel who covered the trial. The newspapers had a field day. It's strange that you never heard about it. What were you doing in November '91?'

Joseph tried to remember, but his mind was a blank.

'It's a long time ago, 1891.'

'Well, have fun. I'm going to get some shut-eye.'

Joseph pushed the plates to one side, cleared up the remains of the meal and put the contents of the file on the table in front of him.

The sheaf of cuttings was in chronological order. On the first one, taken from *La Justice*, he read:

15 November 1891
Tomorrow (Monday), the Crown Court of the Seine, presided over by Judge Robert, will begin its examination of the abortion case which may well last as long as fifteen hearings. There are fifty-two defendants . . . The female defendants are a varied group, including servants, shopkeepers, manual workers, bread sellers . . .

Le Figaro for 16 November announced:

TRIAL OF THE CHILD KILLERS

There they are, three rows of them, overflowing into the journalists' benches, some of them dressed in black, but the majority wearing their best clothes. There is a sea of beribboned hats, feathers and flowers, or bonnets covered with jet beads, which shine in the dim light of the courtroom. Some are little more than girls, some are sixty if they are a day. A refined blonde who describes herself as a painter of miniatures sits next to a cook; further down there are a couple of servants, the husband very respectable and neatly shaved, the wife looking thin and lost, wrapped up in one of Madame's old coats. What were they supposed to do? They worked for middle-class families who didn't want any children around . . . So the woman went to see Madame Thomas . . .

Joseph scanned an article from *Le Temps* dated 18 November.

Thirty-six names were placed in the urn, and fourteen names were drawn: twelve to be actual jury members, and two in reserve. Among those not chosen were the painter Jean Béraud, the sculptor August Cain and the lawyer Clément Royer, who is the leader of a prominent Bonapartist group . . .

The cuttings formed a large pile. Journalists had come up with article after article about the trial, with readers lapping up the salacious details. It was a truly sensational case, a sordid tear-jerker, rather like a story by Eugène Sue. Joseph picked out another article at random, from *La Gazette des Tribunaux*, dated 16 and 17 November.

> The hearing began at half past twelve. The accused were presented to those assembled in the courtroom … Ugly and vulgar, they all belong to the same class: most are servants or manual workers. There are also some men among them.
>
> The usher asks them the usual question, and they give their names:
>
> Marie Constance Thomas, forty-six.
>
> Abélard-Sevrin Floury, thirty-one.
>
> Delphine Céline, married name: Couturier, concierge, fifty-two.
>
> Marie Naïs, married name: Vire, cleaning lady, thirty-eight.
>
> Marie Honorine Duval, servant, twenty-two.

Joseph ran his finger down the list of the accused. Suddenly, he gave a cry and, moving the lamp closer to the table, remained deep in thought for a few moments.

'Where did I put my fountain pen? Quick, some paper!'

He bent over the table and began to fill up sheet after sheet.

'Find anything?'

Joseph started, and made a large blot on what he had just written. Gouvier settled himself in an old armchair.

'I can't sleep. It's twelve years tonight since I lost my wife. She left me on 21 February.'

'I-I'm so sorry, I didn't know,' Joseph stammered.

'Oh, she's doing very nicely. She's set up home with a butcher. She got tired of living in this shambles. She wanted a tidy little life, her house all spick and span, you know. She used to make me wear slippers, and she'd spend all day polishing and dusting. We never got on. Look, here's a picture of her.'

He pulled a wallet out of his jacket pocket and showed Joseph a grainy photograph taken at a fair. In front of a backdrop painted with a mountain scene, a man and a woman, their arms dangling awkwardly by their sides, stood to attention, gazing fixedly at the camera.

'Is that you?' said Joseph incredulously, amazed to discover that Isidore Gouvier had once had a relationship with a woman.

'It most certainly is, young man. Thirty years younger, with a spring in my step. You can't believe your eyes, can you? The years have their way with us all, in the end.'

He began to sing.

> *'Old age! You might as well be dead!*
> *It makes you ugly, makes you weak,*
> *Adds some wrinkles on your cheek,*
> *And takes some hairs from off your head.* [42]

'I didn't know you were a poet, Monsieur Gouvier.'

'A friend of mine wrote it. Have you found what you're looking for?'

'I certainly have, and it's really important! It's all still confused in my mind, though.'

'Don't worry, M'sieu Pignot, just evaluate the situation as calmly as you can. When we want to find something out, we need to be patient. Little morsels of information always come your way in the end. I spend as little time as possible at the editorial offices: all those meetings with Clusel calling the shots are just too boring. The atmosphere at press conferences reminds me of a bullfight, when you're never quite sure if people want the bullfighter or the bull to be killed. I'm not ashamed to admit that I always hope that the toreador will be gored. You have to be heartless to enjoy watching an innocent beast suffer, don't you think? Shall I make us some coffee?'

'I wouldn't say no.'

'Why are you taking the trouble to copy all this out? You can take the file away with you and give it back to me when you've finished. It's eleven o'clock and there are no more trams. Why not sleep here on the sofa? I'll wake you early tomorrow morning.'

Joseph couldn't get to sleep. Suddenly, he remembered the writing Victor had seen in the Baron de La Gournay's secret chamber: *In memory of Brumaire and the night of the dead* ...

He felt a rush of excitement. The trial had taken place in November '91. Loulou and three Sophies had been among the accused ... and also Mireille Lestocart!

'Brumaire means November! And the night of the dead is All Saints' Day, and All Saints' Day is in November! My dear brother-in-law isn't going to believe his ears!'

It was past midnight when Victor and Tasha devoured André Bognol's ragout without even bothering to heat it up. The opening had been a success, and most of those present had been full of praise. As well as Anatole France, two other people had bought paintings, and Mathilde de Flavignol had taken a fancy to a photograph of a merry-go-round that she had promised to pay for very soon.

Tasha piled some mincemeat onto a plate and put it down next to Kochka, who was curled up in her basket next to the bed. The cat only condescended to open her eyes for a moment and sniff at the offering, before falling asleep again.

As always, Victor folded his clothes carefully as he took them all off except for his flannel underpants. When he had placed them on a chair, he climbed into bed. Tasha unpinned her hair, dropped her clothes on the floor and lay down next to Victor, who began to kiss her, unable to resist a small caress despite their exhaustion. Nestling next to her, he explored the neckline of her nightdress until he found a way in and stroked his fingertips over one of her breasts, feeling her nipple respond immediately to his touch. She grasped his hand, murmuring, 'Three sales, five counting your photographs. I only sold the pictures of fairgrounds, though – it's a shame that—'

She was interrupted by a hoarse cry, and sat up so suddenly that she banged her head against the wall.

'What was that?'

'The cat,' Victor groaned.

Tasha felt her way over to the lamp on tiptoe. She stumbled twice, tripping over her own clothes, but eventually managed to find the box of matches. Just as she lit the wick, Victor gave a horrified cry.

'Oh no! I'm drenched!'

The lamplight fell on the guilty feline stretched out on Victor's lap. Her waters had broken.

'She's going to have her kittens!'

Feeling nauseous, Victor took refuge in the bathroom. Kochka let out a series of pitiful wails as Tasha stroked her reassuringly.

'I'm here, puss. Go on, push! You're nearly there.'

Kochka panted, her ears flattened and her pupils dilated.

Victor reappeared, wrapped in a towel. He turned away from the bed, transformed into an impromptu maternity ward, and began to put his clothes back on.

'How many is she going to have?'

'It depends. Two, perhaps three . . .'

A terrible vision appeared before him, of Tasha propped up in the bed, nursing three screaming babies.

'Why don't you go over to the studio? I'll come and join you as soon as it's over.'

'Will it take long?'

'I don't know. I've never been a midwife before.'

He made good his escape, thankful that they had a second place to sleep. At four o'clock in the morning, Kochka gave birth to a black and white kitten.

'I was right. You've been fooling around with the tailor's moggy,' said Tasha.

She felt very moved, and twenty minutes later, a second damp ball of fur appeared, this one with stripes. After another quarter of an hour, Kochka made a final effort and the last kitten, a black one, emerged.

Trembling with emotion, Tasha went to wash her face. When she came back, Kochka was licking her little brood, who had found their way to her teats and were feeding greedily.

'They look as though they're pressing on the pedal of a sewing machine. They're going to work you hard!' Tasha remarked.

It was as though Kochka had understood this, and was rebelling against such harsh treatment: although still weak, she managed to get up and, seizing the stripy kitten in her mouth, jumped to the ground. She went and stood in front of Victor's wardrobe.

'Are you sure that's the home of your dreams? Your daddy isn't going to be very happy about that,' Tasha said.

The cat stayed where she was, unperturbed, while the two other kittens miaowed themselves hoarse.

'All right, I'll try to talk him round.'

Leaving Kochka to settle into her new home, Tasha began to search for something to wipe the bed down with. She found an old newspaper that had fallen out of Victor's coat pocket. She tore out a page, and as she crumpled it up something caught her eye. The word 'murdered' was just visible in a fold, which she smoothed out.

GAÉTAN, THE COUTURIER, MURDERED

The police have searched his home at 43a, Rue de Courcelles, in the hope of …

'43a, Rue de Courcelles. I've heard that address recently. Who said it? André? Euphrosine? Iris?'

All of a sudden, she remembered: Joseph, that very morning. She'd cornered him just as he was about to go and talk to Victor. The suspicions she had dismissed earlier became certainties. A murder. Perhaps two, if she counted this Loulou that Mimi had mentioned.

CHAPTER 12

Thursday 22 February

Exhausted after his sleepless night, Joseph ran all the way from Châtelet to Rue des Saints-Pères, grumbling as he went. He carried on grumbling when he reached the apartment and encountered his mother, who welcomed him with a lyrical tirade.

'Oh, Monsieur has deigned to come back, has he? Not a moment too soon!' she barked. 'Did you sleep tight? I'd be ashamed of myself, if I were you! Like father-in-law, like son-in-law!'

With an immense effort of self-control, he resisted the urge to bang the door, so as not to wake Iris, and bounded down to the bookshop, eager to avoid Kenji. He opened up the shop without any of his usual care, decided that the dusting would have to wait and rushed down to the little basement stronghold where he stored his private papers.

He lined up all of his scrapbooks in chronological order starting from 1889, the year of his first investigation, and consulted the one labelled '1891'.

'Here it is! I've found it! I must be going soft in the head – how could I have forgotten? In November, Victor and I were tied up with other things!'

He jumped. Somebody was watching him. He spun round, banging his nose on a shelf laden with encyclopedias.

'Is that you, Victor?'

'Yes. What are you up to?'

'You could have warned me! This is going to swell up now. People will take me for a drunkard!'

'Blow your nose and tell me what you're up to.'

Joseph felt the blood rise to his cheeks.

'I've found the pot of gold. The trial was in 1891, the same year as we carried out the Montmartre Investigation.'

'Which trial?'

'What's wrong with you? The one that the mad fellow who sells stale bread was talking about. It was an abortion trial, and it caused a big rumpus. All the newspapers, from *La Gazette des Tribunaux* to *Le Père Peinard*, wrote pages and pages about it. Some of the crimes went back as far as 1885 or '86. Most of the women who'd got into trouble and been to see Madame Thomas weren't rich: servants, seamstresses, workers' wives, not earning more than one thousand five hundred francs a year. Madame Thomas had her premises in a room she rented from a wine seller in Clichy. She lived with Abélard-Sevrin Floury, a man fifteen years younger than her. He worked as her assistant, and was the one who had to get rid of the "leftovers" after operations. I'll spare you the detail of all the hearings, which lasted two weeks, and cut to the verdict. It ended with Madame Thomas being sentenced to twelve years' hard labour. Floury was given ten years. The other forty-five defendants got off. I had a look through their names, and among them I found Louise Fontane, Mireille Lestocart and three Sophies, all working for the same boss: Sophie Dutilleul, Sophie Guillet and . . . Sophie Clairsange, seamstress.'

'Mimi kept all this to herself.'

'Were the Baron and Gaétan the seducers in the case? Could the girls who were seduced have been taking their revenge?'

'And could one of them have bumped off Louise Fontane?'

'Perhaps she had been trying to blackmail her seducer?'

'Two and a half years later? And what about the mysterious Sophie Clairsange? And the limper? I'm going to have to give Mademoiselle Lestocart a grilling.'

'And what shall I do?'

'As soon as you've shut the bookshop this evening, go straight to the Hôtel de l'Arrivée and check that Sophie Clairsange is still there.'

The doorman at the Hôtel de l'Arrivée, who was seven foot tall and three feet wide, said, 'Good morning, Monsieur,' somewhere above the crown of Joseph's bowler hat in the featureless monotone of a mynah bird trained to trot out the same phrase at each turn of the revolving doors.

Joseph made a beeline for the reception desk.

'Mademoiselle Clairsange is expecting me.'

'She isn't here, Monsieur. The chambermaid said that her bed had not been slept in.'

'Has she checked out?'

The man attempted a sympathetic smile.

'Her belongings are still here, and she had paid until the end of next week.'

'So she's going to come back?'

'I couldn't say, Monsieur. Guests are free to come and go as they please.'

The man had been sitting attentively upright, but he now shifted into a more relaxed posture.

She's one step ahead of me again! Joseph thought to himself, as he scratched his neck, nonplussed.

Suddenly, an idea came to him. He asked for an envelope and addressed it 'For the attention of Madame Sophie Clairsange', and then went out onto Rue Strasbourg before turning down Boulevard de Magenta and looking around him. He soon spotted a young fop of about fifteen lounging on a bench, cigarette dangling from his suavely sardonic lips as he watched the women go by. Joseph sat down next to him and struck up a conversation. After a few minutes, the artful dodger nodded his head and pocketed a coin and the envelope before sauntering nonchalantly towards Rue des Vinaigriers, with Joseph following at a safe distance.

214

Madame Guérin was on watch in the sweet shop. Joseph saw the fop hand her the letter then slip out again. Madame Guérin opened the envelope, which was not addressed to her, and looked in vain for a letter inside. She went quickly to the door and pressed her face up against the glass, and then extinguished the lamp, left the shop and fastened the shutters. Walking hurriedly, she made for the house on the corner of Rue Albouy. A light came on in the entrance hall. After a moment, the light in the first-floor window went out. Joseph saw two figures silhouetted on the blinds of one of the ground-floor windows.

Maurice Laumier left the Bibulus where, as was his habit, he had spent an hour or so propping up the bar with a group of his fellow artists, and made his way back to his home on Rue Girardon. He was surprised not to see a light in the kitchen. He looked in the bedroom and the studio: nobody. Mimi must have gone out for a walk. He lit the fire and settled down to work on the portrait of the writer Georges Ohmet, which he was due to deliver at the beginning of March.

Half an hour passed, and then an hour. He began to worry, and went over in his mind all the reasons why Mimi might be late. He couldn't think of any very convincing ones. It was a quarter past seven in the evening. He became more and more anxious, and went to ask the grocer on Rue Norvins if he had seen her, but he hadn't. Perhaps she had had an accident. He ran over to the police station. Nothing. Not knowing where to try next, he returned to Rue Girardon, automatically checking the letter box as he went in. There was a sheet of paper inside:

Goodbye. I'm leaving. You can have your little affairs in peace now. Don't try to . . .

He couldn't bear to read any more! He threw himself on the bed and sobbed into the pillow – her pillow!

Somebody was knocking at the door. He jumped up. Mimi!

Victor Legris stood before him.

'Laumier, what's happened?'

'Mimi's left me.'

'Where could she have gone?'

'Well, she can't have gone to her cousin Loulou, because she's dead. Except for her . . . there is a friend of hers who poses for Lautrec.'

'Where does this friend live?'

'10, Rue Saint-Vincent, third floor on the left.'

'I'll bring Mimi back, don't you worry. Just try to be a little more understanding and stop the Casanova act.'

'She's imagining things. Since we've lived together I've never once—'

'What about my sister, Iris?'

'Oh, that was just a bit of fun.'

Victor made his way through a maze of tortuous alleys overhung with branches growing above fences and walls that were daubed with declarations of love and obscene graffiti. Lines of washing hung above disintegrating stairways and untended gardens. A few housewives wrapped up in coats and scarves, and the odd long-haired, baggy-trousered artist, were to be seen picking their way through the muddy streets. There was a sprinkling of snow on the roofs of the tumbledown houses, some of which had been converted into bars and whose windows threw pale, flickering lights onto the streets. The lantern at number 10, a hotel, looked like the dim light next to a sick bed. Victor climbed to the third floor and knocked. A girl in a dressing gown opened the door and went straight back to stirring a stew in a room hardly bigger than a pantry, furnished with wooden crates.

'Mimi? You'll find her at Adèle's, at 4, Rue des Saules.'

Halfway up the hill whose summit was crowned by the intricate scaffolding around the Sacré-Cœur, Victor found the place once

216

known as the Auberge des Assassins,[43] now called À ma Campagne. It was a small building with a tiled roof, and in front there was a terrace with an acacia tree. Victor examined the sign painted directly on the wall, which was the work of the painter André Gill and depicted a rabbit jumping out of a cooking pot, a bottle of wine clutched in its paw. The animal had given the cabaret its nickname of the Lapin à Gill or, as it was jokingly called, the Lapin Agile. Adèle worked as a dancer at the Élysée-Montmartre music hall and was the companion of the chansonnier Jules Jouy.[44] She had converted the Lapin Agile into a popular cabaret, where she served excellent food and regaled the customers with old French songs in her harsh, haunting voice.

Victor entered the bar, which adjoined an enormous room full of polished tables, benches and empty barrels. A large fire was burning in one corner. Some local shopkeepers, a few poets and several bareheaded girls were sitting around playing manille and drinking glasses of grog. Soon, in an atmosphere full of camaraderie, they would be joined by locals from La Chapelle and La Goutte d'Or, and everybody would start singing the choruses of Adèle's well-loved songs in unison.

Victor sat down opposite Mimi, who was huddled in a chair next to the fire.

'M'sieu Legris! How did you find me?'

'Laumier told me I'd—'

'Did he ask you to come?'

'No. I'm investigating the murder of your cousin, don't forget. I've got the distinct feeling that you haven't told me everything. If you want me to solve this case, you're going to have to help me.'

'What do you want to know?'

'At the trial of Madame Thomas, in 1891, you—'

'What has that got to do with anything?'

'A name or a tiny detail could prove to be a vital clue in the hunt for Louise's killer. Please, don't be shy. You can confide in me

217

and I won't repeat a word of it to anybody. Did you used to know Richard Gaétan?'

'Yes. What a nasty piece of work. He'd take advantage of the women who worked for him, especially the young, innocent ones, and then they'd be out on their ear! I know from experience. I used to work for him and a friend of Loulou's nearly died there. And, yes, I visited Madame Thomas too. Are you happy now? She was arrested after one of her patients died, and she denounced us all. I had no choice: the cupboard was bare and there was no way I could bring up a child. And, anyway, unmarried mothers don't have an easy time of it!'

'Did you work for him at Rue de la Paix?'

'Loulou and I started out as errand girls at Larive, a dressmaker's near La Madeleine. We delivered the finished creations. We'd spend all our time rushing from one side of Paris to the other, always on foot. We spent our first pay packet on a hat – a silly extravagance, but we'd never had anything pretty of our own. When men saw us in our hats, they'd turn round, and try to talk to us.'

'And that's when—'

'We were stupid enough to give in to the husband of a customer, a saucy devil with a posh name. Not together, mind! It was his wife who gave us Madame Thomas's address.'

'What was this promiscuous gentleman's name?'

Mimi's cheeks turned bright red.

'I don't like to tell you, because the Baronne was good to us. She got us jobs as seamstresses at Le Couturier des Élégantes.'

'Was her name Madame Clotilde de La Gournay, by any chance?'

'Are you clairvoyant or something?'

'Why didn't you tell me about all this?'

'It's nothing to boast about. There were lots of us: poor women, workers, seamstresses, embroiderers, housekeepers. All of them had a hard life, I can tell you! And some of them were richer, had never even worked, but they didn't have it easy either. And all because they'd wanted their little moment of happiness. And then of course there are the ones who actually have the babies – they suffer too. We paid the price, but it wasn't all our fault: what about the lovers, and the husbands? They were just as guilty as we were. They got us pregnant and they were usually the ones who told us we should get rid of the result! Yes, I went to Madame Thomas, and I didn't die. Or at least, only a little bit.'

Mimi's cheeks were wet. She realised that she was crying and wiped away her tears furiously.

Victor tried to say something to comfort her, but was tongue-tied.

'How long did you stay working for Gaétan?'

'I lasted a year and then I found a job cleaning silk hats with lead salts. The girls who worked there didn't last long. They'd all fall ill and be dismissed. The boss could have avoided killing them if he'd replaced the lead salts with zinc salts, but it would've eaten into his profits, so he didn't. When I realised what I was heading for, I got out of there sharpish and got a job as a model instead. I could earn just as much doing that as I did from sewing. Then I met Maurice, and he asked me to pose for him. He didn't have a penny, but I did it anyway. And then, eventually, we got together – it's funny looking back on it now. Oh, it wasn't exactly a life of luxury, but I wasn't complaining. He was nice, Maurice. He did his best, even though he did run after women all the time. He's a man, and men . . . But I've had enough of that now. I want to be respectable.'

'Did you ever know a young woman called Sophie?'

'Loulou had a good friend she'd grown up with. They used to play together when they were girls. I think she was called Sophie.'

'Sophie Dutilleul, Clairsange or Guillet?'

'Clairsange, that was it, Sophie Clairsange. I remember her – she was pretty. She used to work for Gaétan too, and she was the one who nearly died there.'

'Why?' Victor asked.

'It was because of the overtime. Oh, yes, overtime. We're all exhausted. More than ten hours on the trot, bent over our sewing, without a minute's rest. We never stop sewing, and we can hardly breathe and our eyes sting because of the gas lamps. It's winter and the heating doesn't work properly and all we can think about is getting outside and being free. You can't imagine how much suffering goes into making rich people's clothes! Half past seven comes, and at last we're free! We've already got our hats on when they announce: "Mesdames, overtime!" We've got a quarter of an hour to bolt down some food, eating it in the workshop, not even in the canteen. They send someone out to buy bread and meat, and then they take it off our salaries. We eat as quickly as we can and then we slave until past midnight. At one o'clock in the morning, how are we supposed to get back to Montmartre, Batignolles, Levallois, or wherever it is we live? There aren't any more omnibuses, and a cab would be far too expensive, so we walk all the way back in the dark. Once, I asked a policeman to walk me home. He said that respectable women didn't wander the streets at that time of night.'

'You haven't answered my question – why did Sophie Clairsange nearly die?'

'Because of the overtime! One evening, a work inspector turned up. Sophie was still underage – she shouldn't have been there. So what do they do? They lock her in a wardrobe. The inspector was an old dragon, and she had a row with the forewoman, and while they were at it we all slipped out. We forgot about Sophie, locked up in the wardrobe. The forewoman only remembered hours later. She told a pack of lies to the doctor, who said he didn't think he was going to be able to revive her. The boss called Sophie up to his office and—'

'Richard Gaétan?'

'The very same. We never knew what happened, but I think we can guess.'

'Guess at what?'

220

'Well … Oh, come on, don't be stupid! Do I have to explain it all? He gave her some money and … do you need me to draw you a picture?'

'Did you ever see her again?'

'Sophie? Yes, at the trial. I don't know what became of her after that. Oh, yes, I do! She got hitched to some old geezer who fell for her during the trial. She went off to America.'

'And what about Louise?'

'I told you – she got a job on Rue d'Aboukir. We used to see each other once a fortnight, and we'd go to dances together. In summer, we'd go up to Nogent and buy ourselves some chips, or go boating on the Marne.'

'Did she have any family?'

'Her mother died when she was twelve, but she got lucky and was adopted by someone who helped orphans, who got her a room in a hostel.'

'She had recently been given a job by a rich American woman. Could that have been Sophie Clairsange?'

'How am I supposed to know? By the time Loulou was killed, I hadn't heard from her for a month. Is Sophie Clairsange in Paris?'

'It would seem so.'

'Do you think that her being here is in some way connected to Loulou's death?'

'Possibly. Come back with me.'

'Are you completely mad?'

'Maurice is heartbroken. He's got his faults, I know, but he does love you. Why did you leave him?'

'We had an argument.'

'He's very sad.'

'Really? The poor suffering mite!'

'Does the name Angelica mean anything to you?'

'Isn't it something people use to decorate cakes?'

*

221

Tasha picked up the telephone. It was Joseph.

'It's your brother-in-law,' she said to Victor. 'What does he want now? When you've finished gossiping, come over to the studio.'

Victor took the receiver and made sure that Tasha was out of earshot.

Joseph told him that Sophie Clairsange had left the hotel suddenly and that, thanks to his stratagem, he was almost sure that she had gone back to Rue Albouy.

'Excellent work, Joseph. You've given me an idea. Have you got a pen? Write this down:

Paris, Friday 23 February
Dear Madame, it is vital that we exchange some important information. Your safety depends on it. Come to the café in the Gare de l'Est at midday. Wear a hat without a veil and a white rose in your buttonhole.

'Put that in an envelope addressed to her, and give it to the maid as early as you can tomorrow morning. Must go – Tasha's back.'

Victor began to speak more loudly.

'How many times do I have to tell you, Joseph! I'll go and see Madame Albouy tomorrow morning. If Monsieur Guérin asks for the travel book *The Blue Chinaman*, tell him that I'm making arrangements with the supplier. I'll see you tomorrow at the bookshop.'

Friday 23 February

Under the impassive gaze of a pneumatic clock that marked out the passing seconds, a noisy, hurrying crowd swarmed over the station concourse. Porters wearing a cap, shirt and belt emblazoned with the initials of the Eastern Railways Company argued with baggage handlers over huge piles of luggage. An endless stream of passengers snaked down the marble staircase. Victor stationed himself in front of the café. He could have arranged to meet Sophie somewhere quieter, but had reasoned that in a station they could easily melt into the crowds, unobserved. He had a commanding view of the huge concourse: a limping man would have his work cut out to go unnoticed here.

Corentin Jourdan walked as fast as his crutch would allow, even though, in a place like this, the most difficult thing wasn't to pursue his quarry but to keep her insight without being noticed. His siren did elude him a couple of times, but by elbowing people firmly out of his way he managed to catch sight of her again. She stopped in front of the café and, obviously on her guard, cast her eye over the people sitting there. Instead of trying to limp as little as possible, Corentin Jourdan exaggerated the movement. His messy hair sprinkled with ash under the battered hat, his unshaven chin and his clothes caked in dried mud made him look like a broken-down old tramp who had had a little too much to drink. He walked along the row of ticket offices and stopped in front of a newspaper kiosk. He saw a man approach his siren and whisper something in her ear. The man from the bookshop! Was Sophie Clairsange about to tell him what had happened at Landemer? What should he do? He didn't have much room to manoeuvre. Unless . . . Yes, he had one card left to play: the third criminal.

Sophie Clairsange walked over to a table set slightly apart from the others, adjusted the white rose in her buttonhole and took off her gloves. Victor looked her up and down: medium height, slim figure, brown curls, and slightly dark complexion — extremely attractive. She was wearing neither a wedding ring nor an engagement ring. He invited her to sit down and did the same himself.

Sophie Clairsange looked Victor straight in the eyes.

She's one of those haughty upstarts who look down on everyone, he thought to himself. I'll let her stew for a bit. If she thinks she can intimidate me, she's wrong.

He began to speak calmly, a slight smile playing on his lips.

'I hope that we can come to an understanding, Madame. There is no point in us both wasting our time. You are in danger, and you are afraid. I'm here to offer you my services.'

'How dare you? Do you really expect me to take you seriously when I don't even know who you are?'

Victor continued in a neutral tone, 'For your own safety, you would do better to take me seriously.'

'Monsieur, whose name I don't know, you've been reading too many novels.'

'Quite possibly: I'm a bookseller, my name is Victor Legris and I have pipped the police to the post in several criminal investigations. Here are my credentials.'

He handed her a sheaf of press cuttings, which she studied minutely.

'This doesn't tell me why you're doing this. I don't need any help, and what have I got to be afraid of?'

'I'm going to be honest with you, Madame. In return, I hope you'll be honest with me. I have been asked to look into the death of an acquaintance of yours, Louise Fontane. She has been strangled.'

'I know. A stranger – you, perhaps – had the good taste to communicate this to Madame Guérin. I was very sorry to hear it. Louise was a childhood friend of mine.'

'Madame Guérin denied all knowledge of her.'

'She wanted to consult me first. I have no desire to get mixed up in this business.'

Victor pulled a packet of cigarettes out of his pocket, met the woman's mocking gaze and put it down on the table.

'Was Louise staying with you on Rue Albouy?'

'Yes, she was.'

'Why didn't you tell the police that?'

'Monsieur, it was purely out of curiosity that I came here to meet you. I was intrigued. Yes, I used to know Louise Fontane, a long time ago. We hadn't seen one another for three years. She lost her job and I offered her somewhere to stay, as is natural. You can report me to the police, but they won't find anything wrong with my story.'

You're lying, my dear, Victor thought. Louise didn't lose her job: you offered her a new one.

'There's no point beating about the bush,' he replied, astonished by her aplomb. 'I know a number of things about you and, seeing as you don't seem to want to cooperate, a few other people might end up finding out about them too. Now, let's start at the beginning. You worked at Rue de la Paix, didn't you, at Le Couturier des Élégantes?'

'I don't see why you're asking me that, given that you obviously know the answer already.'

'What is your married name, Madame Clairsange, and what are you doing in Paris?'

She flushed with anger, but answered without objecting.

'My husband, Samuel Mathewson, died six months ago. He owned several orange plantations in California. Once I had set everything in order, I decided to return to France. I was homesick.'

'Where were you the night that Louise was killed?'

'At home, in Rue Albouy. I have witnesses.'

Victor lit a cigarette without bothering to ask her permission.

'There's something else I know that I didn't mention before. You were a defendant at Constance Thomas's trial in November 1891. Your maiden name appears on the list of the accused, along with those of Louise Fontane and Mireille Lestocart.'

'Mireille Lestocart? Who's she? Yes, I was tried. I couldn't keep the child. I was acquitted, like all the rest.'

'Who was the father? Richard Gaétan or the Baron de La Gourn...'

225

His voice trailed off, but the implication was clear.

'How many women have you abandoned without giving a thought to whether or not they might be in trouble?'

'Richard Gaétan and the Baron de La Gournay have been murdered.'

'Do you suspect me? Monsieur, you lack imagination. Everybody knows that Richard Gaétan regularly exercised his *droit de seigneur* on the women who worked for him. As for the Baron, he used to get up to the same tricks behind the scenes at Le Couturier des Élégantes as he did at the Opéra and the Folies-Bergère!'

'What do you know about Richard Gaétan?'

'I only know what anybody can read in the gossip columns. He worked first as a pattern cutter, and then he became a tailor at Larive, near La Madeleine.'

'I suppose you're familiar with the name, the Black Unicorn?'

'Everybody has heard of it, and the way it takes money from so many people. Richard Gaétan, the Baron Edmond de La Gournay and Absalon Thomassin are its co-founders.'

'The Great Absalon from the Winter Circus?'

'Yes.'

'How did Gaétan become so renowned? Did the business at Rue de la Paix simply fall into his hands?'

'In 1888, when he was at Larive, he did some work for Absalon Thomassin, who had just come back from a tour of India where he had gone to study the techniques of self-taught acrobats. Richard Gaétan dreamt of rising to the top, but although he had the technical skill he lacked creativity. Absalon Thomassin agreed to hand over the sketches of exotic costumes that he had made during the course of his travels. He was a talented artist and had an eye for choosing the right material. Richard Gaétan created a dress inspired both by the sketches and by Thomassin's advice ... Oh, I've had enough of this!'

'Please go on.'

'If you insist ... In August 1889 there was a big reception for the

Shah of Persia. The president was there, along with lots of ambassadors and the cream of Parisian high society. Madame Clotilde de La Gournay made a dramatic entrance wearing Gaétan's famous creation, which he called the Dress the Colour of Time, inspired by Perrault's story "Donkeyskin". It was a wonderful thing, in gold and blue brocade. She caused a sensation, and Gaétan's name was on everyone's lips. Add to that the cachet of his aristocratic clients, and Le Couturier des Élégantes was guaranteed success from that moment. I remember what Thomassin said at the time: "I hope I'm not like that donkey which got skinned even though it made so much gold." Have I made myself clear?'

'No, I still don't see what you mean.'

'Have you read Perrault, Monsieur the bookseller? In Perrault's tale, the princess wears the skin of a magic donkey which, when it was alive, had produced droppings of pure gold. The poor donkey was sacrificed – it saved the princess's skin by losing its own. And you call yourself a sleuth! Everything you've said has been much too fanciful. Just think about it: there were three of them, and now there's only one left. Absalon was the truly creative one, and he didn't see a penny of the profits. Gaétan made very sure that the business belonged to him and him alone.'

'So you think it was Thomassin?'

'The big fashion houses are like extended families. It's better to keep some secrets under your hat if you want to hold on to your job.'

Victor hadn't foreseen this hypothesis, and he paused for a moment to take it in.

'Tell me about the man with a limp who's been following you from one hotel to the next.'

Sophie Clairsange-Mathewson's expression darkened for a moment, but she soon regained her confident air.

'A man with a limp? Is that one of your little helpers, hired to watch me wherever I go? Why should I believe that you are who you say you are?'

'You seem to be angry.'

'Angry? What a nerve! You barge into my life, and stick your nose into my past. Haven't you got anything better to do with your time?'

She fixed him with an intense gaze, pleased with her performance.

'Goodbye, Monsieur the bookseller. I'm going now.'

'Just one moment, Madame,' said Victor, who had decided to play his final card. 'Did you know that the Baron de La Gournay's precious collection of unicorns was found completely destroyed?'

'Well, what about it?'

'Somebody had written on a mirror in the room, "In memory of Brumaire and the night of the dead."'

'Now that really does sound like something from a novel.'

'There was a signature, "Louise".'

'Obviously a trick, that's all! Louise had been dead for eight days by that time.'

She seemed completely calm as she said this, but the colour had disappeared from her cheeks, and she was frighteningly pale.

'Goodbye, Monsieur.'

Victor grasped her arm.

'What does the name Angelica mean to you?'

She shook him off and disappeared into the crowd. She had forgotten her gloves.

When she got outside the station, Sophie Clairsange-Mathewson managed to contain her anger. She needed to keep walking to empty her mind. Everything would be all right. It had to be.

The bustle of Rue du Faubourg-Saint-Martin seemed far off. Things were taking a turn for the worse. Suddenly, she understood, and the realisation made her catch her breath. She had to stop and lean against a wall. It was glaringly obvious what was going on and the thought of it overwhelmed her. She couldn't trust anybody. She had set off a chain reaction even though, on paper, everything still seemed to fit together.

An old invalid leaning on a crutch overtook her and went down Rue des Récollets. He followed a barge that was making its slow way along the canal. As he watched it, Corentin Jourdan thought of his past life, disturbed by ripples like the surface of the Saint-Martin canal. In what unknown port would he finally drop anchor?

When Victor got back to the bookshop, he found Kenji doing battle with Euphrosine, who was working herself up into one of her apoplectic rages. Joseph had taken refuge near the fireplace, and was looking on, biting his lip.

'So Zulma makes better tea than I do, does she?' growled Euphrosine. 'Can you be more specific, Monsieur Mori? For example, does the spout of your teapot need to face north, south, east or west? And do the tea leaves have to be picked at full moon? And, tell me, does the milk need to come from a particular cow? Do you have a favourite?'

'I leave the milk to the English, actually,' Kenji replied evenly.

'Oh, do you? I'm so sorry – you drink it black, do you, like the Cossacks, or the Archduchess Fifi Maximova? One sugar, or two?'

'Madame Pignot, you seem to be somewhat bad-tempered today,' Kenji observed, sitting down at his desk.

'With good reason! When I think that that cunning little Zulma Tailleroux had the nerve to try her hand at cooking! If you all die of food poisoning, don't come crying to me!'

'Madame Pignot, let's keep things in proportion. You were out and I simply asked Zulma to boil some water for me.'

'Boiled or not, water is my department!'

'What's the matter?' Victor asked Joseph.

'Oh, a big fuss over nothing! Zulma dared to set foot in the kitchen while Maman was out at the market. Did you see Sophie Clairsange?'

'We had a most interesting interview. She told me a pack of lies. All credit to her! She's got nerves of steel.'

'Do you suspect her?'

'I think she's involved somehow. She has an obvious motive.'

'Such a beautiful woman!'

'Appearances can be deceptive, Joseph. Our first impressions are often wrong. She's a widow, and her married name is Mathewson. When I told her about the writing in La Gournay's secret chamber, she turned very pale.'

'Hmm. Well, that solves the mystery of the Mat anyway! Bricart was right – it's a name that doesn't sound the same as it's spelt! In any case, we can be sure now that there's a link between the abortion trial and the murders. November 1891 . . . Brumaire, the night of the dead . . . It would make a good title for a story. Something doesn't seem quite right, though, Boss . . . I mean, Victor. Why was Loulou killed? Did she know too much? Was she an inconvenient witness? Are we getting out of our depth? It might be best to tell Inspector Lecacheur about the whole business. I don't want my son to grow up an orphan.'

'You're not turning into a bourgeois stay-at-home, are you, Joseph?'

'I'm tired of hanging around on street corners! And what about the limper, what's he got to do with it all?'

'Madame Sophie Clairsange-Mathewson avoided the question.'

CHAPTER 13

Saturday 24 February

The first glimmers of dawn were showing at the window when Corentin Jourdan heaved himself out of bed, still half asleep. He looked in the cracked mirror. An exhausted face that hadn't shaved for several days stared back at him. Forcing himself into action, he lifted up a jug, poured some water into the basin and took up his shaving brush. He was about to raise it to his chin, when he stopped short.

'I'm poor Ben Gunn, I am,' he muttered. 'I'm marooned, mate!'[45]

Disconcerted by this eerie comparison, he contemplated the solitude in which he was fated to live out his days and wondered how he would stand it. He shook his head, trying to rid himself of the thought. He felt as though he were simultaneously an actor on stage and a member of the audience, and that neither actor nor spectator was particularly enjoying the story.

'Go home.'

Like a naughty child, he refused to obey his own instructions. He had got himself caught up in this impenetrable Dostoevskian tangle, which could only end in more suffering. There was something mysterious, even to him, about his own obstinacy. All he had to do was break out of the vicious circle that was drawing him further and further in, pack his bags and go back home, but an inexplicable force kept him inside the circle. He had to find the third criminal.

The cries of children chasing each other down the stairs were unwelcome. Outside, the street was coming to life, as the daily grind began all over again. People were opening up shops, running errands or going to work. All these people, humble folk, shopkeepers, housewives, led ordinary lives from which he was excluded.

He took out a map of Paris and located Rue des Martyrs.

The shifty-looking cab driver had been reluctant to drive all the way to Rue de Belleville, but a generous tip had done much to improve his temper. Joseph made a mental note to thank Victor for paying for the cab, and began walking up the street through the crowds of hawkers. He was disappointed to see that this neighbourhood looked just like other poor parts of the city, with its launderettes, chemists, herbalists, haberdashers, locksmiths and other small businesses. He had hoped that the American quarter would be more foreign and exotic.[46]

Struggling just like the Belleville-Lac Saint-Fargeau omnibus, Joseph finally reached the top of the hill, where the twin spires of Saint-Jean-Baptiste church rose above the city. He couldn't spot anyone dressed in Bricart's distinctive blue belt and red shoes in front of the large neo-Gothic door, an imitation of a thirteenth-century sanctuary.

Joseph asked a man hard at work in a china mender's shop for directions to Sentier de l'Encheval, and he gestured vaguely towards Rue de Palestine.

When he had walked past the school that Sylvain Bricart had mentioned, and got as far as Rue des Solitaires, Joseph lost all sense of direction and asked two young laundresses carrying heavy baskets for help. They burst out laughing and made off. He persisted, first asking a woman sitting outside a shop repairing the seat of an old chair, who turned out to be nearly deaf, and then a crowd of apprentices hanging about in front of a bistro. Eventually, he gleaned enough information to make his way to Rue de la Villette, where a round-faced concierge with an impressive bun and a spotted apron directed him towards a little dead-end alley. There, he suddenly did feel transported to a foreign land, but it was far from being the

America he had dreamt about. He climbed four steps. In front of him was a row of decrepit wooden shacks and brick hovels facing one another, separated by a stream of dirty water. This was home to several families who managed to survive here in abject poverty. A few ragged children were playing alongside a group of hens pecking about between the tumbledown dwellings. Dogs barked, a cow was mooing and a cockerel aimed several vicious pecks at Joseph's calves before he managed to escape to the relative safety of a small courtyard. A woman and two little girls, all shivering with cold, were fetching water from a well and pouring it into a tub for their cow, a black and white Normande.

'She's lovely,' Joseph remarked, relieved to be safe from the ferocious fowl.

'She's our saviour: without her milk we'd starve to death, all of us.'

'Is this drinking water?'

'I think so – it tastes better than the stuff that comes out of the well in Rue de l'Atlas: that smells of rotten eggs! We only use that to water the vegetable patch. Would you like a glass?'

'Thank you, but I'm not thirsty. Do you happen to know where Sylvain Bricart lives?'

'The Millionaire? At the end of the alley – you can't miss it. His is the biggest house by far. It's made of stone too, and always locked up tight. He's afraid of burglars.'

The cockerel returned for a second attack, seeing that the cow didn't seem to pose a threat, but the girls chased him away and drove him into a coop further down the alley.

'I'm sure he can't be as rich as all that. He only sells crusts of bread,' Joseph said, keeping a close eye on the girls to make sure that they shut the door of the coop firmly.

'He makes a fortune from it, believe you me. But he's not a bad sort, I must say. My Théodule got the sack from the workshop a while ago and since then he's had to find whatever work he can, unloading barges down on the quayside, or working at the station putting foot warmers in the first-class carriages. Well, all that time, Monsieur Sylvain has been helping us out. Only yesterday he gave me a big bag full of stale brioches. You just dip them in some milk and they're delicious. It's difficult to get any credit with the butcher or the coal man, and I've already pawned almost everything I own.'

'So he's a kind man then, this Bricart.'

The woman told him that local gossip had it that the Millionaire had a big country house in the Berry region, and that it wouldn't be long now before he retired there, to live out his old age in peace.

'Mind you, he deserves it. He works like a Trojan, and he hasn't even got any other mouths to feed,' she added, looking at her own offspring.

Joseph had a sudden vision of a slant-eyed baby with a mouth gaping like a baby bird's, and he hurried off towards the end of the alley.

She was right: this is more like a fortress than a house, he thought, when he found himself in front of a cement block with a metal front door.

He knocked several times before a little spyhole opened.

'Oh, it's you,' said Sylvain Bricart, opening the door a crack and showing his craggy face with its protruding jaw. When he was sure that Joseph was alone, he allowed him to cross the threshold.

'Why do you take so many precautions?'

'You can never be too careful. When people know you've got a bit of money, they come sniffing around.'

The enticing odour of warm bread wafted from one of the rooms. Joseph imagined an oven filled with marzipan pastries and spiced buns, two of his favourite things, and his mouth began to water. He reached into his pocket and pulled out a book that had been rather hastily wrapped up in brown paper.

'I've got a delivery for Sophie Clairsange – or rather Mathewson. I've discovered what the rest of her name is, since that day when you told me the first syllable.'

Sylvain Bricart scratched his greying head. He wasn't dressed in the flamboyant outfit he wore for work, but in an old shirt, patched trousers and a pair of worn-out boots. He was covered with a light dusting of flour.

'Why are you giving it to me? You might as well deliver it to the hotel!'

'Mademoiselle Clairsange has disappeared.'

'In that case, why not take it along to the sweet shop?'

'Which sweet shop?'

'The Blue Chinaman, on Rue des Vinaigriers. It's run by Hermance Guérin.'

'The thing is, my boss is going to get angry if I'm late back. I told him I'd only be gone for a short while.'

'And I've got a pile of bread in the oven, Monsieur, so if you're wondering whether I'm about to go trotting off to Rue des Vinaigriers, the answer is no way! To tell you the truth, her ladyship the owner sends me packing half the time anyway. There's no getting away from it: women become madder as they grow older. What is it? A novel?'

'*The History of a Crime*, by Victor Hugo.'

'Ah, Hugo! I once spent the night in a prison cell because of him. I'd been kicking up a bit of a fuss with a gang of students because the government had banned a play Hugo had written, *Ruy Blas*.[47] We exchanged a few blows, the police and I. There was some strong stuff in that play, it has to be said:

> 'Bon appétit, messieurs!
> Ô ministres intègres
> Conseillers vertueux! Voilà votre façon
> De servir, serviteurs qui pillez la maison![48]

To Joseph's dismay, as soon as Sylvain had finished this declamation, he made as if to leave, eager to return to his oven. Joseph had to find a way of getting the conversation going again.

'Those lines are still relevant today because in fact the bigwigs who run things are still fleecing us … Congratulations on remembering them – you must have been very young when you heard them last!'

The Millionaire succumbed to the flattery.

'Well, I do have a natural flair when it comes to acting. I should have trodden the boards myself. I was as good-looking as I was popular in those days. I used to toil away in a sweet shop, earning next to nothing, but I had a thing for the girl who worked there. She was eighteen, comely and not shy with it. She preferred my friend to me, though. That's life.'

'What was her name?'

'Hermance.'

'Like the woman who owns the Blue Chinaman?'

'The very same, with a few extra years, a few extra pounds and some wrinkles.'

'And did she marry your friend?'

'Did she hell! As soon as he'd got her in the family way, he packed his bags and left. The little mite was only a month old when her father enlisted and went off to fight in the Battle of Sedan. War might seem very moving when we hear songs and stories about it, but when it comes to actually having a bayonet stuck into you it's a different story. I went to my mother's in Bordeaux and managed to lie low until things calmed down.'

'What happened to your friend?'

'He disappeared without a trace in all the fighting. He always wanted to be as good as Velpeau. In the end, no doctor could bring him back.'

'And what about you – are you married?'

'Married? You must be joking! There are too many women on earth – I can't marry them all. Now, young man, it's nearly time for my first round.'

'I'd like to come along with you.'

236

'I thought your boss was pining for you.'

'Let him wait! Down with the bigwigs, that's what I say!'

'Bravo! That's fighting talk. But I'm warning you, you need legs of iron for this job. I do it all on foot! Wait there – I'll go and get changed.'

He soon reappeared, dressed in his black, blue and red uniform, his eyes partially covered by the brim of his top hat. He piled several crates full of warmed-up bread into his cart, covered them carefully with a blanket, and they were off.

An hour later an exhausted Joseph was doing his best to keep up with the old bull terrier, who was feeling rejuvenated by a good morning's business, which had filled his purse and emptied his cart of almost all its load. At this rate, Sylvain Bricart would soon have the wherewithal to add another wing to his country residence.

'We've done well, my boy! Let's drink a toast to our success!' the Millionaire suggested.

They ended up at an inn, where the landlady served them two small measures of beer, all the while casting flirtatious glances at the stale-bread seller.

'It's not my handsome face she's interested in, it's my loot,' Sylvain Bricart whispered.

'You had a good idea there. Selling stale bread is a fine profession: you're free to come and go as you please,' said Joseph, happy to be back in the warm and off his feet.

'I'm as free as a bird. I started once the war was over and I got back to good old Paris. There wasn't any more work for yours truly at the sweet shop. Hermance had just got married to the boss, Marcel Guérin. She did start to take more kindly to me, though. She wasn't so young and carefree any more! When her dear beloved Guérin snuffed it without warning, he left her with a lot of debts. Hermance had to mortgage the business. It was then that I bumped into her one day in Les Halles, and she told me the whole story, with that expression of hers like a lost kitten. I didn't stand a chance. I paid off the mortgage, and paid for the shop to be renovated. I even painted a new sign: Hermance insisted that the shop be called the Blue Chinaman.'

'Why blue?'

'In memory of her father, who kicked the bucket in China in 1860, on the banks of the Yangtze River, or the Blue River. It cost me a pretty penny but Hermance was grateful. I moved in with them in the end and we were like a proper little family. So Sophie's like a daughter to me.'

'If Madame Guérin is her mother, why is she called Clairsange?'

'That's Hermance's maiden name. Marcel Guérin refused to let the child take his name.'

'But you don't live with Madame Guérin any more?'

'All these questions! Are you thinking of writing our life stories, or what? A tale of two idiots, you could call it! We stayed together for ten years, and then that minx went and fooled around with some other man! I decided to call it a day after that, but we've stayed more or less friends, and in the end it's probably for the best.'

'And what about the trial? You helped Sophie then, didn't you?'

'That was a nasty business! Those judges couldn't stand the fact that a few women, some rich but most of them poor, had dared to end pregnancies that would have produced a brood of unwanted children. I pleaded her cause and I'm proud of it, even though it did mean that my name was mentioned in the papers!'

He produced a tattered notebook full of press cuttings. His name appeared several times in the list of witnesses for the defence, along with that of a missionary who now looked after vulnerable orphans, and a seamstress who claimed to have witnessed the rape of one of her friends.

'My day isn't over yet – the second round's about to start! I'm off home. Bottoms up, young man!' cried Sylvain Bricart, draining his glass.

Joseph did the same, and the room began to spin. Unable to move, he shook the hand that the Millionaire was holding out to him and remained slumped on his chair, aware that the landlady's covetous gaze had turned to him in the absence of any other eligible male.

When he finally managed to control the shaking that had kept him glued to his seat, Joseph took advantage of a moment when she was looking the other way and staggered out onto Rue de la Villette, where he hailed a cab and asked to be taken back to Rue des Vinaigriers.

I need to strike while the iron's hot and talk to this Madame Guérin, he thought. If she's been concealing the fact that Sophie Clairsange is her daughter, then she must either be covering for her, or have something to hide herself.

Falling suddenly into an alcohol-induced doze, he found himself on a battlefield where a gigantic cockerel called Velpeau was pursuing the dastardly Zandini, who was disguised as a black and white Normande cow.

'Are you deaf? We're here!' bellowed the driver, shaking Joseph's arm.

Feeling dazed, Joseph paid the driver, forgetting the tip this time. He ignored the string of insults that followed.

The Blue Chinaman lit up the dreariness Rue des Vinaigriers like a beacon in the gloom. The shop, with its combination of stucco, marble and mirrors, provided a pretty and elegant setting for the tempting sweets lined up on the counter. And there was Hermance Guérin behind the till, her black lace bonnet bent over the knitting that kept her busy when the shop was quiet. Joseph was pleased to see that there were no other customers. When she heard the bell tinkle, Madame Guérin lifted her faded doll's head and blinked her blue eyes, as though she were slowly coming back to reality.

'Can I help you, Monsieur?'

'I'm looking for a present for my wife. She's expecting a baby and has cravings for sweet things. What would you recommend?'

'I can give you an assortment: pralines, fondants, humbugs . . . Does she like mint?'

'I think so.'

'Then I'll add some mint drops and some marshmallow. Ah, and a few violet pastilles. When is it due?'

'What?' Joseph said, transfixed by a huge jar of caramels.

'The baby.'

'Oh, not till July.'

'Have you chosen a name?'

Hermance Guérin's interest was tinged with polite indifference.

'If it's a girl, Évangéline, and if it's a boy, Sagamore.'

'Are those real names?' she asked, taken aback.

'My parents-in-law are American. Oh, I nearly forgot – have you got any angelica?' he asked nonchalantly, fixing her with a hard stare.

'It's more the sort of thing you'd find at a baker's.'

'Yes, exactly; my mother wants to bake a cake and if I don't manage to find some angelica for her . . .'

'I haven't got any, I'm afraid. Will that be all?'

'Yes. I'll come and buy some sugared almonds when it's time to celebrate the birth.'

'Do you live around here?' asked Madame Guérin, as she counted out his change.

'We moved to Boulevard Magenta a month ago. It's rather noisy but very comfortable. That reminds me: my wife sends her regards to your daughter, Sophie.'

The ruse was so unexpected that for a fleeting moment Hermance Guérin let her professional mask slip. She mastered her emotions almost immediately, but her voice still trembled when she replied, 'You must be mistaken; I haven't got a daughter.'

'But I'm sure I can't have got it wrong. It was old Sylvain who told me, and he wasn't drunk, as far as I could tell. He gave me your address because, believe it or not, my wife is an old friend of Sophie's.'

'As I said, you are mistaken.'

'I understand that you might not want to admit it, after all the fuss during the trial, but, seeing as we're talking about the past, I may as well tell you that my wife was one of the accused too. You see, we're in the same boat, you and I.'

Hermance Guérin had turned pale and fiddled nervously with a strand of hair.

'Who are you?' she murmured.

'A friend of the man with a limp.'

She shook her head.

'Leave me alone. Go away.'

'You're hiding your daughter Sophie here, Madame Guérin, admit it. We know why she came back from America. Tell her that. Thank you for your help!' he concluded, waving the parcel with its pink ribbon.

The boss — I mean, Victor — won't half be pleased with me. I did really well! Joseph said to himself as he set off in search of an omnibus.

Strangely, though, when Joseph recounted his story in the basement of the bookshop, Victor frowned.

'You've stirred up a hornets' nest and now they're all going to be terrified — the widow, her daughter, the limper and goodness knows who else! You acted rashly.'

'I might have known it! I get up at the crack of dawn, I go all the way to Belleville, I get some really first-class information out of the Millionaire and you—'

'It's true, you did gather some very important information,' Victor said, with a rather forced smile. 'Well done, Jojo.'

Joseph considered this grudging compliment to be far less than he deserved, and left his brother-in-law standing in the basement. He decided to go upstairs and see Iris, telling Kenji that he would soon be down to help out in the shop. When he got upstairs, he found Zulma beating a hasty retreat while Euphrosine, a carrot in one hand and a knife in the other, shouted after her, 'Go on then, tell tales on me if you like! I don't care! I'm the one in charge here!

241

I'll get that into your head if I have to use a hammer to do it!'

Joseph greeted his mother and gave her a kiss in an attempt to calm her down. He was about to leave the kitchen when he suddenly had a thought.

'Does the name Velpeau mean anything to you, by any chance?' At this, Euphrosine dropped her carrot.

'I'm at the end of my tether, and all you can do is ask me silly questions! The cup of my bitterness runneth over! Jesus, Mary and Joseph!'

Joseph slipped out before Euphrosine started to expand on the weight of her cross. As he went into the bedroom, Iris quickly hid a notebook, in which she had been writing the story of the dragonfly and the butterfly, behind a cushion.

'I've finished typing out the third chapter of *The Devil's Bouquet*,' she told her husband.

Meanwhile, Victor was still down in the basement, thinking.

What did Joseph tell me that was actually important, in amongst all the gibberish? The Millionaire was a witness at the trial along with a missionary who went on to help orphans. Mireille Lestocart also mentioned someone who looked after orphans, who got Loulou a place in a sewing workshop ... Who was it who said he'd been a missionary? ... Father Boniface! Yes, that's it. He helped Louise Fontane. What an imbecile I am – why didn't I think of him before?

'Victor, do you happen to know where we put Hippolyte Castille's *Political Portraits*?' Kenji called.

Victor went back up to the shop and managed to find the books underneath a stack of Marmontel's complete works. Kenji was eager to get rid of these tomes, which had proved difficult to shift, and was doing his best to work his charm on a young, prosperous couple who wanted to fill their empty bookshelves with some pretty volumes that smelt of leather.

Joseph came back downstairs. Victor pulled him into a corner and whispered, 'I'm off. Make up something to tell Kenji ... I'm going back to Fort Monjol. I've been thinking over what you just told me, and I need to go and see Father Boniface.'

'What am I supposed to do? Just twiddle my thumbs?'

'After lunch, you have a special mission: go to the Winter Circus and talk to Absalon Thomassin.'

'Aren't you taking your bicycle?'

'No – I'd have to drag it right past Kenji.'

The Winter Circus ... That would be a great setting for a scene in my novel, thought Joseph, feeling frustrated that he could not devote more time to his literary endeavours. And, anyway, who is this Velpeau? An explorer? Some kind of intellectual?

He was about to look up the name in an encyclopedia when Kenji called for his help with a customer.

Despite the leaden sky and a biting wind, there was an air of celebration in 'the Monjol'. Its narrow streets, heavy with the odour of grilled herring, alcohol, cigarette smoke and rubbish, were tinged with gold from the light of the paraffin lamps filtering through the windows. The crossroads where Rue Monjol met Rue Asselin was brighter and more sheltered from the wind, and here a crowd of brats had gathered, and were amusing themselves by balancing corks on the necks of empty wine bottles and using catapults to try to knock them off again, smashing a good number of the bottles as they did so. Behind them stood a long line of prostitutes, snaking along in front of the decrepit houses and hotels, waiting for the Saturday regulars who would come from all over La Villette and Belleville. The women chattered amongst themselves or with their pimps. One of them waved to Victor and he recognised Marion, the woman with the baby whom he had met in Father Boniface's dispensary.

'What are you doing around here again?'

243

Before he could reply, a voice squealed, 'Hands off, you! He's mine!'

Victor spun round. It was La Môminette, her eyes heavily made up and her lips bright red, her frail figure wrapped in a woollen dress that was too low-cut. Marion walked menacingly towards her.

'If you lay a finger on me, I'll scream for help!' La Môminette hissed.

Victor stood between them before they could come to blows.

'I'm not here for . . . that. I'm looking for Father Boniface.'

The two women eyed one another, looking suddenly shame-faced, silhouetted against the deep-red wall of the Hôtel du Bel Air like bacchantes on a Greek amphora.

Marion pointed to the Hôtel des 56 Marches, at the top of the flight of steps at the end of Rue Asselin.

'He's gone to see the Giraffe.'

Nonplussed, Victor wondered what such an animal could possibly be doing in this melting pot of crime and poverty.

Seeing his puzzled expression, La Môminette explained, 'That's what we call Joséphine Pégrais, because she's as tall as anything, and skinny as a rake!'

'Ever since her pimp dropped her for another girl, Ravignolle, who's much younger and has got a better figure, the Giraffe's been sleeping rough most of the time and not eating anything. Soon we'll be able to see right through her,' added Marion.

Victor took his leave of the women rather awkwardly and hurried away before one of the pimps spotted him. Out of breath, he climbed to the top of the road and then went up the steps of the hotel, which were swarming with pimps, beggars pretending to be crippled and a few unemployed workers.

When a deep voice called, 'Come in!' Victor pushed open the door of a garret room whose only furnishing was a large basin and a rough mattress laid out on the floor. A woman with an emaciated figure was lying there, covered in a dirty sheet. A sour smell reached Victor's nostrils and he began to sneeze violently.

244

'I do apologise, Monsieur ... I'm sorry, your name escapes me. I must have been rather too liberal with the vinegar. I've been using it to try to get rid of the bedbugs. They're taking over the whole neighbourhood at the moment,' Father Boniface explained, getting up from where he had been crouching next to the sick woman.

'That's all right,' replied Victor, holding his handkerchief to his nose. 'My name is Victor Legris.'

'Yes, I remember now. It was you who told me about Loulou's death.'

'That's right; in fact, I've got another question about her. During my investigations, I discovered that she had been living with an old friend and workmate on Rue Albouy.'

'I wasn't aware of that.'

'I also discovered that Loulou and this friend of hers, Sophie Clairsange, were both caught up in an abortion trial, and that you were cited in the list of witnesses for the defence.'

Father Boniface didn't bat an eyelid. He bent down to wipe away the saliva that was dribbling from the woman's mouth, and straightened up with a grimace of pain.

'My back's in a terrible state, what with all this crouching. Yes, that's right, I was involved in Madame Thomas's trial. I did what I could to help those poor women, especially Loulou. I'd managed to find a place for her in a sewing workshop.'

'I'm surprised that a religious man should condone such practices.'

'Protesting against social injustice and condoning the crime are not the same thing. I was taught to be compassionate. I lived in Africa for a long time. There, life is hard; here, it's sordid.'

'Loulou? Is that what you call Louise?'

'I always knew her as Loulou. When I began to help her, she didn't have a birth certificate.'

Father Boniface stopped for a moment to open a skylight and let some air into the attic room.

'I am quite sure that our Lord would not condemn these girls, victims of men's lust and violence.'

'Excuse my indiscretion, but could I ask where it was that you studied medicine? Which university?'

'University?' Father Boniface repeated. He burst out laughing. 'The university of books and practice, dear Monsieur. I have no official diploma.'

'Is it not illegal to—'

'Begging, vagrancy, prostitution, infanticide, abortion and suicide: the law is most efficient in prohibiting them. I do my humble best to make up for its negligence. When a man is dying in poverty, we lend him a hand, do we not?'

Father Boniface looked at him, and his eyes seemed to challenge Victor to disagree.

'Tenacity, skill and experience are all that matters,' he continued. 'I wanted to help my neighbour. I dreamt of becoming a surgeon – I was especially fascinated by trepanation. I used to read specialist works on the subject . . . My parents were poor, though, and I had to go out to work when I was still very young. In the end, I went off to make my own way in the world and landed up on the other side of the Mediterranean.'

'Was that after you fought in the 1870 war?'

'No, long before. I was lucky enough not to take part in that butchery.'

'But Sylvain Bricart told me that he knew you then.'

'Sylvain Bricart?' Father Boniface closed the skylight and scratched his cheek. 'Really, I must be losing my memory. That name doesn't ring any bells at all.'

'He was also a witness at the trial. Try to remember: he was Hermance Guérin's lover, and she seems to be the mother of Sophie Clairsange.'

Father Boniface shook his head.

'I'm sorry, Monsieur Legris, but I really don't remember any of those people. That doesn't mean that I never met them. It's a terrible handicap, growing old. I might remember in the end, though, so don't hesitate to come and talk to me again. Now I need to try to give Joséphine something to eat. She's had nothing since yesterday.'

Victor realised that he was no longer welcome there. He took his leave and, getting away from 'the Monjol' as quickly as he could, made his way back to Rue Bolivar. His only thought now was to go and find Tasha at the *Revue Blanche* offices and take her out for lunch, as they had arranged. He would have to telephone the bookshop later and give Joseph a summary of the fairly paltry information he had managed to extract from Father Boniface. What a strange man ... He seemed to be sincere, and to be skilled in looking after the women in his care. But carrying out operations without being properly qualified? Who was to be believed, Father Boniface or Sylvain Bricart? A cab finally deigned to pull up alongside him and he slumped down on the seat, wishing he could accompany Joseph on his mission. Just as long as Joseph managed to speak to the Great Absalon ...

Joseph's stomach was protesting loudly against the bream with chickpeas that Euphrosine had made for lunch, but he ignored its complaints. He admired the rotunda of the Winter Circus with its two low-relief friezes depicting the art of horse riding. The dastardly Zandini also craned his neck to look at the bronze statue of an Amazon that stood to the left of the main door. Taking her chance while Zandini's back was turned, Carmella slipped into the crowd on Rue du Temple. A gurgle alerted Joseph to his stomach's continuing distress. He assumed a more authoritative attitude, dismissed his characters and went round to Rue de Crussol where he walked up to the door labelled 'Circus Manager'. A servant with the impassive visage of a Roman statue indicated that he should sit down in a small waiting room, and a few minutes later, Joseph was shown into Monsieur Franconi's office. The manager was en-

247

sconced behind an enormous table covered with green baize that was almost invisible underneath a jumble of posters, some old and yellowing, some still garish. He gestured to the unwelcome visitor to take a seat in a mahogany armchair and rested his chin in his hands with a resigned expression, ready to answer whatever absurd questions might be about to come his way. His expression brightened immediately when Joseph said, 'I'm not going to take up too much of your time, Monsieur. I've simply come to request an interview with Absalon Thomassin.'

'He's due back in Paris today, having spent some time away from the capital rehearsing his act. I expect to see him here tomorrow morning, when he'll be working on the finer details of the show. He's performing in the afternoon. The best thing would be for you to go and see him at his home at 2, Rue des Martyrs.'

If Victor Franconi was hoping that this advice would rid him of his visitor, he was about to be proved wrong. Joseph remained firmly settled in his chair, unconscious of the disappointment he was causing. It wasn't every day that Joseph had a circus manager at his disposal and he was eager to glean some professional secrets that could feed his literary creation.

'The readers of *Le Passe-partout* are hungry for any information about goings-on in the artistic world. Might I be so bold as to ask you for the latest news on the Great Absalon's next show? The sheer genius of his acrobatics has earned him many admirers among our readers – especially the ladies.'

'He is an outstanding acrobat, it's true. But, at the risk of disappointing his female admirers, I must admit that I can't help you there: he still hasn't told me anything about his plans! He is a rather capricious man – don't write that in your newspaper. There's his contract, for example: it originally stipulated that his costumes would be ordered by the management, but he insisted that this particular clause be modified. He rather fancies his own skills as a tailor! And, however talented he is, the public are beginning to tire of his death-defying leaps. They want something new. Our poor old lions and tigers aren't enough to entertain people any more. How are we supposed to compete with the music halls? Look, here's an advertisement in *Le Mirliton*: "The Olympia is proud to present Beloni, Marietta and their performing parrots, alongside the famous marksman, Caballero Garcia, assisted by his dog, William Tell"!'

'What you need is someone like Annie Oakley! But she has already been recruited by Buffalo Bill unfortunately.[49] She's so handy with a rifle that Sitting Bull himself calls her "Watanya Cicilia", or "She who never misses"!'

'Congratulations on your mastery of the Sioux language, young man,' the manager replied sarcastically. 'Nevertheless, I don't think the time has yet come for us to dismantle our premises and transport them all the way to the banks of the Mississippi, where the floating circus is by all accounts a great success.'

'That's a shame,' Joseph replied seriously. 'I wonder – would you mind if I had a look behind the scenes to get some material for my article?'

'Be my guest!' Victor Franconi urged him, eager to draw the interview to a close.

There was only a small courtyard separating the offices from the stage door. The manager accompanied Joseph as far as the prop room and took leave of him there.

Joseph wandered along a narrow corridor cluttered with piles of miscellaneous objects, as trapezes and rings swung gently in the air above his head. He walked past several cages where foul-smelling animals lay dozing. A tiger suddenly hurled itself savagely at the bars of its cage and growled. Joseph hurried away towards a corridor full of children practising acrobatic routines and horsewomen dressed in sparkling costumes. Finally, he came to the ring, where a group of Chinese jugglers wearing caps and short jackets were putting the finishing touches to a routine. In the red and gold seats of the stalls, two Italian clowns were playing dominoes. One was dressed in an ornate riding jacket and wide trousers, the other in a pistachio-green silk suit with a belt round his waist and a small pointy hat on his head. Joseph walked over to them.

'Do you know the Great Absalon?'

Wide Trousers shrugged his shoulders to show that he didn't speak French. Pointy Hat attempted a sentence.

'I have hear he very good, but we . . . we *migliori*! Better!'

He winked at Wide Trousers and, without warning, jumped onto his partner's shoulders before bounding over the chairs and into the ring, where he executed a series of somersaults that an agile monkey would have been proud of. Wide Trousers soon caught up with him and they threw themselves into a balletic performance of virtuoso leaps and rolls.

'*Ecco!* This is how we do!' gasped Pointy Hat, out of breath. '*Il vero* . . . true acrobats!'

'"My son, you must be as agile of mind as gymnasts are of body,"' Joseph repeated to himself in the omnibus. The quote was from Barbey d'Aurevilly, and he was certainly right. Except, Joseph mused, if I wrote as fast as those two tumble, all I'd get would be blots!

At 2, Rue des Martyrs, a sour-faced concierge informed him that after Monsieur Thomassin had been away he would often keep very unpredictable hours on his return, which was only to be expected from one of his artistic profession. The upshot was that Monsieur Thomassin was not at home.

Joseph had invented an appointment to inspect a set of books at a stall on the Seine and had promised to return to the bookshop as soon as he had finished. Disappointed, he ran to catch an omnibus that had stopped to make way for a removal cart belonging to a certain Lambert.

Corentin Jourdan was counting the number of carriages that went past in an attempt to forget the icy wind whistling around Notre-

Dame-de-Lorette church. A yellow carriage driven by a pallid coachman in a white hat brought the total to nineteen. A milk cart speeding towards Rue Saint-Lazare didn't count. An old wreck of a thing with a postilion all in green with a black leather hat made twenty. When would that ridiculous man finally come back to the pretentious building he called home? What was it that the poster had said?

ABSALON, KING OF ACROBATS,
ACROBAT OF KINGS

Pathetic!

Corentin felt a lump in his throat at the sight of the Pigalle–Halle aux Vins omnibus, which was toiling up Rue des Martyrs. He had witnessed the scene twice already: a man[50] would attach an extra horse to the original two sturdy animals, so that the heavy, swaying omnibus could be dragged up the hill to Montmartre. He would never have dreamt that horses could be so ill-treated in Paris. Evidently, there was no limit to people's cruelty; they abused animals while pretending to protect them. For example, the men employed to do this maintained that they were alleviating the horses' suffering. In that case, why not simply ban omnibuses from going up these steep streets? Let the intrepid travellers get out and walk! He thought of his own dear Flip and felt a surge of anger. The fate of these animals had nothing to do with the task he had set himself, but the rage it provoked in him confirmed his determination. He must succeed no matter what, for the sake of Flip, and for Clélia, another victim of social hypocrisy . . .

The sight of a smartly dressed dandy in a checked jacket and trousers leaping out of a coupé interrupted his musings. It was him: he recognised the neat moustache and carefully trimmed beard. The man was followed by a servant weighed down with suitcases. They went up the steps to the porch of number 2.

Corentin Jourdan forced himself to be patient. Hurrying now would only cause the man to panic. Far better to let him make himself comfortable, and then go in by the servants' entrance and carry out his plan.

As he waited, he began to count shoes instead of carriages, just for a change. A pair of grey ladies' boots with square toes. Two patent leather shoes – that made four. Two more boots, spattered with mud, six. Two cracked galoshes, eight. Two delicate slippers, offering little protection against the cold. Two heavy postilion's boots . . .

Absalon Thomassin placed his top hat carefully on a bedside table and put on his flannel-lined slippers with a sigh of pleasure. Despite the persistent anxiety that had been eating away at him ever since he had heard of the deaths of Edmond de La Gournay and Richard Gaétan, it was comforting to be back in his own apartment. There, he rediscovered the well-ordered security that he had missed during his long stay at his family home in Chantilly where, surrounded by cloying memories, he had perfected a complex new acrobatic routine.

He closed his eyes, conjuring up the series of daring moves that he was now able to perform with absolute accuracy. They would guarantee his success at the Winter Circus where, after the rehearsals that were due to begin the following day, he would be the star of the new season.

The acrobat's butler unfolded his employer's favourite dressing gown and announced that he was going out to run some errands.

Feeling suddenly anxious again, Absalon Thomassin paced up and down the large sitting room full of Oriental carpets and furniture, trailing his fingers over an ornate hookah. The newspaper articles about the murders had mentioned a message scrawled in Gaétan's chamber, signed Angelica. It was enough to drive him mad. But, in the end, there was no reason to panic. It was perhaps a simple case of a woman's revenge, which would hardly be surprising, given Richard's sexual habits. Moreover, La Gournay's murder could have been the work of a crazed individual, and the similarity between the two murders just a coincidence rather than some intricate plot. Absalon could thus reasonably conclude that this terrible business had nothing to do with him and look forward to becoming the sole head of the Black Unicorn. He had already sent his condolences to Clotilde, but he would have to meet her and find out more about the circumstances of her husband's death. The newspapers had hitherto not mentioned anything about his collection of unicorns being damaged. And unless Absalon was much mistaken, the chamber also contained manuscripts and rare ancient works which Clotilde, who cared nothing about them, would probably agree to sell to him for a very small sum. She would also hand over all responsibility for the occult society to him, and might stop resisting his advances now that her wan charms were no longer the sole property of Edmond. Should he marry her? It wasn't impossible. He was rich enough to pay off the dead man's debts and even to buy his title. Baron Absalon de Thomassin had a nice ring to it.

He removed several sketches that he had made during his exile in Chantilly from the parcel in which they had been carefully wrapped. There were three in particular of which he was very proud: the costume adorned with small paste jewels that he would wear for his dramatic swallow dive, a scarlet and silver creation for the horsemen in a future equestrian show and a richly embroidered Hindu snake charmer's dress, which he would offer to Nala Damajanti, a dancer at the Folies-Bergère.

He heard a noise.

'Léopold, is that you?' he said.

There was no reply except for the murmur of the noisy street outside. Feeling worried, Absalon walked down the long corridor which led to the servants' entrance and his office.

He entered his office and stifled a cry of fear. It was as though a scarlet rain had lashed down on the whole room: the boxes where he stored his sketches, the drawings pinned to the walls, the two dummies draped in shimmering tunics and the sketchbooks filled with watercolours that provided the inspiration for whole troupes of jugglers, clowns and dazzling horsemen were all stained red.

He touched the spine of one of the books with his index finger then sniffed the finger, feeling sickened. Blood. He crossed the room and, opening the window, leant out. A man emerged from the servants' entrance and hurried, limping, towards the porchway. Absalon was about to cry 'Stop him!,' but he held back: it was too late. He turned round. That was when he saw the letters traced in white paint above the dark blue mantelpiece.

YOU LET THE SEED DIE.
PREPARE TO DIE YOURSELF.
LOUISE

'W-what can it mean by "seed"? Louise? Who is Louise?' he stammered, his voice trembling.

He had had many mistresses in his time, like all men. He tried to remember their names: Catherine, Georgina, Aliette. Then there had been a Scottish lion tamer called Helen MacGregor. Sophie, Philomène, Cécile. But, as far back as he could remember, there had never been a Louise.

Joseph pulled down the first of the shutters and wished Victor a good evening. Madame Ballu was on watch outside the large main door. She waved to Victor absently as he walked down the street towards Quai Malaquais, but then her gaze returned to the carriage on the other side of the street.

'First it was a removal cart and now it's a carriage! But what does he want from me?'

Euphrosine's cruel comment was still ringing in her ears: 'My poor Micheline, if you hadn't already had the change, I'd say you

254

were having some kind of hallucination. Why on earth would any man follow you?'

'Is it so impossible that a man should follow me? Hallucinations, my foot! There's no age limit on seduction! She's just a bitter old harpy. She's full of airs and graces, but she started off working at a market stall. Ever since her boy married the boss's daughter, she's been lording it over us all. But someone is spying on me, that's for sure. It's not as if I enjoy being spied on anyway!' she muttered, locking herself in her room.

She was in urgent need of a drop of vintage port from her late husband Onésime's stash and didn't notice the carriage moving off at a jog trot.

Victor was lost in thought and had just passed the Temps Perdu café when something white flew down in front of his nose and landed at his feet. A rose. He turned round quickly. A cab had come to a halt a few feet away. The door opened and someone called his name.

'Monsieur Legris! Get in – I've got something to tell you.'

He hesitated.

'I'm alone. Make up your mind; I'm not going to put a spell on you!'

Victor jumped up onto the running board.

'Good evening, Madame Clairsange, or should I say Mathewson? Am I being kidnapped? This isn't the Wild West, you know!'

'I'm not interested in your pleasantries, Monsieur. I don't know why you have decided to harass me, but I beg you to leave my mother alone. Earlier today your assistant—'

'Just one question: why are you lying to me? I know you were the one who got Loulou out of her job at Rue d'Aboukir. Why did you do that?'

She was certainly a fascinating mixture of innocence and daring. She remained silent, deploying her full armoury of smiles, lowered eyes and delicate hands nervously smoothing her gloves. It was a charming spectacle even to someone familiar with her techniques.

255

'Oh, Monsieur Legris,' she cried, 'you're the only person I dare speak to. If I tell you my secret, will you help to protect us from any scandal?'

'Possibly. I'm curious to hear your version of—'

He stopped short, confused by the direction his own thoughts were taking. She let out a heavy sigh and knocked on the glass to attract the driver's attention.

'Close the door, Monsieur Legris. Let's drive on for a while,' she murmured.

Victor turned to the window. He knew that Sophie Clairsange's actions were all perfectly calculated and that she was observing him coldly from underneath her lowered eyelids.

'Poor dear Loulou! It was all my fault. What I'm about to tell you is all so extraordinary that I couldn't possibly have made it up. After the death of my husband, Samuel Mathewson, I dreamt up a plan to wreak revenge on two men who had ruined what should have been the most carefree years of my life. I wrote all my plans down in my diary. I wanted Richard Gaétan and Absalon Thomassin to get their comeuppance. The first raped me and the second turned me out on the street when I was pregnant.'

'And the third, the Baron de La Gournay?'

'He got Loulou, my best friend, pregnant. I wanted to ruin their reputations, but never for a moment did I dream of murdering them.'

'Absalon Thomassin isn't dead yet, as far as I know!'

'And I hope he lives to a great age.'

Victor was startled. It was strange to hear this woman, who had been so wronged, say such a thing. She fixed him with a worried gaze.

'Let me tell you the whole story,' she said, 'because I still think you don't believe me. My plan was simple. I asked Loulou to come and live with me on Rue Albouy. I told her about my plans, and she agreed to play her part. I made sure that the three devils were still

256

living where they always had, and then I wrote to Gaétan, saying: "I am in Paris. If you want to avoid trouble, do exactly what I tell you." I signed the letter "Angelica".'

'Why Angelica? And what did you tell him to do?'

'He would always give his victims pet names that made them sound like sweet treats. Mine was Angelica, but there were plenty of others: Mirabelle, Clémentine, Cerise, Amandine ... He really was a strange man. Loulou looked quite like me, except that she had blonde hair, and, in order for us to be able to do what we intended to do, she had to look just like me. So she dyed her hair. We agreed a time and place for the meeting with Richard Gaétan, in an out-of-the-way spot. We needed to get him a long way away from his home so that I could carry out my plan. Loulou was to pretend to be me, and he wouldn't know the difference. While she was meeting him near the La Villette rotunda, I went to his house at Rue de Courcelles. I got rid of the butler with some excuse or other, opened the door to the secret chamber where he kept his precious collection of dolls and didn't hold back.'

'You were the one who vandalised it?'

'Yes. Then I wrote a warning on the wall. I wanted him to know who had done it, but I used the name Angelica so that the crime couldn't be traced back to me if he reported it to the police.'

'And what was Loulou supposed to say to him?'

'That she was going to expose the fact that he'd never designed the dresses he produced, that the creations he was so famous for were not his own – that he would be a laughing stock. It was a game, and I never thought of taking it as far as murder! I went back to Rue Albouy and waited in vain for Loulou to come back. The next day, I read in the newspaper that a woman had been found strangled near the La Villette tollgate. I realised what must have happened and I was devastated. The brute! I suppose that when she told him what she knew, he must have panicked and killed her, thinking it was me he was murdering.'

She wiped her eyes. Victor thought over what she had told him. He wanted to believe her but doubted her sincerity, influenced by his own prejudices against women who seemed to him too arrogant. Perhaps his judgement was biased against her because she was so obviously attractive and at the same time so condescending towards him. Where was the clear-sightedness that he was usually so proud of? Modesty: that was what he liked in a woman.

'A second person appeared at the scene of the crime,' he replied, more gently now.

'I don't know him, I swear. I have suffered, Monsieur, and suffering can lead you to follow dangerous paths, but you must believe me. I had nothing to do with these murders. Somebody must have got wind of my plans and carried out acts which I would never have dreamt of committing.'

'You must have spoken about it to someone.'

'Only Loulou knew what I was doing, and she died before the Baron de La Gournay and Richard Gaétan were killed.'

'So how do you explain—'

'The blue notebook – my diary. Several people could have read it without my knowing.'

'Who? Do you have any idea?'

'In January, the schooner on which I was travelling from England to France was wrecked, and a man saved me from drowning. I spent some time at his home, but I only have very hazy memories of it. He could have read my diary. He left me in the care of a convent in Urville, but the nuns refused to tell me his name. Later, I encountered him at the Hôtel de l'Arrivée. He told me that he was the man who saved me and I believed him. He was in a terrible state: he had been attacked just outside my bedroom door. He seemed to want to protect me, and told me to go and hide in the house on Rue Albouy. That evening, Richard Gaétan was murdered.'

Victor was silent for a moment. Why would a stranger encountered in such singular circumstances have become some sort of redresser of wrongs? he thought to himself. And was she guilty, this woman who was now supposedly confessing all to him? Was she a criminal? A liar?

'Who else could have read your diary?' he asked.

'Soon after I returned to Paris, I had a relapse: it was pneumonia, brought on by having been in the sea for so long. I was delirious for several days. A friend of my mother's was often at my bedside.'

'What was his name?'

'Sylvain Bricart.'

'Was he the only one?'

'There was the doctor, of course, and my mother, but they can hardly be suspected.'

'A mother is capable of committing all sorts of crimes in order to protect her children.'

'Don't be ridiculous!'

'You're right – we are straying from the point. Let's forget about your diary for a moment. Yesterday, you said that Thomassin had a lot to gain from the early demise of his two associates.'

'Yes, of course. But he would have had to know who Loulou was, and nobody ever formally identified her body.'

'Or perhaps he knew that Richard Gaétan had killed a woman?'

'Impossible! Why would Gaétan confess to a man who was blackmailing him?'

'Ah, now there's something else you forgot to tell me. So Thomassin was blackmailing Gaétan?'

'Well, it goes without saying! Why do you think that Le Couturier des Élégantes was still producing new designs after so many years? So, Monsieur Legris, what do you think?'

'I need some time to reflect. I'll contact you when I'm ready. I'll get out here.'

'Don't you want me to ask the driver to take you back to where I found you?'

'No, thank you. I'd like to stretch my legs.'

He crossed the Seine, kicking a stone absent-mindedly as he went.

'A pack of lies,' he said to himself. 'That woman is leading me up the garden path.'

His nimble mind tried to follow several trains of thought simultaneously and he got muddled up. He recited the names of all the people who could have read the diary in which Sophie Clairsange claimed to have written down her far-fetched plan. He talked to himself as he walked, occasionally stopping and then setting off again.

'The mother, Madame Guérin: possible. Sylvain Bricart: also possible. The limper: what would his motive be? Why are there two names, Angelica and Louise? I can't work it out. Joseph's right: we should pass the whole business over to Lecacheur . . . No, not yet, there's still Thomassin to think about. Is he involved? Is he a potential victim? I need to meet him, and quickly.'

Victor looked up and realised that he was on Rue de Rivoli. He hailed a passing cab.

CHAPTER 14

Sunday 25 February

Escaping from Tasha's arms without waking her was a delicate operation. Victor began to inch away from the tight embrace in which they had been sleeping. A groan and a sharp intake of breath, and he froze. The soft, warm sheets seemed in league with his sleeping wife to persuade him to stay in bed. With an effort, he escaped their dual charms, put his feet on the icy floor and looked behind him. Tasha's eyes were closed and she was lost in a dream that he would never know about; she moved occasionally, and her damp lips were half open in a mute dialogue with an invisible presence.

He dressed quickly, scribbled a note in which he apologised for having to go out on a Sunday morning to attend a meeting with a client that he had forgotten to tell her about and assured her that he would be back before midday. If he had to stay away longer, he could always invent some excuse.

He found some bread and an apple to take with him. Kochka, warm and cosy in her wardrobe, was purring contentedly, her three kittens suckling quietly. She gave a small miaow by way of good-bye.

Rue Fontaine was only just coming to life. The few passers-by zigzagged along the street, buffeted by the wind, looking more like wisps of straw than human beings. Cycling to the circus on a Sunday; it was like being a child again. But he remembered how much he used to hate the clowns that the other children loved so much. He always found them uncouth and menacing ...

*

Locked in his dressing room, Absalon Thomassin had put on his costume and applied a layer of white make-up to his face, which he was now covering with powder. The Winter Circus was empty except for the manager, come to watch the rehearsal of the much-anticipated new routine, a few stagehands, a scattering of circus performers and Vassili, the young acrobat trained by Absalon himself.

When Absalon had gone down into the bowels of the circus building, the familiar smells of sawdust, animal droppings and dust had momentarily eased the lead weight in his stomach.

Now that he was alone, looking at his lavishly dressed reflection in the rectangular mirror, he let his guard down, and the fear that had tormented him all night took hold again. The haunting vision of his drawings splattered with blood, and of the inscription on the mantelpiece, brought such a lump to his throat that he could barely breathe. He inhaled deeply, and breathed out through his mouth, feeling a sudden thirst. Neither the deep breath nor the glass of cold water that he drank could calm the pounding of his heart.

Already, Vassili was knocking at the door and telling him that Monsieur Franconi was getting impatient. He tried to clear his mind, as though he were about to dive into a deep lake. But it was impossible to shake off the feeling that he was going to faint.

Victor managed to get into the circus easily. He slipped down a corridor leading to a flight of stairs surmounted by an equestrian frieze and found a seat as close to the ring as he could. He wanted to be able to speak to Absalon Thomassin as soon as the rehearsal was over.

The only lamps were in the small arcades near the entrance, and these lit the lower part of the arena and the ring, where a group of stagehands was setting up a safety net. Up above, the flies were lost in darkness, and the highest galleries could just be made out emerging from the gloom, rows of red velvet seats with their wooden backs painted white.

A man in a bowler hat and tailcoat came and took a seat in the stalls. Victor looked at him curiously, guessing that this was the manager Joseph had met the previous day. Then a movement high above caught Victor's eye. Without any fanfare, a figure had appeared, spinning on the end of a rope and looking more like a fluttering leaf than a human being. With his white face thrown back and his teeth clenching a bar at the end of the rope, the acrobat began to spin faster and faster, and his jewelled costume glinted in the lights, finally blending into one dazzling streak of light. He gradually slowed down until he came to a complete stop and, seizing the rope, moved his taut body away from it until he was entirely vertical, the muscles in his arms bulging with the effort.

At almost the same moment, a young assistant began to swing two trapezes so that they travelled back and forth a few feet below the Great Absalon. Just as the first trapeze came perpendicular to the ground, the acrobat let himself drop into the void and caught the bar as he flew. A lightning change of hand position allowed him to turn and face the second trapeze, which was now heading towards him. He swung forward and seemed to freeze for a fraction of a second. Something shot through the air, and Absalon Thomassin dropped like a stone into the net, struck on the back of the neck by a black ball.

There was a stunned silence, then a murmur of alarm, and a confusion of cries and panicked movement. Victor leapt up and scanned the tiers of seating. Behind one of the thin metal pillars, he could see a figure hurrying towards the exit. He sprinted off in pursuit, elbowing performers and stagehands out of his way, and eventually emerging on Boulevard des Filles-du-Calvaire, where he had left his bicycle. He was just in time to see a man with a limp haul himself up onto the seat of a cart, which had the words 'Lambert Removals' painted on the side in green, before it galloped off at top speed.

The limper! So it was him, Victor thought, as he, too, rode off as fast as he could.

Luckily, the weather was dry and the traffic was moving smoothly, enabling Victor to keep his prey in sight. The cart took the first road on the left, quickly merging with the traffic on Boulevard Richard-Lenoir.

Did the limper know that he was being followed? There was no reason why he should. It wasn't surprising that a murderer should flee the scene of his crime. The bridges and locks along Quai de Jemmapes flashed past too fast for Victor to admire them, but his photographer's eye unconsciously noted the potential of the passing scenes: washing flapping in the wind on a barge, a barrel-organ player swearing at a dog that had just cocked its leg against his instrument, a soldier in red trousers embracing a buxom woman.

The cart swerved onto Rue des Écluses-Saint-Martin. Keeping his distance, Victor skirted round a coal cart and rode along next to it in the gutter. He had only gone about twenty feet like this when the back tyre of his steed suddenly burst. Feeling rage and frustration welling up inside him, he saw a post office and began to run towards it. As he did so, he spotted a boy of about twelve leaning against a building with his arms folded, looking the picture of indolence.

'Hey, you, do you want to earn yourself some money?'

'Maybe.'

'I'll give you half now, and half when you get back.'

'When I get back from where?'

'You see that cart over there, stuck at the crossroads? You run after it, and if it stops you look at the name of the road and you come back here and find me in front of the post office. Hurry up!'

With Victor's coins clutched in his hand, the boy hared off with surprising speed for such a sluggish specimen. Victor reflected that the chances of seeing him again were small: even if the boy was interested enough to come back for the second half of his reward, he might well end up following the limper as far as Pantin or goodness knows where. Another coin persuaded the woman working at the ironmonger's next to the post office to look after his bicycle. At this rate he'd be a pauper before long.

Kenji put down the receiver, feeling worn out. Would the Comtesse de Salignac ever accept the fact that the bookshop was closed on Sundays? This woman whom Kenji, too, secretly thought of as the 'battle-axe' kept on demanding that a book about education be delivered to her immediately, even though she knew perfectly well that it had already been ordered.

No doubt she's impatient to read it because her own education was so lacking, he decided, going back up to his room.

His daughter and his son-in-law were still sleeping. Euphrosine had, mercifully, been invited by an old friend from Les Halles to go to Châtelet Theatre and swoon over *The Treasure of the Rajahs*, and would therefore not be gracing them with her presence.

He ran a steaming-hot bath. Feeling lethargic in body and mind, he settled down to imagining Djina shedding her clothes in the intimate interior of his new studio flat in Rue de l'Échelle, where the damask curtains were now hanging in all their glory. The final layer of clothing was about to fall to the ground and reveal a stiffly boned corset which sat low on the hips and squeezed the bosoms, just like the ones he had seen out of the corner of his eye in a shop window on the Boulevards. Somebody knocked at the door. He didn't react. They knocked again. Annoyed, he pulled on his dressing gown and dried his feet on a bath mat to avoid dripping water all over the tiles.

'It's Sunday,' he grumbled, when he saw Joseph in the doorway, fully dressed and looking sheepish. 'Is something wrong?' he added, suddenly worried about Iris.

'I've been dreaming about it all night. I can't get it out of my mind. Do you know who Velpeau is, by any chance?'

'Are you joking?'

'No, honestly, I'm not. I would have gone and looked it up in one

265

of the reference books in the basement, but I don't like going down there at night. And as you're a living encyclopedia, I thought …'

Flattered, Kenji swallowed his irritation.

'He was a famous surgeon who specialised in trepanations. Why on earth do you want to know about him?'

'It's just something to do with my book. Thank you so much.'

'Go and answer the telephone,' Kenji muttered, and disappeared back into the bathroom, fearing that it would be the Comtesse de Salignac again, returning to the fray.

Joseph went slowly down the spiral staircase, engrossed in a mathematical formula that was obscured by a fog of confusion. It was Tasha on the telephone, suspicious and upset. Was it really true that Victor had no choice but to be away from home on a Sunday morning because of some errand for the bookshop? A vision of the Winter Circus appeared in the middle of the dimly lit shop. Joseph cleared his throat and claimed ignorance, before shouting, 'Yes, darling, I'm coming! I'm sorry, Madame Tasha, but Iris is calling me.'

He had only just replaced the receiver when the telephone rang again. This time it was Victor, sounding agitated.

'It took me ages to get through – the line's been constantly engaged! Are you listening? Absalon Thomassin was attacked during his rehearsal, and he's badly injured, perhaps dead. I followed the attacker and it's the limper. I had to give up the chase because I got a puncture and … don't go away.'

Joseph heard his brother-in-law talking to somebody, and could just make out a piercing voice. Victor came back on the line, sounding even more worked up.

'I got a boy to follow him and he tracked him to Rue Burnouf, just next to Rue Monjol! I'm going straight there – come as quickly as you can.'

'Rue Monjol? That's not where he lives …'

All of a sudden, the fog cleared and the answer was there, as clear as daylight.

'Victor! I think I've found—'

Too late. His brother-in-law had already put down the receiver.

'Oh, the stupid idiot!' he cried. 'He never listens to me! If I don't get there straight away, he's going to find himself in a terrible mess, the lunatic . . . Now, where did he hide it?'

Joseph remembered that, after their last investigation,[51] he had seen Kenji hiding a pistol at the back of one of the drawers in his desk. He opened them one after another, resisting the temptation to turn everything upside down. He found it at last, hidden underneath the accounts register from 1880, and put it in his pocket with the trepidation of a new recruit about to take part in his first skirmish. Only one thing worried him: he had no idea how to use it. If only he could have transformed himself into the dastardly Zandini, who was far more expert at handling a gun than his creator.

'There's going to be trouble,' he murmured, as though just saying the words could imbue him with a little more courage and a little more expertise with firearms.

He slipped back the bolts on the door, hoping that no opportunist pilferers would steal the books while it was left unlocked, and, by making himself as thin as possible, managed to slip out without the bell tinkling.

Iris felt as though she were living through some sort of nightmare. She had been standing at the top of the stairs for some time and had heard part of Joseph's conversation. Rooted to the spot, she had watched him search the desk and witnessed his furtive departure. She felt a terrible weight of guilt descend upon her. It was her fault: she had suspected for some time that Joseph and Victor were caught up in another investigation, but she had refused to intervene. How could she make up for her mistake? In bare feet, wearing only her camisole and slip, she ran to the telephone and asked for a number. Tasha answered almost immediately, and when Iris had finished relating what had happened, she let out a cry of anger.

'I suspected as much! That night at the exhibition, Laumier's mistress was saying all sorts of strange things to Victor. And Joseph gave himself away by accidentally telling me the address of a couturier who had been murdered. So they're at Rue Monjol, are they? Where's that?'

'Tasha, I'm so afraid. Joseph's borrowed Papa's pistol—'

'Who wants to borrow my pistol?' asked Kenji, appearing behind Iris.

Iris jumped, and dropped the receiver.

'Joseph. He's already taken it … Oh God! What if they're injured?'

'Who are you talking to?'

'To Tasha.'

He seized the telephone.

'Tasha, it's Kenji. I'm going to call the police. Goodbye.

'Are you sure he said Rue Monjol?' he asked Iris.

Iris nodded. He dialled another number.

'Mademoiselle, get me Inspector Lecacheur's office – 7, Boulevard du Palais. It's a matter of life and death.'

He waited, tapping the edge of the desk nervously.

'My dear, you must go back to bed. Think of the baby,' he said to Iris. 'Hello, Inspector Lecacheur? This is Monsieur Mori.'

Victor reached 'the Monjol' after a mad dash in a cab. Having hoped, not so long ago, never to come back to this sordid area, he was becoming very familiar with its miserable streets. He was sprinting towards Rue Burnouf when he noticed two young rascals shooting at a pigeon with catapults. He stopped short, indignant.

'You should be ashamed of yourselves!'

'What about it? We're training! Father Boniface told us the story of David and Goliath! It's from the Bible! It's a great story!'

Victor set off again until, as he had foreseen, he caught sight of the Lambert Removals cart outside the clinic. He banged on the door. No answer. He grabbed the handle and the door opened easily. The waiting room was empty except for the pretty little girl with the blue eyes and the one-legged doll whom he had met on his first visit.

'Have you seen Father Boniface?'

'Yes. He was in a rush. He took off his surplice and shut himself inside the room where he sees the patients. Then the other man knocked on the door, and knocked and knocked. Then he bashed the door open, but Father Boniface had jumped out of the window, so the other man jumped out of the window too, and he nearly cracked his head, because of his funny leg.'

'Where did they go?'

The girl shrugged her shoulders.

'They didn't tell me!'

Discouraged, Victor felt in his pockets for a coin.

'Here, buy yourself some sweets,' he said, handing her his last coin.

'Oh, thank you, Monsieur! If I were you, I'd go and look in the grotto.'

'The grotto?'

'In Buttes-Chaumont park. When the police are about, Father Boniface tells everyone to go and hide in the grotto,' she explained, as she ran her dirty fingers through her doll's hair. 'It's a good hiding place. There's a waterfall. In summer, it's fun – we go under the spray. In winter there's never anyone there, so when the pimps want to have a fight that's where they go, because the *flics* . . .'

She realised that as she looked down at her doll she had started to dribble. She jerked her head up and saw that the man was gone.

Corentin Jourdan was paying the price for all the weeks he had spent pacing the streets of this rainy, unwholesome city. His foot was in agony, but he still refused to give up the chase. Despite his age and heavy build, the man he was pursuing was astonishingly

269

agile. He had shot up the steps on Rue Asselin as quick as a flash, and then run along Rue Bolivar as though Genghis Khan and his marauding army were hot on his heels. A stab of unbearable pain forced Corentin to pause for a moment, and he tried to get his breath back and gather his strength.

The man now had a good lead on his pursuer, and he carried on running, never looking behind. Corentin quickened his pace and saw his prey jump over a gate and disappear into a large area of wasteland. Keeping his arms close to his sides, panting with exertion, Corentin followed him. He found himself surrounded by tall grass and little stones, on which he slipped several times, twisting his ankles. Ahead of him, the other man seemed to be moving without any difficulty at all, and he eventually climbed over a small stile and disappeared. Corentin swore. His shoe slipped and he felt himself thrown forward. He only just had time to stretch his arms out in front of him to break his fall. He was overcome by a sudden rage. He got up as quickly as he could, climbed a hillock and saw below him a man-made lake with an island of rocks in the middle, on top of which stood a small Corinthian temple. Some ten yards below, there was a metal bridge. He felt as though he had been transported far away from Paris. In the time it had taken him to get his breath back, his prey had vanished into thin air. Where should he search for him? Had the man melted into the undergrowth, or had he crossed this little oasis in order to lose himself in the metropolis on the other side?

'I know you're here somewhere,' Corentin said. 'You must be just as exhausted as I am. Go on, get your breath back, but don't think for a second that I'm going to give up and go home.'

He collapsed on a bench and allowed himself to relax. He could see a few people strolling in the park, despite the biting east wind. Most were braving the cold for the sake of their dogs, who were busy marking their territory.

He gritted his teeth in an attempt to distract himself from the stabbing pain in his foot. To give up when he was so close to his goal would be to go back on his promise. He had vowed to achieve his end, whatever the cost, and he must remain impervious to the pain and explore the park with the same dogged persistence with which, years ago, he would have triumphed over a stormy sea.

Although impeded by his limp, he nevertheless succeeded in walking all the way round the lake, with its scattering of ducks. Next, he climbed a hillock planted with cedars. A mossy path led him to a deserted café. The bronze sculptures dotted among the trees observed his progress with their empty eyes. Suddenly, there was a shower of sparks, and a train pulling several carriages emerged from a tunnel. What was the use of searching when the railway skirting the park had probably provided the fugitive with a convenient means of escape?

From his high vantage point, Corentin noticed the entrance to an artificial grotto where a waterfall gushed down the side of a fern-covered ravine. He ran down the path towards it. The interior was dark and damp, and the grotto, with its stalactites, looked just like a real cavern. A purplish light glinted on the edge of a well covered in lichen and creepers. He waited for his eyes to get used to the darkness. There was a noise to his right. For a fraction of a second, he was aware of a shape looming up beside him and he was just in time to fend off a blow that he barely saw coming. Two strong arms wrapped round him and forced him to stagger backwards. He struggled violently, but as soon as he broke free and turned round to face his attacker, a second blow sent him sprawling against the rough wall of the cave. He fell to the ground. Fingers were closing round his throat. He braced himself and sprang up again, ready to confront his opponent.

The dastardly Zandini would have laughed in the faces of these sinister-looking bruisers with their carefully groomed sideburns, who formed a protective ring round the prostitutes who plied their trade in front of the Hôtel de Bucarest. Zandini would have drawn his knife as ostentatiously as could be, and casually begun to pick his teeth with it. Joseph, on the other hand, was not feeling at all equal to the situation. He kept on repeating the answer to the mystery to himself, as a sort of comforting incantation, hoping fervently that he would stay alive long enough to find Victor and communicate the solution to him. He touched the weapon which was making his pocket bulge and told himself he would at least put up a good fight.

'C-could you tell me the way to Rue Burnouf?' he finally managed to stammer to a girl who looked slightly less threatening than the rest.

'What do you want to go all the way there for, love? There's everything you could ever want here! Isn't he a little sweetheart?'

She stroked his cheek. He turned scarlet and turned away, only to find himself surrounded by more of the intimidating creatures, who clung to him and shot vicious, competitive glances at one another.

'I've always wanted to go with a hunchback. Is it true that it brings good luck?' one of them squawked, sinking her talons into his shoulder.

'Put a sock in it, Charlina. You're so fat there's no room in your bed for anyone else anyway!' screeched another.

'Don't you listen to them,' a third advised. 'They're just a lot of selfish vultures. They drown themselves in perfume and cover their nasty faces in powder, but when you get them home you realise they're all rotten on the inside!'

'You take it too far sometimes, Rincette. You drink so much that a man risks his life just giving you a peck on the cheek. She only has to breathe on a punter and he falls backwards onto the bed! Mind you, it saves her having to actually do any work – she'd fall asleep on the job if she did!'

The conversation was taking a worrying turn: as the women got angrier, they tugged violently at Joseph and he began to think he would be torn apart. Before that could happen, a tall man wearing a red scarf stepped into the fray.

'Shut up, the lot of you. This mummy's boy isn't here to listen to your bickering. Go and fight somewhere else. Monsieur is obviously here to try his hand at winning a few francs.'

He saw off the women, who were still angry but quickly obeyed the heavily built man with his shaved head and defiant expression. Joseph felt that he had been delivered from the frying pan only to step into the fire.

'Here's what I suggest, my friend. We'll have a drink together – I'm sure you won't object to standing me a glass or two – and we'll play some cards. Just so we're all above board – something tells me that you're a bit of a slippery customer – let me introduce myself: Auguste Balandard, rag and bone man, buccaneer of the canals, and occasional chimney sweep, but only in my free time. And you, Monsieur?'

'Jo— Joseph Pignot, bookseller.'

'Well, Jojo, I'm pleased to make your acquaintance. Cough up the cash and I'll get us some red.'

Too polite to refuse, Joseph was already fishing out a coin when the sound of a shrill whistle plunged the street into turmoil.

One word was on everyone's lips: police! It was as though a candle had been snuffed out: within seconds, the street was empty of its motley inhabitants, as everyone tried to get away before the forces of law and order could do their worst. Whether actually guilty of illegal activities, or just frightened by the very idea of authority, they were all united in a common aim: escape.

Joseph was not sorry to be free of his chimney sweep, who jumped over a fence in his eagerness to avoid a run-in with the police. In his relief at being spared the humiliation of being cheated out of his money, Joseph stood brandishing his pistol with the air of a privateer who has single-handedly seen off a band of pirates. A voice behind him said, with heavy irony, 'Be careful, Monsieur Pignot. Those things are tricky to handle. As long as you've remembered to load it, of course!'

Inspector Lecacheur smoothed the frogging on the lapels of his hussar's jacket pensively. All around, his men were fighting hand to hand with pimps armed with clubs and sticks. Windows smashed, and stools and chairs flew through the air. Policemen hanging on grimly to crooks and prostitutes slipped in piles of rubbish. A dog bared its teeth and an old lady shook her stick above her white hair and shouted, 'The army! We need the army!'

Inspector Lecacheur's impassivity commanded respect.

'So, Monsieur Pignot, what's all this about? Things must be rather serious for Monsieur Mori to have demanded my immediate assistance. Apparently, you and Monsieur Legris are in mortal danger. Where is Monsieur Legris, by the way?'

Joseph had put the gun back in his pocket and he affected a sudden deafness, casually smoothing down a stray lock of blond hair.

'Do you have a speech problem, Monsieur Pignot?'

A little girl with periwinkle-blue eyes slipped between two brawling groups and stopped in front of the inspector. Swinging her one-legged doll in one hand, she announced at the top of her voice, 'I know where the men went.'

Victor felt as though his heart were about to explode. He bemoaned the loss of his bicycle and had a vision of himself dropping dead of a heart attack. What sort of funeral would they give him? Who would mourn him? Tasha, certainly, Kenji, Joseph, Iris . . . Who else?

When he got within sight of the grotto, his legs were almost numb but he was still alive. Through the mist which seemed to be floating in front of his eyes, he could make out two figures. One had his foot on the other's chest and was pinning him to the ground. With a supreme effort, Victor threw himself into the mêlée. His arm flailed in thin air, and he received a swift upper cut right on his jaw. He seized his assailant's hair and pulled hard. The man staggered and just had time to deliver one more swinging blow before falling backwards and sitting down hard. He stayed there on the ground, lips swollen, one eye half closed and his shirt in tatters.

'Unmasked at last!' Victor cried.

Father Boniface picked himself up. His expression changed immediately, but, beneath his angry grimace, Victor saw a flicker of irony.

'Who would have thought it, Monsieur Legris? Oh, your nose is bleeding. I must have hit you a little too hard.'

He pointed to the figure hunched up on the ground. 'Don't worry. He's just a bit stunned – he'll get over it. He only got what he deserved. After all, he's been getting under my feet ever since the beginning. The funny thing is, I don't even know his name.'

'Perhaps it's Lambert – that's what it says on his cart. So, you're the shepherd, the future King David?'

'I'm sorry?'

'"And David put his hand in his bag, and took thence a stone, and slang it ..."'

'"And smote the Philistine in his forehead . . ." Congratulations, Monsieur Legris, the Old Testament is obviously familiar territory to you.'

'My father was extremely strict in the matter of his son's religious education.'

'How long have you suspected me?'

'Not long at all. I just met a gang of boys throwing stones at pigeons. You're a true commander of soldiers.'

'I can't claim all the credit. I grew up in the countryside.'

Without his surplice, he seemed younger and more debonair.

'I loved Loulou dearly. She was my protégée. I knew that she and Sophie were playing with fire, but I never imagined . . .'

Father Boniface's voice was calm and neutral. He was as impassive as a statue.

'There's something about you that isn't quite right,' Victor said. 'Something that doesn't ring true. I can sense it.'

'I should have suspected that I couldn't get the better of you on that count. You're an expert in human nature, Monsieur Legris, and you're dying to know what my motive was, aren't you?'

Father Boniface's smile was broad, but there was a calculating look in his eyes.

'Hermance Guérin asked for my advice. She had committed the indiscretion of reading parts of Sophie Clairsange's diary while the girl was ill, and she was worried. It seemed to me to be nothing more than a girlish joke, a just revenge on those who had wronged her. I couldn't warn Sophie of the dangers without betraying Hermance's confidence, and I certainly never foresaw the fatal turn that events were about to take.'

'You know Madame Guérin! You told me you had no idea who she was!'

'I needed a little more time so that Thomassin could be caught in the middle of his final somersault! Hermance Guérin is a friend of mine. We got to know one another during the trial, in 1891, and she asked me to come and look after Sophie. I am a doctor, after all. Not a properly qualified one, I admit, but anybody can learn how to apply a poultice. It's your fault, Monsieur Legris: none of this would have happened if you hadn't told me about Loulou's death. You set the whole thing in motion. As I had no idea which of those three scoundrels had committed the cowardly crime, I murdered them all in order to protect Sophie. La Gournay was the only one I made a mess of, but even though he didn't die straight away he did eventually shuffle off his mortal coil.'

'And you, a man of God – to have come to this!'

'We are all God's creatures, Monsieur Legris. You are an intelligent man but you rely too much on appearances. It's so easy to pull the wool over most people's eyes simply by wearing a certain kind of clothes.'

'You're not a priest!'

'Have you any children, Monsieur Legris?'

'No ... that is, not yet.'

'One day, perhaps you'll understand that a father's love may lead him to commit all sorts of crimes. I'm not usually given to quotation, but I am rather fond of Lactantius, "the Cicero of Christianity", as he is sometimes called. Do you know what he wrote, more than one thousand five hundred years ago? "Some men, though only a small number, began to stake a claim to all that was most necessary to humanity ... they placed themselves above all others and set themselves apart by their clothing and their weapons."'

Father Boniface stood absolutely still, leaning forward slightly. There was something triumphant in his expression.

'I "set myself apart" in order to survive. War tore me away from my woman and my daughter, and a dark chasm opened up between us. My sole aim during my years of exile was to see them again. I leave morality and the Litany to those who lay down the law in the false name of justice.'

While they had been talking in whispers at the entrance to the grotto, Corentin Jourdan had recovered his senses. He stayed where he was for a few moments, before stretching slowly and, with his back still bent, making his way to the darkest corner of the grotto.

'Why was the message you left in the Baron's room signed "Louise"?'

'You're certainly meticulous, Monsieur Legris. I followed Sophie's plan to the letter, and I knew that she intended to ruin these distinguished gentlemen's collections under the pseudonym of "Angelica", but I couldn't guess whom she had intended to visit first, so I signed the name "Louise", in order to cover my tracks.'

'And how did you manage to get into the Baron's house on Rue de Varenne?'

'That was easy. I told them I was the parish curate's cousin, and that I had come to give the Baron the last rites. It was he himself who told me where he kept the key to his secret chamber.'

'I suppose you did the same at Richard Gaétan's house?'

'No, I couldn't get in there – the police were already on the scene.'

'And what about Thomassin's house?'

'That was risky, and it took me a little time. I wedged the servants' door of his apartment open, and just as I was running away our friend here ... Where's he gone?'

They turned round. The grotto was empty.

'He can't be far,' Father Boniface said.

'If you're talking about me, look no further!'

Surrounded by a cohort of police officers, Inspector Lecacheur was eyeing them coldly. Half hidden behind the inspector's stout frame stood Joseph, his face lit up by a triumphant smile.

'I cracked it, when you telephoned me, Boss ... Victor! Medical student + Velpeau + trepanning = Father Boniface! A nice formula, don't you think? And Father Boniface is Sophie's fa—'

Victor silenced him with a menacing glance. The inspector gave them a pitying look.

'Messieurs, it's time we all went down to the police station for a little chat,' he said, popping a handful of lozenges into his mouth as he did so.

Father Boniface, in handcuffs now, climbed into a police van.

After they had gone, a little girl with periwinkle-blue eyes remained standing in front of the cave, rocking a one-legged doll in her arms.

'There were three men, though ...'

CHAPTER 15

Thursday 1 March

'I need a cognac,' Victor declared.

'I think I'll settle for your favourite tipple. A vermouth cassis, please, with rather more cassis than vermouth,' Joseph ordered prudently as they sat in the Temps Perdu.

For the third time since they had left the police station, Victor quizzed his brother-in-law about the version of events he had given to Inspector Lecacheur.

'But I keep telling you, my story tallies perfectly with yours!' said Joseph. 'Have some faith in me – I've learnt my lesson, and in record time!'

'Did you mention Loulou?'

'Yes, but I pretended not to know anything about her. Let's just hope that Mireille Lestocart and the customs man . . . that Ganache, don't let the cat out of the bag.'

'Gamache, not Ganache. Mimi is terrified of the police, and Alfred Gamache is too afraid of losing his job to tell them anything. As for Martin Lorson, he's disappeared off the face of the earth. Did you take all the blame then?'

Joseph raised his glass with a melodramatically self-pitying expression.

'I sacrificed myself. I told Lecacheur that I was so keen to find material for my new novel that I dragged you into this mess despite your objections. I said I noticed a story in the newspaper about the murder of a young woman near the La Villette tollgate, but that, try as we might, we couldn't find out who the woman was. It was then that I got interested in the Baron de La Gournay, who'd been knocked off his horse in the park . . . All down to my little habit of collecting newspaper cuttings, of course!'

'So you told him that you did a little bit of investigating by yourself, into occultism and the Black Unicorn,' Victor added, sipping his cognac.

'Exactly. But going to the unfortunate Baron's funeral didn't make the story surrounding his death any clearer – far from it! Next, my taste for murders led me to Richard Gaétan. A journalist contact of mine let me know, even before the police were aware of it, that Gaétan had fallen off his perch, or, more likely, that someone had pushed him off.'

'I assume that you categorically denied having visited Gaétan's place on Rue de Courcelles?'

'Naturally. However, I did explain that once we had discovered that this Gaétan was completely devoid of any talent and that it was his friend, the Great Absalon, who designed his creations, I suggested that you should go and talk to this famous acrobat at the Winter Circus. There, you witnessed the tragic event when Thomassin took his final tumble.'

'And I ran after his assassin, this Father Boniface, who led me to Fort Monjol, where I telephoned you for assistance. I think that all fits together – my version seems to tie in with yours.'

'He didn't half give me a talking to, Inspector Lecacheur!'

'Me too, but it was thanks to us that he got his man. We make a good pair of liars, Joseph.'

'Yes, well, telling the truth can get you into all sorts of trouble – prison, for example. But what if Sylvain Bricart or Hermance Guérin blow our cover?'

'Bricart is far too clever for that – he won't want to jeopardise his chances of retiring to the country. As for the widow, she will protect her daughter, and Sophie knows that the best way of doing that is to keep a low profile.'

'And the limper?'

'He remains a complete mystery to me. He must be one of Sophie's former lovers. She certainly beats us hands down when it comes to being mysterious!'

'And don't forget Baronne Clotilde, what about her?'

'I haven't forgotten her,' Victor replied. 'She refused permission for an autopsy to be carried out on her husband. She hasn't the slightest interest in what actually happened to him. It seems clear that all she wants is to spend the rest of her days with her son and her needles, relying on her husband's family to settle her debts.'

'So we've tied up all the loose ends! Still, it's a stroke of luck for Father Boniface that we've kept our mouths shut about him!'

'Yes, but the same goes for us: he hasn't said a thing about our role in this whole affair.'

'But we did conceal the fact that he also murdered the Baron de La Gournay!'

'What would be the use of adding yet another crime to Father Boniface's record? I understand his motives.'

'It's always the same with you — the murderers are always in the right! You're weird. You hunt them down and then you almost forgive them! He bumped off three men!'

'He did it to protect his daughter. He loves her, even though he didn't bring her up. He wants her to be happy. I've got him one of the best lawyers in Paris, and I'm sure he'll be eloquent enough to get the jury on his side by telling them how he heard about Loulou's murder—'

'How can he tell them that, given that nobody officially identified the corpse with the dyed black hair?'

'— that having learnt about Loulou's murder from a boy from "the Monjol" whom he'd been paying to follow her in secret, he decided to apply the old law of an eye for an eye and a tooth for a tooth.'

'You've really got a knack for bending the facts to fit your story! I can't drink any more of this.' Joseph pushed away his half-empty glass, feeling his head already beginning to spin. 'Now we can finally get back to normal life,' he added.

'Speak for yourself,' said Victor. 'There's one last visit I want to make.'

'Who do you want to see?'

'Madame Guérin. You see, Joseph, I may be a consummate liar, but I do want to get to the bottom of this mystery that has preoccupied me for so long. There are still lots of blanks in the narrative, and only this upstanding woman can fill them in.'

Torn between two desires, Joseph only hesitated for a few seconds. Victor was about to cross Quai Malaquais when Joseph caught up with him.

'Lovely peas, only five sous a pound!'

'Eight sous a lettuce! Choose your own!'

'Take a look at these – Fontenay potatoes! They practically peel themselves! And if you buy five kilos of them we'll give you the butter to cook them in absolutely free!'

The stallholders' cries flew back and forth across the street as Victor and Joseph walked past the stalls that lined Rue de Lancry. Closing his eyes and breathing deeply, Joseph savoured the smell of roasted chestnuts mixed with the sweet hint of vanilla coming from a waffle stand. As they passed a barrel organ playing *La Fille du Tambour-Major*, they saw an old man carrying two books with gilt-edged pages and arguing with the owner of a bric-a-brac stall.

'Two books by Paul Féval only ten sous? Are you pulling my leg, young man?'

'If you don't want to sell them, take them home and use them as a footstool, Grandad!'

I must remember that for my next story, Joseph thought to himself. There's nothing better than scraps of real-life dialogue.

'Come on,' Victor said. 'We need to catch her unawares before she closes the shop.'

When they reached Rue des Vinaigriers, it seemed strangely quiet after the bustle of the market.

'It's closed,' said Joseph, pointing to the Blue Chinaman.

'Then let's go to Rue Albouy.'

They rang the bell several times before one of the ground-floor windows opened. Hermance Guérin fixed them with a hostile gaze.

'What do you want? Haven't you caused enough trouble already?' she shouted.

Victor took off his hat and nudged Joseph, who did the same.

'Madame Guérin,' said Victor, 'we are here to apologise. It was a terrible misunderstanding. We would very much like to speak to your daughter Sophie.'

'She isn't here any more. Go away!'

'Please – I have been in touch with Masson, a great lawyer. He's very renowned. I'll pay his fee. He has agreed to defend Father Boniface.'

Hermance Guérin frowned and pursed her lips. Her expression remained doubtful.

'Madame Guérin, Father Boniface sent us here. He mentioned a diary. Please, it's really very important. I assure you that neither you nor your daughter will be mentioned at the trial. Please let us in.'

'Give me one good reason why I should trust you,' she said.

'I've got a letter here from Monsieur Masson, and one from Father Boniface – you know his handwriting. The police have no conclusive proof against him, only circumstantial evidence. His only mistake was admitting to the murders of Richard Gaétan and Absalon Thomassin. He confessed spontaneously. I've spoken to him, and he wants the trial to go ahead.'

'What will the verdict be?'

'Given the circumstances, the jury will probably be sympathetic towards him. You won't be asked to give evidence, and neither will your daughter. Your names will never be mentioned, and Monsieur

Masson will avoid bringing you into it. We speak for him and we guarantee that your anonymous revelations will be used only to protect Father Boniface.'

Hermance Guérin looked at them for a moment, seemingly unmoved. She closed the window. The front door squeaked on its hinges.

They entered a small sitting room where the ticking of a marble clock on top of the piano was the only sign of life in the sleepy silence. Hermance Guérin invited them to sit down on a small sofa, while she perched on the edge of an armchair.

'Still,' she murmured, examining the two letters, 'it doesn't look very good, does it, given that he confessed?'

'Madame, there is still hope. Tell us everything.'

'Are you really interested in the story of my life?'

Even as she said this, memories began to swarm into her mind. She was seventeen, naïve and enthusiastic. Without thinking, she took up her needles and began to knit.

'I hardly knew my father. He died when I was eight, and my mother was left to bring up five children. I got a job as a shop assistant working for Marcel Guérin, who owned a sweet shop in the Latin Quarter. He was a friend of my father's, and had another shop on Rue des Vinaigriers. When you're young, you don't mind hard work, but you want to have a bit of fun too. We were all good friends, working there, and we'd go out in the evening. I met Julien Collet like that. He was a handsome boy, only twenty years old. His best friend, Sylvain Bricart, worked at the shop on Rue des Vinaigriers, and he always wanted to court me, but I preferred Julien. Julien wanted to be a doctor, but he didn't have any money so he used to study in the evenings, from books. During the day, he worked for a glass blower. At the end of 1869, we set up home together. I got pregnant and Sophie was born a few days after France declared war on Prussia. Julien signed up ...'

The knitting looked like an old, ragged piece of clothing with fraying sleeves.

'I only ever got one letter from him, just before the Emperor surrendered. I waited for a year, and then another year. He had disappeared. So when Marcel Guérin proposed to me, I accepted. He let me keep Sophie, but he wouldn't recognise her as his own because he hoped to have his own children and pass his money on to them. In March 1873, he had a heart attack and I became a widow, up to my neck in debt. I had to sell the apartment and the shop in the Latin Quarter, and take out a mortgage on the shop in Rue des Vinaigriers. It was Sylvain Bricart who helped me out in the end. He found us a place to live on Passage Dubail. I wasn't in love with him – I just needed protection and a little bit of kindness. I had never really accepted that Julien was dead, though, and part of me still hoped that he would come back. When there's no proof of death, you dream of a miracle.'

The knitting came to life again, like a cat waking up and stretching. The needles began to click quickly again.

'When Sophie turned twelve, I decided it was time for her to have a proper education. I put her in a convent at Épernon. One of my brothers lives there. I hated being apart from her. I had eventually managed to save up enough money to buy the house and garden on Rue Albouy. One morning, I received a letter in which Julien's name was mentioned. I thought it was some kind of horrible joke at first, but I went to the meeting place specified in the letter. There was a man waiting for me there who I would never have recognised he had changed so much. He was wearing a surplice, like the ones the White Fathers wear. It was my Julien. He told me that he had hesitated for a long time before contacting me because he was afraid of turning my life upside down, and my daughter's. There he was in front of me, thirteen years later! And it all came back – the same feelings, the same desire . . . He had deserted and travelled south. In Marseilles, he had got a job as a ship's cook and sailed to Algeria. He stayed there for a year, doing all sorts of work, but he always had one aim, and that was to get back to Paris and find me. But after the Commune and all that followed, it was too dangerous for him to come back to France. He feared for his life and retreated to the countryside. He met a White Father on his way to work as a missionary in the desert. They travelled together for a time, but the White Father (whose name was Henri Boniface) was bitten by a snake. Julien did all he could to save him, but in vain. Father Boniface died. So my Julien had the idea, there and then, of taking the surplice and becoming somebody else. Nobody would find out, because Father Boniface had no family.'

Hermance Guérin held up her knitting and shook it out, before placing it back on her lap.

'When Julien got to the missionaries' camp, there was no one left except for a few black slaves who had taken refuge there from the raids. He stayed with them and helped to build a hospital. One day, a long time afterwards, some French soldiers arrived. That was how he learnt that there had been an amnesty for deserters. He decided to come back to France and see his daughter, even if it was without her knowing. He went to live in "the Monjol", where nobody cares about anybody else too much. He devoted his life to the poor, and to the children there. We used to meet at his house. Bricart left me. I don't know whether he was jealous or whether he'd had enough of our life together.'

The knitting slipped to the floor, unnoticed.

'When Sophie and her friend Loulou went on trial in 1891, Julien, or Father Boniface, was a witness. Sylvain didn't suspect that it was Julien, and Sophie never knew that this priest was her father. When she was ill, after she came back from America, it was he who looked after her. He would dress in ordinary clothes to come and examine her. When I read my little girl's diary, I was so frightened. I talked to Julien about it and he read it too. He told me that it was all just a girl's silliness, and that he would watch her and make sure she didn't do anything stupid. Except Sophie and Loulou were too quick for us, and—'

'Have you still got the notebook?'

'Why should I give it to you?'

Victor feigned indifference, and Joseph bent forward to inspect the pattern on the rug more closely.

'There is a certain person who has been following Sophie, and you too sometimes, Madame Guérin. He limps,' Victor said, quietly. 'Where does he come in? Did he also read the diary?'

He noticed a fleeting gleam in the blue eyes. She replied wearily, 'It's more than likely. How else can you explain why he was spying on Sophie? He saved her life, apparently.'

'May I look at the notebook? That's where everything started, isn't it? It must be destroyed, but first, if you will allow me, I'd like to see it.'

'It's private.'

'Madame, I feel responsible for this. Worse, I feel guilty. There's nothing forcing you to show it to me – you can burn it here in front of us if you want to. But I would hate not to know the whole truth, given that I was the one who started the whole thing off with my blundering.'

Hermance Guérin shot him a mocking glance. She rose, tucked in her skirts and, with surprising agility, climbed onto a chair, felt around on top of a cupboard, seized a blue notebook and jumped back down.

'Here you are, Messieurs. But let me say this: everybody has their own way of doing things. Life is like a piece of ribbed knitting: the stitches are different depending which side you're looking at.'

She held it out, an old school exercise book, with some of its pages held together by hairpins. Victor noticed a sharp, hard look in the doll-like face. She was sizing him up. Reassured, she nonetheless added, 'I was the one who encouraged her to write a diary. It meant she could see how she was getting on. She inherited her impulsive character from her father. I thought I was protecting her … The pages pinned together are personal things that have noth-

287

ing to do with all this,' she added. 'You can read it aloud, so that he can hear it too,' she said, indicating Joseph.

Victor nodded. The first few pages had been inserted at a later date.

1893. I shall begin at the end.

30 July
The clouds are like enormous white waves. The orange groves extend to the foot of the mountains, and the air is full of their scent. Everything is calm. The silence eases the pain. I have lost a friend. Where are you, Sam? Are you floating between two worlds in this blue evening light?

2 August 1893
Everything is settled now. I have received all the insincere condolences, and the funeral was solemn and sumptuous, just as my detestable brother-in-law, Arthur Mathewson, wished it. I managed to maintain my dignity as the family all trooped past looking gloomy. They always look gloomy anyway, so it wasn't so difficult. Dear Sam, if you were looking down on us from wherever you are, this whole charade must have made you laugh.

4 August
I can't stand living in this enormous house any more. I intend to leave the Mathewson clan to do with it what they will. I shall take nothing away with me; everything is in my heart. As for the apartments in Regent Street and the money in the London bank, I must remember to send a cable to Sam's lawyer, Osborne, and ask him to meet me at Southampton.

Here, a pin held together a small number of pages covering the years up to summer 1889. The handwriting was slightly different.

July 1889

Maman has managed to buy a house on Rue Albouy. The business isn't doing very well and I decided to try to find a job so as not to be a burden to her. She agreed to the idea, but she wanted me to help her in the shop. I wanted to get my own job, though. I've been taken on at Le Couturier des Élégantes, on Rue de la Paix. I'll work hard: Sister Jeanne always used to say, 'It's harder to work your way up in life than it is to get to heaven.' I don't care about heaven, though! I want to live, and to be in love, but not like the Princesse de Clèves or Madame Bovary.

20 September 1889, Rue Albouy, my room, 9 in the evening.

This afternoon, on Rue de la Paix, I was just coming out of the storeroom when I bumped into Monsieur Thomassin, Monsieur Gaétan's business partner. He smiled at me, and raised his hat just as he would have done to a client. I blushed and ran away. He's so handsome and elegant!

22 September

I managed to arrange things so that at five o'clock, Mademoiselle Valier, the head seamstress, sent me to the storeroom again. I was hoping to bump into Monsieur Thomassin. And I did, but I was so shy that I didn't even dare return his smile. I was trembling and my heart was pounding. He caught up with me at the top of the steps because I had deliberately dropped some receipts, which he picked up for me. This evening, he was waiting for me in a carriage when I came out of the workshop. He took me back to Rue Albouy without asking me to do anything except agree to see him again. I haven't slept a wink all night.

25 September

Monsieur Thomassin asked me to call him Absalon. I'll never dare. Maman doesn't suspect a thing. We meet in carriages.

10 October

I told Maman that I was going to work overtime and that I would sleep at the workshop. I met Absalon at his home on Rue des Martyrs.

Here there were several more pages pinned together, and then:

2 November 1889

I'm so sad. Absalon is going away for a few weeks. Yesterday evening, Loulou came and stayed the night at Rue Albouy. I told her everything, and all she said was that I should be careful. She told me that the person who designs all the clothes at Le Couturier des Élégantes isn't Richard Gaétan at all, but Absalon, but it's a secret.

8 November

I don't know what to do. The day before yesterday, we worked overtime. They hid me in a cupboard because the inspector turned up without warning. The next day, Monsieur Gaétan asked to see me. He showed me into a pretty little boudoir and I sat down. He offered me sweets and told me that I was as tempting as an almond cake covered with angelica. He filled two little glasses with some green liqueur and insisted that we drink a toast. It was strong and it stung my throat. He leant over and passed me an envelope. He said, 'Here, buy yourself some trinkets.' I was feeling giddy by then. He began to be more insistent and told me that if I was good then I wouldn't be fired. I heard the other girls leaving the workshop and old Monsieur Michon starting to do his rounds checking the stoves. I got up to go, but Monsieur Gaétan was looking at me in a funny way. He came towards me and pushed me back onto the sofa. I started to scream, but he put his hand over my mouth and took me by force. Since then, I haven't stopped crying.

25 November 1889

If I tell Absalon about what happened in Monsieur Gaétan's boudoir, who knows what might happen?

30 November
I'm three weeks late.

15 December
Monsieur Gaétan threatened me and I had to go and meet him at his house on Rue de Courcelles. It was that or be fired. I need to work, so I went. He showed me his collection of dolls. He's obsessed — it's disgusting.

20 December
Still nothing. I'm nearly six weeks late now. I'm going to have to tell Absalon.

22 December
Absalon says it's all over. He doesn't want to see me ever again. He said some terrible things, that I was stupid, nothing more than a common baggage, and that the streets were full of hussies like me. I'm devastated. I cried and begged, but he told me never to go back to Rue des Martyrs. Anyway, he's going away on tour soon, far away, to the other side of the world.

10 January 1890
I can't eat, and I can't sleep. I don't even know who the father is. I went to meet Loulou on Rue d'Aboukir, and she noticed straight away that something was wrong. I told her everything. She comforted me. 'Only eight weeks — it can still be sorted out. Swear that you won't repeat this to anyone, because it's serious, do you understand? I could get into trouble with the police.' She said, 'There are women who, for one reason or another, don't want children, or can't look after them, so they have abortions. I did it last year. Do you want me to help you to have one?' I said yes. I was terrified, but I didn't hesitate for a second. When we went to Constance Thomas's rooms, it took me an hour to calm down and lie on the bed. Madame Thomas put a handkerchief between my teeth so that the neighbours wouldn't hear me scream. Loulou held my hand. It hurt a lot.

291

Victor skipped another few pages that were pinned together, and started reading again.

November 1891

This terrible trial! The newspapers aren't talking about anything else. Loulou's godfather made a big impression. He used to be a missionary and he wasn't afraid to say exactly what he thought.

An American man sent me flowers just before the jury began their deliberations. He's called Samuel Mathewson and he has an orange plantation. He noticed me at the trial. He seems kind. He's old enough to be my father, except that I never knew my father, of course.

We were acquitted. I will be tarnished by this for ever. I have terrible migraines, so painful that I want to bang my head against the wall to make them stop.

There followed several more private pages, and then:

10 January

Samuel wants to marry me. I'm going to go a long way away, to California.

Still more pinned-together sheets, and then one page written in purple ink.

San Francisco, at the hotel. 20 November 1893

I'm taking the train tomorrow, for a long journey across the United States. I feel as though I'm coming back to life. Money can do anything, they say. They're right. I'm going to have my revenge on those three beasts. They'll all get it: Absalon Thomassin and Richard Gaétan for me, and Baron Edmond de La Gournay for Loulou. At last, I'm going to do something: everything's planned and Loulou has agreed to do her bit. We'll destroy their treasures. Oh, if only we could see their faces when they discover the carnage! Loulou is going

to come and live with me on Rue Albouy while we carry out our plan.
This is what we're going to do …

The final pages had been torn out. Victor was disappointed. There wasn't a word about the limper. He handed the notebook back to Hermance Guérin.

'Burn it,' he said, pointing to the stove.

CHAPTER 16

Saturday 13 March

Joseph snuggled up to Iris. She was sleeping curled up, with the sheets wrapped around her. The night before, they had begun a conversation that had lasted long into the night. Explanations, apologies and promises never to put himself in danger again had been pretexts for forgiveness, consolation and embraces.

'Would it be unwise to …' he whispered as Iris, nestling in his arms, nibbled his ear lobe.

'Dr Reynaud says that it's all right, as long as we're careful.'

He was tempted to reply that her caresses were making him want to be anything but careful, but he thought better of it, not wanting to alarm her.

How lovely it would have been to laze in bed this morning! Alas, he had made a solemn promise to Kenji that he would distribute all of the orders still awaiting delivery that very day, and he was determined to keep his word. His father-in-law had, in fact, given him to understand that a change of attitude would be not only welcome but necessary.

'You're going to be a father by the summer. Do you want your child to lose his father before he's even learnt to say "Papa"? And my daughter – have you thought about her? My patience has run out. This latest investigation bordered on madness. What were you and Victor thinking of? Chasing a scoundrel disguised as a priest, and then being nabbed by the police in a hideout for criminals! What good publicity for the bookshop, of which you're about to become one of the owners!'

'It was all a terrible misunderstanding. I only wanted to study the street life in Fort Monjol and ... What did you just say?'

'We're going to become partners, you, me and Victor. Victor insists upon it. Until now, I've put it off, but as it's clear to me that I'll never be able to knock any sense into him, I'll have to rely on you. Next September, we'll employ a new assistant, and we'll just have to find the money somehow.'

'I swear that you won't regret it!' Joseph had cried, overcome with gratitude.

He kissed his wife on the forehead and said, 'I'm going to start by doing the rounds of the battle-axes: old Salignac will finally have her precious book on education. And after that, guess what, darling? I'm going to deliver a book to Émile Zola himself while he's having a meeting with his publisher, Fasquelle! It's a collection of essays about Rome!'

This reference to the famous writer made him pause for a moment. How would he find the time to write his stories when he would have so much more work to do in the bookshop? Iris would help him, of course, but she would be spending most of her time looking after their little offspring.

'Where there's a will, there's a way,' he said to himself as he shuffled to the bathroom in his slippers.

Iris let out a groan and turned over onto her other side.

When she woke up an hour later, she lifted her arms over her head and gripped the bars of the bedstead, stretching luxuriously. She felt a faint movement inside her: the baby was waking up too. She was certainly hungry enough for two. As though she had read Iris's mind, Euphrosine came in, looking cross and carrying a heavily laden tray.

'Would you like to eat your breakfast in bed? I'll plump up the pillows for you.'

'No, thank you, I'll get up. Are you all right?'

'How could I possibly be all right when my boy causes me such terrible worry? At his age and in his position, wrestling with criminals in a neighbourhood full of streetwalkers, and then going and getting himself arrested! His picture will be in the papers – there's no doubt about it!'

'But his next story will be in the papers too, *Thule's Golden Chalice*. You should be proud of him.'

'Proud! I certainly am! My son has got something published, and there are people who buy *Le Passe-partout* just because of his stories, it's true. But what are they going to think when they hear that the author was arrested armed with a pistol?'

'They'll be thrilled by his daring, and will read his stories even more avidly than before.'

'You make a joke of it, but their monkey business could have made you a widow! And me, what would become of me without my Joseph?'

Her cheeks red and her eyes moist, she wrung her hands just as the heroine of *The Treasure of the Rajahs* had before she was tied to the stake to be burnt.

'Joseph survived, he's still alive and he's going to settle down and devote himself to his writing. He told me so.'

'His writing . . . stuff and nonsense! He should be looking after you and your little boy!'

'Or little girl, Euphrosine. I've got a feeling that it might be a girl. As soon as she's born, Joseph will calm down.'

'You're very optimistic. I suspect that they may be beyond help, Joseph and Monsieur Victor. Jesus, Mary and Joseph, sometimes my cross is too heavy to bear! Have you got enough toast there?'

Iris nodded, her mouth full.

'In that case, I'll be off. I want to get the shopping done before Zulma finishes cleaning Monsieur Mori's room. I need to check that she's done it properly, the clumsy girl!'

'You look very handsome! Have you got a meeting?' Iris asked Kenji, who was finishing his breakfast in the kitchen.

He was wearing a new white silk shirt and a pair of woollen trousers. Over his double-breasted waistcoat with its two rows of buttons, he had tied an elaborate knot in his cravat. His calfskin boots were polished, the jade knob on the end of his favourite cane shone and he smelt distinctly of lavender. He deposited his teapot and bowl on the draining board and put on his suede gloves.

'I've got a whole series of meetings in my new office. You look very elegant too.'

She had put on a deep-purple watered-silk dress, which was loose enough to conceal her new curves.

'You work too hard. I don't like it.'

'There are worse things to worry about in this house!'

He had his black frock coat over his arm and was trying to make for the door, but Iris blocked his way.

'You mean so much to me, my beloved Papa! Overwork doesn't do you any good. I'm not the only one who has been worrying about their parent's health: Tasha is afraid her mother is wearing herself out too.'

'But her mother looks wonderful. She certainly doesn't show her age – anyone would think she was her daughter's older sister,' he said enthusiastically.

'Oh, so you've seen her recently?'

'Yes, at Tasha's exhibition on Rue Laffitte.'

Iris looked at him in consternation. For a while now, she had suspected that an affectionate relationship was developing between her father and Djina. As far as she was concerned, love was a sentiment strictly reserved for those under the age of thirty-five, and it was bordering on indecency that these two should feel anything like it. But it would really be beyond a joke if that love should actually involve physical attraction between two such old people. How could this father of hers, with his greying hair and a few wrinkles, be capable of exciting the passions of a respectable mother? And could it possibly be right that he should feel the same about Djina?

She desperately wanted to tell him that she knew what was going on and that she was strongly opposed to it. But she guessed what his reaction would be, so she simply said, 'It's difficult to imagine that I'll be fifty one day.'

'If you're referring to Madame Kherson, let me tell you that she is only forty-eight.'

'That's the beginning of old age.'

'I could resent that remark, given that I'm nearly fifty-five!'

'You're a father. It's different.'

'I'm going to let you in on a secret: a father is a human being like other people. Even though I may look different, the young man I was before you were born is still there somewhere inside me.'

She threw her arms round his neck, suddenly upset.

'Life goes by so quickly. I'm afraid of getting old, of dying—'

'Put your fears aside for now,' Kenji advised her, smiling. 'When the earth has gone a hundred more times around the sun, you and I, and all those who are dear to us, will be ghosts in the palace of dreams, free from our cares and waltzing to the sound of an ethereal music, not one bar of which is audible on this troubled earth. That is why it's useless to worry about the future. Speaking for myself, my only ambition is to be as happy as I can, and to seize moments of joy when I can, without hurting anybody else along the way. Is there anything wrong with that, now?'

He had taken her gently by the shoulders, and his wry expression made him look so youthful that she dared not say anything in reply.

'Go downstairs and find your brother. He's working until midday, and then he's going back to Rue Fontaine to see Tasha. I hope that Joseph will be back by then, unless he has been hypnotised by the illustrious Émile Zola.'

Kenji slipped out of the first-floor-landing door so as to avoid seeing Victor, whose recent conduct he found so irresponsible. He could not, however, escape the menacing glare of Madame Ballu, who was polishing the banisters. Ever since her row with Euphrosine, she had been nursing enough rancour to encompass the entire extended family of her ex-friend. In his hurry to escape, Kenji tripped over a step, much to the satisfaction of the concierge, who was sure that she was possessed of special evil powers.

Djina hurried up the stairs, hoping that none of the other tenants had spotted her. The small apartment smelt strongly of fresh paint. Despite the cold, she opened the windows, stopping to run her fingers over the curtains that brought back such sensual memories. She twirled around happily and then stopped short. The bed, with its virginal white sheets, seemed to mock her.

What was going to happen? Was she making a terrible mistake?

If you had any sense at all, she told herself, you'd get out while there's still time! Don't even take your hat off! Run!

Deaf to her own reasoning, she took off her hat decorated with cherries, a present from Tasha, and smoothed her hair, which was carefully done up with combs. Was she giving in to simple curiosity, or to the desire to develop, at long last, an intimate relationship with a caring man, even though he could only spend one day a week with her?

No, you're not being fair, she thought. You were the one who insisted that the two of you should only meet once a week. It's true that he didn't protest much…

She suddenly remembered a decisive moment from her past, in Odessa. She had been leaving the Rousseau library on Richelieuskaya, a book clutched to her chest. Pinkus had been running down the street in the opposite direction, and they had collided. As he picked up the catalogue of Rembrandt's works that she had been carrying, he had been impressed by her taste in art and invited her to have a glass of mineral water with him at the café in the park. That evening, they had gone to an open-air concert together, and afterwards he had hired a landau to drive her back to her Aunt Clara's house, in the Moldavanka district. A week later, he had asked her to marry him. She loved the artist in him, but the man had disappointed her: he was too brusque and too capricious, but, more importantly, he was too overbearing.

This time, it was different. There was no use tormenting herself about it: Kenji's good temper and her good sense would go well together. And, this time, it would be on her own terms.

She untucked the ivory satin bedspread and folded down the edge of the sheets under which they would soon be lying. When she tried to imagine their two bodies together, all she could conjure up was a blurred picture in which only Kenji's laughing eyes were clear and compelling.

'My Mikado! What a piece of luck! I was just thinking that I must come and see you!'

'What a surprise, my dear! Are you staying long?'

As taken as he was with Djina, Kenji felt a pleasant flutter of excitement when he saw Eudoxie Allard, alias Fifi Bas-Rhin, now Archduchess Maximova, weighed down with parcels and hat boxes as she walked under the arcades of Rue de Rivoli.

'I intend to stay for some time. I've had enough of Russia. It's not a country, darling, it's an icebox! And so dull! I was growing ill, simply wasting away. The doctor told me that I should go abroad. Don't you think I look terrible?'

He looked at her glowing complexion, her slim waist shown off to advantage in a beige fur coat with a large collar, and replied that she seemed a little tired but that it did not detract in the slightest from her beauty.

'Oh, you still know how to flatter me, you rascal! Will you walk with me?'

'I'm afraid I have an appointment . . .'

'With a woman, no doubt! Ah well, I was never a jealous woman. In case you want to pay me a call, I'm at the Hôtel Continental, number 3, Rue Castiglione. My suite has windows overlooking the Tuileries Gardens. You'd like it, my Mikado.'

He kissed her hand and set off towards the Palais-Royal, not wanting to go to the apartment in Rue de l'Échelle while there was any chance that she might see him.

After she had handed her parcels to a page-boy and jumped in a cab, Eudoxie drove across Paris feeling only half awake, but none-theless vaguely regretful: she should have followed Kenji.

'I shall solve the mystery another day. There's no hurry,' she murmured, yawning.

For now, she was going to spend the afternoon in the amusing company of a young dandy she had been flirting with the previous night at the Moulin-Rouge. What was his name? Amaury de Champlieu-Mareuil – a ridiculous name, but he did have a wallet simply overflowing with cash, and it seemed a shame not to help him spend some of it.

She stopped the cab at Rue Lepic, where the young whipper-snapper had rented a bijou apartment at his parents' expense.

In his impatience to reach the top of the hill, Maurice Laumier bumped into a woman wearing a beige fur coat and was severely reprimanded by its imperious owner. He increased his pace, curs-ing the steepness of the hill, all the while savouring the good news he was about to communicate. Not only had Georges Ohmet paid him handsomely for the completed portrait, but he had also intro-duced him to a couple of friends of his who had recently moved into a large house in the Plaine Monceau district, and who wanted full-length portraits of themselves, in order to impress their future visitors. They were a pair of imbeciles, but they'd pay him well. And, in any case, the woman wasn't bad-looking. A rather disap-pointing bosom, but nice hindquarters. That look she had given him out of the corner of her eye seemed to suggest that their sit-tings might not be entirely devoid of interest.

301

He turned onto Rue Girardon, singing a song he had composed himself:

> *'I'm in the money,*
> *Joined the gentleman's club*
> *But I want to stay an artist,*
> *There's the rub!'*

He burst into the studio and bellowed, 'Mimi! We're rich!'

A piece of paper held in place by a glass told him that his beloved was not there.

> *My sweetheart, I have gone to see your friend Legris. I thought I should at least go and thank him. Many kisses.*

Maurice Laumier threw himself on the bed without taking off his shoes and lit a cheap cigar. The smoke rose in sensually curvaceous wisps that Raphael himself would have been proud of.

'I hope I haven't woken you?'

'No, this is just what I wear when I'm painting.'

Dressed in an old shirt, with her hair pinned up messily, Tasha was loath to invite Mimi in, especially as Mimi was dressed up in her finest clothes.

'Can I speak to your husband?'

'He isn't here,' Tasha replied tersely.

'When will he be back then?'

'He's being questioned by the police, and it's all because of you, Mademoiselle. He might even be put in prison.'

'Oh, honestly? That would be awful.'

'Quite.'

Mimi twisted the string on the little box she was carrying. She handed it to Tasha awkwardly.

'It's for him . . . to say thank you, because of Loulou. You can have some as well. It's some chocolates, Swiss ones, expensive too, not just any old sort! Well, bye then. Tell him that Mireille Lesto-cart sends her best wishes. And if he gets put in jail I'll bring him some oranges.'

Feeling rather ashamed of herself, Tasha hurried back into her studio in order to avoid André Bognol's silently reproachful look. The former butler had an astonishing ability to express his emotions without opening his mouth. His imposing height, his slightly balding head, his carefully tended handlebar moustache and his neat beard made him look like a clergyman. But this dignified exterior concealed a rather shy man who was extremely intimidated by women, strange creatures who filled him with confusion. He found domestic work both enjoyable and reassuringly predictable.

Tasha cast a critical eye over the watercolours she had produced for Iris. Would they suit the delightful story, *The Dragonfly and the Butterfly*, that the young woman had written for her child? What a shame that she refused to show her writing to Joseph and Victor! This feeling of artistic inferiority was common to so many wom-en ... I shall encourage her to continue and eventually to publish her work, Tasha said to herself. Yes, these illustrations are rather good. I hope she likes them.

She wrapped the sheets in brown paper and went over to André Bognol.

'Could I ask you a favour? Would you deliver this parcel to my sister-in-law, and make sure you go to her apartment, and not to the bookshop? You can take a carriage, of course.'

'As soon as we have finished dressing the salad, we shall be on our way.'

André Bognol had assumed that Madame Pignot herself would answer the door, not this young girl with a freckled face and huge hazel eyes.

'Who … who are you?' she stammered.

'Get out of the way, you oaf! Go away, Zulma! What can I do for you, Monsieur?' Euphrosine simpered, doing her best to persuade some dimples to appear in her fleshy cheeks.

'Madame Legris asked us to deliver this parcel directly into the hands of her sister-in-law.'

'We?' said Zulma. 'Who's we? Are there more of you?'

She craned her neck to see.

'It's just a turn of phrase, you silly idiot,' snapped Euphrosine. 'Leave it to me, Monsieur. I'll give it to Madame Iris. I am her mother-in-law.'

Still standing stiffly to attention, André Bognol looked stubborn, and did not obey.

'Give it to me, I say!'

'Madame Legris gave us very specific instructions, from which we would be wrong to deviate,' he enunciated calmly.

'So I'm not trustworthy then? Well, if that's the way it is, then you can go and find her, scatterbrain – I need to get back to my oven!' Euphrosine shouted at Zulma, before turning on her heel and disappearing.

The maid gave an ecstatic curtsy, utterly fascinated by André Bognol, who, for his part, fell prey to a violent emotion hitherto unknown to him. Zulma retreated backwards down the corridor and disappeared into the apartment, before Iris emerged in her turn.

'Zulma tells me you have a parcel from Tasha?'

He handed it to her with a grave bow. Iris only just managed not to burst out laughing, and ran off to shut herself in her room.

In a trance, Zulma flicked the furniture uselessly with a feather duster, murmuring to herself, 'So that's how it feels, love at first sight!' while, still barricaded in the kitchen, Euphrosine fumed with frustration at not having got her way.

'The first thing I'll do when I get home will be to write about him in my diary, the pretentious lackey!'

Iris marvelled at Tasha's watercolours, with their delicate blue and green colour scheme. She would put together a book just like the beautiful volumes from the Middle Ages and would read it to her daughter every night. When she heard Joseph approaching, she quickly hid the pictures under the mattress, with the notebook.

'My darling, he spoke to me as an equal and he encouraged me to carry on writing! He even said that I could sign a copy of my novel for him!'

'Who did all this, my love?'

'Monsieur Zola! Just as I was leaving, I was struck by inspiration – this is how I'll finish *The Devil's Bouquet*: the dastardly Zandini, having been locked up in Toulon prison, will be freed by the beautiful Carmella dressed as a gypsy. He will fall in love with her, give up his idea of killing her and the two of them will set sail for Argentina.'

'Wonderful! Just like the hero of the Rocambole stories!'

While Iris was planning to write a second story about a donkey who dreamt of running in the Derby, Joseph was wondering whether he should have given Carmella red hair, like Madame Tasha's. From there, his thoughts began to wander to his old sweetheart, Valentine de Pont-Joubert, but he soon pulled himself together and decided to write a letter to Émile Zola. Busy composing a dramatic opening sentence, he snatched up his pen, not noticing that it was leaking and leaving blots all over the page.

Micheline Ballu was fuming. That man who looked like a cross between a waiter and a policeman had dirtied her clean staircase with his muddy boots! She hammered on the door of the Pignots' apartment and, when Euphrosine answered, launched into a bitter tirade on the general lack of respect for her work and her lumbago.

'That awful man with the beard, he went up to your apartment – I saw him!'

'That servant? He's a cretin of the first order, just as ill-mannered as that noodle Zulma!'

Comparing notes on the fools they had to deal with, the two women were soon the best of friends again. Madame Ballu almost hugged Euphrosine when she suggested that they should read extracts from Joseph's work together every evening.

By the time Victor had put his bicycle away and opened the front door of the apartment, Tasha had got dressed and laid the table. She kissed him fondly before admitting that she had behaved unjustly towards Mimi.

'The poor thing, she must have spent a fortune on those chocolates. You've really made a conquest there ... '

'Well, this is a turn-up for the books – you're jealous! For once it's not me who's guilty of being possessive.'

'You're guilty of much worse. When will you stop trying to pull the wool over my eyes? You're a liar!'

'We haven't been married long enough for you to make an unpleasant scene, my darling.'

'Oh, that's it, try to wriggle out of it, as always. Ah, Kochka, at least you haven't got to deal with a husband who treats you like part of the furniture!' she cried to the cat, who was in the process of transferring her brood from Victor's wardrobe to the bathroom.

'Oh no, not there – we'll keep stepping on them!'

Victor put his arms round her and whispered, 'And upon whom are we planning to bestow these lovely little balls of fur?'

'Inspector Lecacheur? He's certainly earned one.'

'I'm not sure he'd be game.'

'Raoul Pérot?'

'Yes, he might be open to persuasion. He's already got a tortoise ...Who else?'

'There are lots of people: André Bognol, Mireille Lestocart – it's the least she can do – Madame Ballu, Euphrosine, the woman who owns the Temps Perdu café ...'

'So many people are queuing up for a kitten? Who would have thought it? In any case, I hope it doesn't happen again.'

'You hope what doesn't happen again?'

'This occupation of our flat by a pack of felines.'

'What can we do about it?' Tasha said, biting her thumbnail. 'Poor Kochka, we'll have to lock her up when she's feeling frisky.'

'How will we know when she is and when she isn't?'

'Well, it's not exactly the same for women as it is for cats, but I'll do my best to show you what it looks like,' Tasha replied.

EPILOGUE

Gilliatt came tumbling out of the cat flap and sniffed the sharp outside air. Although the frequent showers made spring seem far away, there were subtle signs that it was waiting in the wings: a dandelion flowering at the top of a wall, the buzzing of an insect, the velvety moss covering the thick thatched roof where the cat took his usual route up to the ridgepole. Over in the pasture full of crooked little apple trees, tiny buds studded the branches, which were already filling with sap. But the clearest sign of new life was the man, who never seemed to stop working.

Corentin Jourdan had so much to do! He needed to cut back the vine and the ivy from the front of the house, and rake over the manure pile where the chickens loved to scratch around in the warm, steamy air. Then he must clean Flip's stable from top to bottom. And the inside of the house urgently needed to be plastered: the lathwork and yellow earth had begun to show through the peeling whitewash. Throwing himself into his work stopped him thinking about what he had lived through in Paris. Sometimes, though, memories would consume him.

When he had finally managed to drag himself out of the grotto where his adversary had dealt him so many cruel blows, he had collapsed behind a rock and lost consciousness. He had been woken from his daze by the terrified cries of a nurse and two children. With some difficulty, he had dragged himself to his feet, beating his dusty cap against his leg. When he touched his face with his hand, he could feel cuts and grazes. He must have bled a lot, judging by the expressions of the woman and the two children.

'It's nothing – I was just taken ill,' he had muttered.

He had gone back to the grotto, which was now deserted, and, kneeling down near the little stream, had dipped his handkerchief in the water and done his best to clean his cheeks and forehead.

He knew that he had to escape, without even stopping to collect his things. He must run to the station and take the next train to Cherbourg, in case the police caught up with him and decided that he was guilty of these murders which he had been unable to put a stop to. Could he go and pay one last visit to his siren? Show her his swollen face and dirty clothes, suffer her indifference or sarcasm, perhaps even suspicion? It was more than he could stand. He would expunge her from his soul just as he had done with Clélia. Then at least he would be free of her during the day, and it was just too bad if henceforth his nights were destined to be haunted by the figures of two beloved women.

Five days later, when he had reached his home, Madame Guénéqué had appeared unexpectedly and let out a series of astonished exclamations. Oh, was this the state people came back in? That horrible, dirty city. She had insisted on rubbing butter into his bruises – a traditional remedy – and had relieved her anger by polishing the pots and pans as though they were personal enemies of hers. He had waited patiently for her to leave so that he could wash properly.

He decided to spend the rest of the morning cleaning the mould from the trough next to the well. He balanced a plate of beef, a slice of bread and a glass of cider on the edge of the well, rolled up his sleeves and prepared to start work. At that moment he heard the creaking of an old cart. He recognised old Pignol's grey mare. Had the man finally decided to repair Corentin's roof? The cart stopped a few feet away from the house, and a woman got out. The roofer handed her a large carpet bag and waved a greeting to Corentin with his whip.

Shading his eyes with his hand, he watched her approaching slowly, wrapped in a long velvet coat with a hood that covered her hair. She stopped a few steps away from him, dropped her bag and waited.

He remained rooted to the spot, thinking at first that this was all a figment of his imagination. Then he realised that the person standing staring at him was no vision. It was her, beautiful, seductive and unattainable as ever.

'Well, are we going to stand here all day? I'm frozen right through and famished,' she said, eyeing his meal.

Clumsily, he picked up her bag and tried to take the plate as well.

'Let me do that! You'll drop it.'

They went into the house, where the fire had died down. Sophie Clairsange looked around the room.

'So this is where you live? It's a real hideaway! Let's have more fire.'

Mechanically, he threw some more logs into the fireplace and blew on them with the help of a tube made from elder wood. Soon, the flames leapt up again. He got up and shut the door, covering the cat flap with the bunch of broom twigs that he hung there to keep out the cold. Finally, he turned towards her. She was standing in front of the fire, she hadn't tasted the food and, still holding herself erect, had only taken off her hood.

'What do you want here?' he asked in a low voice.

'I want my blue earring back. Did you pick it up, by any chance?'

He walked over to the sideboard and, from among the pile of pipes and tobacco pouches, extracted a small pillbox of dull silver. He took out the jewel.

'I thought as much,' she murmured. 'Why?'

'Why did I keep it?'

'Why did you follow me all the way to Paris? Why did you try to foil those crimes?'

'I had read your diary. I was very touched by what you had been through, because a long time ago a woman who meant the world to me died after having an abortion.'

He ran his fingers through his hair, still feeling dazed by emotion. The young woman with her golden skin was listening to him attentively. He stared at one of the copper pans and went on in a voice full of emotion.

'I got myself a room next door to the house where you were hiding. I knew what you were planning to do, and I was worried that you would put yourself in danger. I was right to worry. Unfortunately, when your friend, dressed in your clothes and with her hair dyed to look like yours, was strangled, I arrived too late. I saw a woman fall to the ground and a man running off. I was paralysed: you had been murdered before my very eyes, and some strange force stopped me moving. The truth was there before me: you were dead – it was all over.'

He looked up, dared to meet her gaze, and continued. 'I refused to believe what I had seen. This terrible crime, which I had been too slow to prevent, had so many strange aspects to it that I was completely confused. When I looked at the victim's face, I'm ashamed to admit that I felt overwhelmingly relieved – full of joy, but anger too. You had begun to carry out a childish plan that was now out of your control. I tried to stop the murderer, but failed in my endeavour. He was always one step ahead of me.'

'Is that such a bad thing? Those men deserved to die. I'm safe and sound, though. You didn't answer my question.'

Puzzled, he moved closer to her.

'But I've just explained—'

'You described what you did, but you haven't fully explained your motives. You went to an awful lot of trouble to help a stranger.'

'I … It was all so similar to what happened to Clélia.'

'When I woke up in the convent at Urville, they told me that a man had rescued me from the sea, taken me to his home, brought me back to life …'

She stroked the four-poster bed covered in a soft eiderdown, and ran her hand over the two snow-white pillows.

'They told me I smelt of alcohol …'

He drew back slightly. 'You were so vulnerable, so soft …'

'I was almost naked.'

'I had to act quickly: I was afraid that you would catch pneumonia.'

'In the hotel that day, when you told me to leave, why weren't you more … explicit?'

She was so close to him now that her face almost touched his.

'I didn't dare. You … you had taken on such importance in my mind. I was afraid that you would reject me.'

He thought of Clélia, and it was a bitter memory, bringing back all the sadness of the moment on that day when he had realised that she cared nothing for him.

Sophie Clairsange was looking at him strangely, as though she was trying to answer a question that was troubling her, deep down.

'You were wrong,' she whispered.

'What do you mean?'

'You understood me, Captain. Do you think I've gone mad? You're wrong.'

'I can't believe it,' he said. 'You're beautiful, so beautiful, and …'

He stopped short.

'It's kind of you to say so, Captain,' she said softly. 'We've both been shipwrecked, you and I, and we're floating on a raft, hoping to reach land somehow … I wanted to forget you, but I couldn't.'

He took her hands, but she held him gently at arm's length.

'This time, Captain, we're going to swap. We've finally been washed up on an unknown shore. You are lying unconscious on the beach. I'm going to help you. But, before I do, I want to take advantage of your weakness, just as you took advantage of mine.'

He offered no resistance as she unbuttoned first his waistcoat and then his canvas shirt, letting them fall to the floor. He took his boots off himself, and she untied the belt of his drugget trousers. Bare-chested now, he abandoned himself to her. She was smiling slightly, with an almost triumphant expression. He leant forwards and caught her in his arms. Their lips met hungrily, then parted, then met again. They fell onto the bed and he began to undress her as she removed the rest of his clothes ...

*

Gilliatt couldn't understand why his cat flap was shut up again. He miaowed and scratched at the door. Madame Guénéqué walked towards him, dragging two heavy bags.

'Well, puss, has he shut you out? Are you being punished, you greedy thing?'

She bent down and put her eye to the keyhole.

'He's got company – that's unusual. Oh!'

She rubbed her back, suddenly feeling flushed. She took a second look, to make sure that she was right, and then, half laughing, said to the cat, 'They're making the beast with two backs in there! You can cry as long as you like – they're not about to finish! I'll leave the food in the stable.'

Resignedly, Gilliatt sat down and began to wash himself. Madame Guénéqué watched him out of the corner of her eye.

'He's putting his paw over his ear! That means it'll rain before the week is out.'

NOTES

1 Now Rue Lucien-Sampaix, in the tenth arrondissement.

2 Now Rue Jean-Jaurès, in the nineteenth arrondissement.

3 French architect (1736–1806). This rotunda is all that remains of the La Villette and Pantin toll barriers, built in 1789 and destroyed by fire during the Commune.

4 A comic opera in three acts, with lyrics by Louis Clairville, Paul Siraudin and Victor Koning, and music by Charles Lecocq (1872).

5 A comic opera in three acts, with lyrics by Henri Chivot and Alfred Duru, and music by Jacques Offenbach (1879).

6 *The Adventures of Sherlock Holmes* was published as a serial in *The Strand* between July 1891 and June 1892. It was published in a single volume in 1892.

7 His real name was Émile Henry. His attack took place on Monday, 12 February 1894 at 8.52 p.m., one week after the anarchist Vaillant was executed.

8 This committee was founded in 1894 by Gabriel Bonvalot (1853–1933), known for his explorations of Turkestan and Tibet. With its headquarters at 16, Rue de Choiseul, the committee produced propaganda promoting the benefits of emigration to the colonies.

9 Thadée Natanson (1868–1951) collaborated on the review with his two brothers, Alexandre, who was the editor, and Louis-Alfred, whose pen-name was Alfred Athis.

10 A French painter and member of the Nabis group (1868–1940).

11 'Les Ingénus'.

12 'Idiot', in Russian.

13 'Goodbye, sweetheart', in Basque.

14 Henri Rousseau (1844–1910) was a Naïve and Primitive artist, dis-

covered by Alfred Jarry. He began exhibiting in 1886, and as a result his recollections of America (where he had fought during the Mexican–American war) became well known.

15 The complete text of Diderot's *Neveu de Rameau* did not appear until 1892, edited by Georges Monval, the archivist of the Comédie Française. He had found, on a quayside by the Seine, a collection of manuscripts which included the complete text of the work.

16 Pierre le Mangeur (1100?–1179?): theologian and author of *Historia Scolastica*, translated into French by Guyart des Moulins.

17 The six tapestries that make up *The Lady and the Unicorn* were discovered by George Sand in the Château de Boussac in 1835 and have been in the Musée de Cluny in Paris since 1883.

18 Louis-Pierre Anquetil (1723–1806).

19 Now Rue Henri-Turot.

20 This neighbourhood was demolished between 1927 and 1928.

21 A song by Frédéric Bérat (Rouen, 1801–Paris, 1855). 'Ma Normandie' was very popular during the July Monarchy, with forty thousand copies sold in one year.

22 Marie Godebska, known as Misia (St Petersburg, 1872–Paris, 1950). An excellent pianist, she was the pupil of Gabriel Fauré and married Thadée Natanson when she was fifteen years old.

23 Music by Consterno, words by Joseph Dessaix, sung for the first time in Chambéry in 1856.

24 Cited by Ernest Raynaud in *Souvenirs de police (au temps de Ravachol)*, Payot, 1923.

25 Gérard Anaclet Vincent Encausse, known as Papus (1865–1916). He published innumerable articles and other works on the occult and founded the Martinist Order.

26 Stanislas de Guaïta (1861–97), French occultist and poet of Italian origin, author of, among other works, *Rosa Mystica*, 1885.

27 See *The Marais Assassin* (Gallic Books, 2009).

28 See *The Père-Lachaise Mystery* (Gallic Books, 2007).

29 A ballroom which was also used as a public meeting room, at 12, 14 and 16, Rue de la Douane.

30 Now called Rue du 8-mai-1945.

31 The hero of Jules Verne's novel *Journey to the Centre of the Earth*.

32 In 1768, Sébastien Érard, the son of a Strasbourg cabinet maker, came to Paris and built his first piano.

33 Marc-Antoine-Madeleine Désaugiers (1772–1827), *Ronde de table*.

34 In August 1889, the decomposed body of a bailiff called Gouffé was found near Lyon. The police discovered that his body had been sent from Paris inside a suitcase. See *The Père-Lachaise Mystery*.

35 By M. Meyronnet.

36 A German engineer (Anklam, 1848–Berlin, 1896), who invented a glider made up of two wings, a rudder and a tail covered in cretonne, or 'shirting'. He died while making his two thousandth flight.

37 Absurd.

38 Victor Franconi (1810–97) directed the Summer and Winter Circuses in Paris and, in 1845, founded the Hippodrome, which was demolished in 1893 but rebuilt in 1900. The Winter Circus building was designed in 1852 by the architect Hittorff, and holds five thousand spectators. It was the last permanent circus building to be constructed in Paris.

39 A song composed in 1893 by Yvette Guilbert which was very successful at the Concert Parisien.

40 Erotic or pornographic books.

41 It was sold in 1894.

42 An extract from 'La Quarantaine', a poem by Charles Frémine, from *Chansons d'été*, dated 1884 and published in 1900.

43 An artist called Salz had decorated the walls with paintings illustrating the crimes of the murderers Lacenaire and Tropmann.

44 1855–97.

45 From Robert Louis Stevenson's *Treasure Island*. Marooning was a punishment meted out by pirates. Someone guilty of a misdemean-

our would be abandoned on a desert island and given nothing but a small amount of powder and shot.

46 This quarter, between Rue de Belleville and Rue Manin, owes its name to the old gypsum quarries, from which stone was exported to America and used for buildings in New York.

47 These protests took place on 18 February 1868, at the Odéon theatre.

48 *Bon appétit, gentlemen! Oh trusty ministers*
   Virtuous counsellors! This is how
   You serve, servants who steal from their master!

49 In 1885.

50 Employed by the Society for the Protection of Animals.

51 See *The Predator of Batignolles* (Gallic Books, 2010).